Dolor and Shadow

Dolor and Shadow

The Seidr Cycle, Book I

Angela B. Chrysler

Dedication

*To my dearest love: my friend, my muse, my Isaac,
my mate. You, who carried me from the darkest
caves, and you, who believed in me when no one else
would, even after reading the first draft...and for that,
I am sorry.*

*To my sweet Tribble, who gave me so much for
seventeen years and who passed away just before the
publication of this work.*

*To the people of Norway whose country and culture I
fell in love with so deeply, it inspired me to recreate
their heritage and, who I hope will forgive me if I got
it wrong.*

Acknowledgments

Here I stand at the end of seven years. A part of me aches to reach out to the organizations and people who made my journey a memorable one. To you I wish to extend my hand, to raise my voice and say thank you.

Greatest of thanks to the staff at Google, who gave me Steve: the little, yellow guy on Google Maps. When you spend that much time with something, no matter how inanimate, you name it. Dropping Steve onto a map and entering worlds at a blink of an eye made so much of my imagery possible. Because of your work you allowed me to walk the streets of Trondheim, to follow the river Glomma, and gaze upon the fjords all without ever stepping foot into Norway. Thank you.

And also to the precious staff at Wikipedia; for the accumulated history, the lists of recommended reading you supplied, and for paving the road of sourced hyperlinks that allowed me to journey back a thousand years. Because of you, I was able to find John Lindow and Snorri Sturluson. Because of you, I was able to enter the world I so desperately needed to create. Thank you for being the scriveners of our time.

My sincerest thanks to the people of Norway, whose passion to capture their love for the outdoors showed me their home through YouTube, Flickr, and Google. To each of you, thank you, for bringing Norway to me.

Eternal thanks to my science consultant and cartographer, Isaac Gooshaw. Without your countless casual crash courses in cell division, hydrogeology, Volcanism, metallurgy, martial arts, and, in general, all things that go boom, a significant sense of realism would have been missing from Kallan's world.

Deepest gratitude goes to my editor, Mia Darien, who polished my manuscript until it glistened. You did such a beautiful job! Warm thanks to Indigo Forest Designs for the beautiful cover. I still love it!

Sincerest thanks to my beta readers for your invaluable input and to all of you on board the HMS Slush Brain. The beautiful C.L. Schneider and Stanislava D. Kohut deserve mention. This is your captain speaking. Both of you did so much for me on my lowest days. I forever look forward to our crazy adventures. Thank you.

Thank you to all of you at Scribophile. So many of you took time out of your day to read and contribute to the shaping of Dolor and Shadow. There really are too many to name you all, but I must recognize Benjamin Scheinfieldo, Jennifer "Sugie" Peltier, Jaselyn B. Taubel, Elizabeth Schyling, and Michael Wisehart. It can not be said enough how much you did for me. Thank you.

Thank you, Angi Dukes, my dear friend, for fullers you deemed "decorative pieces." And my beloved sister, Alicia, who loved Bergen first. Thank you. I love you, Pea-Brain.

Sink into my books with me,
I will show you what I see.

Prologue

"How fare the gods? | How fare the elves?
All Jotunheim groans, | the gods are at council;
Loud roar the dwarfs | by the doors of stone,
The masters of the rocks: | would you know yet
more?"*
- The Poetic Edda 48th stanza

"Think back to the oldest era your mind can fathom,
back beyond everything we can remember, when
gods were still men who had not yet lived the deeds
that would deify them." Gudrun's aged gold eyes
peered from behind her curtain of long, silver hair.
"Think back before the time when the Aesir and the

Vanir were still men who had settled here on ancient Earth, ages before their war."

"Back when the Earth was new?" Kallan asked, looking up from the vellum scroll before her on the table. The tips of her tapered ears poked through the brown hair she had tied back to avoid the candle's flames.

"Was it?" Shadows flickered over Gudrun's face and shelves full of jarred things. All sorts of unusual jars of powders and exotic roots had been crammed into every available corner. Dried herbs hung from the crossbeams. The light from the candle and small hearth fire mingled and added a heavy thickness to the room that smelled of boiled heather and sage. "The Earth was still very old by the time the gods found it," Gudrun said. "By then it was already ancient soil, which stirred beneath their feet. Can you see it, Kallan?"

The girl closed her eyes, an iridescent blue like the lapis stone, and thought back to the earliest memory she could recall, back before the Great Migration, when the gods lived in the Southern Deserts and the Land of Rivers. Back before the Great War between the Aesir and the Vanir.

"I can," Kallan said.

The old woman kept the dry sternness in her voice. "These are the antiquated stories that predate the empires of men. We have studied the Vanir and their ways, their medicines and herbs. Now think of the gods of our gods, the gods so old that we have forgotten. The gods our gods once taught to their young.

And think of their ancient stories and their myths, the legends they once revered before they themselves became myth. And think of everything now lost to time."

Kallan nodded. "I see it."

"The Seidr is older still," Gudrun said. "Like veins, it flowed from the Great Gap, spreading through all elements of the Earth, stretching out, threading itself into the waters, the air, and earth."

Kallan opened her eyes as she drew the connection to the tri-corner knot enclosed in a circle hanging from the chain on her neck. Gudrun smiled, confirming that Kallan's conclusion was correct.

"Your mother's pendant," she said. "*Na Trionóide*: the three united. The Seidr fused itself to the elements, until it lost itself inside the Earth, becoming a part of it, flowing with the waters, churning with the soils, and riding on the wind through the air. The Seidr is still there sleeping, waiting for us to remember."

Kallan shifted forward in her seat.

"When the Vanir found the Seidr, they recognized it. In secret, they honed it and mastered it. They hoarded it, keeping it concealed from the Aesir." Sadness hovered in Gudrun's tone. "Afraid the Aesir would learn of their treasure and exceed them in power, the Vanir refused to divulge their secret."

"What happened to the Vanir?" Kallan asked.

Gudrun visibly fought back the bitter sting of tears. "They died." Her voice was low. "Doomed to be forgotten, and living only within the ancient stories now nearly extinct."

Kallan bit the corner of her lip as if biting back a question.

"Deep within the earth, beyond the sea to the west, they met their end," the old woman continued. "Some say they perished far beyond the western-most reaches of the world where the beginning formed. There where the Seidr emerged from the life source and fused to the elements and life itself. The Seidr now resides dormant in all of us. However, for most of us, it sleeps, available for the host to use, but never awakened, its keeper unaware of its presence.

"But don't think its power is lost," Gudrun said. "Even dormant Seidr, ripped from its host, will de-stroy the life line that has formed around it. It lies sleeping within every man born to Midgard. Just as the races of Men have it, we elves have it—"

"Elves?" Kallan repeated.

"Alfar," Gudrun clarified, forgetting the word was foreign beyond the Ocean Isle where she had lived for the past three hundred years. "The Dvergar, the Svartálfar. Even the Ljosalfar—"

"They have it?" Kallan interrupted. "King Tryg-gve?"

Gudrun nodded. "King Tryggve and King Eyolf—"

The name of her father sharpened Kallan's atten-tion. "Father has it?"

Gudrun continued, not daring to encourage the princess's interruptions.

4

"As do the reindeer that migrate across the valleys of King Raum in the north and the elk birds that fly across the southern realms of King Gardr Agdi. The sea worms that swim, and the pines that grow tall in these lands. However, among us all, Men and the three races of the Alfar, only a rare handful are still aware of its existence. Of those precious few, only some can waken it. Fewer still can wield it."

After concluding her lecture, Gudrun spoke faster, more sternly, leaving behind the mysticism of the storyteller.

"To wield the Seidr is to pull on the lifeline that has formed within the confines of your center. To master the Seidr is to pull on the threads that have woven themselves within the elements. Find it!"

As if suddenly aware of the stuffy room, Kallan narrowed her eyes to better see the Seidr that was somehow there suspended in the air. This time, Gudrun's smile stretched across her wrinkled face.

"Start small," she said. "The Seidr around us has not conformed to the order of a path and goes where the elements take it. Try to find the Seidr within you, at your center. That is where it sleeps. That Seidr will know you and be the first to obey you."

Slouching, Kallan nodded and closed her eyes, then changed her attention to the center of her body.

"Once you master your own Seidr, you can reach out to the Seidr in others. It won't be as willing to obey as your own, but it too has adapted to the confines of a living being."

Kallan opened her eyes, eager to collect the knowledge that always seemed to pour out of Gudrun. "Is it within the fire you summon?"

The old Seidkona shook her head.

"Fire is not an element, but a reaction, like when the cook blends stews or when I mix spells."

"Like bubbling water or brewed tea?"

"Exactly," Gudrun said. "Fire is only present when other actions bring it out, whereas soil, wind, and water are always there, maintaining a permanent state that defines the Seidr." As she listed each element, Gudrun pointed to each point of the pendant hanging from Kallan's neck. As she finished, she traced her finger around the circle enveloping the knot. "The elements don't require fuel. However, Seidr is living. It is a life form made of pure energy. Compress enough Seidr, and it will release heat. Compress it more, and it will become hot enough to produce flame."

"And hotter still produces your lightning." Kallan grinned.

"Exactly."

Part One

Chapter 1

Lorlenalin

Aaric, the king's high marshal, towered over the refugees in Lorlenalin's keep as he made his way through the moonlit halls. Sleeping families had done their best to nestle up for the night on the stone floor. Every passage and stairwell overflowed with Alfar. No one had room to stretch out. His men performed well considering the circumstances, but still.

Ninety thousand.

He glanced into one of the countless rooms filled with more than two dozen people. Only this morning he had used most of the rooms for storage. Now, children slept sitting upright against their mothers.

Ninety thousand.

He couldn't believe the report when he heard it two weeks ago. He and his men did well to prepare, but seeing this many refugees arriving at the steps of his keep without home or food had been enough to shock him into the reality of the numbers. His keep simply could not house them all. Outside, his men erected tents, thousands of tents, along the outer battlement. Alongside the river and even the waterfall, they had pitched rows upon rows of tents that would serve as permanent housing for the Svartálfar until his men could build proper establishments.

He still wasn't sure where he was going to put them all until then. The spring nights could get cold.

Aaric stopped at a closed door in the hall where orange light seeped through the crack at the floor and spilled onto the stone. The quiet whimper on the other side pulled at his broad chest. He uneasily shifted the sword on his hip and pushed the door open.

The room was laden with simple fixings fine enough to belong to a field marshal: a desk, a table, no ornamentation. On the wall beside a door that led to a balcony hung a tapestry embroidered with the Svartálfar seal: a hammer intertwined with a tricorner knot. The same seal the smiths had engraved into the armbands worn by all of the king's men. On the bed, Kallan sat sobbing softly on King Eyolf's lap. From the red of his dry eyes, Eyolf had found more tears to shed for his wife.

Kallan stared wide-eyed, her lapis eyes swollen and red like her father's. The child lay with her fist pressed into her mouth, uninterested with anything he had to say.

"Daggon's ready," Aaric said.

Eyolf dug at his eyes and nodded. Despite having reached his elding ages ago, gray now streaked the black of his shoulder length hair and his full beard. The eternal youth of the king had waned since last they met. Exhaustion pulled on his face and made him appear much more like a middle-aged human instead of an Alfar king blessed with the eternal life of his people.

Eyolf returned his hand to his daughter's back. "How is everyone?" he asked. "Have the Dokkalfar settled?"

Aaric furrowed his brow. "Dokkalfar?"

"That's what the Svartálfar who followed started calling themselves," Eyolf said. "I'm not sure when, really. Along the way, they started, I think. The name just stayed with them."

"We found everyone a bed. My men are still working on the latrines. I have another group working on food supply."

Eyolf nodded wearily.

"What of the others?" Aaric asked. "Have you heard anything?"

"No. The Svartálfar who stayed behind were not happy with my decision." Aaric watched Eyolf tighten his mouth. His lip had started to shake. "I urged them to come with us, but they wouldn't abandon the fight."

"How many?" Aaric asked.

Eyolf rubbed his face. "More than half. One hundred and twenty maybe."

Nausea flipped Aaric's stomach. "One hundred and twenty thousand left in Svartálfaheim?" He tried to imagine the number of Alfar who had chosen to stay behind as the city went up in Seidr flame. He and Gudrun alone knew it was Seidr flame. He was certain to keep it that way. Aaric shook his head. "They won't make it."

"They wouldn't listen." Aaric heard the grief swell in Eyolf's voice. "And if I stayed to fight that battle..."

Kallan sniffed and Aaric watched a tear spill down her nose. "I had no choice, but to protect those who I could," Eyolf said.

"How is she?" Aaric asked, nodding to the child.

Eyolf made a conscious effort to rub her back again. "About as tired and scared and grief-stricken as the rest of us."

"I have time," Aaric said. "I can take her if you wish."

Eyolf nodded and placed a hand on her head. "Kallan." Aaric watched her eyes wander then focus. "I have to go."

"No." She sat up, her lip trembling as she looked to her father. "No—I don't—"

"Aaric is here," Eyolf said. "He'll watch you."

"No, please...What if—"

"I'll be right back." For his daughter, Eyolf forced his best smile. "You must be strong."

"I'm not strong." Kallan shook her head. "I'm not."

Eyolf planted a kiss on the top of her head and stood from the bed. "I'll be right back," he whispered and nodded to Aaric before heading out the door, down the hall.

Aaric watched the princess pull her legs into her chest as she gathered the furs around her and dropped her face to her knees. Her long brown hair fell to the bed, shielding her face from the light.

"Kallan." Aaric walked to the bed.

"I miss Ori." The furs muffled her voice.

Aaric sat on the bed in front of her.

"I know, Kallan." He tried to smile. "But he'll be alright."

"And Grandmamma," Kallan continued.

Aaric nodded. "Gudrun will be here soon."

"I miss Mommy."

Tremors tightened his body. Kallan looked up from her knees.

"I want Mommy."

Aaric clenched his teeth until he was certain they would break and held his breath until the pain eased enough for him to speak.

"I know." He swallowed the knot in his throat. "We all do."

"I couldn't save her."

"No one could," he said.

"But I really couldn't." Kallan tipped her head, insisting. A beam of light caught her eyes, illuminating the rings of gold encompassing her iridescent irises. Aaric caught himself from exclaiming.

"I wasn't strong," Kallan said. "Father says I am, but I'm not." Another tear. "Mommy wasn't strong either."

Kallan buried her face back to her knees and cried.

She mustn't know.

Aaric leaned closer. They were no longer alone.

"Kira was strong, Kallan." *Kira was.* His eyes burned. "Very strong."

"Not like Daddy," Kallan said, raising her face to Aaric's. "Not like you or Daggon..."

Aaric gently cupped Kallan's chin, which appeared dwarfed by his fingers.

There was no mistaking the prominent ring of gold. If she hadn't been crying, if Eyolf hadn't been grieving, they all would have seen it too.

"Kira had strength, Kallan."

"Then why is she dead?" Her eyes searched his face as if she would find the answers there. "If she were strong, then why?"

A tear escaped him and Aaric closed his eyes, cursing Eyolf. He never should have left her. Not when he knew Danann was hunting them. He was a fool for obeying his king.

Kallan pulled her chin away and dropped her face back to her knees.

"I want to go home."

She needs to forget.

"And what would you do there? Hm?" Aaric asked.

She must forget.

13

"I could find her." Kallan sniffed. "Ori and I would find her."

Aaric watched her silent thoughts fly and Kallan descended into another bout of crying.

If she forgets, her grief will end. "Come here, Princess." Aaric beckoned and, picking up the child from his bed, he pulled her into his lap where she curled up into a ball.

"It hurts so much," she said. "I just want it to stop...to cut it out of me. If I were stronger..."

"And what if you were stronger?"

Aaric rocked.

"Then I could go back and get her. I could have saved her."

Not all her memories, Aaric decided. *Only some. And her Sight. Surely her Sight must go. If she Sees, then she'll know. And if she's anything like her mother...*Aaric continued to rock her back and forth.

There are things she can not know. She already knows enough to figure things out when she gets older. If she remembers. She can not remember.

"Aaric?"

"Yes, Princess."

"Princesses aren't strong," she said. "Do you think I will be strong?"

"Yes, Princess," Aaric said. "You will be strong."

"Like you and Daggon and Father?" He felt her hair brush his chin.

"Yes, Princess. Just like Daggon and Eyolf."

"And you?" she asked.

Aaric placed a hand to her forehead.

"And I," Aaric whispered. Threads of gold, like sand, flowed from his hand and encompassed Kallan's head. Through her body, he reached with his Seidr until he located and linked the golden strands within that harbored her power. One by one, he tugged on the strands, and pushed his own Seidr inside them until his Seidr bound hers and pulled and changed its direction.

"And Gudrun," Aaric said. "Just like Gudrun."

He withdrew his Seidr, leaving hers alone to flow in the new direction. Already, the child slept. Carefully, he laid her back on his bed, pulled his furs up around her neck, and kissed her brow.

"Goodnight, Princess," he muttered.

Several times, he rubbed his hand over his face and made his way to the balcony.

He needed air.

The sea crashed upon the jagged rocks that made up the base of the keep carved into the mountainside. The black waters greeted him as coldly as a late winter chill. Aaric breathed deep the sea air, expanding his chest as far as it would go. Before he released that breath, he knew she was there.

"What did you do to her?" Fand said.

Slowly, Aaric turned his head to the woman leaning too lax against his balcony. Her golden irises gleamed with that same nonchalance that urged him to attack her.

"I sealed off her memories," he answered with a tone of disgust and pulled his attention from the goddess.

Fand tucked a strand of black hair behind her white, tapered ear.

"It won't work," she chimed, too happily for the dreary mood of the keep.

Aaric stared at the generous curves of her body.

"What are you doing here, Fand?"

"You didn't kill her."

Aaric looked back. The nonchalance was gone. In its place, fury peered from her golden eyes. "Our agreement was that you kill her."

"I didn't agree, you proposed," Aaric said. "I'm not going to kill a child."

"She won't always be."

Aaric took a step toward the railing, adding several feet of space between them.

"She's hidden," he said. "Danann won't find her. She doesn't even know Kallan exists."

"You think Danann won't find out?" Fand pushed off the railing. "Granddaughter to the Great Drui and you think Danann can't find her."

Fand stepped in, closing the space Aaric had reserved between them.

"Kira is dead," Fand said, shoving her face uncomfortably close to Aaric. "Danann is hunting you and Gudrun."

Aaric's throat tightened at the sound of Kira's name.

"Kira didn't make it," he said and formed a fist when Fand cocked her hand and feigned pity.

"Oh, so sorry."

"We've blocked Danann's vision," Aaric said. "We blocked her sight. Danann can not find us."

Fand shrugged with a grin that encouraged Aaric to leap off the balcony.

"There is still Volundr," Fand said.

Aaric's back stiffened as he held his breath. "Volundr is—"

"Unpredictable." Fand smiled. The moon did well to illuminate her face. Aaric had to force himself to look away.

"He doesn't know where Kallan is," he said, knowing how little that mattered.

"It's Volundr," Fand said. "He will find out."

"Gudrun and I are both with her."

"Gudrun isn't." Fand tipped her head ever so slightly. The black strand of hair fell back to her face. "Where is Gudrun, Aaric?"

"I don't know."

He felt her eyes scrape over him.

"You're telling the truth," she said. He could hear her smile fall. "You really don't know."

The space between them eased as he felt Fand back away.

"That child is better off dead than alive to me," Fand said over her shoulder. "If Danann even suspects there was a child—"

"You will not kill Kira's daughter," Aaric said, meeting Fand's narrow eyes.

"She would never have you."

Fand turned and walked to the edge of the balcony. The wind whipped her black hair about.

"Where are you going?" Aaric called.

"If the mood suits her, Danann can track me," Fand answered, staring out over the sea. "If I stay too long, it will raise questions. Once Danann withdraws her troops from Svartálfaheim, she will begin looking for you. And Gudrun. Once that happens, if I go near that child, Danann will find her."

"You will not kill Kira's daughter."

"You can have your precious princess," Fand said and released a chuckle. "But the moment Danann finds her, the moment that child knows...I'm coming for her."

Aaric paid no mind as Fand took the shape of a raven. With feathers as black as her hair, she flew into the night, leaving Aaric alone with his princess.

Chapter 2

Gunir

Ten years later...

Swann pushed open the heavy oak door of Rune's chambers. The hinges whined and her silver eyes peered through the crack. The sitting room was empty.

Braver than she had been a moment ago, the girl threw open the door, slipped into her brother's bower, and quietly closed the door behind her with her back pushed flat against the oak.

The hem of her silk chemise caressed her bare toes. Her golden locks framed her slender face before falling to her knees. A soft smile pulled her lips and, as she pushed herself off the door, she brought her hands to her front, clasping a small box filled with her newest treasure.

Skipping lightly, she crossed the Eastern rug that spanned the length of the grand sitting room. Dyed with reds and gold, the rug filled the sitting room with regal warmth and caressed the tips of her toes as she made her way to the dresser to rummage through her brother's things.

Rich wood decorated every corner and ornamented the wardrobe, the tables, and the mantle. The desk, the chairs, even the wooden framework surrounding the doors and each of the four windows was ornamented with the craft of the Ljosalfar woodcutters. Few could claim their equal.

Humming a ditty, Swann arrived at her brother's desk and riffled, combed, and turned over each artifact.

"Sing and skip o'er Faerie mounds," she sang as she inspected a broken piece of thick, green glass that had come from the Desert Markets. "O'er the hill and through the dalr."

Swann moved on to the center window and welcomed the earliest of morning light. A recurve bow and quiver resting in a chair didn't interest her. Nor did the collection of sharpened swords splayed out on a corner table.

With a deep breath, she leaned out the window. Ignoring the courtyard below, she looked to Lake Wanern where the longboats creaked in port. Swann widened her smile at the sunlight and morning breeze as she turned her gaze to the east, beyond the city's end and across the river to the Alfheim Wood.

A groan from the bedchamber pulled her from the window, and Swann grinned with rejuvenated excitement. Pushing off the window's sill, she ran to the bedroom as if ready to burst from the news she was eager to tell.

Encumbered with sleep, Rune lay buried beneath a mountain of blankets, furs, and pillows.

"Rune," Swann said in singsong.

He knew her voice, but couldn't move to answer. A weight in the dreaming was holding him still.

"Wake up," she said.

But Rune didn't wake. Instead, the voice penetrated his dream and became part of it.

"Rune," she said as she climbed his body like the steps of Jotunheim and sang, her voice as crisp as fresh fallen snow on ice:

"Sing and skip o'er Faerie mounds,
O'er the hill and through the dalr,
Where sleep's joy spins my dreams.
There the moonlight finds its beam."

Clutching her small box, Swann slipped on Rune's hip and caught herself before breaking off into the second verse.

"Sing and skip o'er Faerie mounds,
O'er the hill and through the dalr,
Where the rolling brook doth play,
O'er the hill and far away."

Without hesitation, Swann projected her voice into the morning air that blew in with the breeze through Rune's chamber window. As Swann climbed and chanted, her locks spilled over the blankets like sunlight. Swann succeeded in perching herself atop Rune and shoved her face so close, the tip of her nose grazed his.

"Rune," she shouted, pulling Rune from his dream.

With a howl, Rune pushed a pillow into his sister's face, sending her falling onto her back with the pillow, her box, and her golden tresses. Undaunted, Swann jumped up and slapped the pillow back on Rune, who had pulled his blankets over his head. Before he could groan, Swann broke off into another verse.

"Sing and skip o'er Faerie mounds,
O'er the hill and through the dalr,
Where the ancient scrolls doth lay.
Think of their secrets far away.

"Ruuuuuuuuune," Swann said, relinquishing the pillow.

"Whaaaaaaaaaaat?" The furs on Rune's head muffled his voice.

Swann grinned.

"Great! You're awake."

Another groan.

With a hop, Swann said, "Rune, come. You must see. You must see. I've found one!"

Swann squealed as she bounced on her knees beside him.

"Found what?" Rune asked, refusing to budge from beneath the blankets.

"A Fae's mound," Swann cried and sang:

> "Sing and skip o'er Faerie mounds,
> O'er the hills and through the dalr.
> Faerie song will lead you there,
> To their sunlit halls so fair.

"Just like what Mother said," Swann exclaimed the moment her song was done. "And 'glowing as if sunlight flowed from the earth,' just like the ones she saw in Eire's Land."

Huffing, Rune threw back his blankets. His blue-tinted silver eyes squinted in the light.

"You found a Faerie mound?" he asked, arching a single brow in doubt.

Swann nodded vigorously.

"Swann." Rune slapped the furs. His lack of enthusiasm did nothing to deter her spirits. "I suppose I'll have to go see."

"Get up," Swann said, throwing her hands into the air and leaping down from the bed. Her hair followed like golden rain.

"Not right away, Swann." Rune swung his legs over the side of the bed. "I have lessons all morning with Geirolf. And if I skip them again, he'll have my hide. Not to mention the Hel I'll get from Father."

Swann dropped her arms and slouched with the box still tucked away in her hand.

"But the holiday," Swann said over a puffed bottom lip. "It's Austramonath."

"Not for another few days. The Dokkalfar haven't even arrived yet," Rune scolded and watched as his sister curled her bottom lip out further. "I'll be around later."

Swann didn't move.

Rune groaned, throwing himself onto his bed and staring at the ceiling.

"When would you like me to be there?" he asked.

"Now," Swann said, making a full recovery from her sulking.

"Swann," Rune said, and she was on the bed again, holding her face upside down over his with a wide-eyed grin that never waned.

Rune batted at one of her locks.

"Go on ahead," Rune said. "Do whatever it is you do in that valley of yours, and I'll meet up with you before the sun is high."

Her joviality fell again, but she did her best to hide her disappointment.

"That's what Bergen said." Swann sat back on her legs and did her best to not look too upset.

Rune crunched his brow. "Bergen's back?"

With a grin, Swann nodded.

"When did he get back?"

"Just," she sang, thrilled to know something her brother didn't. "Look what he brought me back from Râ-Kedet," she said and shoved her precious box into his face.

Rune sat up, turned himself around, and flipped up the latch. The hinges creaked. Inside, nestled in red Eastern silk, an egg gleamed in the light.

Vibrant, yellow circles capped each end where lines like sunbursts spilled into a black base coat. The rays met the peaks of deep, blood red mountains that encircled the egg. Their bases stopped where a wide strip of black enveloped the egg's center. There, within the strip of black, a red circle drew Rune's attention.

"It's a worm," Rune said as he made out an image of a snake, twisted into a signet until it had formed a circle. Two black slits, like eyes, peered from in between the snake's body. A single yellow eye dotted its head and its tail and Rune turned the egg upside down.

"With two heads," Rune said, seeing the dotted tail was indeed another head. He turned the fragile jewel over to find a second signet snake that mirrored the first. "Where did he get this?"

Swann bounced as if she would burst. "Bergen said it was a gift."

Rune turned the egg over again, clearly unable to tear his eyes away.

"Did he now?"

"He said, 'it was a gift from the queen, who ruled the lands below the White Sea'." Swann repeated Bergen's words verbatim with an air of mysticism as she stared at the ceiling in thought then leaned over Rune's shoulder and added in a normal voice. "He said it came from a Sklavinian ship."

"Sklavinian," Rune said. He knew the name too well.

"Bergen gave you this?" Rune peered up at Swann. "All the more reason why you should heed Bergen's request and go play in the valley." Rune grinned and Swann sighed, taking back her egg with an eye roll that became a head roll. Carefully, she returned it to its silk and latched the lid like a treasured secret.

"You're older," Swann said. "I was hoping you would override Bergen's instructions."

Rune smiled. "Older by moments."

"Enough to be heir."

"Perhaps," Rune said. "Besides, no one really tells Bergen what to do. Not even Father."

"Before the sun is high?" she asked, looking up from her box.

Rune nodded.

"Promise," Swann said, "and you'll bring Bergen too."

"I do and I will," Rune said.

"*Hala*," Swann announced and slid off the bed. As she ran from the room, she sang:

"Sing and skip o'er Faerie mounds,
O'er the hill and through the dalr,

Where the mystical spriggans play,
O'er the hill and far away."

Forced to pull his body from bed, Rune stumbled into his garderobe and began to ready himself for the day.

A gift from the queen, who ruled the lands below the White Sea.

Austramonath was no excuse to skip lessons today, but Bergen's return from Râ-Kedet was. If he hurried, there was time enough to hunt a bear and slip a little something into Bergen's bed.

Chapter 3

At the end of a barren road, a dilapidated stable stood as private as one could hope. Moss and turf more than an arm's length in height buried the sagging roof. The sound of the city had long since vanished. Here, beside a fisher's daughter, Bergen lay, his broad shoulders made wide from hours spent wielding a sword. Thoughts of a pair of deep black eyes, an intoxicating laugh, and the glow of copper skin had followed him all the way back to Gunir from Râ-Kedet.

A pain pulled at his chest and he shifted his head to the maid asleep beside him. Her back glistened white beneath a ray of sunlight. Strands of yellow hair flowed down her bare shoulders to spill over onto the furs.

For a moment, he imagined her hair black, and he shook his head to forget.

Her Nordic skin had never seen the unforgiving sun of Râ-Kedet. Had she lived in the desert lands, she almost would have the same glow as Zab—

Bergen pinched the bridge of his nose. He couldn't lay there much longer. Another time and he would have thought of little else. Another time, and he wouldn't have permitted the maid rest. Today, he was a fool for trying.

Taking great care to not disturb Helga, or Hilda, Bergen shifted himself from beneath the blankets and pulled on his trousers. His black, shoulder length hair fell forward, blocking the girl from view. For that, he was grateful.

Coming here, trying to forget—

For two years, he had done little else.

Bergen took up his tunic and pulled it over his head.

"Hey, Bergen."

The girl groaned.

Taking up his bag, Bergen turned for the door before his brother could—

"Bergen!"

Bergen stumbled out of the stables, dropped his bag at his feet, and gazed at Rune, who stood as tall as he.

"Ssssssh!" Bergen hissed, buckling his belt. His menacing silver-blue eyes, so like his brother's, caught the sun's light, making him appear more threatening than usual.

Rune grinned. "Not back half a day and already you lure one of your mistresses-in-waiting to your shack."

Rune slapped his hand down on his brother's back, hugged him briefly, and released him.

Bergen abandoned his feigned irritation for a wide grin and returned a slap to Rune's shoulder.

"She was there on the docks when my ship came in," Bergen said. "Now, dear brother, what would move you to disturb my lovemaking?"

Rune rested his backside against the little that remained of a weathered fence. "Another maiden has beckoned us to call," Rune said.

A twinge of relief pricked Bergen's chest, welcoming any delay from returning home where solitude waited to torment him.

"Swann," Bergen said, doing his best to appear annoyed. He looked back to the stables. Without word or protest, he took up his bag and slung it over his shoulder.

"What about—?" Rune nodded at the stables as he pushed himself up from the fence.

Bergen glanced back at the doorway then shrugged. "She'll forgive me," he said and joined Rune down the dirt path toward the stone bridge that would carry them from Gunir into the forest to the valley.

"What news?" Rune asked, once the stables were well out of sight.

Bergen stared off to the end of the road that twisted behind a grove of birch trees as he sank back into memories of the last five years. *How to begin*, he mused.

Words would barely begin to describe the beauty of Râ-Kedet with her white sands turned gold in the sun. The alabaster palaces surrounded by the sea of sand-brick buildings, bristling with bustling markets that thrived on the trade ships coming in to port on the White Sea. Statues carved from limestone and ebony alabaster and great white pillars adorned every hall. Papyrus and palm gardens burst with life along the shores of the city and within the gardens of the Serapeum.

Everything was there, anything could be found in those markets, from Sliders and pet desert spiders to Eastern silks and fine curved blades from the Mountains of Khwopring. The ports overflowed with the latest innovations and astounding theories from the Deserts.

'*The city of gold*,' Bergen had often called it. "Hm," he grunted.

Rune creased his brow and shifted a suspicious eye to Bergen. "Gone five winters and all you have to show for it is a grunt."

"Not much to say," Bergen said, batting at a low hanging branch still dripping wet with cool, morning dew. "Glad to be out of the desert heat."

Bergen felt Rune scrutinize his cold demeanor before changing the subject as if deciding on a different approach.

"How was the Academia?" Rune asked, stepping over a root in his path.

"Burned," Bergen said. "Three years ago."

Rune tripped over his own feet.

"Burned three years ago and you're only getting home now?" Rune asked. "What kept you?"

Bergen thought for a while before answering. "Obligations."

Bergen felt the hesitation as a knot formed in his throat. So much for keeping his secrets.

"Obligations," Rune said. His tone confirmed he doubted Bergen's half-truths. "It wouldn't have anything to do with a 'queen from the lands below the White Sea,' would it?"

Bergen stopped dead on the trail. His lips tightened with the snarl he suppressed. At once, his thoughts drifted to a pair of black eyes and skin as gold as the sun. He was unaware that he had clenched his fists.

Zabbai.

A bird chirped, breaking the silence.

"Where did you get the egg, Bergen?" Rune asked.

The corner of Bergen's mouth curled and he resumed walking. "Didn't Swann tell you?" he asked with a hint of humor that told Rune he was in for a runaround that would delay the topic as long as a fortnight if he let it.

Rune shrugged. "No matter. I'm sure Mother would love to hear that you could have been back nearly three winters ago if a certain lady hadn't detained you."

"You're a whelp."

Rune grinned. "I am."

Bergen inhaled the cold, sharp air of the Nordic winds that blew in off Lake Wanern. He released a long, quiet breath. "The Academia wasn't just an academia. It was a shrine. There were days it felt like it damn near made up the entire city of Râ-Kedet. It had its own community that answered to its own laws. There were streets filled with dorms, gardens, markets, lecture halls, theaters, a museum—"

Rune arched his brow. "Museum?"

"The Muse's Hall. It was the wing dedicated to the study of metric speech."

"Music," Rune said.

Bergen nodded. "Among other areas of interest. And a library, the largest this side of the Silk Roads."

They followed their path toward the stone bridge that carried them over the river Klarelfr.

"The library is what kept me," Bergen said.

Rune didn't answer.

"Since its construction, the Academia has grown as the center of education in Râ-Kedet," Bergen continued. "With the Muses and the extended teachings of Pl—"

"You're losing your audience, dear brother," Rune interjected. "I already skipped my lessons for the day."

"The scholars collected everything that came into port," Bergen said. "And everything that came into port was added to their growing Serapeum. Anything that could be used for study was taken. Every artifact was confiscated and housed in the museum, every written word taken and copied in the library.

33

When my ship pulled into port five years ago, so were my manuscripts."

Rune gave Bergen a solemn look.

"They took everything," Bergen said. "Even letters. They gave us coin for our troubles, and the writings were eventually returned to us, but..." He shook his head. "...they would only return the copies the scriveners made. They kept the originals to be added to their library."

"Your notes even?" Rune asked.

"Gone," Bergen said, unable to meet Rune's eyes. "All of them."

"Naturally, you wanted them back."

"Well, yeah," Bergen scoffed. "So, I did what I do."

"You caused a commotion," Rune said.

"—which drew the attention of the woman who ran the place." Bergen beamed.

"You didn't," Rune said with a feigned look of surprise.

"You're mocking me."

"I'm sorry," Rune said as Bergen watched a pair of male sparrows land in the road, locked at the beaks. Wings flailed, throwing up a small puff of dirt, and by the time they were airborne again, their mood had subsided.

"So what happened?" Rune asked.

Bergen shrugged. "I found the school, enrolled, and traced my manuscripts back to the library where I got a job as a scrivener."

"And the woman who ran the place?"

Bergen pretended to be interested in the trees ahead while he collected the courage to speak. "Turned out to be the queen of Râ-Kedet." The knot in his throat returned.

"And the egg?"

Bergen shrugged. "Didn't get to lay her." His jaw tightened.

"The *egg*, Bergen," Rune said.

"As common in Râ-Kedet as the Sliders for sale at market."

"Bergen."

Bergen sighed.

"The woman, who took my manuscripts—"

"—the queen—"

"—had found the egg on a Sklavinian ship." Bergen shoved a branch out of his way.

"How did *you* get the egg?"

Bergen knew that flux in Rune's tone and was suddenly aware of how much he had missed it. Rune wasn't going to buy any story he manufactured, but he was going to try.

"She gave it to me."

"Just like that?" Implausibility dripped from his tone.

"Right after the hunting and drinking," Bergen said, smiling through his lie.

Rune raised a doubtful brow at Bergen.

"The Queen of Râ-Kedet went hunting and drinking," Rune said, "with you."

Bergen nodded. *At least that part of it was true.*

"She did," he said, still grinning.

Rune threw Bergen a look that told him he knew better, but Bergen held his gaze on the path ahead.

"Sklavinian artifacts are notorious for curses," Rune said.

An old memory surfaced and Bergen failed to suppress a grin.

"I've had my share of experiences with the Sklavinian," Bergen said. "And the artifacts release the curse only on those who steal from them. Besides..." Bergen waved his hand. "I've carried that thing now for three years and nothing's happened to me."

"How did you get the egg, Bergen?"

Bergen took a long moment, recalling the breeze that blew in from the sea that night. The desert moonlight had filled Zabbai's chambers. Her cheeks glowed with a red that poured down her bronze neck, flushed from too much wine. Her eyes, like black pools, pulled him in too easily, even for him. Her lips...There wasn't a day he didn't regret not kissing those lips.

Bergen fisted his hand and did his best to ignore the tightness in his chest. If he had known then that his two years with Zabbai were at an end—

"She gave it to me in exchange for a promise."

"Before or after you bedded her?" Rune asked.

Bergen flashed Rune a somber look, drawing Rune's eye. "I didn't bed her. Not this one." Bergen returned his attention to the road. "No one did."

Rune took an extra-long step over a bare root.

"Râ-Kedet has always...attracted...a lot of attention ever since trade was established centuries ago," Bergen continued. "War is always on the horizon there with the rising Western threat that the Gutar brought with them across Danu's River."

"The Gutar?" Rune asked. "They were there?"

Bergen nodded. A shadow had fallen over his face.

"They destroyed the Great Temple not three winters before my arrival."

Rune stopped and grabbed Bergen's arm, nearly pulling him to the ground. His face had fallen white. "The Great Temple?"

Bergen nodded. "Destroyed."

There was a pause while Bergen waited for Rune to find his feet again.

"Tension on the trade routes was high," Bergen said once they started again down the road. "Still is. Two years after my arrival, the Empire in the South invaded Râ-Kedet. It ransacked the city and set the Academia on fire. We managed to put out the flames, but the library was beyond repair."

The sudden stench of camel flooded back to Bergen, bringing back every detail of that night. His stomach felt like it would fall out of him as he recalled the brush of Zabbai's breast on his arm when he hoisted his Lady—*not my Lady, never my Lady*—onto her camel. The high moon seemed to have filled her black eyes. She was still flushed red from the wine and tipsy when they started out across the endless dunes to the Ufratu River. It was there on the banks of the Ufratu that they departed. There, that she gave him the egg, and there he gave his promise.

It was there that he left her for dead.

Fire nipped the tip of Bergen's nose as he tightened his jaw and swallowed the bitter bite in the back of his throat. There was too much he wasn't saying, too much he couldn't say.

"When it was over, I gathered up the last of the surviving scriveners and we moved what was left to the new library," Bergen forced out the end of his story.

"And your manuscripts?" Rune asked.

"Lost in the fire," Bergen said.

There was a moment of silence as if grieving the loss of his works.

"What happened to your queen?" Rune asked.

A disquieted look blanketed Bergen's face. "The last time I saw her, the emperor had her walk the streets of the Imperial City."

Wearing nothing but chains of gold, Bergen couldn't bring himself to say and instead fell silent as he recalled the shimmering gold in the desert sun and her dark, bronze skin. Her hair had fallen down her back like black rain that barely covered her rounded backside.

She held her head high even then, he recalled.

"And so you stayed," Rune finished for Bergen, pulling him out of the withdrawn daze he had drifted into.

Bergen nodded. "To care for what little was left."

There was another prolonged silence as they made their way deeper into the wood.

"What aren't you telling me, Brother?" Rune asked.

Indifference blanketed Bergen's eyes, but Rune didn't seem to notice.

"There was another fire."

Rune kicked his own foot and stumbled, then regained his balanced.

"It's why I came home," Bergen said coldly. "The emperor got to it. There's nothing left."

A breeze swept their path, giving Bergen a chance to breathe in the fresh Nordic winds he had spent five years missing.

"I got to see the Lighthouse of Râ-Kedet," Bergen said.

"How was it?"

Bergen shrugged. "Big."

Rune dropped his shoulders. "Oh, is that all?"

"Almost as big as the pyramid I saw in the Black Land across the River."

Rune made a sound that combined a loathsome grunt and an impressed scoff.

Bergen fell silent again.

"What does it look like?" Rune asked.

Bergen scratched the unshaven, black bristles on his face.

"Wet."

"Not the river," Rune said. "The lighthouse."

Bergen shrugged as if it was every day he saw a behemoth rise from the sea. "A tower extends from a white octagon that stands on a square base. There's a room at the top where they use a kind of metal plate to catch the sun. At night, they light a fire."

"Your description exceeds your skills," Rune drummed sarcastically.

"Four statues adorn the octagon," Bergen said, "and Odinn stands at the top, welcoming the ships to port."

"Your words move me," Rune said as they entered the edge of the valley.

A cold, empty smirk pulled at Bergen's mouth. "Also saw the Statue of the High Mountain and the Mausoleum at Halikarnas."

"I hate you."

"You missed me."

In the valley, Swann made her way up a lively little brook, stepping lightly upon the stones poking out from beneath the water. With her precious egg clutched in one hand and a bundle of pussywillows bunched in the other, Swann swayed as she balanced barefoot on each moss-covered stone. As she hopped from stone to stone, she sang her sweet song, skipping to the next stone on the downbeat of each new phrase:

"Sing and skip o'er Faerie mounds,
O'er the hill and through the dalr,
Where the Fae King's halls are gold,
Where they sing their songs of old."

On the final downbeat, Swann slipped and fell, ankle deep, into the water. Hopping back to the stones, she continued with the chorus, undeterred by her wet feet.

> "Through the wind the spriggans play,
> O'er the sea where they stay.
> The queen of Fae, she sits there still,
> Tending the earth beneath her hill."

On the last three words of the verse, Swann leapt from the stone into the cold water, and giggled, delighted at her own game. With branches fisted in hand, Swann hiked her skirts to her knees and sloshed her way to the bank of the brook, then stepped onto dry land. Skipping ahead through the birch trees, with her golden hair streaking the forest, she sang:

> "Sing and skip o'er Faerie mounds,
> O'er the hill and through the dalr,
> Where the mystical Fae King's throng,
> Fills the earth with ancient song."

Swann timed her song so that, at its end, she fell to her knees on the ground before a mound of dried leaves and dead branches. Setting aside the willows and gently placing the egg's chest into the grass beside her, Swann hummed as she cleared the leaves away until, bit by bit, a golden light seeped then threaded itself up and out of the earth like a spring of gold water.

"Through the wind the spriggans play,
O'er the sea where they stay..."

With a wide grin, Swann fixed her silver eyes upon the golden light and sang quiet and low beneath the wind:

"The Faerie queen, she sits there still,
Tending the earth beneath her hill.

"Beneath her hill," Swann whispered as she pulled away the last of the branches.

Too entranced by the shimmering spring, too enthralled by the glittering gold, Swann failed to see the shadows lurking as darkness moved in.

The clouds overhead had filled the sky, blocking the sun's warm light and casting a dismal gray over the earth. A cold, lifeless wind swept through the valley and Swann shivered as she hummed her song.

From the corner of her eye, she saw, too late, the glimpse of a shadow. Startled, she turned, opened her mouth, and screamed as the darkness filled her lungs, plunging itself down her throat to her belly. Engulfing her, it left her screams to fill the valley.

Chapter 4

Lorlenalin

Kallan breathed in the fresh morning air from her balcony. The clear skies permitted an unobstructed view of the jagged precipice that plunged into the waters below where the ocean's waves slammed into the mountainside. Unyielding, Lorlenalin's foundation stood strong against the sea.

Kallan grinned. The scent of sea and spring and holiday clung to the winds that tossed her hair about. She was certain she could smell Cook's cloudberry glaze dripped over holiday breads and custards.

The feasts of Austramonath.

Her smile widened and in a sudden bout of energy, she sprinted into her bower. Taking up her boots, she dropped to the elaborate chest that ran flush with the foot of her bed and pulled them on. Still grinning, Kallan grabbed the sword from her bed and fled from the room, leaving the main doors of her chamber wide open.

Down the hallway, Kallan ran down the steps to the main corridor that encircled the Great Hall. Inside, the servants and Cook were preparing the last of the delights for travel. Nearly three hundred wives had already left with their children and a small guard. Today, she and her father would be leaving to join them in Gunir, located on the other side of the Alfheim Wood where the northernmost tip of Lake Wanern met the forest. There, on the eve of Austramonath, they would break bread with King Tryggve and his kin. Still, she had time to get in a morning's worth of swordplay.

Too eager to find Eilif in the city's hall of records, and too impatient to stop when one of the kitchen servants offered her a handful of cloudberries, Kallan dashed down the hall to the courtyard, which buzzed with a liveliness only an approaching holiday could bring. The first warm spring day had lured everyone into the streets where Dokkalfar women were busy decorating Lorlenalin in the festival colors of Austramonath.

Piles of branches bursting with pussywillows lay beside children who had followed their mothers into the sun-filled courtyard. Strips of fabrics dyed with bright reds, yellows, blues, and greens hung balls of evergreen sprigs. Wreaths of flowers and wild branches covered one side of the battlement. It would take the next day to hang the rest, just in time for the holiday.

Kallan ran past the piles of branches and skirted around the children running about, before cutting across the vast center square that brimmed with village life. Everywhere, Alfar bustled, doubling up their chores to complete them in time for the celebrations.

Decorations trimmed the streets, feeding the excitement that flowed through the city. At the town's center beside the vast fountain, Freyr's Pole stood. Like a beacon, it fed the people's enthusiasm as it waited, erected for the feasts of Austramonath.

All week, Kallan had stopped to gaze at the ribbons and colors that decorated Freyr's Pole. Today, Kallan paid no mind as she hurried toward the barracks on the farthest end of the square. The stone streets, the distant 'plink' of the smith's hammer, and the stables did nothing to deter her from her goal.

With ease, she fastened the sword to her waist as she came to a stop at the barracks' door.

Breathe.

Kallan eased her excitement and slowed the beating of her heart until her hands were steady and her nerves unyielding. She unsheathed her sword, enjoying the pure ring of the metal, and she placed her hand to the door. Kallan pushed on the wood, and the door swung wide. Kallan raised her sword above her head, angled the tip to shield her face, and entered.

The room appeared empty. Swords hung on the stone walls. Barrels of training swords remained undisturbed in a corner where a line of dummies, beaten to all sorts of conditions, spanned the farthest wall. The occasional round shield rested in waiting propped against the wall. Streaks of sunlight poured through the windows onto the floor. She watched the sun dust settle.

Empty.

Still holding her sword in position, Kallan returned her hand to the door, drew in a long deep breath, and threw her body into the door, slamming it hard into Daggon on the other side.

Daggon howled and Kallan swung the sword down toward Daggon's red head. He raised his sword and blocked her strike, forcing Kallan to take several steps back. She poised her blade, blocking her torso as Daggon stepped from behind the door and matched her position.

"Princess," Daggon said with a grin buried beneath the wild red mass of beard and hair. He lunged, thrusting the blade for her shoulder.

"Kallan!" she corrected, swinging her blade for the exposed artery in Daggon's leg.

Her sword crashed into his and Daggon bore his blade up, forcing Kallan to leap back. She swung her blade up for his neck then down for his head as Daggon moved with her.

He deflected her sword and mirrored her attack, swinging his blade down as Kallan raised her palm flush with the end of her blade. She blocked his attack, then shoved it aside and smashed her pommel up into his face.

As Daggon stumbled back, blood gushed from his broken nose. Knowing his skills with the blade, Kallan gave him no time to recover. She swung for his shoulder as he dabbed at his nose.

Daggon blocked her attack then hooked her hilt with his cross-guard. He reached across her arms and grabbed her hilt, which held her in place as he spun and slammed his back into her front.

"Thank you!" he said, giving a yank and relinquishing the sword from her hands. He shifted his weight and Kallan fell to the ground in a heap.

Daggon threw back his head and laughed long and loud as Kallan sat grinning from the floor.

"You think you have time to smile, Princess?" he jeered.

"Kallan," she corrected again. "And fools are meant for smiling at."

"Fool?" Daggon wiped the moisture from his amber eyes and dabbed at the blood on his nose. "You're the one sitting on your arse."

Kallan widened her grin. "You're the one with your guard down." She flicked her wrist and Seidr flame burst to life in her hand.

"By Baldr," Daggon cursed and leapt, taking up a round shield from the wall as Kallan sent her Seidr streaming for Daggon's torso.

Neither saw King Eyolf standing in the door.

Fire rolled off the edges of the wood while Daggon cowered behind the shield. Kallan's flames grew hotter.

"Kallan!" Daggon shouted.

"Kallan! Stand down!" Eyolf ordered and Kallan extinguished her flame doing her best to already hide her waning strength.

"Do you yield?" she asked, staring at the shield charred black.

"No!" Daggon said and threw the wood at Kallan.

Kallan raised her arm and caught the shield with her elbow. Blocks of blackened charcoal fell to the floor and Daggon charged, his sword positioned to impale Kallan as she mustered the last of her strength, readied her Seidr, and braced for the impact.

Sweeping her feet out from under her, Eyolf dropped Kallan to the ground in a pile.

"First rule of battle, Kallan," Eyolf said, putting his full weight onto her. "Don't turn your back to your opponent!"

"Get off!" Kallan shouted, squirming between the floor and her father.

"Say it!" Eyolf said, indifferent to his daughter's wheezing.

"No—Ow!" Kallan bellowed.

"Quit squirming and say it!"

Kallan raised her head to Daggon who threw back his head and laughed, then sheathed his sword.

"You're next, Daggon," she said. "Now help me up so I can kick your a—"

Daggon threw his hands in the air. "I can't help you, Princess. My orders come from the king."

"And why is that, Kallan?" Eyolf said as if they were seated in the war room. "Why do Daggon's orders come from the king?"

Kallan slapped the floor, doing her best to pull herself out from under her father. But the Seidr left her too weak to fight him.

"Because," Kallan gasped. "Daggon is your captain."

"That's right," Eyolf said, patting her head like a dog. Kallan growled.

"And what am I?" Eyolf said.

"I won't say it!"

"Say it, Kallan."

"No!"

Eyolf picked his foot off the floor, adding more of his weight to her.

"Argh," Kallan dropped her head and answered into the floor. "You are my king!"

"Good girl," Eyolf said with a victorious grin. "And...?"

"No!"

"Give in, Kallan," Daggon shouted over Kallan's screams. "You overspent your energy again using too much of your Seidr on me. You've exhausted yourself because you lack the endurance to fight."

"And besides," the king said, shifting his weight, "my backside has you pinned to the floor. Now say it."

"I won't!"

"Say it," Eyolf said patiently.

"Never!" Kallan punched the floor and winced.

"Say that you eat dragon dung," Eyolf instructed.

49

"No!"

"Say it!" Eyolf gave a light bounce.

"Squish me," Kallan gasped and relaxed on the floor.

Eyolf smiled. "Stubborn," he said and pulled himself up, leaving Kallan free to stand.

Kallan didn't move. Her breathing punched the air as she lay.

"You can't rely on your Seidr," Daggon said, attempting to wipe some of the blood away with his sleeve.

"I can—" Kallan gasped.

"Not until you work on your endurance," Eyolf said.

Kallan lay, focusing on the Seidr she felt brewing inside her. Brewing, but locked somehow as if in a vault somewhere deep within.

"I can do this," she said. "There's more in me. I just can't..." Kallan brushed the long, brown locks from her face. "I can't get to it."

"You're not Gudrun yet, Kallan," Eyolf answered. Kallan cringed at the severity in his voice. "You can hardly hold a stream longer than a handful of minutes. And when you do, it leaves you exhausted."

Kallan rolled her head to the side to better look upon Daggon. "Daggon. Tell him."

"I will forever side with my king, Princess."

"Kallan," Kallan corrected. "You always side with him."

"As it should be," Eyolf added.

"Until you are queen," Daggon said, "my services belong to the king. I'm going to see Gudrun to fix my nose then I'll ready the horses. My liege." Daggon nodded to Eyolf and winked at Kallan. "Princess."

"Kallan!" she shouted after the captain who had already left the barracks.

Daggon threw his hand to the air in goodbye. "When you are queen, Princess, that can be your first order to me."

Kallan sighed and turned her head to the rafters. "Stubborn."

"Like you," Eyolf said and took Kallan's hand, helping her to feet.

"Eilif doesn't call me princess," she said, combing her hair from her face.

"Eilif is a boy who doesn't fight in the service of the king," Eyolf said.

Kallan collected her hair then gave it a snap so that it fell in an orderly fashion down her back. "Well," she said, picking her sword up from the floor.

Eyolf arched his brow too noticeably. "Well?" he asked.

"You're hiding something." With her skirts, she wiped down the blade and studied the elding steel closely. Unlike the iron blades, hers remained without chipping. "You came to the barracks for a reason and seeing as how you didn't follow Daggon to the stables..."

"That obvious, huh?"

"Only to me," Kallan said and sheathed her sword. Noting the delay her father was relishing, she picked up a bit of broken shield and turned over the black bit of charcoal.

"We're meeting with King Tryggve for the festival," he said at last.

Kallan looked up from the wood.

"We are." She waited, holding her attention on him.

"Aaric's done a lot of work, arranging this holiday with the Ljosalfar."

"He has." Kallan didn't flinch.

"They kept out of our way while we..."

Kallan watched her father inhale uncomfortably, not daring to meet her eyes. "We invaded their land in a way...We were vulnerable. They could have wiped us out without any trouble and didn't—"

He rubbed his beard, black and streaked with silver, once, twice...

"Father."

"Hm?"

"You're evading."

Eyolf furrowed his brow. "Am not."

"You are. You're using that tone you use when you're hoping I won't notice you're evading if you use just the right flux in your voice."

Eyolf pinched the end of his beard in thought. "I have no flux."

"You flux."

"I don't think I flux," he said.

"You flux," Kallan said. "Out with it."

Eyolf scratched his forehead. "You're about the same age your mother was when she and I..."

Kallan continued to peer over the charcoal.

"I'm just saying you're almost old enough to..."

She didn't move.

"Try to look nice for the holiday," Eyolf finished.

Kallan arched a single brow. "Do I not look nice?"

Eyolf frowned.

"Do I get to bring my sword?" Kallan asked, deciding to rescue him from having to answer that question.

"If you wish," he said.

"Alright then."

Kallan wasn't convinced.

"Tryggve has two sons, you know," Eyolf rattled off.

Kallan felt the blood leave her face. "That's what you wanted to discuss?"

"I'm just saying they may not be..."

Kallan dropped the charcoal to the floor and tried quelling a groan on top of the rising pit in her chest.

"Kallan, you're well past the age to be thinking about marriage," Eyolf said. "And a marriage would do well to unite our kingdom with Gunir."

"I don't have time for boys," she said. "I have lessons and...lessons."

"You have time for Eilif," Eyolf said.

"Well, Eilif is different."

Kallan stared into the courtyard. A warm breeze blew through the barracks, tousling her hair with her skirts.

"In another year, you'll have less of a choice," Eyolf said. "In another two, you'll have no choice. We have very little options available. The boys are about your age."

"How much older?" she asked, turning her head from the door.

"Five...ten years older. I'm not sure."

"They're old," she muttered, knowing her father wouldn't believe her lie but trying anyway.

"I'm old," Eyolf said.

"You've reached your elding," she said and felt a bit grateful he had waited until Daggon had left to discuss this matter with her.

"And soon, so will you...as will Tryggve's sons. The aging will stop, and it won't matter your age from theirs."

Kallan released a slow breath, knowing she had little room to argue. The political advantage was too clear. Kallan nodded. "So...you want me to look nice."

Chapter 5

Gunir

The high morning sun bathed the castle gardens of Gunir with a touch of gold. King Tryggve breathed deep the warm spring air. The willow trees wept with streams of fresh buds. Their whip-like branches draped over the garden's lake. He watched with a contented grin as a lone swan plunged its head into the water and up again, its silver eyes glistening in the sun. Beads of water rolled down its white back.

The swan caught sight of Tryggve and he watched her swim to the edge of the lake where the water was most shallow. Her feathers ruffled, her head bowed, and he watched, entranced, as the swan shifted its form into that of a woman with generous curves and perfect skin as white as the bird. Her hair, as pale as spring sunlight, fell down her shoulders, breasts, and back. She raised her head and smiled at him.

Her teeth, like pearls, he thought and felt his breath leave his body.

He watched enraptured as she walked from the lake to a small stone bench beneath the willow where she had abandoned her robe an hour ago.

With graceful ease, he watched his wife wrap her body in the robe. His eyes followed the slender curve of her face, her eyes, and the locks she pulled free from the fabric.

"Your eyes still take my heart as completely as the day we met," he said as she made her way toward him. "Caoilinn." He took up her hands and placed his mouth upon her palm.

"Such words," she said, smiling.

"True words," he corrected and pulled her into him. "You take my breath from me." He buried his face into her neck and she laid her head onto his. "The children are gone," he whispered.

"So you shall have me. Is that it?" she asked.

"Always have. Always will, so long as you'll let me." He grazed her neck with gentle kisses.

"*Is breá liom tú*," she whispered back and Tryggve exhaled, pulling himself from her neck so that he could look into her eyes.

"You know I can't understand a word of your sweet tongue." He kissed her mouth. He released her and kissed her brow.

"I know that," she said.

"Say it again." He kissed the lids of her eyes.

"*Is breá liom tú.*"

He smiled and kissed her mouth again hard and deep until he had his fill.

"Tryggve?" she asked when he returned to her neck. "The children are gone, you say?"

"Hm." He kissed her neck deeper and wrapped an arm around her waist. "Swann is off where Swann always is, in the valley." He kissed the tip of her nose. "Rune has vanished."

Caoilinn shifted to better look into his eyes.

"Where is he?"

"Geirolf said he skipped out on his lessons." He raised her palm and kissed her wrist.

"Will you reprimand him?" Caoilinn asked.

"I will..." Tryggve kissed her brow again. "...not care."

She smiled and Tryggve kissed her mouth.

"What aren't you telling me, husband?"

"Later," he whispered.

"Tryggve."

He sighed, ceased his kissing, and wrapped his other arm around her.

"Rumor has slipped from the docks." He hated himself for saying it. "It would appear that our son is home."

"Bergen?"

Tryggve nodded, knowing his plans for the morning were quickly slipping from him.

"Bergen is," Tryggve nodded.

Caoilinn beamed and heat flooded his insides.

"Where is he?"

Tryggve sighed. "I have a suspicion that Rune has taken it upon himself to find him."

"Well then, why are we here?" she said and was off, free from his arms as she ran across the gardens toward the keep.

"Yes, love." Struggling to think of little else but the curve of his wife's backside, Tryggve ran his hands over his face and turned to join his wife. "Whatever you ask, my love, I shall give it."

Tryggve took a step and stopped. She stood stiffly, her head bowed, frozen as if in pain.

"Caoilinn?"

She turned, her eyes brimming with fear.

"Something is wrong," she gasped.

Only once before had he seen her like this. Once, years ago, and she hadn't been wrong then either. Tension pulled his back taut with worry.

"What is wrong?" he asked. "Caoilinn?"

"The children," she muttered. Before Tryggve could run toward the keep, Caoilinn shifted back into a swan and took flight.

From the gardens, she flew over the parapet to the courtyard while Tryggve fled up the steps to the kitchens. Panting, he threw open the door, slamming into the cook while he made his way up the steps to the Main Hall.

Paying no mind to the décor or the feast, Tryggve charged the great oak doors. Geirolf called, but Tryggve ignored him and punched open the doors to the courtyard.

"Please." He heard Caoilinn's plea, and the color drained from his face.

Upon the steps, wrapped in the remnants of a gown, lay Swann, naked and drained of blood that now covered her young body. From her navel to her chest, her body had been cut, gutted like one of the animals brought to slaughter. A handprint of dried blood marred her face where her lifeless silver eyes stared into nothing.

Beside her, Bergen and Rune waited while Caoilinn splayed her hands onto Swann and sent streams of gold into the lifeless child.

"Caoilinn! No!" Tryggve cried and fell to his knees alongside his wife and daughter. "You can't give too much. You'll die."

Caoilinn increased the flow of her Seidr.

"Caoilinn." Tryggve clutched her arms and tried to pull her away.

"*Le do thoil,*" she said. "*Ní le do thoil bás.* Please." But she drew too much. And when she linked her Seidr to Tryggve, she was unaware of the life she took from him.

Tryggve felt his arms weaken, his head spun with darkness, but Caoilinn didn't break the link.

"I can save her," she muttered, but Swann lay unmoving, not breathing while the Seidr drained from Caoilinn.

Tryggve released his wife. His Seidr came back, his eyes focused, and he watched Caoilinn pour her life into Swann. The child lay on the courtyard steps.

"I can...*shábháil*..." Caoilinn muttered. "*Ní le do thoil bás.*"

She was pale now. "I can sa—" The Seidr line broke and Caoilinn fell back into Tryggve's arms.

The red of her lips was almost white. The gleam in her eyes was fading.

"S—She's given too much," Tryggve said. He brushed her waxen face with a shaking hand. "Geirolf," he muttered. "Where's Geirolf?"

The king searched the many faces that had gathered to see. Too helpless to change the fates, too stunned to cry or weep, they only looked on in silence and dismay.

"Caoi—"

Her skin was gray. Her breath was broken. The light in her eyes was fading.

"*Ní le do thoi—*" And she gave her last breath.

Tryggve's head spun.

My wife.

He touched her white lips.

My daughter.

He turned to Swann, seeing, but not understanding.

"Rune?" Tryggve said. "Bergen?"

Neither moved.

"What happened?" Tryggve asked. "How..."

Geirolf was there, leaning closer to inspect the queen.

"We found her," Rune said. "The valley."

Tryggve gazed upon Swann, so like her mother, blood covering her pale skin.

He shook his muddled head and shifted his gaze to Caoilinn, waxen and gray in his arms. His hands had grown cold.

He felt Geirolf shift to touch her neck, and the king raised his bewildered eyes to the old man. "Geirolf?"

Geirolf's eyes glazed over with a wall of tears and he looked to his king. With a quivering lip, Geirolf shook his head and Tryggve felt his sanity leave him.

With trembling hands, he raked his scalp and pulled at strands of hair, one hand still clamped to his wife.

"W—who...?" He couldn't finish. He couldn't speak. "W—why...?" Tryggve turned his attention to his daughter, his wife, his sons.

Bergen stood shaking, breathing as if chilled by a mountain storm. Rune stood beside him, his fingers clutching something until his knuckles were white beneath the blood. Blood covered their faces, their clothes, their hands. Blood now covered Caoilinn. Swann's blood.

"W—ha..." Tryggve could say no more.

Shaking, Rune extended the white-knuckled hand that clasped a silver band of metal. It struck the courtyard stone, punctuating the silence like a deadened weight.

Tryggve shifted his crazed eyes to the object. An elding armband engraved with the tri-corner knot and a hammer.

"Dokkalfar," Geirolf sputtered.

"Eyolf," Tryggve muttered.

Rage consumed him and pushed the confusion and grief aside until only fire burned, and it severed his senses. Wild rage, cold hate took Tryggve and ripped his mind from him. With a single thought, he raised his eyes to the south.

Lorlenalin.

"Get my sword."

Rune gazed at the lifeless faces staring up at him, paying no mind as his father called for his sword and ran to the stables. Torunn had joined them and muffled her sobs into her skirts. Gently, she wrapped the bodies in cloth while Geirolf took up Caoilinn's body.

"Take care of Swann," Geirolf muttered to someone, but Rune heard nothing.

Bergen remained at his side, his shoulders shaking, his hands curled into white fists. His hair hung over his face, hiding the rage that shook him. The shock was wearing off. The wave of crying had begun. Someone took up Swann's body and carried her into the keep. The sky was gray. Blood, Swann's blood, stained the steps of the keep. The armband lay where it had fallen.

Forcing his body to move, Rune took up the band and trudged down the steps and started for the barracks.

The door creaked. The barracks were empty. Rune stopped in the doorway and gazed at the collection of swords and armaments. His eyes stopped on a single sword. Still clutching the armband, he withdrew it.

Hate boiled, rage rose. Rune screamed and swung the blade. His shoulders shook, and he swung again. Images of his sister's body stripped and broken, bleeding and dead, swarmed him. Her body left to die in a pool of her own blood.

He swung the blade again and again.

Bergen had roared and taken up Swann's body.

Rune had dug at the earth with his fists. He didn't know how long they sat there screaming over her body.

Rune swung the blade. He roared, letting his voice shred his throat with the same agony that clawed his chest, and lunged, swinging again and then bringing the blade down into a table, down to the wooden floor.

He remembered the armband lying in the grass.

Rune swung the blade and it shattered in two. He dropped to his knees and stabbed at the floor with a half-blade while the tip clamored to the ground somewhere.

The dagger used to gut her had been left. Rune had run off, shouting to the murderer to come out while Bergen rocked sweet Swann and roared.

Rune dug at the floor over and over until the blade broke again. With his fists, he punched the floor and dug at the planks until his knuckles bled.

And then Mother.

His mind couldn't process. Anguish clamped his chest and dug itself into his heart.

Rune shook his head and punched his brow. He pulled at his hair and dug at his scalp, desperate to find the Dokkalfar and kill him.

The barracks door struck the wall.

Rune remained, kneeling on the floor, yearning to find another sword and slash away at the world.

"Father's gone," he heard Bergen say. "I'm going after him."

"Where?" Rune asked. Screaming had begun to pass over Gunir.

"To hunt Dokkalfar," Bergen said.

Rune raised his face to his brother. Cold hate penetrated the silver blue of Bergen's eyes.

"I'll get the horses."

The wind howled over the hundreds that lay dead on the forest road. Rune tightened his hold on the reins. He couldn't see the end of the massacre through the steam.

Too stunned to speak, he stared at the Dokkalfar women, the children, the soldiers, and horses as Bergen spoke.

> "Hundreds lay dead for me.
> Silenced, they weep for thee,
> Blood spilled where ne'er they'll be."

A raven cawed. The first of the flock were gathering.

"Silence the hundreds."

The stench of the dead was growing. Within the hour, the field would be crawling with scavengers. This was how King Eyolf would find his kin. There was little time to act.

Rune turned his horse around. All taste for vengeance had left him.

"What are you doing?" Bergen asked and turned his horse to follow.

"There will be war," Rune said. "The Dokkalfar king won't dismiss this, nor should he."

Bergen pulled back on his reins and looked to the dead.

Rune stopped his horse and turned. "Bergen," he said. "We need to go back. We need to find Father before the Dokkalfar do."

Bergen stared, not moving, the hate in his eye unyielding.

"Bergen," Rune said.

It was another long moment before Bergen steered his horse back around to follow his brother.

Chapter 6

Kallan smelled the death before she saw the amassed bodies that lay, hewn in pools of their own blood and excrement. Steam rose from the bodies of children, dismembered and disemboweled beside the mothers who had thrown their broken bodies onto them. The steam now formed a thick fog that appeared to have rolled in. Interspersed with meat, drink, and gifts carried for Austramonath, three hundred lay dead.

In silence, Kallan stared from atop her horse. The ravens made feast where piles of pussywillows lay beside children. Alongside the corpses of horses and Alfar, wreaths of flowers and wild branches littered the ground.

Eyolf's saddle creaked as he lowered himself from his mount. All eyes scanned the dead that spanned the caravan.

"Eyolf..." Daggon spoke, releasing the Dokkalfar from their spell. Numb to the horror that blinded her, Kallan slid from Astrid. Her legs jelled and buckled beneath her.

"F—Fathe—" Her voice cracked. A raven took flight and circled the air. "Were there no guards?"

Eyolf shook his head, unable to speak.

"There were," Daggon said.

The raven circled and landed upon a small, bloodied mass: a boy. It pecked the corpse then pulled at the boy's head until it had a mouthful of strands.

"Stop it," Kallan muttered.

The raven pecked at a stub where an arm should have been.

"Stop it," Kallan said.

The raven did not obey.

"Stop it!" Kallan shrieked and, scooping up a rock from the ground, she chucked it hard at the bird. "Stop it!" She took up another and, this time, she ran. "Stop it!"

The second rock fell short like the first, but, as she approached the body, the ravens took flight and left the corpse to Kallan.

"Stop!" Kallan screamed and threw her third rock into the air. It fell to the ground with a soft thump. Beside the boy, Kallan stood where the stench of death was stronger.

Behind her, Eyolf and Daggon led the king's warmen into the dead. In silence, they walked, some bodies too mangled to identify. A few men, some guards lay on the ground, but mostly women and children made up the dead.

"Daggon," Kallan heard the strength in her father's voice falter. "Have one of your men take Kallan home."

"My king." His voice too had weakened. "Kallan."

Kallan wasn't sure how long she gazed into the steam that rolled in the wind. A shadow moved and a soft sob filled the massacre that was Austramonath.

She watched the malformed creature whimper as it hobbled over the dead. It sobbed as it stumbled and babbled intermittently with disconnected slurs and cries until a boy, bathed in blood, emerged from the fog, cradling the remains of a second much smaller boy.

"Mother said..." he muttered. "I will...He'll be alright." He stumbled and the corpse he grasped swayed, allowing Kallan to make out that the body was missing an arm and its tiny spine was cloven in two where entrails hung from its back.

"Mother said..." the boy muttered. "I can watch him. I can...I'm here...I did like you said, Mum. I'll take care of him..."

His eyes focused as he emerged from his madness, and he noticed Kallan. "You can save him...you're Seidkona. You're...You can save him!"

Kallan stared, unable to speak, unable to offer words to the child whose mind had long since gone.

"Save him." The child shoved the remains of his brother at Kallan. "You can! I know you can! You can...Mother told me...A Seidkona can save him!"

Kallan shook her head and forced the words to form. "I can't."

"You can!" The boy was standing close enough for Kallan to make out the blood that flowed from the child's head and the one ruined eye now coated white. "You must!"

"Daggon," Eyolf said.

"You aren't even trying!" the boy screamed and Daggon reached to take him by the arm.

"Come along," Daggon said.

The boy shrieked at Kallan. "You'll kill him!"

Daggon grabbed the boy and firmly pulled him away from Kallan.

"You killed my brother!" The boy's voice filled the stiff air.

"Daggon," Kallan said and the captain froze. "I will take him."

Daggon shook his head. "Kallan. You can't help him."

"I can't bring his brother back." Her knuckles were white as she dug her fists into her skirts and stumbled over the blood-soaked ground. "But I can help him."

Chapter 7

Bergen sat on the steps of Gunir's keep. Resting his arms on his knees, he supported his hunched back and shoulders. In one hand, he clutched the Sklavinian egg until his fingers were numb. In the other, he loosely held the neck of a bottle still full with mead.

Sklavinian artifacts are notorious for curses.

Rune's words echoed back as Bergen stared at the stone courtyard bathed in moonlight and blood, Swann's blood. He recalled Zabbai's bronze body glistening in the sun of Râ-Kedet, naked and pure and perfect and chained. For two years, he had thought of little else.

Zabbai.

Swann's death brought everything from Râ-Kedet flooding back.

The bottle slipped from his fingers and struck the stone with a thud. Red mead flowed down the steps of Gunir. Bergen didn't move to stop it.

He could still smell the death on her.

And then their mother—

"Bergen."

Bergen sat up. Like he, Rune looked beaten down and broken beneath the grief that had penetrated the city. Everyone felt the effect of Swann's death. No one was immune to that loss. And Caoilinn's death, at least that was one they could explain.

"Did you find him?" Bergen asked. The sound of his own voice felt foreign to him.

Rune shook his head as he watched a drop of mead cling to the lip of the bottle still resting on the steps. "Geirolf is looking with Torunn," Rune said. "They haven't seen him since..."

Rune dug his fingers into his eyes and Bergen stared at the city, too grief stricken to cry, too tired to sleep, too much death to live without hate.

Hate.

Bergen turned his thoughts to the fire that burned in his chest. That was something he knew and welcomed. He would need it where he was going.

Bergen shoved his hand through his short black hair and rubbed the back of his neck, then took up the bottle from the steps and shoved the egg into his pocket.

"And what of Mother?" Bergen asked, rising to his feet. "Has her body—" Bergen lost the words in his throat. There was no more room for grief, no more room to feel anything anymore, but hate.

Rune shook his head and wearily climbed each step to the great oak doors of the keep. "According to Geirolf, Father's orders were to leave her."

"We can't just leave her," Bergen said. The hate swelled again.

"What will you have me do?" Rune said, turning back to his brother. "Swann is dead...and Mother. Father is missing. After finding their kin slaughtered...the hundreds that lay dead..." Rune rubbed his hand over his face. "The Dokkalfar will want answers. They won't stand for this, nor should they."

Rune continued up the steps.

"Why should I concern myself with their misery when it was their kin who started this?" Rune gazed down upon his brother. "When it was they who took our Swann from us?" Bergen asked.

"Would you have war?" Rune said. "Would you see more dead? The Dokkalfar are strong."

"We have numbers." Bergen took a step closer.

"They have a witch, Brother. A Seidkona."

Bergen's face fell as he assessed the Dokkalfar's strength against their numbers.

"One Seidkona doesn't make an army," Bergen said and turned away, but Rune's hand flew to Bergen's arm.

"They have weapons," Rune said. "Forged from a steel the likes I have never seen before. If there is war..." Rune shook his head and left the thought unfinished. "We can't win this."

"There are others," Bergen said. The rising darkness within him blanketed his face as his thoughts turned to the mountains.

"What others?" Rune asked.

"Rune. Bergen."

Torunn stood on the steps of the keep. Her dainty shoulders sagged from the insurmountable grief they all bore these past few days. Her long black hair, always so neatly twisted and fastened to the back of her head, was disheveled, making her appear almost crazed.

"Your father," she said. Her lip quivered. "He's here."

"I've never seen him like this," Torunn whispered as Bergen and Rune entered the corridor behind her. "He came in, mumbling such madness. It's like he's gone. I can't get him to talk to me. He won't speak to Geirolf."

"Where is he, Torunn?" Rune asked as she wrung her hands together.

Torunn stopped before their mother's bower. The door was open just enough to make out the endless babble that accompanied the uttering of a mad man.

Rune pushed on the door and entered with Bergen following close behind. The candles were unlit. The hearth was cold. The queen's bower was dark save for the streak of bedroom light that spilled into the sitting room.

The smell of death grew stronger as they drew closer to their mother's bedchamber. The inane ramblings became clearer until they approached the threshold where they could hear the words.

"Please forgive me...Caoilinn? Please...I didn't mean to—I didn't mean..."

Rune pushed open the door. On the bed, his mother lay. And on the floor, by her side, sat his father. Weeping, Tryggve clutched his wife's cold hand.

"Swann...Sweet Swann," he muttered, smiling at Caoilinn's lifeless eyes. "With silver eyes..." he said. "So like yours. They glisten like pearls. Can you see them, Caoilinn? See them." His lips quivered and his face turned down with anger. "Won't you look at me? Look at me. Please look at me, Caoilinn. Please? It's because I killed them, isn't it? That you won't talk to me?"

Bergen stopped at the door beside Rune and both brothers watched, unable to speak.

"I killed them..." Tryggve said. He stroked her golden hair. "I killed them all...every child...every mother...every soldier...I killed them all. I had to. They killed our Swann...our precious..." Tryggve pursed his lips. "Please talk to me, Caoilinn. Talk to me...Won't you speak to me? You're mad at me. Because I couldn't...Forgive me? You must forgive me. Please forgive..."

Bergen turned without a word and stomped back through the sitting room to the corridor. Down the steps into the Great Hall, he ran, not bothering a glance to the empty throne seated between the High Seat pillars engraved with wolves.

His hands struck the great oak doors and Bergen ran down the steps, past the stream of mead into the courtyard to the stables around the west tower.

"Bergen!"

Bergen paid his brother no mind.

"Bergen!" Rune was already closing in on his heels, but Bergen kept running. "Where are you going?"

"To the mountains, Brother."

Rune stopped at the stable door as Bergen began saddling his horse.

"The Dvergar," Rune said. "Bergen. You can't go. They'll kill you."

"Their enemy is my enemy," Bergen said. "They will help us."

"They will kill you!"

Bergen stepped in so that he stood face to face with his brother.

The soft sob at the stable door quelled the argument and drew their attention to Torunn. A beam of moonlight flooded her reddened face enough that they could see the fresh wave of tears. He knew that shadow that clung so desperately behind her eyes.

"The king..." she spoke between sobs. "Your father...he..."

Shaking her head, Torunn turned. Hugging her arms, she wandered back to the keep alone.

"No!" Bergen screamed and lunged right into Rune's fist. Bergen fell back, shook the initial shock off and returned a punch to Rune's jaw. Before Rune could recover, Bergen slammed himself into Rune, who dropped his hands hard onto Bergen's shoulders and held him there.

"He isn't!" Bergen growled and Rune dropped his brow to his brother's. "Not Father! Not..." Bergen's breath punched the air as his head spun as if desperate to find something to cling to.

Zabbai.

His chest throbbed with that pain that twisted his insides.

Swann.

Rage burned his skin from the inside out.

Mother.

"Breathe, Bergen," Rune said.

Now Father.

"No!" Bergen shouted and shoved Rune back. "I will go to the mountains!"

"Bergen, they will kill you," Rune said.

"I have no choice!"

"You always have a choice."

Bergen shoved his hand through his hair again and again, each time he saw Zabbai then Swann then Caoilinn...

"Do I?" Bergen gasped. "What choice is there? To stand here and watch you die? Do you call that a choice?"

"It's a risk I must take as king," Rune said.

Bergen studied the silver-blue eyes so like his. Apathy was taking his brother, the king. Bergen knew the signs well. Rune, who spent his youth training for this day. His brother, Rune, King of Gunir. Choice and risk were two things Rune would never have the luxury to exercise.

"I am not king," Bergen said. "I don't have to risk."

"There is another way," Rune said. "War isn't our only option."

"Isn't it?" Bergen said. "And will you be here when the Dokkalfar find their dead and come to tear down our walls? Will you stand by, idle and ready to negotiate while they carve open your back and tear out your ribs?" Bergen shook his head. "No, Brother. I will not be one who stands and fights to die. You said yourself that their weapons are too great and they have a Seidkona."

"The Dokkalfar will come and we will defend ourselves," Rune said.

"They started this!" Bergen shouted. "When they took Swann's life from her, they took the very spirit from this city. Just like Zabbai!"

A familiar cold plunged itself through Bergen's rage as he realized what he had just said.

"Bergen," Rune said.

Bergen's throat clamped shut and he turned his attention to his hate and the saddle.

"Bergen, what happened in Râ-Kedet?"

"I'm going," Bergen grumbled.

"Bergen."

Bergen raised his eyes to his brother and shook his head. "I can't stay here." He pulled himself into the saddle and pulled back the reins, steering the horse from the stall. "I'm going for help."

"Bergen."

"Goodbye, Brother." And snapping the reins, Bergen sent his horse cantering out of the stables.

"Bergen!"

Rune fell to the courtyard of stone.

My sister. My mother. My father. My brother.

His back hunched as a shadow crept in. He felt it like fingers twisting its darkness through him, cutting off his air. A cold chill, a dark pain remained in its wake like a wraith.

Rune gasped against the pain, insurmountable pain that made it hurt to breathe. His body shook as he battled back the shadow that threatened to take him.

And why shouldn't it?

He stared at the stone. He wanted to die, to rise up and kill, to avenge.

This shadow.

He watched it twist its ugly darkness into his mother in a matter of moments until she succumbed to its plague, its vile filth. He watched it consume his father, who rose up and slaughtered the children. And now it took Bergen.

"Rune?"

Rune ignored Geirolf's quaking voice.

"Rune."

This is how it will be: the shadow and me.

"Your Majesty."

The title pulled Rune's attention back to Gunir. "What is it, Geirolf?"

No answer.

Rune pulled himself up from his knees while wrestling back the shadow that had beaten him down to subservience.

"Geirolf. What is it?" Rune said and looked to Geirolf.

As white as his hair, Geirolf stood sick with fear, his attention not on the west where Bergen had fled or on the new king beside him, but the Dokkalfar army that filled the horizon to the south.

Eyolf.

At the bottommost depths of Rune's being, a fire sparked to life and he raised his eyes to the horizon. The shadow within swelled, urging him to fight, to avenge, and to spill the blood of those who killed his sister. That was what the shadow wanted.

Rune focused all his energy on the flame that churned his insides.

The shadow did this. The shadow did all of this.

"Your Highness?" Geirolf asked.

Rune looked at Geirolf and raised his head with the command taught to him by his father. "To war," Rune said as the Dokkalfar war horn sounded.

Part Two

Chapter 8

995th year after Baldr

Olaf listened to the sweet voice flowing down the limestone cave lit with torches. The usual stench of bat feces, ammonia, and dampness was strangely absent, just as it had been a moon ago when he had last visited the Seidkona's domicile. Nevertheless, he pulled his fur and hide coat tighter around broad shoulders made wide from three decades of swordplay. His long, blond beard protruded from the fur lapels of his coat as his blue eyes scanned the darkness.

He proceeded as cautiously now as he had then, each step landing him in the small stream that trickled its way deeper into the cave. A misplaced step caused him to favor his left leg. The wound that nearly cost him his life a month ago had not yet fully healed. When the faint glow of firelight reached him from around a sharp turn, relief relaxed him.

The scent of stew teased Olaf's appetite when he turned the corner and ducked to enter the small, shallow room. Accessories, furniture, and décor dressed the limestone cave, making it into a proper home.

In the center of the room, a small fire crackled beneath a large soapstone pot fixed on an iron tri-stand. The Seidkona had shoved a table and chair against the cave wall along with barrels of food. Herbs and spices hung on a rack she positioned in place from the ceiling, although he couldn't quite see how. Tapestries and hides dressed the walls to hide the jagged façade and warmed the feel of the room. The Seidkona had a handful of candles burning on the table between two empty wooden bowls.

A large hide hanging from the cave wall served as a door to what Olaf could only imagine was a second room as comfortable as the first. It was there he could hear her voice glide almost like a spell that fogged his mind and threatened to leave him senseless. He found himself fighting it to preserve his angst. He didn't have to wait long for her voluptuous frame to emerge from that passage.

"You came back." A pleased smile pulled the corner of her red lips. The firelight danced in her round, gold eyes and, for a moment, he forgot to answer.

"I did."

She tilted her head and Olaf watched her long, black hair fall down her curves where his eyes lingered. He wasn't sure if her song had stopped, but still found it hard to focus. The air was heavy with spell.

"Now you believe?" she asked.

Her question jogged his memory.

"You said my men would betray me...that I would be near death."

A pleased smirk pulled the corner of her red lips.

"And you were," she replied.

Olaf nodded. "I was."

He recalled the raid a moon ago soon after he had challenged her skill. He still felt the laugh in his throat when she had warned him that his men would betray him. Not a day later, they turned on him and he barely escaped with a wounded leg. He almost lost the leg. An arrow had nicked the artery. That laugh now felt like bile stuck in his throat. He also recalled her other words of prophesy.

"You said that I would be a great king," Olaf said.

"I said you would be renowned. Not great," she answered, walking to the fire where the stew bubbled.

Olaf stepped closer and felt the spell-air thicken as he watched her bring the ladle to her lips.

"My father..."

She sipped.

"I know who your father was." She sipped again, then stirred the stew. "And his father before him." She hung the ladle on the lip of the cauldron and looked to Olaf's blue eyes and long blond hair, so much like his father's father. She looked at him as if she was seeing far more than a usurped king on a broken throne.

"I know who you are, son of Trygg, son of Olaf, son of Fairhair."

Olaf stiffened and she smiled.

"Yes, I know about Fairhair and how he killed the great High King of Alfheim and Viken."

Lodewuk. That elf had done well to ensure Alfheim remained under the rule of his kin, the Ljosalfar in Gunir.

"And now you wish to reclaim what once was yours," the woman said.

"I wish to reclaim my father's throne," Olaf answered.

She grinned. "Liar."

The spell-air thickened as she moved around the cauldron to stand closer to Olaf. Her head reached his shoulders. "You wish to know about your beloved. Your Geira."

Olaf's back straightened at the sound of his wife's name.

"You wish to know what killed her," the Seidkona said.

"She was young," Olaf said, sharper than he had intended. He couldn't afford to anger the witch, and forced his voice steady. "And healthy..."

The Seidkona tipped her head in thought as if delighted with unearthed knowledge in which to savor. "And with child it would seem."

Olaf tried to shake his head. No one had known about the child. "My Geira didn't just die."

"No. It would seem she didn't."

She turned her back and circled the fire, taking the spell-air with her. He felt his tension return.

"Tell me what to do," he said.

The Seidkona stared. He felt her eyes on him as if she had undressed him and had seen every flaw, every scar, every secret he harbored. He remained unmoved, unbroken as she gazed long and hard. When she spoke at last, it was with careful precision.

"Seidkona have unearthed the secrets to a forgotten power that sleeps. It is best for everyone if this power remains..." She pensively sucked on her bottom lip. "Forgotten. One of them carries a pouch."

Olaf furrowed his brow. "All Seidkona carry a pouch."

The witch grinned.

"This Seidkona carries a pouch that holds an endless supply of Idunn's apples."

Olaf's mouth fell open.

Here in Midgard. Idunn's apples.

"Idunn..." His mouth watered with greed. If he had had those apples, his leg would have healed weeks ago. Not just healed, but completely restored as if there had been no wound at all.

"You know what those apples can do," she said.

Olaf nodded, swallowed the mouthful of saliva and answered, "I do."

"Kill every last Seidkona in the lands to the east. Find that Seidkona and bring her pouch to me. That is my price."

"Seidkona are rare and hard to find," Olaf answered.

"So they are." She took up the ladle again and stirred.

"Consider it done," Olaf said. He almost turned to leave.

"Son of Trygg," she said and gazed at him with golden eyes that made Olaf want to take her. "If you eat of the apple, I will kill you."

Olaf watched her blow onto the stew in the ladle.

"To eat of those apples is to gain immortal life," he argued and felt her spell-air thicken.

"There are ways to end an immortal life." She grinned and gazed up at him. "If you eat of those apples, I will kill you."

He nodded. "I understand."

Eager to get gone and leave the witch to her brew, Olaf turned for the door.

"There are others who knew of Geira's child."

Her words slammed the air from his lungs and he looked back.

"Word travelled from Eire's Land and reached the King of Dan's Reach," she said.

"Blatonn," Olaf whispered.

The Seidkona shook her head. "Not King Blatonn. His son."

"Forkbeard." He remembered the stern gaze of that spoiled prince born to the son of Gorm.

"Geira's grave is not yet cold, yet Forkbeard has inherited your wife's land and the crown of Dan's Reach," she said. "Forkbeard, the king's son who knew your wife was with child." The Seidkona stirred the stew again. "If you wish to take back your throne and avenge your wife's death, assemble an army. Start with Forkbeard's vassal, Hakon. He resides in your father's land west of the Northern Way in Nidaros. There, he plays puppet king to your people."

Would she have me march to my death?

"Forkbeard is strong," Olaf said. "His armies are great."

"So they are."

"I can not take him alone," he said. "Not with all the aid of Eire's Land."

"You can when you kill all who worship Forkbeard's gods."

Olaf's thoughts wandered to the kingdom of Asgard and the gods seated there in halls of gold.

"The Vanir," he whispered. "You would have me target Odinn, Thor, and Idunn?"

The woman shrugged and slurped more stew. "Baldr has fallen," she said. "There are greater kings with greater powers who look to bring new gods."

"Destroy the old for the new," Olaf said.

The woman grinned.

"Very well," Olaf said and made his way back to the passage. At the edge of the room, he gazed at the witch. Her black hair rippled in the firelight. "How will I know her when I find her?"

She stirred the stew so long that Olaf thought she hadn't heard and opened his mouth to ask again.

"She's the Seidkona without gold eyes."

Olaf flinched, taken aback by such a concept. All Seidkona had gold eyes. Everyone knew that. Their bodies consumed by so much Seidr...For a Seidkona to not have golden eyes...

Olaf grunted, unsure of what to think of such things. "What do I do with the Seidkona once I have her pouch?"

The Seidkona shrugged and peered up from her brew with a grin. "Whatever you wish."

The Seidkona watched the Norsemen with a satisfied gaze as he slipped back into the cave passage. Turning her back on the fire and stew, she strode to the makeshift door where she had emerged not long ago. She pulled back the hide and paid no mind when the hide became a sheet of fine, blue silk. She dropped the silk behind her and breathed in the thick spell-air of Under Earth. Skies made blue by earth and shadow and lit by veins of Seidr ignited every bit of this realm with its energy. The elding balcony where she stood twisted a path of steps down to the garden below and a lake as clear and as blue as the wings of the azul flutter-by.

Green grass grazed the soles of her bare feet. Soft fibers clung to vibrant pink flowers and succulent orange petals dripped with dew.

With her prized grin, she eyed the wide, bare back by the lake. His black hair ended at his shoulders where vines of tattoos and runes spilled down his shoulders, biceps, and back. She hungrily studied his form before moving closer.

"Took you long enough," Aaric said, looking at her. "Anything of importance?"

Fand shrugged. "Simple mortals looking to fix simple problems."

She eyed the patterns of black that trailed down his chest.

"Are you done?" Aaric asked.

Fand ignored the impatience in his tone and took up his shirt from the ground.

"Nearly," she said, taking the liberty of eyeing the patterns she had spent hours imprinting onto his body. "Danann still hasn't found you and this should be enough to keep it that way awhile longer."

She dragged a single slender finger down his chest until he yanked his shirt back and slapped her hand away. As he pulled his shirt over his head, she widened her grin at his defiance.

"If it weren't for these, I wouldn't come here it all," he said.

Tipping her head to the sky, Fand stretched her arms overhead. A long strand of black hair fell from her face.

"Such anger," she cooed.

Aaric fastened his sword to his hip then took up his hide coat and pulled that over his shoulders.

"What of the brat?" Fand asked.

"Kallan is well," Aaric mumbled, feeding his belt through the buckle.

"Still ignorant and naïve?" Fand smiled. "Still alive?"

"What do you want, Fand?"

She savored her grin and met his eyes, heartless and cold as always.

"Danann knows," Fand said, savoring the sick look that colored Aaric's dark skin white. "She suspects the Drui are still alive after all," she added and looked at the lake speckled with starlight and Seidr dust.

"What did she say?" Aaric asked.

Fand shrugged. "They're sending out mercenaries."

She studied the cold gleam in his eye.

"You're lying," he said and shoved his way past her, back to the steps.

"How can you tell?"

Her nose burned from the prick of annoyance. Aaric was on the first step.

"I want the girl, Aaric!"

Aaric stopped on the elding steps. "You can't have her."

"That wasn't the deal, Aaric. I want Kira's daughter." Fand strode to the steps and stood so that her head was forced back, exposing her slender neck. "She's too old. The girl has reached her elding. She'll know soon enough. She needs to return to Under Earth before Danann finds her."

"It isn't that simple," Aaric said. "I can't just take Kallan and move her... Eyolf would never let her go."

"Then get rid of him."

"I won't listen to this." Aaric continued up the steps.

"Aaric, your time is up!"

Aaric stopped.

"For nearly an age, I heeded your mindless, petty request." Fand watched the veins in the side of his neck pulse. "You've played with your princess. Now bring her in."

"I won't."

Fand ground her teeth. "Then I will kill her."

"No!" Aaric slammed Fand into the stone, his hand on her neck.

She felt his fingers tighten, hungry to squeeze. She smiled her sweet smile, delighted in watching the beads of sweat build on his brow.

"I can lick them off for you," she whispered.

Aaric released her neck and punched the wall with his fist, missing Fand's head by a breath. Blood trickled down the stone where he held his knuckle and Fand listened to his breath slow then steady.

"You can't...you can't kill her," Aaric said.

Fand leaned in until her lips grazed his ear.

"Bring her in," she whispered.

Aaric raised his eyes to Fand. The defeat she had milked out of him was there right where she wanted it.

"Eyolf won't let her go," he said and Fand shrugged.

"Then get rid of him."

"I won't."

He had moved to continue up the steps when Fand clasped his arm. "Get rid of him, or I will kill her."

Chapter 9

Streets of white stone twisted through homes buried between Lorlenalin's towers. The late morning sun that bathed the city in streaks of orange vanished among the dark alleys and winding side streets.

From beneath a black hood, Kallan peered through the grim lane. She didn't see the unusual blackness that twisted its way through the alley behind her. It stopped when she stopped and moved again when she pulled her cloak tighter and continued through the maze of back streets. Her feet slapped the stone, adding an articulated footfall to the silence. Behind her, the Shadow loomed.

The Seidkona descended a collection of small steps and turned into a darker passage where frequent clusters of weathered, gray planks augmented the drab of Lorlenalin's warrens. Walls loomed over her, forming a labyrinth of gorges from towers built too close together.

At the end of the narrow alley, a small door, fashioned out of warped planks and held together with fraying twine, leaned against a dilapidated frame. The Seidkona pulled at a rusted bracket, bent and turned upside-down. The Shadow watched and waited as the aged, makeshift handle rattled in her grasp. The door hinge whined and shifted. The last of the nails had come loose again. Without hesitation, she slipped through the small doorway and descended an immediate three steps into the ground, and the Shadow descended too, seeping its way down the steps behind her.

Broken barrels, weathered planks, and graying scrap wood from the docks filled the small room. A serpentine path wound its way through the maze of wood. In the far corner, near the back of the wall, the tallest of towers obstructed the path from view. With a flick of the Seidkona's wrist, blue Seidr light burst from her hand and formed a hovering orb that lit the room. The Shadow swelled and wove itself in between the planks and barrels, spilling in and around the room's natural darkness, where it concealed itself just as the Seidkona gazed over her shoulder.

Blue light touched her pearl-white skin, accenting her high cheekbones and delicate jaw. She scanned the room as her hand moved to the sword at her waist. The air was thick. The Shadow waited. Her grip tightened on her hilt when, from behind the tower of broken barrels, a boy emerged and charged the Seidkona.

He swung his stick high in the air and ululated his best battle cry. Kallan released her hilt and raised her palm where silver-blue Seidr flowed, forming a shield. At once, Kallan drained her strength into the Seidr-shield. By the time the boy brought his stick down into Kallan's ward, the Shadow was gone.

"Oh." The boy's shoulders fell and he pushed out his bottom lip. "I wanted to duel."

"Geir," Kallan said. "I am not going to raise my sword to you. Stop trying."

"You're scared I'll beat you," Geir said. His head almost reached her waist.

"You know what—" Kallan flicked her finger, sending a speck of Seidr through the air harmlessly striking his cheek.

"Ah," he cried. "That's a challenge!" He raised his play-sword again.

"Kallan!"

A girl squealed and charged, fastening herself to Kallan's ankle. The child grinned through blemishes of dirt and tangles of blond hair.

Geir groaned and lowered his stick again. "I just accepted her challenge, Kri," he said and slumped back off behind the barrels, dragging his stick behind him.

With a smile, Kallan brushed back her hood and crouched down to the child attached to her leg.

"Is Eilif here, Kri?" she asked with a gentle grin.

"He's in the back with Latha," Kri said, refusing to relinquish Kallan's leg.

"Is his nose bleeding again?"

The child nodded.

Slipping her hand into the folds of her cloak, Kallan presented a green apple that filled her palm.

"My leg for an apple?" Kallan said as the lantern light caught the white elding bracelet dangling at the end of her wrist. Intricate etchings of eternity knots and runes spanned the length of the jewel, but the apple alone drew Kri's eye.

Bristling with joy, Kri released Kallan's leg. Snatching the apple, she bound their contract and sank her teeth into the fruit. With a flourish, Kallan pulled her cloak from her shoulders, revealing a large basket crammed with herbs, fruits, breads, and salted meats. Her long brown hair fell down her back and, after draping the cloak over the basket, Kallan held her hand down to Kri.

"Let's go then," she said.

On cue, Kri leapt from the floor and snatched Kallan's hand.

Making their way around the barrels, Kallan came to a second door. This one was newer and stronger than the first, with proper hinges and a sturdy, shiny handle freshly nailed in place. Orange light poured from the cracks of the wood and streaked the shadows with a happy glow that seemed unnatural in this part of the city. Pushing open the door invited a flood of squeals and hullabaloo that accompanied a bombardment of minute Alfar children swarming Kallan's feet.

Over the sea of heads, Kallan scanned the wide, warm room laden with thick, lavish blankets and elegant furs. A large fireplace crackled beneath a soapstone cauldron that filled the home with the scent of stew. Piles of bedding were scattered about wherever there was room. Beside the hearth, the youngest child slept beneath her blankets.

"Again?" Kallan called over the children's heads to Eilif, who stood pinching Latha's nose beside the only table in the room. Clad in his plain brown robes, the scribe peered beneath the rag held to the face of a lad sitting on the table.

"Again," he said, leaving Kallan to free herself from the rabble.

It took Kallan several insane minutes to quiet the children and disperse the crowd. Exclaiming, they huddled around her basket in the center of the room, and gleefully picked through Kallan's gifts as the princess tended to Latha's nose.

"It looks like you've just lost some blood," Kallan said and shrugged, shaking her head at Latha. "That's it."

"Will it come back?" Latha asked, his round, brown eyes peering over the rag.

"I don't know," Kallan said and pulled a gold apple from the pouch fastened to her side. Unsheathing a dagger, she sank the blade into the apple's golden flesh.

"Here." Kallan offered a slice and, heaving, lowered him to the floor.

"You're getting big," she said, emphasizing a grunt. "Now, go take a look at the basket."

The boy beamed as he scarfed down the apple slice and scurried off to find a place around the basket.

Kallan was back on her feet when she felt a tug on her blue skirts.

"Kawin."

Kallan crouched to the ground.

"Yes, Rind?" she asked a girl no more than three winters old. Appearing too small for her age, and with eyes larger than her starved, sunken face seemed to be able to hold, Rind wrapped her arms around Kallan's neck and snuggled her face into the Seidkona.

Grinning, Kallan stood, taking the girl with her.

"How did Father and Daggon's clothes work out?" Kallan asked Eilif as Rind shoved a thumb into her mouth and plopped her head down on Kallan's shoulder.

"Perfect," Eilif said, fascinated by the children who were currently shredding a loaf of bread into pieces. "I used most of them to replace some of the tunics. I also made trousers for the older ones who've outgrown their rags."

"And Herdis?" Kallan asked, nodding to the sleeping girl who had not awakened despite the commotion.

"She's resting well enough now," Eilif said. "Your concoction seems to have worked. It brought the

97

fever down and it broke this morning. The infection also seems to be clearing up. The smell is gone."

Kallan nodded, hearing the relief in his voice.

"It'd be easier if I were further into my studies," she said, detesting her own limits. "Another day and I would have taken her to Gudrun."

"What about the food?" Eilif asked. "Did Cook catch you this time?"

"No." Kallan grinned. "I used a spell."

Eilif chuckled, bouncing his body with the rhythm of his laughter.

"Don't laugh," Kallan said, smiling. "That spell has saved me more times than anything else I've learned."

"I just remember Aaric and Cook protesting that you not learn it for this very reason," Eilif said, still chuckling.

"Not this reason, exactly," she said.

"But one like it," Eilif reminded her.

"I like cloudberries," Kallan said, watching the last of the bread vanish as the children started on the fruit. "Besides, this is a good reason."

As Eilif's face split into a wide grin, the door opened, emitting a brief creak that drew Kallan and Eilif's attention to Daggon, whose wide frame filled the doorway. His wild red hair spilled past his shoulders and into the wiry red beard that framed a pair of copper eyes.

"Daggon?" Kallan said.

"Yep," he said and stepped aside. Behind him, Eyolf stood as tall and as wide as Daggon with a fur and hide coat that added to his size.

"Father," Kallan said as Eilif bowed his head in genuflect.

"Kallan," Eyolf said and nodded to the scribe. "Eilif."

"Stand down, Princess," Daggon said, closing the door.

His armor clinked and moved with him as he followed behind Eyolf, who walked around the children as if they had been Kallan's gowns strewn about her chamber floor while she played with spells and swords.

"Still robbing Cook's kitchens?" Eyolf asked.

With a scrunched brow, Kallan assessed the layer of chain mail Daggon and her father wore, then studied the swords secured at their sides.

"You're armed," Kallan said. "I was told of no battle."

A smirk pulled at the edge of Daggon's mouth as Eyolf took up Kallan's hands and planted a kiss to each.

"Told you she would notice," Daggon muttered.

"I'll pay you later," Eyolf said, not bothering to hide his remark.

"What is that supposed to mean?" Kallan said as Daggon scrutinized Geir's trousers that looked too much like a man's tunic...his tunic.

"Still looking for a fight, Kallan?" Eyolf said.

She flashed him her best smile. "Always."

"Well, don't," he tried his best to scold her. "A woman of your age should be enjoying far more than just fighting."

"You taught me little else." She beamed and the firelight caught a gleam of mischief in her eye.

"You're too old to care only for swords and battle," Eyolf said.

"I care for other things," Kallan said.

Eilif stifled a bout of uncontrolled chuckling.

"And you." Eyolf peered at the scribe. "You shouldn't encourage her."

"He doesn't encourage me, Father," Kallan said, passing Rind to Eilif. "He enables me."

Eilif took the child and carried her to the basket of goods where he could escape the talk that was due between Kallan and the king.

"I'll ready the horses and leave you to your daughter," Daggon said, evoking a scowl from Eyolf.

"What was that about?" Kallan asked and her father shrugged.

"Daggon wants me to marry you off to King Ethelred of Engla Land."

Kallan flashed her best unimpressed look and took up her cloak from the table as the door closed behind Daggon.

"You must have something of importance to discuss to track me to the warrens," she said.

"I did," Eyolf said, releasing her hands as he walked around the table to put distance between themselves and the children.

"About?" Kallan asked.

"I'm marrying you off to King Ethelred of Engla Land."

There was silence and the fire popped as Kallan felt the warmth drain from her face. Eyolf grinned. "I'm kidding."

Kallan released her breath and attempted a smile back.

"We just received word that King Rune is preparing another attack."

"Again," Kallan said. "When do we leave?"

"We don't."

Kallan opened her mouth to argue.

"King Rune is growing more desperate," her father said before Kallan could intervene. "The Norns have helped you this far—"

"The Norns have nothing to do with it," Kallan said. "I'm that good."

Eyolf shook his head. "I can't let you go, Kallan."

"But I'm good," Kallan said. "You know this. I've never been wounded."

"Because you're not a target. Not yet anyway. Once they catch on that the Seidkona's apprentice is the king's daughter, the Dark One...that berserker will stop at nothing to get his hands on you. It's too dangerous."

Kallan's shoulders fell with her spirits and mood, and she gazed at the children huddled about the basket.

"They've lost so much," she said. "The least I could do is avenge their fathers for them."

"By taking their hate on for them, you hope to ease their suffering, is that it?" Eyolf asked and brushed Kallan's chin.

She looked up at his old gray eyes, weathered from stress and war.

"I can't have you fighting alongside me anymore," he said. "Don't follow. Not this time."

Kallan nodded and lowered her eyes, but Eyolf caught her chin.

"Promise," he said.

"I promise."

Eyolf kissed Kallan's brow and wrapped her in a warm hug.

"How long will you be at the keep?" she asked into the furs.

"Most of the day," Eyolf said. "I'll be back in time for sup."

Kallan nodded.

"This is just a routine inspection. I need to make sure Thorold has the troops ready. They'll be our first defense when the attack comes. Besides..." Eyolf peered down at Kallan, who looked up from the furs that tickled her nose. "Don't you have a lesson today?"

Kallan's eyes widened. "The forge. I forgot!" With a hurried kiss to his cheek, she turned for the door, then stopped at the basket of food and the huddle of children.

"Hey, Geir," she called.

Geir poked his head up just as Kallan flicked her finger. As before, a speck of gold Seidr flew through the air and harmlessly smacked Geir on the other cheek.

"Hey," Geir shouted and was on his feet, running for his sword.

With a grin and a flourish, Kallan wrapped her cloak around her shoulders and glided toward the door in a sweeping display.

The door closed with an impertinent click behind her.

"Hey! Come back here," Geir called and threw back the door. In short order, he followed behind her with his stick.

"Hel's gates," Eyolf muttered.

From the floor, Eilif smiled. "Kallan is who she is, Your Majesty."

Eyolf watched the scribe tear apart a loaf of bread for Rind.

"You're not children anymore, Eilif," he said. "If Kallan doesn't learn to expand her interests beyond orphans and swords and spells, I may just have to force the issue through marriage."

Eilif respectfully nodded and passed Kri her own helping of bread.

"You have Kallan's respect more than any of us," Eyolf said. "Perhaps you should do your part to encourage her proper behavior before I am forced to find her a husband who will."

Eilif looked up from the children.

"For her sake, Eilif. Please."

Eilif nodded to the king. "Yes, my lord," he said, leaving Eyolf to his silent contemplations.

Chapter 10

The forge glowed white from the constant heat of Kallan's flame. Beads of sweat poured down her brow as she steadied the endless stream of Seidr flowing from her hands. The smith gave another gust from the bellows, forcing air into the small pipe that fed the heat and Kallan's flames.

"Keep it up, lass," Uthbert said and gave the bellows another squeeze. "Almost there."

"How are you holding up?" Eilif asked through the heat. The young scribe maintained his distance, ensuring that Latha and Geir kept theirs. The boys sat pressing their faces into the fenced barrier, peeking hungrily between the spokes. For the moment, they seemed far more interested in Kallan's Seidr fire than the forge itself. Despite having to squint against the blinding yellows and whites mirrored on the white stone that made up Lorlenalin, the boys had sustained their audience well for the past three hours.

"I'll make it," Kallan said, battling through the exhaustion that endlessly sapped her strength. Her neck had stiffened, but it was nothing compared to the burning ache in her arms and shoulders from standing at Uthbert's forge for more than half a day.

"We're almost there," Uthbert said, sending another blast of air into the fire. "A few more degrees and we'll have an elding ingot on our hands."

The status encouraged Kallan to bear in, sending a refreshed surge of Seidr flame into the forge.

"Lady Gudrun, couldn't you just use your Seidr?" Geir asked, unable to look away from Kallan's flame.

The old woman seated in the chair behind Kallan snorted at the suggestion.

"I could," she said. "But if she ever wants to improve her own Seidr, then there's no better teacher than endurance. And so, Kallan..." Gudrun leaned closer. "...endure it!"

"You're almost there, Kallan," Eilif said over the fire's roar. "You can do it."

"Of course she can," Gudrun scolded. "I'm a damn good teacher, if I do say so myself."

"Come on, Kallan," Uthbert said. "One more should do the trick."

Kallan bore down, focusing the last of her energy into the forge, and Uthbert grinned.

"There we are," he said. "Alright, Kallan. You're done."

On cue, Kallan extinguished her flame and dropped her stiff arms. She swayed, taking in the extent of her exhaustion.

"Easy now," Gudrun said, standing up from the chair. "Here."

Gudrun withdrew a small apple from her pouch. "Get this down...now." Sunlight struck the fruit as Gudrun handed it to Kallan. A thin layer of purest gold seemed to make up the apple's skin, but when Kallan sank her teeth into the flesh, the fruit snapped like any ordinary apple would.

At once, the ache from her arms and back dissipated. The severe weakness gave way to renewed strength. With every bite, her strained muscles rewove themselves, leaving her feeling as if she hadn't just spent fourteen hours heating Uthbert's forge.

Kallan wiped the sweat from her forehead, leaving a streak of soot smudged across her brow.

"How does it look, Uthbert?" Kallan asked as the smith used his hammer and tongs to pry off the bricks and baked mud from the forge that encompassed the mold within. The boys were at their limit. After sitting for so long, they leapt up and scrambled around the forge and Uthbert, barely keeping a safe distance.

"Geir! Latha!" Eilif warned and followed the boys, ready to enforce their boundaries.

From the forge's belly, Uthbert pulled a single white crucible from the furnace. He furrowed his brow as he rested the crucible on the edge of the forge.

"Did it get hot enough?" Latha said as Uthbert smashed the ash and clay crucible away to reveal a bright yellow ingot that glowed like the sun.

"Well..." Uthbert said and shifted the ingot to an anvil beside the forge. He struck the ingot hard. Almost no slag jumped from the hot metal. He struck it again then proceeded to hammer the ingot, forcing it to conform and stretch to his design. "Looks that way," Uthbert said. "In a couple of days, Kallan, you'll have an elding war dagger on your hands. What'll you name it?"

"*Blod Tonn*," Kallan said, unable to hold back a grin.

"Blood Tooth," Uthbert translated and smiled at his work. Already the ingot looked elongated. "Is that your father's sense of humor in you?" he asked, shoving the metal back into the furnace.

Kallan raised her hands and gave the furnace another brief blast until Uthbert grunted, "Good." He returned the metal to the anvil.

"It's only fitting," Kallan said, resisting the urge to bounce on the balls of her feet. "His sword is *Blod Hjerte*. Mine should be *Blod Tonn*."

"Where is your father anyway?" Eilif asked over Uthbert's hammering. "I'm surprised he isn't here to see this."

Kallan watched the ingot clamped in Uthbert's tongs.

"He went with Daggon and Aaric," she said. "They're making a run to the keep."

"What for?" Gudrun asked. "An inspection isn't due for another moon."

Uthbert struck the ingot, stretching the hot metal into what started to resemble a flat strip.

"With the constant threat from King Rune, Father wanted to be sure the keep is armed and ready."

"And you're not with them?" Eilif asked.

Kallan shrugged.

"It's not a fight. It's just a standard troop check."

"Besides, you needed the training," Gudrun grumped. The twinkle in her eye assured Kallan she was in for a fight.

"I'm not half bad," she said to her grandmother.

"You can also do better," Gudrun replied, goading the argument from Kallan.

Kallan's mouth was agape, ready to rebut, when the sudden stomp of a horse's hooves pounded the white stone of the courtyard.

Kallan and Eilif jumped and looked to the worn rider, the forge forgotten. From atop Astrid, the king's horse, Aaric stared down with troubled eyes. A fresh cut seeped blood down his tattooed left arm.

"Aaric?" Kallan asked, perplexed at the large figure and his unprecedented arrival.

"It's your father," Aaric said. "There's been an ambush."

The high summer sun beat down as the wind burned Kallan's ears. Astrid's hooves struck the ground and she snapped the reins, urging the horse on through the barren fields to the outpost at the edge of the forest.

Within minutes, the Dokkalfar keep was in sight, and with it, the swarm of Ljosalfar surrounding Daggon, who battled them alone. At his feet lay dead the two dozen that had accompanied Daggon and King Eyolf that morning. Pulling Astrid to a stop, Kallan slid from the dark, reddish-brown horse and strode to the raid ahead. Only a handful remained. The ring of her blade announced her arrival and attracted the first of her enemy.

Tightening her grip on the hilt, Kallan raised her elding sword and pivoted as a Ljosalfr brought down his blade. She blocked and sunk her blade into the soldier. Kallan caught a flash of steel. With a heavy thud, he dropped to the ground. She had no time to study the frozen fear that peered up from the lifeless young face before another charged her, as eager as the last to boast a Seidkona's death.

With careful calculation that allowed her to predict their actions, she dodged each swing.

Kallan plunged her sword into another warrior, who fell to the ground. She scanned the field, assessing the number left standing as she raised her sword and charged.

"Daggon," Kallan called to the redheaded mammoth. "Where's Father?"

With his sword raised for the blow, a Ljosalfr charged Daggon.

"I saw him go into the keep," the captain shouted back over the clang of Ljosalfr iron against Dokkalfr elding steel.

Kallan gave her blade a final thrust as the life withered from a Ljosalfr. Withdrawing her sword, she turned and sank the blade into a Ljosalfar preparing to throw his spear. Over-eager pride blanketed his face as the spearman slumped to the ground. Another Ljosalfr charged as the salt from Kallan's sweat burned her lips. With axe raised, he set his interests on the Seidkona whose sword remained buried in the soldier's chest.

Turning up her wrist, Kallan pulled from the energy produced in her core. Seidr flame burst to life in her hand and she fired, catching the Ljosalfr in a torrent of flame, all before his blade could cleave her head in two.

His screams lasted as long as his stubborn refusal to relinquish his weapon. She held him there until he released the axe. Kallan extinguished her Seidr as the scent of roasting flesh churned her stomach, and the charred body slumped to the ground. The final wave of soldiers charged with weapons raised.

Leaving the blade to rest in the spearman, and with both palms ablaze, Kallan brandished her arms and unleashed her Seidr. Like dual whips, her fire cut the air, searing a spearman to the far right, while, behind him, another advanced. Ceasing her fire, Kallan reclaimed her sword and turned in time to plunge the blade into an advancing warrior.

"There," Kallan cried as a Ljosalfar lunged, but Daggon had already seen the last of them, who had taken off on horseback. His armband bearing her father's crest glistened in the sun's light as the captain mounted Kallan's horse, intent on pursuing the rider into the forests bordering Midgard.

Kallan's broken breath unsettled the silence that stretched over the dead as she took in the carnage. Systematically, she assessed the many faces lying in pools of their own blood.

"Father?"

The rustling wind rolling over the bodies was the only answer, confirming the onslaught of troops had ended.

Kallan studied the tall stone tower beside her.

"Father," she called again, remembering Aaric's report.

"It was just a routine inspection. We weren't ready. We didn't even see them coming."

Aaric had rushed through the update as Kallan mounted her father's horse. *"Daggon and your father were holding them off well enough on their own, but there's no telling if more are right behind them!"*

"Go on ahead. I'll gather the war-men. We'll be right behind you."

But there were no war-men.

Pushed haphazardly by the wind, the door of the keep clanked against the stone and, flexing her grip on the hilt, Kallan brandished her sword and vanished into the darkness.

Chapter 11

A thick, heavy cold enclosed within the keep added to the stagnant dampness that enveloped Kallan. Light fought to invade the darkness, casting splashes of sun onto the stone. Lines of water were visible where moisture had collected down the gray walls.

Kallan raised her sword and relaxed her shoulders, despite the gnawing suspicion that she was very much alone. Keeping her senses sharp, she made her way up each step, straining to hear the slightest sound. The warm summer air billowed up the stairs, catching her skirts in the breeze.

At the top of the stairs, slivers of light spilled over the top step onto a platform where a door swung ajar. Kallan flexed her fingers around the hilt, assuring herself that her sword was ready. She stepped onto the platform. As gently as a gust of wind would rustle the needles of a pine, Kallan pushed against the door and entered the room.

An upturned chair lay on its side next to a small table pushed awkwardly into a corner. Droplets of red spattered the floor and mingled with vellum maps ruined with blood. The only movement was the dust visible in the stream of sunlight pouring in through a window and streaking the stone floor.

Dropping her arms with a sigh, Kallan sheathed her sword and moved to the window where she hoped for a better view in which to find her father. A breeze swept across her face as she looked down where the dead littered the ground. She breathed easier once she saw that her father was not one of them. In the west, beyond the hills of Alfheim, pines reached to the clear sky where the edge of the wood became Midgard. Across the extensive plain, grass rippled like the sea beneath the low winds.

Centuries had passed since she had wandered beyond the West Wood where the thin air burned the skin with winds too cold to breathe. From the trees, Kallan looked to the south. Towering mountain peaks guarded Lorlenalin. Her eyes trailed down from the fields streaked with green, to the plains of Alfheim. It was there, in the distance, over meandering lakes and streams, that she saw them: four Ljos-alfar, riding for Gunir in the east. She didn't have to meet the elusive King Rune to know it was him. Her stomach churned as heat climbed to her throat.

"Coward," she muttered and averted her thoughts to the numerous dead, disposed for his convenience, at the foot of the keep.

Kicking a chair across the floor, Kallan strode from the room as it smashed into pieces against the wall.

"Father," Kallan called as she plodded down the stairs, filling the keep with echoes.

Her ever-rising anxiety did nothing to quell her nerves.

"Father," she cried and bit her lip in angst. "F—"

Kallan gasped.

With a trembling hand bathed in blackish red, Kallan's father, King Eyolf, clutched the side of the keep. Drained of color, his skin was a waxy, yellowing hue. His cold, empty eyes reflected his waning life as the king battled to stabilize his breath through a mouth blackened with blood.

"F—Father?"

The great Dokkalfr shook as he released the door and fell into his daughter's arms. Taking her sanity with her, Kallan sank to the ground, doing her best to hold him off the cold earth.

Liquid pulsed from his stomach, filling the air with the stench of pungent metal.

"Father?" The word scraped her throat.

Desperate to keep him alive, Kallan fumbled with the pouch at her waist. With a shaking hand, she dug mindlessly among the contents, thinking only of the soft round treasure that could save him. Dread clouded her senses as her trembling fingers found the single gold apple.

Pulling it from her pouch, she held it to her father's bloody lips and, at once, her mind went blank.

She did not know the incantation.

Words and spells flooded her mind, providing no aid while she held the precious fruit to her father. Hope diminished with every spell Kallan discarded, her desperation rising until her mind was frozen, devoured by a dark void.

Kallan could not feel his heavy body resting in her arms. She could not smell the metallic stench of blood. She could not think.

"K—Kallan." Eyolf's white lips trembled as he spoke her name. His body convulsed as he fought to stay beside her, desperate to speak the words that would not come.

Kallan held the apple, her eyes widened in horror, confounded at his idleness, waiting and believing that a single bite would be enough to stay Death's hand if only she could remember the right words.

The sun's light warmed her, but Kallan felt nothing. There she sat, until King Eyolf's breath left him. Still she held him, offering the apple smeared with blood and willing herself to mutter the words she had never learned, the words that could no longer save him.

Kallan did not see the vast clouds move in from the sea in the south as they flooded the skies with a gray chill that consumed all of Alfheim. She did not feel the strands of hair sting her face like tiny whips thrashed relentlessly by winds that raced through the plains carrying the crisp scent of unfallen Nordic rain. She did not hear Daggon's distorted cries, or feel the earth shake from the pounding hooves of the war-men.

Kallan, daughter of Eyolf, felt nothing. Not when Daggon's large arm wrapped around her waist and lifted her from her father's side. Not when he sat her down in front of him, nor when her limp fingers released the golden apple that fell to the blood-soaked earth and came to rest beside her father's body.

"It was just an inspection."

"Dozens swarmed them from nowhere."

"No notice. No warning."

"She didn't see who did it?"

"She had gone into the keep."

"Stabbed from the back."

"Found her holding him."

Kallan couldn't identify the voices. Countless hands led her to her room then bathed and dressed her. She could not see that Daggon guided her to the courtyard before the Dokkalfar. She could not feel the weight of the silver circlet on her brow or the wind as she stood on the shores, watching her father's body set ablaze in a ship sent to sea. She did not hear when Gudrun called upon the gods to guide Eyolf to Odinn's halls. Kallan, daughter of Eyolf, Queen of the Dokkalfar, stood cold, empty, and oblivious to the weight of the signet ring bearing down on her finger.

The room was dark, save for the moonlight that stretched across the stone floor of Kallan's chambers. Still dressed in ceremonial gowns of white and silver, with faceted blue gems, Kallan stared across her room and out her window, to the north and Gunir. Her blackened wall of ice was complete, allowing her to think again without having to feel anything beyond the heavy numbness pulling down on her body.

She took a step. Her shoulders were stiff, her feet like weights. She could still feel her father's kiss on her brow from that morning. An invisible blade impaled her and twisted its way into her chest. Kallan closed her eyes and amassed her pain, her hurt, her grief. With it, she built a vast, black wall around memories that would be the death of her. Higher, thicker, colder, she secured the wall until she was numb and hate alone remained on the outside.

Bury the memory. Bury it all.

She pulled in a deep breath, filling her mind with simpler thoughts, safe thoughts, and forced the slew of memories behind the wall where, one by one, time would erase them. Opening her eyes, Kallan took a second step toward the window.

Numbed to the grief she refused to feel, she was free to think again, and replayed recent events.

The reports are always consistent. Rune always reports to the Southern Keep...on every moon. Father—

Her insides screamed and tightened. Her eyes burned as she gulped down a hot ball in her throat. Her hand curled into a fist as she crammed the memories deeper beneath the wall.

"All of them," she breathed and stifled a sob. "Everything."

She forgot her father's goodnight kiss. She forgot his morning hug. She forgot the gleam in his eye that followed her every question. She forgot the warmth of his voice, until the blade in her chest had dulled and the agony eased.

Kallan opened her eyes and took another step toward the window.

After every inspection, Rune meets the Dark One at Swann Dalr in the Alfheim wood.

She absorbed the cold that numbed her grief and slowed her pain to a silent standstill. Kallan built her wall higher.

That is where we'll strike, she decided as her thoughts finally flowed free of pain.

A chill webbed through Kallan's spine, but she did not shudder. Her iridescent eyes sparkled as she raised them to the moon's light and knew exactly how to proceed.

A cold, dark smile spread across Kallan's face.

With the pieces aligned, the plan was perfect, and, this time, King Rune would die.

Chapter 12

The acidic venom collected at the tip of the snake's fang and then splattered onto Loptr's brow. The poison seared his flesh, and he howled with a rage that shook the rocks that bound him.

The pain subsided and Loptr inhaled sharply, releasing his breath. The snake tied to the stone above his head hissed. Another drop was already forming on the serpent's tooth, promising another wave of agony.

Loptr shifted his body on the rock bed and winced. Fresh cuts sliced his back and split the old ones. Struggling to lift his head, Loptr searched the black rocks and boulders that made up his earthly prison.

The sudden sound of splintering wood pulled his attention to the large, winged worm that raised his black, stone-like eyes to him. Its jaw moved with lethal precision. Blinking curiously, the worm studied the giant chained to the stones and then returned to his meal of Yggdrasill root. Its large talons clung to the wood that protruded from the mountain's side.

Loptr pulled his attention from the black worm to the pile of discarded clay bowls. Sigyn was not back yet. She would be back. She always came back. Nevertheless, the venom dripped and Loptr's hatred grew ever more for Odinn.

The giant gazed at his bonds. Odinn's words still echoed in his mind.

"*Special bonds,*" Odinn had called them. "*Unbreakable.*" He had given Loptr that contemptible grin. "*Made by the Dvergar.*"

"And with elding, no doubt," Loptr grumbled aloud while inspecting the silver sheen that glistened on the black metal.

The worm munched his meal with disinterest.

Loptr had spent the first of several months fighting the bonds that held him. The enchanted metal showed no signs of wear. If anything, it appeared to be stronger, thicker.

"*I had them forged just for you with what little remained of your sons,*" Odinn had said.

Raw hate twisted Loptr's insides with the flood of memories that invaded his senses. He remembered the random adventures spent in Odinn's company, when they would end the day exchanging women, story, and mead.

Another drop fell from the snake's fang and Loptr howled, shaking against the pain.

Sigyn would be back soon.

"Sigyn," he whispered. She has suffered so much already. Odinn had killed their sons. Loptr would be sure to return the favor.

The giant pulled on the chains again, still seething with rage. Another drop of venom fell and Loptr bellowed, trembling against the pain. Again, the pain subsided and only the shadow remained while he lay stretched on the stone, panting. His black hair covered his face like long, menacing fingers. Loptr opened his vivid, green eyes and gazed at the snake hanging above him.

He would find a way to escape and he would see to it that Odinn suffered as much as his beautiful Sigyn.

Yes. Odinn would suffer.

Chapter 13

Kallan sat among the fire's glow as Aaric unrolled a map on the table in front of her. Bracing his weight on the back of her chair, the high marshal leaned over Kallan's shoulder and tapped the lines that were the forest of Swann Dalr. The inked etchings on his hand moved with his finger in the orange light.

"The Ljosalfar have returned from the Southern Keep with the king," Aaric said. "Everything is on schedule."

"What are their numbers?" Kallan asked, studying the marking that was the Ljosalfar's keep positioned on the southernmost borders of Alfheim in the east.

"Daggon's advance there has decreased their numbers to seven thousand," Aaric said. "The march back to Swann Dalr has left them weak. They haven't the stamina to sustain a fight. They've secured their camp for the night and our scouts report that most of them now sleep."

Kallan shifted her gaze to the Ljosalfar keep north of Gunir marked, in faded ink.

"And what of the Dark One?" she asked, gazing up at Aaric. A set of war braids framed his face.

Aaric pulled his hand from the map. "Reports confirm he is still at the Northern Keep where you left him."

"And their numbers?" Kallan asked. "Do they look to recover and join King Rune at Swann Dalr?"

Aaric shook his head. "The ruse was a success. The Dark One arrived as you predicted. Scouts reported that he and his army left the Northern Keep before Gudrun's spell wore off. The Dark One rides now to Swann Dalr. He carries word that everyone at the Northern Keep is dead. It will be another two days before the Dark One arrives."

Kallan nodded. "We'll be long gone by then. And King Rune?"

"He suspects nothing, nor has he reason to. The diversions we implemented were successful in convincing Rune's scouts that we pulled back to Lorlenalin."

Kallan stood, forcing Aaric to stand upright. Absentmindedly, she turned over the white elding bracelet on her wrist.

In the center of the room, the tall fire brazier crackled, exuding its warmth as she crossed the bearskins splayed on the floor of her tent. The table, a chair, and a suit of plain, unmarked armor composed her simple accommodations along with a bed and a chest of clothes. Thick tapestries woven from deep blues and gem-like greens lined the walls besides the occasional standard hung on posts. They added the only color to the brown, earthen room.

Beside the map table, she had tucked away a box with a brass latch. Daggers, swords, and a shield covered her bed.

"What of the Dark One's scout?" she asked, coming to stand beside the brazier in the room's center.

"Dispatched," Aaric said. "King Rune waits for word in Swann Dalr, but assumes no more than the usual skirmish has happened at the Northern Keep. The Dark One believes our troops to the north have withdrawn to Lorlenalin."

Kallan returned to the map table.

"Notify Daggon," she said. "I want to depart before dawn. We must be in position and move in while they still sleep. We'll move the twelve-thousand in here..." Kallan tapped a finger to the west of the words 'Swann Dalr.' "...and here," she said, tapping to the south of the words. "I want Gudrun in position with them."

"What about the north side?"

Kallan shook her head.

"That side is too steep to climb and forms a natural barrier that closes them in. By leaving the east side open, they won't grow desperate before they realize what's happened. What hour is it?"

"The moon has arched," Aaric said. "Another three hours before dawn."

"Before dawn," Kallan muttered.

Replaying the strategy over once more, Kallan returned to the fire. Orange light flickered across her face. Hours ago, she had blocked out the tension and unease felt by her war-men. To her, this was a game and she, too clearly, could see its end. In her mind, King Rune was already dead.

"Kallan." Kallan ignored the strain in Aaric's voice. "You know my thoughts on this," he said. "It isn't too late to back down."

Kallan took her eyes from the fire. "We've been through this, Aaric," Kallan said. "I did not spend the past year aligning my men, risking my war-men, and scouring Alfheim to find Rune's base in Swann Dalr all to back out now."

"The effort hasn't been for naught," Aaric said. "You've shown the Ljosalfar what you're capable of this past fortnight. In four days alone, you've sent Daggon's army against Rune's Southern Keep while Gudrun single-handedly wiped out the four-thousand to the north, giving you the chance to find Swann Dalr. We can go home and spare the lives, recharge, re-plan, and strike again bef—"

"A move now will clinch this," she said. "We have a chance to live without war."

"But why waste the lives, when we have an opportunity to extend a hand for peace?"

"It's been done," Kallan said, raising her voice. "We've been to war, pulled back, offered peace, and sent out the army against the king's advancements, losing more numbers in the process. Thousands could have been saved if we simply moved when we should have ages ago."

"The troops are anxious," Aaric said. "Tension is on the rise, what with Eyo—"

Kallan stared at Aaric with a cold look of madness.

Aaric tightened his jaw. A hot ember in the fire popped and Kallan relaxed her shoulders.

"I'm sorry," Kallan replied and returned her gaze to the flames. "Leave me."

The rugs dampened Aaric's heavy footsteps and a cool breeze infiltrated the tent as he dropped the hide flap behind him.

Orange light colored the room. Kallan stared into the fire. Inhaling deeply, she pulled her attention back to the present situation and released a long sigh.

The latched box beneath the table caught her eye. After rolling, wrapping, and storing the map, she pulled the box from the floor and emptied its contents onto the table. Within moments, the rich aroma of sweet lavender, sage, and valerian root filled her tent. She positioned various herbs and bottles around a pestle and mortar alongside the trinkets and treasures she pulled from the box. As if her fingers moved without consciousness, Kallan swiftly distributed the powders among a collection of tiny bowls. With a firm hand, she began powdering and combining ingredients that she then sifted into folded packets.

After a long quarter of an hour, Kallan looked up from her work. The troops outside were quiet, like the calm that always came before every storm.

"Swann Dalr," she whispered and permitted her thoughts to wander to the King of Gunir.

The opportunity was prime. The chance of failure, slim.

To see the face of the man who killed my father...not broken and beaten...but as a king...as his men see him.

"And then I'll kill him," she muttered.

Eager anxiety filled her and she decided.

Throwing open the lid of the chest nestled at the foot of her bed, Kallan dug beneath her gowns and collected the Ljosalfar apron dress, the cloak, and the pair of brooches she had secreted away. Placing her pouch onto the table, she stripped her gown and dumped it over the back of the chair.

Gudrun can kill me later, she mused, pulling the plain brown dress over her chemise and fastening the straps with the brooches.

After pulling the signet ring from her finger and the white bracelet from her wrist, she placed her mother's pendant on the table beside the ring. Wrapping the threadbare cloak around her shoulders, Kallan freed her hair, and shuffled the contents of her pouch. She found the folded packet among the contents almost immediately and scrutinized the brown powder she poured into her hand like sand.

More than enough for two applications and Astrid.

Bringing her hand to her lips, Kallan blew the powder into the air. With her palm still open, she muttered a spell under her breath. Golden Seidr rolled from her hand in puffs of cloud. It enveloped the powder, then carried it up and around her like a blanket as Kallan whispered the words, all before the powder could waft to the ground. She whispered until a layer of Seidr wrapped and concealed her.

Pushing aside the tent's hide flap, Kallan peered into the Dokkalfar camp. Soldiers said little as they hovered around fires. Some sharpened swords while others slept, eager to catch a few hours of sleep before battle. In the distance, too far to see, a rigid laugh cut the weight in the air. Aaric was right. Tension was high.

Several paces away, Kallan spotted Daggon with Aaric. The black runes that began on Aaric's knuckles stretched up his arms and across his shoulders, down to the curve of his back. Daggon shoved a nervous hand through his red hair as he listened to Aaric's report. Gudrun was nowhere in sight. With a deep breath, Kallan slipped into the camp and rounded her tent to the trees where Astrid grazed beside his tethered tree.

Kallan held her breath, then waited. Once she was certain her passing had gone unnoticed, she made her way to her horse.

"Sh. Sh. Sh," Kallan hushed as the stallion snorted. After enclosing Astrid in the same blanket of Seidr that concealed her, she pulled herself into the saddle and rode from the Dokkalfar camp to Swann Dalr.

Chapter 14

Kallan stared from the trees of Swann Dalr. Ljosalfar spanned the valley out as far as the darkness allowed. Hundreds of lights from campfires and torches peppered the camp. Kallan watched, hidden away in her enemy's shadows, her whispers heard only by the rolling wind beneath the midnight moon.

"Seven thousand sleep. Seven thousand fathers...seven thousand sons whose wives and mothers will weep, all unaware of their fate the dawn will bring."

Kallan memorized the face of a lone soldier who sat polishing his sword before a fire.

"Are your thoughts filled by a wife, a lover, your child? When this battle ends, and you, my friend, have fallen, what children will be left to die in Gunir's streets?" Kallan watched his scarred hands as they slid up the blade with care. "How I hate to kill you," she whispered. "How I hate more that you seek to kill me, and how I hate most your bloodthirsty king who orders the slaying of my kin."

Kallan blinked back her hot tears. "How I hate the actions he evokes from me...the life he bestowed upon me. How I hate he, who has made orphans of the children and of me."

Seven thousand.

All would be dead by morning.

The king's army slept soundly, some outside around the campfires that still burned, while others slept peacefully within the confines of their tents. Not even a dozen meandered about the camp. Fewer still were posted on guard and walked the perimeter, but that wasn't why she was there. She was there for him.

Abandoning the safety of the empty mead barrels, Kallan walked a final round through the Ljosalfar camp, desperate to find the king's tent, desperate to see the face of the man who killed her father, eager to sink her Seidr into him. Kallan searched the Ljosalfar camp nestled within the crook of Swann Dalr, but the black of night had begun to wane as it counted down her last hour.

An hour away, barely more. The spell will be wearing soon.

Suppressing a loud sigh, Kallan bit the corner of her bottom lip and made for the trees. She stepped around a warrior and studied his sleeping face.

Somebody's son. Somebody's father.

130

She frowned at the waste.

This one will be wriggling on the end of my sword soon enough.

Kallan doubled her pace. The trees were just in sight.

A guard walked by and stopped, studying the soil where Kallan's foot had touched the ground. She held her breath, afraid to move while he searched for the source of her print.

He raised his eyes and looked right through her, peering hard into the shadows where she was heading.

Only when Kallan felt his eyes pierce her beating heart did he move on, leaving Kallan free to breathe and a clear path to the wood. She softened her footfall and hastened her step. Within twenty paces, she had exited the camp. Another ten and the spell wore off. Five paces. A lone Ljosalfr out for an early hunt had spotted her. Two paces more and he was following her.

Kallan decided not to kill him. She wanted to. It would be too easy. A flick of the wrists and he would be dead on the forest floor where only a skilled tracker could find him, but she knew better. A missing hunter in these woods, on this night, was the last thing she needed.

She diverted her path, hoping to lose him yet again. Despite every attempt made, she failed to shake him. Kallan listened to the forest behind her. She had to strain to hear the offset rhythm of the Ljosalfr within the subtle winds. Only Daggon had ever given her such trouble.

Whoever trained him, trained him well.

Kallan clutched her fists, forcing her arms stiff at her side. The Ljosalfar clothes fooled him now, but the moment she summoned her Seidr, he would know she was no common peasant.

Dawn would soon come, and Daggon would be ready to ride into battle. She was running out of time. Kallan stopped and stepped to turn, to confront him, but in that moment, the silence changed.

The shapes within the trees shifted, and a new chill brushed her skin. Kallan slowed her breath as she fought the urge to attack...not the Ljosalfr behind her, but the sudden whispers in the shadows within the forest's umbra. A shiver ran along her spine, her insides quaked, and her hand flew to her neck for the pendant that was not there. A cold crept down her face as the remembered.

Mother's pendant is on my desk.

She tightened her hand into a fist.

Five. She counted as their indecipherable whispers awakened ancient dreams she could not remember.

Kallan leaned closer to the nameless shapes, desperate to hear what words they spoke, eager to force the forgotten memories as the Ljosalfr watched from behind. Closer, they moved, the whispers growing with the darkness. The shadows withdrew as an animal snorted. Kallan spun about and froze.

A wild boar, displaying its teeth behind its tusks, stared with beady, black eyes. Undaunted by the fact that the beast outweighed her by three hundred pounds, Kallan raised her hands as the animal pawed at the ground.

A single pulse through its heart is all I need. If I can just touch it...

The boar squealed then charged. Its muscle rippled as its hooves pounded the ground and Kallan, holding her breath, braced for impact.

A sudden squeal became a scream, and the boar hit the ground, sliding to a halt at Kallan's feet as it kicked the air, twitched once, twice, then no more. A Ljosalfr arrow, perfectly positioned behind the boar's front leg, protruded from its heart.

Discretely, Kallan drained the Seidr from her arms and spun to the Ljosalfr, who had stepped from the forest.

Clad in brown leather armor, he lowered a bow to his side that he gripped with gloved hands. A quiver hung from his belt next to a small hunting dagger. Had it not been for his large arms, honed from years of swordplay, she would have mistaken him for an ordinary hunter.

"You're a long way from home, princess."

His words fell like ice down her spine and she fought the urge to attack, to kill, and run. Kallan swallowed the lump that had risen in her throat. She raced through a number of possible replies, each one as unlikely as the last. The back of her neck burned with rising panic.

"Everyone knows the forest is out of bounds." His stern, silver-blue eyes held her full attention. "What coerced you to break the king's law?"

He doesn't know. She swallowed the scream that had filled her throat as his voice rolled over her like Odinn's thunder, and her shoulders dropped. She drew breath again while she scrambled for a credible answer to give.

"Your men," she said. "They followed me."

The hunter raised a curious brow.

"We are alone," he said.

"Five, at least, stood among the brushes." She pointed toward the trees. "Only moments ago. Your comrades."

She ensured her voice remained strong.

The Ljosalfr moved his hand to his dagger as Kallan listened for the Shadows, but the whispering had ceased and the night's bottomless black had ebbed, leaving behind the last of the usual forest shadows of the night.

The Ljosalfr shook his head. "I came alone."

Kallan studied his face for deception, but his vow was adamant. He spoke the truth or lied well. The empty trees rustled then stilled.

"I felt their eyes," she whispered. "They were there, whispering, their voices riding on the wind."

Dismissing them as the Ljosalfr's comrades had seemed such a simple explanation, but he appeared more perplexed about their existence than she did.

"I...but I...I felt them," she said.

Placing a hand to her shoulder, the Ljosalfr pulled her beside him and looked hard into the darkness. The trees were eerily void of wildlife.

"You think I'm mad," Kallan said, but the hunter shook his head.

"The forest is too quiet." The hunter searched the empty black. "Whatever was there is gone now," he said, still holding her.

Kallan shrugged to push him off and failed.

"Release me." She spoke with the regality of someone used to giving orders. He met her eyes.

"No." He smiled.

Kallan sent her hand flying, but the Ljosalfr clamped her wrist, stopping the blow inches from his face. His instant response confirmed her suspicions.

"You move too efficiently to be a mere hunter...and don't underestimate me."

The Ljosalfr and the Dokkalfr assessed one another. After a moment, Kallan's face split into a wide grin, and the Ljosalfr shook his head.

While appearing to restrain a chuckle, he released her wrist and ripped his arrow from the boar's carcass.

Kallan twitched with the temptation to attack as a streak of moonlight spilled over his back.

"What were you trying to do, anyway?" he asked, wiping the blood from his arrow onto the boar before sliding it back into his quiver.

"Kill it," she said.

"Kill it." The Ljosalfr grinned. "A little thing like you?"

Kallan barely caught the resounding 'yes' she almost threw back at him as the Ljosalfr shook with a chuckle that tweaked Kallan's patience.

"You don't happen to have a sword beneath those skirts, do you, princess?"

The pet name burned her blood and the beginnings of a smile softened Kallan's face from contempt as she entertained the idea of frying his smug grin with her Seidr.

"No," she said. "I was going to use the sword under *your* skirt."

The hunter refreshed his laughter.

"Why were you following me?" she asked, eager to end his amusement.

He proved just as eager to play her game. "Why were you leading me in circles?"

"Why are you so difficult?"

He shrugged. "A man has to have his hobbies."

Kallan narrowed her eyes.

"Don't you have a wench to woo or a boar to clean?" Kallan said, attempting to be serious.

"Don't you have some husband to please?"

Kallan straightened her back in defiance. "I don't do well in confinement."

The hunter arched a single brow. "You don't?"

Kallan shook her head. "Hate it," she said, his temperament putting her at ease again, the approaching dawn forgotten.

"And are you?" he asked. "Confined, I mean."

"Too often."

Kallan grinned again as she cocked her head at the Ljosalfr. The first of the birds had started to sing.

"Why are you here if the forest is so forbidden?" she asked.

With the bow's stave, the hunter tapped the dead boar.

"The king would be most displeased," Kallan said.

The hunter shrugged. "The king can be forgiving."

"I've known a different king," she said and sauntered away from the boar.

"Do you?" The Ljosalfar fell in step beside her. "Know the king?"

Kallan stopped, her thoughts adrift in better places. "I know the children his war has left behind," she whispered.

"Children?" The Ljosalfr furrowed his brow and stepped closer.

"Countless children," she said, "made orphan by the slaughtering of their kinsmen and left to die."

Lost in thought, she paid no mind to the lock of her hair he brushed back. Startled, she turned and met his eyes. Like ice, they shone with silver blue.

"Too long, I've held them in my arms...watching helplessly as death takes them."

"They mean so much to you?" he asked.

Kallan nodded. "I am one of them." A breeze passed, sending a shiver up her spine. "What of you?" she asked. "Have you had the pleasure of meeting 'His Majesty'?"

The hunter shrugged. "On occasion, I've had the pleasure."

Kallan scoffed. "Is he as obtuse, cowardly, and spoiled as his men say he is?"

The hunter came to attention. "What men say this?" he asked, looking about as if these men would at once appear.

"Or does he spend his days justifying the blood-bath of our people?" Kallan said.

"No, truly," the hunter asked. "What men say this?"

Kallan couldn't help but chortle as she continued her stroll back toward Swann Dalr.

"The king is kind," the hunter said.

Kallan furrowed her brow.

"Kind?"

"And attractive," he said, evoking an eye roll from Kallan.

"Women swoon," he assured her.

"I'm going to be sick."

The Ljosalfr stepped closer. "You're not interested in strong, powerful men who've dedicated their lives to honor?"

"Oh, no," Kallan said. She held his gaze, letting him take in her striking lapis blue eyes that reflected the moonlight like gems. "I love honorable men. The greatest of my respect is reserved for such men, but I see no honor where that man is concerned."

The smile fell from the hunter's face. "I'll bear that in mind when next I see him."

Pleased with herself, Kallan bounced on the ball of her foot, content to be free of all burdens, content to forget everything out there in the wood, including the time. Her merriment left her oblivious to the Ljosalfr's sour mood.

"He's a sight better than the Dokkalfr queen hiding behind the Seidkona who slaughters our thousands."

Kallan's mouth was open for the rebuttal then froze. A single word would betray her. The careless refute would end everything. She closed her mouth and swallowed her words and his insult.

"Although," the hunter mused, "she is better than her father was. That man had a blood thirst tha—"

"Don't!"

Sudden darkness cloaked Kallan's face. She was too angry to realize all of what she was saying. The hunter looked on with an expression contorted between confusion, curiosity, and something else she couldn't quite place. With fists clenched white, Kallan forced her nerves to still and looked to the sky. The white moon was fading and the palest of morning blues was waxing.

"The skies are clear tonight," she said. The hunter took a step closer. "They won't stop until they're dead. All dead," she whispered, "and for what?" Tears glistened in her eyes, holding small images of the paling moon. "I don't even know what we're fighting for...why the children are dying."

The dawn was near.

"I have to go."

"Please." The Ljosalfr grasped her fingers and shook his head. "You shouldn't be alone right now."

For him, Kallan managed a smile.

"And what do you know about being alone?" Kallan asked. Out here away from all else, he felt less and less like an enemy.

The Ljosalfr didn't smile, but shook his head again. "You shouldn't be alone right now."

"I have to go," she said, pulling away.

"You speak differently."

Kallan stopped, her fingers still caught in his grasp.

"I speak—"

"Your dialect," he said.

She would have noticed the urgency, but her face burned. Her speech would betray her. "Northumbria," Kallan recovered. "I...studied in Northumbria."

"Engla Land." He sounded impressed. "What did you study?"

His question eased Kallan's breath.

"Writing, words, mostly. Runes. Although..." She furrowed her brow. "...I remember so little about the runes."

She tried to recall those lessons. "It's so hard to remember sometimes."

"Remember?"

"Like sheets of black, it spans my mind," she whispered.

The hunter was quiet as she thought. The birds were waking.

"What else?" he said.

"Medicine and swordplay."

"Swordplay?"

The gleam in her eyes returned with her smile. "I love my swords."

"I prefer the range of the bow," he said, "but my brother has a sword, a two-handed great-sword. Stunning piece. He picked it off a Dokkalfr. Elding forged right into the steel and folded with carbon. And the size..." He whistled. "...longer than my arm."

Kallan did well to disguise the bitter distaste that filled her mouth at the sound of 'picked it off a Dokkalfr.'

She cocked her head, pretending to be curious instead. "Your brother?"

The hunter scrunched his brow in suspicion. "You haven't met my brother, have you?"

"No." She shook her head. "I don't think—"

Kallan marked the twain of a snapping twig, a voice rose, and the hunter looked to the trees behind him as she pulled her hand free.

Before he could turn and reach for her, Kallan withdrew a spell from her pocket. By the time the hunter looked back, she was gone, leaving only the black trunks interspersed with moonlight that cut through the darkness, and streaking the Alfheim Wood in strips of shadow.

Chapter 15

I know too well the shadows that lurk within. I've spent most of my life looking into empty faces. Every one of them veiled with the same deadened look. I've seen the insatiable rage that comes next.

Rune searched the darkness and dropped his shoulders. Despite his training, he found no trail. The blue of her eyes was as dazzling as the lapis gem Bergen had brought from the Eastern roads. Eyes he wouldn't soon forget.

"Your Majesty," the scout shouted, his voice on the edge of panic.

Rune turned his back to the wood where the girl had been standing a moment ago.

"What word, Joren?" he asked, pulling the gloves from his hands.

Panting, the scout emerged dressed in light leather armor and covered in a layer of dust from the road and a hard ride.

"The Dokkalfar," Joren said. "She's here."

"Who's here?" he asked, fixing his attention on Joren.

"Queen Kallan."

The words dumped a cold chill down Rune's back, pushing all thoughts of the maiden aside. "When?" Rune asked.

"Dawn," Joren said, "with the rising sun."

Rune looked to the sky. Daylight would be upon them. "And the Seidkona?" he asked, his deepest worry setting in.

Joren was already nodding. "She rides with them."

He closed his eyes and pinched the bridge of his nose. The silver of his signet ring shimmered. "Where...is Bergen?"

"Two day's ride from here," Joren said. "Even if I leave now, I won't catch him in time."

The last of Rune's hope vanished as the forest spun around him. For the first time in a year, he saw everything and understood. "By the fires of Muspellsheim," he cursed, opening his eyes. "She planned this."

"My king?" Joren asked.

"All of it." Rune crammed his gloves into his belt. "Our fight alongside Roald left us too weak to send aid to Thorold. We had no choice but to send Bergen. She knew he wouldn't be back in time to defend the valley and we would be too few in number here, too weak in arms to stop her. The march alone left us too weak to battle, and she knew this. And now she strikes, when we are most vulnerable."

Joren was whiter than the moonlight on his face. "But how did she find the valley?"

"We don't stand a chance against that Seidkona of hers without him." Rune shook his head at the hindsight, deaf to Joren's question. "I hate that bitch."

"But we won the battle of the Southern Keep."

"And lost significant numbers in the process," Rune said. "By keeping the Southern Keep, we have lost the valley. And the war."

In silence, they stood, battling back waves of panic. They were dead if they retreated to Gunir and dead if they stayed to fight. They were dead without Bergen's army.

"We can fall back to Gunir," Joren said, desperate to stop the inevitable.

In silence, Rune reviewed his options. His knuckles popped as he tightened his fist, detesting the options the Seidkona had left him. After a moment, he settled on the one choice that would move him where he knew the queen wanted him.

"The Dokkalfar come for Gunir's king," Rune said. "If not in the valley, then they will march to Gunir, cross the Klarelfr, and rend her walls. They will take me from my city...through the spilled blood of Gunir's children and her daughters, if they have to. No." Rune shook his head. "We will stay in the valley, and we will face the Seidkona. Without Bergen."

Sweat glistened on Joren's brow. "But how? With Bergen gone—"

"I don't know." Rune rubbed his hand over his face as he scrambled to collect a thought. "Carry word to Bergen. He must be warned of the massacre he'll find when he gets here. I will return to Swann Dalr and ready the army for battle. If we can hold them off long enough, maybe we can. Maybe Bergen will arrive in time."

"But it's two days' ride at least," Joren said. "He won't make it. Regardless of how quickly I move, Bergen won't make it to the valley in time."

"We have to do something!"

A bird screeched, rustling the trees as it flew.

"The Dokkalfar queen has positioned everything flawlessly. They march to slay Gunir's king. No matter how we assemble the pieces, I shall fall in the end." The declaration of his death sparked a wild determination within.

"If it is my head she comes for, then she shall have it," Rune said. "But the price of my head is the heart of her Seidkona. If I fall, so shall her servant. I will cut that Seidkona's heart from her chest with my sword. Without her, Bergen will have a fighting chance to reach the queen."

Rune's words ignited the same fighting spark in Joren, and the scout lifted his head with the want to prevail.

Nodding, Joren disappeared into the trees, ready for the two-day ride to the Northern Watch and Bergen.

Rune glanced over his shoulder, hopeful to see what he knew wasn't there when he caught sight of the dead boar forgotten on the ground. It seemed like a different time and place when he had killed it only a few moments ago.

The casual curiosity that impelled him to follow the maiden paled in comparison to the dread he saw in her eyes. Too well, he knew that darkness. Too well, he knew the hole it would leave as it ate its way through her. Too many memories of his own raced back as he shook his head at the boar. There was no time to drag a four hundred pound boar from the forest and dress it. After administering Freyr's blessing upon the animal and grieving the wasted life taken, Rune followed Joren into the trees. He vowed to come back for it later, if he survived the day.

Kallan bit the side of her bottom lip, cursing her own foolishness as she rode. The Dokkalfar camp came into view where barely a corner of light from her tent was visible, and she pulled back the reins, slowing Astrid to a light canter.

In a matter of minutes, she slid from the saddle, tethered the reins to a tree, and stroked the horse's dark bay coat. The stallion snorted and nuzzled Kallan's waist.

"I'm sorry, Astrid," she said. "I don't have my pouch with me."

Mindlessly, she patted the horse's brown nose and added a kiss to the velvet as he snuffled for an apple. Her insides twisted with the pressing dawn. She gave a final pat on Astrid's neck and slunk unseen toward her tent.

A different silence filled the wood and Kallan turned to the forest. Desperate to see through the dark, she ignited her palms with Seidr flame and studied the black silhouettes of foliage and pines behind Astrid. Her heart pounded through the silence. Converting her panic to patience, she scanned the shapeless black that rustled in the Nordic winds.

She could feel them. This time, she was certain of the nameless spirits that watched from the trees, if only she could see them.

"Where are you?" she whispered, scanning the blackest darkness.

Astrid pawed at the ground and shook his head, disturbed by an invisible pest. The leather bridle slapped the branch. The metallic jingle of the bit broke the tension in the air, and with it, the weight of the Shadow's eyes. In that instant, the tension released and the forest returned to its calm.

Sighing, Kallan extinguished her flame and dropped her hands. She studied the trees a moment longer, until she was certain that whatever it was that had been there was gone. Without a second glance to Astrid, Kallan pulled back the tent's flap.

The fire crackled in the center of the room, filling the air with a stuffy warmth. Aaric, like a large, tattooed sentry, brooded by the fire. Saying nothing and paying him no mind, Kallan strolled to her bed and sat down on the furs.

"One hour, Your Majesty," Aaric said.

Kallan clenched her teeth at the formal title, but kept her head bent over her boot as she unlaced the leather strings.

"One hour," he said. "Could you please explain why the queen of the White Opal could not be found until one hour before battle?"

Her foot smacked the floor and Kallan raised her fearless eyes to Aaric.

"A queen's head is worth its weight in gold," Aaric said as Kallan studied the newest of black lettering etched into his shoulder.

She shrugged at the statement, and loosened the laces on her boot.

"I went for a ride," she said.

"On Astrid."

Kallan dropped her boot to the floor and crossed the bearskin rug to the table at the opposite end of the room, knowing where this was going. Pulling the chair from the desk, she dropped herself down.

Kallan looked over the mortar filled with powdered sage, the pestle she hadn't cleaned yet, and numerous herbs scattered about, until she located the single most precious possession laid out before leaving.

"Astrid is the only horse of his kind," Aaric said. "You know that, and the enemy has long since learned to associate his presence with you, Seidkona," he all but growled the word. "He'll be the first to betray you."

"*If* he's seen," she said, fastening her mother's necklace around her neck. "I used a spell on him," she added before Aaric could roar a rebuttal.

"Well, thank the gods you had sense enough for that," he said.

Hoping to discourage Aaric's well-rehearsed rant, Kallan ignored the lecture and gathered the maps from the floor. She gently splayed them over the supplies, careful not to spill the inkwell she had abandoned earlier along with the paperwork.

Aaric relaxed his shoulders. The raging sea had ebbed.

"Kallan," he said. "We were worried."

We.

The lone word caught her ear, and she peered over her shoulder.

"You told Gudrun."

Aaric narrowed his eyes.

"Gudrun taught you that spell. Do you think I had to tell Gudrun?"

She didn't have time enough to answer before a chill swept the room. Throwing back the tent flap, Daggon entered, followed by a streak of silver and a flash of gold.

"Where is she?" the old woman said. "I'll kill her."

Behind her, Daggon dropped the tent flap.

Pushing out her thinned bottom lip, Gudrun looked Kallan over from her feet to her face.

Gudrun grimaced. "You've met someone."

Kallan felt her face burn red as Aaric took his leave, shaking his head.

Daggon shifted his eyes, feigning interest in the sword on Kallan's bed as Gudrun burrowed her fierce, golden stare into Kallan.

"Well, that explains that," the old woman said, not noticing the change of tension in the air.

"Daggon," Kallan said, doing her best to divert the subject to the captain's corner of the room. "Where is the Dark One?"

"Just two days' ride from here," Daggon said, eager for the change in topic himself.

With a nod, Kallan averted her attention back to the map.

Gudrun's eyes peered closer to better scrutinize every movement of Kallan's face. "Who is he?"

"Woman," Daggon howled from across the room.

"I've my rights," she spat back.

Kallan's face flushed a deeper red as she bit her lip and shuffled to bed.

In silence, she stared at the orange light splayed across the silver-black blades, remembering her father's smile.

Deeper into darkness, her memory pulled her as she ignored the bickering that unfolded between Daggon and Gudrun. Her mind drifted as far from her room as her meandering thoughts could take her where the cold slowed her grief until it stopped. There, deep in the back of her mind, buried behind an iron black wall, Kallan couldn't feel. There, she ceased to remember.

"Kallan?" Daggon's gentle voice didn't reach her.

Flames flickered in the silence, casting shadows Kallan didn't see. She was somewhere else, stretched deep in the darkness of her mind where images lurked as she drew the blanket of cold around her, slipping further into the void, numbing her emotions, shutting him out, shutting everything out.

A gentle hand brushed her shoulder, jolting Kallan back to hear Daggon's consolation.

"It was not your fault," he said.

She flinched as his words drove a sharp pain through her.

"There was nothing you could have done to save him," Daggon said.

Kallan's eyes burned and the walls thickened, rising higher than before. She couldn't breathe. "No," she gasped. Tears burned her eyes. Her lip quivered.

"Shutting yourself in will not bring him back," he said.

His words sliced their way deeper through the wall and a scream caught in her throat. Kallan threw her hands to her head and dug her nails into her scalp, desperate to shut out the memories that flooded back. A stream of blood flowed down her face, but she only felt her heart ache as she remembered her father's laughter. Kallan's hands wouldn't move. Daggon held her wrists and he pulled her hands from her head. There he held her, staring inches from his face.

He had stopped talking and neatly, Kallan tucked the images and memories back behind the wall where they were safe and she could breathe again.

"Leave me," she said, shaking beneath her rage.

Anger flushed her face where tears refused to flow and Daggon searched her hardened gaze.

"I still see the soft, gentle princess who broke every rule in jest and pilfered my wardrobe for clothes in which to dress the orphans," Daggon whispered. "Where are you, Kallan? Where is the girl I once knew? Where has that princess gone?"

Kallan searched his copper eyes.

"You have no idea how much I wish to reach you," he said, "to take you away from the void."

Kallan's rage recoiled and the hardened shell of the grief-stricken queen remained.

"You will not be able to maintain your focus in battle if you do not control your emotions," he said, repeating Eyolf's words to her.

But Kallan held her stone gaze fixed on her captain, who, at last, released her wrists.

"I'll ready the men," he said. Without a word, he lowered the hide flap behind him.

"He was a Ljosalfr, wasn't he," Gudrun said.

Kallan jerked her head around. The silence was all Gudrun needed to confirm what Kallan didn't deny.

"I didn't dare say anything to the men," she said. "I felt you had enough to deal with from Aaric's lecture. So," Gudrun sighed. "Who was he?"

"A mindless oaf out hoping for a quick romp," Kallan said. "He saw me and thought I was one of them."

Gudrun nodded.

"He was an ass," Kallan said.

Gudrun smiled. "Was he now?"

Only after Kallan was thoroughly uncomfortable with the topic did Gudrun sigh.

"Never mind," she said and helped Kallan peel the Ljosalfar clothing from her body. "Not my business so long as you maintain your focus and don't let feelings get in the way." Gudrun droned on, lulling Kallan back to Daggon's words.

Kallan closed her eyes against the pain and forced herself to breathe as Gudrun prepared her for battle.

Focus, she chided. *The war. The plan. King Rune.*

She felt the cold of her elding sword. Kallan opened her eyes and raised her blade before her until the double-edge reflected back the fire's light. Kallan tightened her grip on the hilt, letting the solid weight ground her back to where she needed to be.

She would lead her army through the pine forests of Alfheim to battle at Swann Dalr. She would fight to take back what she had lost. She would fight to usurp their king and then she would kill him.

Chapter 16

Daggon stared over the darkness draped upon the Ljosalfar's tents. Dawn spilled blotches of blue, gray, and black light that stretched into the trees where he waited. Many would die that day. Not a part of him cared anymore. There was only one other left who he bothered to concern himself with.

He shifted his gaze to Kallan, who had long since administered her orders to the commander of her second division. With her amadou pouch fastened beside the steel and elding dagger at her waist, Kallan wore leather and mail beneath her full set of elding plate armor. Her helmet encased her head. The nose guard distorted her face so much that he could barely make out her eyes peeking through the mail-lined helmet where she had tucked her hair. Standing beside him, she looked like one of her men.

"It is time." Kallan's cold voice cut the air.

"What of their sentries?" he asked.

"Silenced."

"The Seidr?"

"My sword." Kallan's terse answer chilled the back of Daggon's neck.

He knew better than to underestimate the delicate frame of the Seidkona. The Seidr was stronger than anything the Dvergar could create in Svartálfaheim. The shield secured to her forearm was unmarked for a reason.

"Gudrun is in position, awaiting the signal, secured within the pines on the cleft."

Daggon peered to the ledge in the distance where Gudrun waited.

"Whenever you're ready." Her instructions were curt, confirming she had closed out the last of her emotion.

Daggon turned to the army hidden within the trees behind him where thirty thousand Dokkalfar waited in the Alfheim wood armed with axe, shield, and spear. Gripping the handle of his broadsword, Daggon shifted his gaze through the forest. Looking to his queen, he nodded slightly.

"Bring me their king," Kallan bade and, with that order, Daggon raised his sword and released his battle cry.

The army echoed his order. Their voices rose from the darkness, sending the signal to the southern cleft where Gudrun raised her arms. With Seidr staff in one hand and Seidr in the other, Gudrun spoke with fervor beneath her breath.

The winds stirred, blowing her silver hair in a wild torrent as she turned her palm out and launched a single stream of lightning into the tents. Fire erupted within the valley and she saw Daggon join the charge, his sword still raised.

Warriors raced by as Kallan summoned her Seidr. With a flick of her wrists, she discharged streams of flame that arched into the camp and set the tents ablaze. Unsheathing her sword, Kallan raised her voice and charged, following her men into the open.

Into the valley, Daggon led the Dokkalfar. Their cries held strong until they stood in the very center beside Gudrun's inferno where, one by one, their voices died out.

All was silent, save for the roaring flames. The dozen soldiers who had run out to meet them had already perished. Not a single Ljosalfar emerged from his burning tent. Not a single retaliatory cry was uttered. The Dokkalfar looked about for the enemy as Daggon assigned half a dozen men to search the tents. The Dokkalfar threw back the tent openings, upturned tables and chairs, and smashed the Ljosalfar possessions. A blanket of confusion settled over the army as Kallan pushed her way to Daggon's side.

"Daggon." Kallan's voice carried over the men. She emerged from the crowd, her sword still unsheathed at her side.

"Where are they?" he asked. "Did they head out?"

"Their tents are still here," Kallan said, sweeping her hand to the abandoned camp as she stepped to the side.

"Then wher—"

A gust of wind and Daggon roared. Kallan looked back to her first commander.

An arrow protruded from his left shoulder. He wrapped his hand around the wood and, wincing, broke off the shaft. A single stream of blood trickled down his bicep where the arrow's head had embedded into the thick of his shoulder and Kallan turned her face to the sky.

"Shields," she cried and, thrusting her blade into the earth, she slammed her hands to the sky, and with it, her Seidr.

From her body an iridescent glow erupted, encasing her in energy. Facing the rain of arrows, the Dokkalfar raised their shields in a wave that started with Kallan's cry.

The arrows shattered against the Seidr, unable to penetrate the shield Kallan formed. She looked to the north where countless Ljosalfar archers unleashed a second volley among the pines.

Releasing her spell, Kallan refocused her energy into her palms and swept her arms, whipping her red flames through the archers. From the cleft, Gudrun uttered a charm. Lightning surged from her palms as she directed her Seidr into the archers, who scattered in a vain attempt to escape. From behind them, Rune's army rose up and charged the clearing where the Dokkalfar met the attack.

Axe cleaved bone and spearmen impaled foes, spilling Alfar blood. In one hand, Kallan wielded her flame while she swung her sword with the other. Securing a wide perimeter around her, she slaughtered any who dared approach her for a chance at the killing and the glory.

Almost immediately, she lost sight of Daggon amid the chaos. Warriors of two, three then five came at her, each group failing to slay her as the red sun rose.

Desperate to take the Seidkona down, Rune fought his way through the battle. He slowed as he approached her, waiting and watching for the chance to move in. Only Bergen had ever made it this close to her. Armed with flame and sword, she left no opening. He assessed her skills, deciding she was equivalent to ten of his best men. She shifted. A warrior lunged and she threw him back. She repeated the process until the rare chance came when one of his soldiers stepped from behind the Seidkona and closed his arm around her neck. Believing the soldier had her, Rune raised his sword.

The Seidkona released a blast of energy, throwing the grappler onto his back and, as she poured her fire onto her assailant, Rune closed in, his sword raised. A flash of iridescent lapis blue caught his eye and, within that time, she knew him, and the Seidkona paused. Her delay was all the time Rune needed. Blade clipped the iron and dislodged her helmet, throwing her to the ground unconscious.

Holding his breath, Rune drew back his sword, prepared to thrust the tip through her heart, and froze. At once, he understood the Seidkona's hesitation. Chestnut hair spilled across the red-soaked earth. Pearlescent skin was splattered with blood seeping from a gash above her tapered ear, and Rune recalled the grief-laden eyes of the maiden.

The mass of his sword weighed down his arm, but he kept the blade suspended. He had sought this Seidkona for years. She needed to die. He tried to convince himself. She had to die, and yet his arm would not obey.

His eyes swept over her, examining the wound he had inflicted. She was losing too much blood. She would die from that wound within minutes if he did nothing. A stab of hate swallowed his guilt. He could not suffer her to die a slow death. His conclusion silenced his conscience, but not soon enough.

A shallow pierce to his neck stayed his hand, and Rune stiffened.

"Give me a reason to cut off your head so that I may hand it to her." The words, laden with the Dokkalfar's brogue, hissed. "Stand down."

Rune held his stance as the warrior's sword cut deeper into his throat. He stole a glance to the armband of silver and elding and Rune knew the queen's captain before meeting his amber eyes. The stream of blood still poured from the arrowhead lodged in his flesh. Three inches to the right and Rune could have saved himself this trouble. He glanced at the woman. She was growing paler.

"Stand down." The captain's voice was colder this time.

Rune's stomach tightened as he eyed the body before him.

I should stab her, he thought.

But the glory of a Seidkona's death no longer carried the pride it had moments ago and death for him was certain.

Unless...

Rune lowered his sword to his side.

Only a few feet in front of him, a Ljosalfr warrior took his last breath, doubled over the Dokkalfar blade that speared his stomach. With that warrior's death, a great wave rippled through the battlefield that would turn the tide of the war. Around him, Rune's men fell, overwhelmed against the odds.

They fought in vain to win the honor awaiting them in Odinn's hall. They fought until the last Ljosalfr of Rune's army perished, and two Dokkalfar seized Rune by the arms. A third took his sword and stripped his weapons, removing them as they found them. Swann Dalr grew quiet. Screams replaced the victor's cry.

The captain held his fiery glare, the tip of his blade still nestled in Rune's throat. More guards raised their swords while others stripped the king's armor. All the while, Rune gazed upon the Seidkona.

She was growing paler by the minute. He wasn't the only one who had noticed. Rune watched as the warrior, battling remorse, fell broken to the Seidkona's side. Gently, the captain lifted her head and brushed back a long, bloodstained lock of hair. His large hands trembled as he slipped an arm behind her back and, as if he cradled a precious jewel, pulled her into him.

A twinge of envy pricked Rune's chest.

"Where's the Dark One?" a Dokkalfr soldier grunted.

Rune made no movement to show that he heard as his thoughts filled with Bergen riding with Joren to the desecrated remnants that would be left of Swann Dalr. He thought of the vengeful eye Bergen would turn to Lorlenalin.

The battlefield had a new sound as the Dokkalfar slaughtered the last of the Ljosalfar. Only the fire continued the battle, consuming the tents.

"Where is he?" the Dokkalfr asked again.

Too clearly, Rune envisioned Bergen's head rolling about in the white courtyard. Blood would streak the stone while he, Rune Tryggveson, the elder son of the great Lodewuk, looked on helpless as his father's kingdom fell, its memory left to the mercy of Dokkalfar bards and scribes.

"Dead," Rune said. Shackles clamped his wrists.

The captain cradled his maiden, taking great care not to jostle the dying woman. He shifted to stand as Rune watched the Seidkona held adoringly by the Dokkalfr. He knew her as either a daughter or a lover, perhaps. Surely, if anyone knew who she was, he would.

"Who is she?"

The captain raised his head. Cold hatred emanated from the Dokkalfr. The silence stretched as Rune waited.

"You don't know," the captain said.

It wasn't a question, but a calm observation chilled and made rigid by the Seidkona's imminent death. The pain in Rune's chest tightened as the captain turned his back to him.

"Dokkalfr," Rune said, drawing his adversary's attention once more. "Her name."

The captain glared and, without an answer, he left Rune to his captors.

Chapter 17

The last relenting flames burned with seemingly less ferocity than they had moments ago. Smoke billowed into the sky above Swann Dalr, casting the early day into dusk-like shadows that mingled with steam from the bodies. Daggon no longer saw where the smoke ended and clouds began through the haze. Behind him, the clink of shackles broke the silence as the Dokkalfar detained the handful of prisoners they had selected to slaughter on ceremony.

The pain from his wounded shoulder had dulled to a steady pulse as he stumbled over the bodies through the morning mist. He no longer tasted the blood and sweat on his dried lips. Kallan was beyond medicine now. If he could save her at all, he would need Gudrun.

"Gudrun!" Daggon's voice shook over the silenced battlefield.

Kallan's limp body swayed with every misjudged step over the dead. He afforded himself a quick glance at the queen in his arms. A single stream of blood flowed across her brow, draining her life with every drop. She was too pale.

Daggon doubled his pace. Catching his foot on a broken shield, he fell to one knee and grunted in pain. His breath punched the air. Gasping, his senses reeled and he shifted Kallan's weight with his as he studied the battlefield for a more definitive path. He pushed himself back to his feet, and took a step, lost his footing, found it again, and continued through the mutilated flesh and broken corpses, abandoning all interest in where his feet landed.

The memory of an infant eclipsed his rising panic.

"*You won't break her,*" Eyolf had barked amid laughter he didn't bother to hide. Desperate to engage his king with political matters, Daggon had pressed the issue.

"*I didn't come to pass my congratulations, Eyolf. The Dvergar King—*"

"*Can wait. Motsognir will do well to learn some patience anyway,*" Eyolf had said. "*Here.*"

Before Daggon could object, the proud king had shoved the fussing infant into his arms.

A hearty laugh mocked his awkwardness, but Daggon had been too busy trying to balance the fragile princess away from his armor to notice. His face had flushed with surprise as he tried to shift the child without dropping her. His tunic had started to stick to his back.

"*It's rare that a captain earns the privilege of humility,*" Eyolf had chortled. "*Usually that virtue is reserved for a soldier of lesser rank.*"

But humility had been far from his mind as the infant ceased her wailing. With her iridescent lapis eyes so much like her mother's, she stared at his large face buried beneath the mass of wild, red hair. He had never held a child before in his life.

Daggon glanced down at Kallan's face. She was white as death.

"Gudrun!"

His voice pierced the chill in the air. Worry gave way to panic as he pondered the chance of Gudrun's death and, at once, started looking among the dead, searching the thousands for a familiar streak of silver hair or ancient, empty eyes no longer glistening with gold.

A distant shape formed within the fog. Daggon strained to see through the steam, the smoke, and the haze. His panting started to regulate into steady breaths when he recognized the minute frame hobbling with a hurried step and a familiar madness. From the edge of the valley where the mist had cleared, Gudrun scurried over the corpses.

His blood raced with relief and he again doubled his pace, tripping as he ran to meet her.

"Out of the way, out of the way," she said as she drew near.

Daggon had no time to explain, nor did he need to. With her hands already upon Kallan's brow, Gudrun dropped to her knees, pulling Daggon and Kallan to the ground with her.

Daggon watched Gudrun's ageless eyes shift about, studying Kallan's waning complexion as she shuffled around the contents of her pouch. With a hand she kept steady, she pulled a golden apple from a pouch secured to her side and sliced into the fruit.

"Can you—"

"Sh. Sh," Gudrun hushed, keeping her attention on the spell.

From the fruit's flesh, golden juice flowed, gleaming with glistening specks of Seidr. Under her breath, Gudrun muttered a series of words Daggon couldn't decipher. The liquid flowed between Kallan's lips as he watched, wringing his fingers.

Time seemed to slow as the color returned to Kallan, bringing her life back with it until she gasped, arched her back, and opened her eyes.

"Kallan. Kallan, can you hear me? Will she be alright?"

Kallan's gaze focused on Daggon, who released a long breath as a single tear escaped his eye. Grinning, he clamped her palm to his lips.

"Daggon?" she said, wrinkling her brow.

Daggon nodded. "Kallan."

Alertness gave way to confusion as Kallan gazed about the silent battlefield.

"They knew," she whispered, playing back her last memory as the exhaustion melted from her bones, leaving a surge of strength that urged her to her feet. She pushed off the ground, motivating Daggon and Gudrun to take an arm and help her to her feet. The Seidr supplied by Idunn's apple surged through her and Kallan breathed the chilled air with the scent of fire that mingled with the stench of burning dead.

In silence, Daggon and Gudrun waited as Kallan scanned the wasteland and assessed the damage. Pockets of orange light in the distance had barely started to fade through the fog. The land was unnaturally quiet, as if Hel had reached up and stilled even the Seidr in the earth. Mid-day had passed, but the haze was too thick for the sun's light to break through. The Dokkalfar had begun piling up the dead. A few pyres already filled the valley with their light.

"The Ljosalfar were ready," Kallan said, looking to Gudrun and Daggon.

With her head high, she resumed her command undeterred, as if she had never fallen.

"Where is my army?" she asked. "Where are my war-men?"

"Your Majesty." Daggon's boot crunched the ground as he stepped forward. "We have apprehended Rune Tryggveson, Ljosalfr and King of Gunir. The men are preparing him for transport as we speak."

A knot formed in Kallan's throat and tightened her insides uncomfortably. Despite her captain awaiting her exclamation of glee, she clenched her teeth and nodded somberly.

"Kallan?" Gudrun asked.

Kallan forced a smile that did little to convince either Daggon or Gudrun of her feigned jubilation and the awkwardness hung suspended in the air, encouraging Kallan to move. With renewed strength, she waded through the dead to Astrid waiting in the trees. Behind her, Daggon and Gudrun followed.

"We ride for Lorlenalin immediately," Kallan said with unusual stiffness. "I want to waste no time in finishing this. Find Aaric. Have him start the preparations for the execution. See to it the Coward King has provisions and any wounds are treated. I want him alive and healthy when we perform the Blood Eagle."

"Kallan," Daggon said. "With the Dark One and his army riding this way..."

Kallan looked at him.

"It's the perfect chance to move in," he said. "Wipe them out while we have the chance."

A sharp stab twisted its way into Kallan's chest. Anxiety settled to the bottom of her stomach and she closed her hand into a fist.

"The Dark One dead would end this," Kallan said. "We'll let him come to us."

She continued toward Astrid. "We'll break camp and prepare for transport," she said, not bothering to turn back. "I want the living and the dead counted. No doubt Odinn will be claiming many of our best tonight."

"Will you come see him before we're off?" Daggon asked.

"Odinn?" Kallan asked.

"The king," Daggon said. "You've never seen him."

Kallan forced down the lump in her throat.

"No," she said. "I have not."

Panic swelled in place of the excitement she had expected and, with it, a realization she wasn't ready to name. "So long I've dreamed of this day," she muttered, staring back at the dead and the pyres, "when I might look into the eyes of the man who killed my father." A foreboding lurked in Kallan's words. "To look down upon him victorious..."

"It would confirm the end of the war," Daggon said.

But I have known nothing else. Kallan's throat was dry as she felt a piece of her slipping away.

"Not yet," she replied, forcing the words out. "There is plenty of time and too much to do. I'll see him later."

Kallan could feel Gudrun's golden gaze scrutinize her, while Daggon nodded and took his leave, eager to carry out her orders.

If the war ends...if Rune dies, what else would there be, but the Dark One? And when he is gone, whose blood then shall I spill to avenge my father's?

Her insides twisted uncomfortably. There was much more at stake. Something beyond the vengeance, which Kallan didn't dare name. Tightening her jaw against the deepening urge to scream, she turned on her heel, careful to avoid Gudrun's eye, and made her way to the trees. Her stride was strong

169

and purposeful. Panic was settling in, and a realization that weighted her down was coming whether she wanted it to or not.

Desperate to escape the end that was closing in, she hoisted herself onto Astrid and sent him into a light canter through the trees to where no one could find her.

Too broken to fight, Rune gazed upon what little remained of Swann Dalr. The only living left among the dead were those too injured to save. The countless corpses made his defeat more real to him than anything he could have prepared for. The last of his hope dwindled, pulling him into despair.

"Leave them," a Dokkalfr called to the queen's men. "Odinn can have his pick of the dead."

All other conversations were too far away to decipher, making it easy for Rune to merge his thoughts until he remembered the chestnut hair that spilled over the blood-soaked earth.

Saved the maiden from the boar to kill the Seidkona whose death took what little victory I had. Rune lacked the nerve to chuckle at the irony. *The queen will be sure my death is a slow one.*

The fire burned to the ground as the Seidr flames consuming the tents started to dwindle. The fog muted the light from the flames. It pained him to breathe. In a senseless hope that he may see a single captain carrying a maiden with iridescent blue eyes over the dead, Rune kept his gaze fixed on the valley.

"You look as if you've lost something."

The voice jarred him from his thoughts. Rune shifted his attention to a Dokkalfr, a warrior.

Soiled and bloodied by battle, the Dokkalfr stood away from his comrades, stiff and cold before the Ljosalfar king. War braids framed a gruff face that cloaked all emotion.

"Haven't I lost everything?" Rune asked, dulled by the shock of his loss.

The Dokkalfr shrugged.

"Perhaps you have. And yet, you still look for hope among the dead."

Once more, Rune looked to the valley, deciding to be uninterested in anything this Dokkalfr had to say. The smoke-filled fog rolled unbroken over the valley.

"If it is Bergen you seek, he has the better part of a two-day-ride before he arrives," the soldier said.

Rune returned his attention to the Dokkalfr. Curiosity awakened his pain, putting an end to his sedated dullness.

"You're Borg," Rune said.

The Dokkalfr's eyes narrowed with the secret they harbored. "I am."

Pensive, Rune started back into the valley.

"A king's head is worth its weight in gold," Borg said. "A kingly ransom for a king's life is only fair, don't you think?" The sharp words were void of emotion and weighted with absolute logic. "How much would you be willing to pay?"

Rune studied the confident grin. A chill swept Rune's spine and he fought the urge to shiver. "You're a mercenary," Rune said with pricked curiosity.

Borg smiled coldly. "Everyone is, at some price. What's yours?"

Kallan slid from her saddle, touching her feet to the forest floor before Astrid had stopped. She was off through the thick pines and over the blankets of leaf litter as she hugged herself against the cold. There, among the thickest of trees, the canopy blocked the sky.

Daggon's words rang back in her head.

"End of the war," she muttered aloud, repeating the words as she pushed a path through the ferns and foliage. She hugged herself tighter.

Another three steps brought her to the middle of a clearing where the lowest of pine branches had died and fallen. Kallan dropped to her knees. Panting, she clasped her hands, tugging at her fingers, desperate for them to stop shaking.

"End of the war." Kallan rocked. The words wouldn't stop, as if they were taking the last of her father away from her. "End of the war."

And then what? When the king is dead, then what would I do? This war is all I've known. This war and death. What am I to do without it?

Digging her fingers into her scalp, Kallan threw back her head and screamed.

Birds took flight, fluttering as their wings beat the air, then cleared, leaving behind an echo.

"If I see him..." Kallan hugged herself, rocking on her knees. "If I see him..."

I would have no choice. To see him, I would end this war. So long as I don't see him... So long as I don't see him...

Through the jumbled words, her father's face appeared. Shaking her head, Kallan pushed the memory along with the pain, back behind her cold, black wall. Her anxiety eased. The forest grew still again, and she regained control of her senses.

I won't see him. I don't have to. Not yet. The war still goes on. And the Dark One will come.

Kallan almost grinned with relief.

The Dark One will come.

Kallan stopped rocking and drew in a deep breath.

So long as I don't remember. So long as I don't see him...

She sat a while longer until the last of her worry had ebbed.

Silent. Cold. Control. Forget. Forget it all.

And there was peace once more.

Having shoved aside the rising panic, Kallan shifted her knees out from under her. She would let the Dark One come to her. The men needed rest. And in Lorlenalin, they could regroup. Kallan shifted, and something through the foliage caught her attention.

Curious, she peered through the brush and leaf litter, and stared at a sow left to rot on the forest floor.

"He didn't take it," she whispered. "Why didn't he take it?"

Chapter 18

The sun settled beyond the trees, spilling the last of day's light into the thick forests of Alfheim. In premature celebration, the Dokkalfar wasted no time erecting fires, stewing meats, and breaking into the mead.

Huddled around fires built a bit grander than necessary, the Dokkalfar war-men passed bowls of stew and exchanged drink with tale as they merged themselves in song and victory. The camp buzzed with a warm joviality that extended well into the night.

Amid the celebrations, unbeknownst to all, Borg made his way through the Dokkalfar camp. The solace of his tent couldn't come quickly enough. Exhaustion from the day's march was noticeable, and he directed his thoughts to the hot mead and meats waiting for him.

A shadow descended with a death-like chill and his breath stilled. Taking care to remain unseen, he redirected his path into the clusters of trees. The ground crunched beneath his boots. The orange glow of the camp faded as he neared the shadows within the forest. The camp was well behind him now.

He swept his gaze over the trees.

"Borg."

Borg stopped. A growl emerged from the forest and he followed the faceless voice into the darkness without hesitation. A pair of deep, black eyes emerged, lined with the frame of a sickly-pale face cloaked in a thick, black beard with wild, wool-like hair to match. The shadows did well to conceal him.

"Motsognir," Borg addressed the darkness where the night was blackest. "You're running out of time, Borg," Motsognir said.

Borg tightened his jaw as cold contemplation blanketed his eyes.

"There's been a delay," he said. "She's alone now."

"In a tent guarded by no less than two guards," Motsognir growled.

Borg didn't miss the bite in his tone. "You were supposed to be providing us with the opportunity. You've been paid to deliver."

"And I gave you an opportunity last night," Borg said. "I signaled you the moment she took off. You could have taken her then."

"She was not alone," Motsognir snarled. "There was another."

Hot hate boiled in Borg's chest and he inhaled, commanding his composure.

"I told you then. I don't know the hunter," he said through gritted teeth. "She was alone when she left here and alone when she returned."

Through the shadows, Borg could feel Motsognir's eyes pass over him, assessing him, ready to pass judgment.

"When?" Motsognir asked.

"We arrive in Lorlenalin in two days," Borg said. "The queen hates confinement. She'll seek to abandon her guard. I can signal you then."

Motsognir examined Borg, who stared back with a determined hate that blocked all other thoughts.

"You have two days," Motsognir said. The shadows shifted and Motsognir was gone.

Alone, Borg stood listening to the rustle of wind as life returned to the clearing. He wasn't sure how long he waited before he willed himself to move again. Abandoning all thought of the idle comforts that waited in his tent, Borg returned to camp, pleased with the evening's events.

Gudrun dropped the tent flap behind her. A few strands of silver hair hung in her face as she pulled close her evening robes against the chill. A single candle burned at the table where Kallan sat staring at nothing beyond the flame. Kallan's thin, white chemise did little against the bitter bite in the air, but she didn't shiver.

As Gudrun pulled her shawl around her shoulders, the single flame flickered, distorting Kallan's face in a myriad of orange and black.

"Kallan?" Gudrun's voice grazed over the queen, who sat motionlessly watching the fire engulf the wick. Gudrun approached her granddaughter, who didn't move to smile or frown or reprimand. She hardly moved to breathe.

"Still fighting to delay the suffocation," Gudrun whispered and brushed back a strand of Kallan's locks. "Fighting and losing to the darkness that will eventually win." Kallan didn't move. "You seek to take shelter within the cold asylum of that void. Sink deeper into the black chasm where all thoughts end and where feelings cease to be. Keep sinking, Kallan, and you will find your Seidr leave you."

Kallan coldly stared.

"You will die, killed by the grief that suffocates you. Kallan?" Gudrun shifted a gaze to the untouched tray of dried fruits and salted meats. "Kallan, you must eat," she said. "It will be another two days before we reach Lorlenalin."

In silence, Kallan stared, oblivious to the world around her.

Gudrun touched Kallan's arm and effortlessly reached into Kallan with her Seidr. Almost at once, she found what she had been looking for. Kallan had already descended into the abyss within that she had made for herself. Her Seidr was cold like winter ice.

Its flow was sluggish, almost stagnant like bog water where no air, no flow, and no life could reach it. In contrast, Gudrun's own Seidr moved with an energy that exuded heat and nourished her lifeline.

She knew what Kallan had done, a dangerous thing for any Seidkona, especially one who underestimated her own abilities. Gudrun focused her energy deeper and, pushing her flow into Kallan's, she forced the immobile Seidr to move and churned the currents with her own.

But something wasn't right. The path flowed wrong. Gudrun furrowed her brow as the color returned to Kallan's face and the life flowed back. In all of Midgard, only two could do such a thing.

Aaric?

The new path was too old to correct. Not now. It would require a lot of work to restore Kallan's Seidr lines.

But when? And *why?* Gudrun pondered as Kallan took in a slow, deep breath. Her chest rose, expanding with air, and Gudrun pulled back, withdrawing her Seidr from her grandchild.

For the first time in hours, Kallan altered her gaze, lifting her face to the old woman whose long, silver hair was braided back, the ends tied at the tip with a bit of leather. Gudrun watched the silenced scream staring back from Kallan's eyes. Wordlessly, Kallan pleaded, while inside she crumbled beneath her grief.

A chill swept the tent and Gudrun stood. Aaric released the tent flap as the old Seidkona studied him. Scowling, she set to work making tea. Water filled the cup. Loudly, Gudrun clanked the cup and dipped her finger into the water, which was boiling in a matter of moments.

"How is she?" Aaric asked, keeping his voice low.

Unable to form the words, Gudrun shook her head and pulled her finger from the water. She knew too little about his reasons to say too much about Kallan's altered Seidr path. Without a word, Gudrun poured powdered lavender, sage, and mint into the boiling water until the aroma hung heavy in the air. The fire crackled and Gudrun provided the cup to Kallan, who quietly took the tea.

Before Aaric could inquire, Gudrun dropped a fur onto Kallan's shoulders.

"I'll be back in an hour to check on you," she said and planted a kiss on Kallan's brow.

Turning, Gudrun mustered up her best fake smile for Aaric and slipped out the door, leaving the high marshal alone with Kallan.

"What do you need, Aaric?" Kallan said over the rim of her cup. Exhaustion weighed thick in every word.

"The prisoner has been cleaned and fed," Aaric said.

Kallan nodded and tipped the cup to her lips. "Is there anything else?"

"There is," Aaric said. "Will you be seeing him now?"

Kallan lowered her tea, keeping her eyes fixed on the candle's flame. She pondered the question, enveloped by the cold panic that swept over her each time she thought of nearing King Rune's tent.

"No."

Aaric nodded in acknowledgment and reached for the flap of hide that was the door.

"Aaric."

He turned back to his queen.

"Daggon should have presented you with letters of execution," she said and took a sip of her tea.

"He did."

"Are they ready for my seal?" She took another sip.

"Kallan." Aaric stepped toward her. "I beg you to think about this. Killing the king will only enrage the Dark One."

Kallan glanced up from her cup. The fire in her eye flared with conflict, refusing to leave the war on the battlefield.

"The Dokkalfar will demand no less than his death," Kallan said, "and with the endless amount of the blood that has been spilled by their warmonger-ing, it leaves me little room to disagree."

"The Dokkalfar are wrong," Aaric said.

Kallan's chest rose and fell with every silent breath. The surface of her tea remained undisturbed by the tremors of temper running through her. The air in the room thickened.

"Mind yourself," she said. "You tread dangerously close to enemy waters. Or have you developed com-passion for the prisoner you were charged to keep?"

The fire popped.

"Have you given any thought to the repercussions of this execution?" he asked. "By killing the Ljosalfar king, the Dark One will rise up in vengeance. Have you given any thought to the rage you'll stir in him if you kill his king?"

Kallan's eyes hardened at the mention of the berserker deemed the Dark One.

"He will come for his king," Aaric said. "It's only a matter of time, and when he does, he will rise up and demand Rune be returned. I promise you. You will want the Ljosalfar king alive to give back to him or he will break every stone of Lorlenalin."

Kallan looked back at the candle. The Dark One's vengeance was exactly what she was hoping for.

"In your eagerness to end this war, you will spark a new hatred within the Ljosalfar," Aaric said. "They will seek to destroy you with a rage that will only be quelled when your blood flows onto the bones of their ancestors."

"The Dokkalfar demand the king's execution," Kallan said. "The people have that right."

"The people are blinded by an ageless hatred for that bloodline."

"Why are you so moved to spare him?" Kallan asked, calming her voice to a whisper.

"Not spare him, Kallan," Aaric said. "Protect you."

Kallan studied his eyes then dropped her gaze to her cup. Sleep was settling in and she started to sip again. She sunk her back into the chair. Gudrun's brew was working well.

"Kallan." Aaric forced his voice low. "I served with your father long before the migration. I've known the Ljosalfar centuries longer than any Dokkalfr has known this land. I once ate with them, laughed with them...slept with them." Kallan peered into her cup. "I promise you, they will rise up and start this war over again."

Her tea had lost its steam.

"The Dark One does not know the way into our city," she said. "Our stronghold is impenetrable. Our fortress, unbreakable."

"He will find a way."

Kallan raised her face to the high marshal. Venom overshadowed her gaze.

"The Ljosalfar king dies in Lorlenalin's courtyard. Do not forget which side you're on, High Marshal."

She spoke each word sharply, confirming the end of the conversation. With his complexion slightly paler than it had been moments ago, Aaric lowered his head and forced an agreeable answer.

"I'll have the letters prepared for the execution."

Chapter 19

Aaric slapped back the flap of Kallan's tent. The refreshing, cold air struck his face, revitalizing his senses after sitting in the warm tent for so long.

As he trudged through the camp, he replayed his conversation with Kallan and her refusal to keep the king alive. Too annoyed to join the festivities, he made his way to the small, dark tent at the far end of camp where Gudrun and Daggon sat exchanging anecdotes.

"How did it go?" Daggon asked, glancing up from the mead he coddled.

"It didn't," he grumbled. "Your turn."

Daggon sighed, ending it with a swig of his drink.

With nothing to say, he studied the nearest fire surrounded by a gaggle of soldiers, bent on boasting their deeds in battle.

"How is she?" Gudrun asked. She wrapped her shawl tighter as Aaric found himself a seat on the ground beside her.

"She's talking now," he said, resting an arm on his knee. He found the same group of soldiers who had broken off into random song, the mead doing much to persuade their pitch.

"Did you talk to her about the execution?" Gudrun asked.

"I did." Aaric didn't nod, but stared, happy to appease her inquisitiveness. Gudrun puffed out her bottom lip with impatience.

A soldier fell over, sloshing his drink down his arm.

"And?"

"She's going through with it."

The old woman didn't answer as she stared off at the farthest tree where the forest jabbed at the black of night. The soldiers had abandoned their song and moved on to downing more mead.

"Will she at least see him?" Daggon asked, rolling the neck of the flask between his fingers.

"I asked," Aaric said. "She refused."

"This isn't looking very hopeful," Gudrun said beneath her breath.

"Has he eaten?" Aaric asked with a nod indicating the prisoner in the tent behind him.

"He?" Daggon passed a calculative look toward the tent and shrugged. "He hasn't spoken or moved since we put him there hours ago."

A disquieting silence settled between the three of them as each stared off in their own direction.

The soldiers began another verse, this one louder and with less pitch than the last.

"She has said nothing all day," Gudrun said. Aaric and Daggon gazed at the woman hugging her legs. "She refuses victory. She refuses meals and sleep." Gudrun stared into the black of night above the trees. "She's regressing and, what's more, she's closed everyone out. No one can get close enough to pull her back."

"What will you have us do?" Daggon asked, ready to receive his orders.

Unfallen tears glazed the gold in Gudrun's eyes. "You were Eyolf's oldest friend," she said.

The name of their late king silenced the group as the source of Kallan's shadow surfaced.

There was a belt of laughter from the cluster of soldiers, barely muted by the distance between them.

"Speak to her," Gudrun said. "She'll listen to you."

Daggon scoffed.

"When has Kallan ever listened to anyone?" he said. "Not even Eyolf could tame that child. You know that."

On the other side of Gudrun, Aaric silently watched the soldier.

Daggon examined his flask as if lost in thoughts, likely of hunting games and swordplay he longed to have again. He threw back his head, taking in a large mouthful of mead.

Gudrun grinned. "Do you remember Kallan putting more effort into using the spells outside of class than the actual time spent in class?"

"Until you taught her the cloaking spell," Aaric said with an admiring grin.

"Yes..." Gudrun frowned. "Which only made her harder to find for her next lesson."

"I told you not to teach her the advanced spells," Aaric said with a twinkle in his eye. "She's too much of someone else I know."

"I know what you're doing, hag." Daggon grimaced at the old woman who was content to ignore him. "It won't work."

"And a little girl trading dresses for smiles in the warrens," Gudrun said.

"She was always fond of those damn warrens," Aaric said.

"Or sparring in her father's trousers and tunics alongside her father's war-men," Gudrun continued.

Daggon gazed at the distant fire with a muted, pained look. "She was forever running in and out of the streets of Lorlenalin in men's clothes and rags, rallying up the orphans she and Eilif found there."

"I have never seen anyone so eager to master the craft and swordplay," Gudrun said.

"She was twelve, boasting battles not yet won and of lands not yet conquered with a garish candor only Kallan could master," Aaric said.

"She stole my clothes," Daggon grumbled. "Twice Eyolf and I woke to find our garderobe bare. We had breakfast wrapped in blankets like a couple of wet nurses."

"Bundles of fruits wrapped in her gowns," Gudrun said.

"Wasted on dreams, plans, and play," Aaric said.

"Until the day I watched her fervor and voracity break beneath the weight of Eyolf's corpse." Daggon's words put an end to their reflections as Aaric and Gudrun watched the captain throw his head back for a drink. A moment later, he shook his head. "I will talk to her...when we're home." Daggon downed the last of the mead and stood, sighing. "But expect no resolution," he said and stumbled off in search of more drink.

Inside the tent, the air was cold. The pair of soldiers sat, staring down at Rune, who made no movement. The shackles that bound his wrists hadn't clinked for hours now. The Ljosalfar king stared at the lantern, refusing to acknowledge his guard.

Outside, the distant laughter rolled through the air. The low whispers of the high marshal, the captain, and the woman clung to the whistling wind and Rune sat, listening to every word.

Chapter 20

From the northernmost ends of the world, over the snows of Jotunheim, down past the fjords of Midgard, the land of Alfheim lay. Her tall, ancient pines stretched across the grass plains riddled with rivers that intertwined through forests and lakes. Rich forests radiated the heart of Freyr's land where secrets were buried within, secrets forgotten even by the Ljosalfar, who had dwelt in the land since it had formed.

To the east, Lake Wanern stretched on like the sea. During the long, cold winters, it iced over so thick, so solid, that kings fought their wars on the surface, which was strong enough to sustain thousands. When standing on the bank, looking out to the farthest corner, one could not see its end. Its primary inlet, the Klarelfr River, flowed from the north and split in two around the island filled with the Ljos-alfar city, Gunir, before pouring into Lake Wanern.

At the southernmost end of the lake, the waters drained into the Gautelfr River. For days it flowed, ending at the sea of the Kattegat. There, the shallow waters clawed and chewed apart a ship's hull, ready to eat away the keel of a negligent crew. Sailors igno-rant of the passing tides would find themselves run aground, or worse.

From the Kattegat, the mountains emerged, reach-ing high into the heavens where the peaks rose and vanished into the lowest clouds. Waterfalls cascaded from the mountains, dressing the rock in glistening streaks, the Dokkalfar's most beloved waterfall being Livsvann that supplied Lorlenalin with fresh water.

There, the Dokkalfar built their mountain city, Lorlenalin, the White Opal. With stones of white glistening in the sun's light, the Dokkalfar's city dis-tended from the precipice with a beauty equaled only to that of the Dvergar who lived in the caves be-neath the mountains to the west. Homes and tow-ers dressed the cliff face overlooking the Kattegat. Winding streets of white led deep into the earth, faceted with towering parapets and balustrades that extended into the clouds.

At the base of Lorlenalin and Livsvann's end, the mountain met the sea. There, the Dokkalfar's ship-yard spanned the docks. There, they constructed great longships, shaped to cut through the waters. They formed their hulls to move with the sea, welcoming its power and using it rather than carving an unnatural path against the currents.

From the docks, the forests began and peppered the crag with speckled green, stretching up and around the elevation where it joined with Alfheim's wood and concealed Lorlenalin. Pines and maples still green with color lined the earth and twisted their way up to the main gates in the back of the mountain.

Before the sun had reached its height, Kallan's army emerged from the forest. In and out of trees, they weaved, crossing the occasional pool of light that spilled across the forest floor. The thunderous rumble of a horn shook the ground in welcome. Kallan slouched back into her saddle, raising a blank set of eyes to the city.

As a child, Lorlenalin had been her playground, bursting with many mysteries she once explored. The older she grew, the more restrictions forced her into the confines of her station. No longer free to run through the streets or crawl into the hidden corners of the market, the pearl-white streets with green décor were forgotten, left there as a painful reminder of the life she no longer had.

The portcullis rose and the bridge lowered like a giant, outstretched hand eager to receive her people. Hollowed and cold, Kallan gazed at the courtyard's façade as she followed her guard into the vast courtyard spanning a generous acre. The city buzzed with excitement around a resplendent fountain of pale green stone that rose at the yard's center. Precious gems glistened from every corner of the citadel, adding an ancient grace that permeated the ample streets.

Cheers echoed through the high buildings as the war-men dismounted, hungrily taking up their wives or the random wench who ran to greet them. Unseen from the dank side streets, hidden among the barrels and shadows, a lone urchin searched the mounted riders. Careful to keep his distance, Latha grinned from the alley, eager to catch a glimpse of the queen before vanishing into the alley back toward the warrens.

Disconnected from the uproar of welcome, Kallan sat, allowing the emptiness to engulf her. She took a moment to watch the children run to their fathers while a few of her men raised a flagon of mead to hail her name. Kallan lifted her eyes to the citadel whose white opal face vanished into the clouds. Three stories above, a vacant balcony ordained with green stone extended over the courtyard. By nightfall, she would receive her people from that balcony, and the king's execution would launch the three-day festivities. Already, her people had prepared an altar for the Blood Eagle.

By nightfall, Kallan thought.

Nausea set in and Kallan lowered her eyes as she steered Astrid through the tumult of jubilation, leaving her war-men to their glory and song.

The corridor filtered the excitement that rolled from the courtyard, easing Kallan's nerves as the light of the late morning faded. An occasional lantern threw a tinge of orange to the stone, lighting her path. Within the labyrinth, she slid from the saddle and gathered the reins, leading Astrid down the hall past the doublewide arch that opened to the Great Hall.

Knowing each crack and each crevice of stone, Kallan walked down the hall. A black void encompassed her thoughts as she strode past the barracks where a handful of men had escaped the courtyard ruckus. Astrid's hooves struck the stone with a deafening clop that set the rhythm of her pace. The horse shook his head and snorted, pulling the reins in Kallan's grip.

At the end of the corridor, a warm orange light poured from the stables where the walls opened to a vast cave that the waters of Livsvann had honed naturally into the mountain. The thundering falls welcomed her and drowned out all outside noise as the water sent a constant hum into the grotto that calmed the fjord horses. A permanent gust of air pushed through the subterranean room and mingled with the scent of sweet hay.

Mindlessly, Kallan stepped over the small, manufactured stream directed off the main river outside the grotto. Its waters provided the stables with a constant supply of fresh, running water made available for watering the animals and cleaning.

Fresh hay covered the floor alongside the stalls built of thick, rich wood. Blankets, bridles, and saddles hung about the cavern on pegs, fences, and barrels. The wrought iron lanterns scattered about gave sufficient light, save for a single path buried in darkness at the back of the stables near Livsvann. To the naked eye, the path appeared to fade behind the falls, but in actuality, it emerged on the outside, leading into a series of courser paths and trails.

Kallan led Astrid down the lines of stalls where more than three dozen fjord horses grazed. Their wide, stocky bodies appeared dwarfed next to Astrid's tall, muscular build of the southeastern deserts. His dark coat and long, black mane contrasted the rows of light cream coats with black and white tails.

Paying the stable master and stablemen no mind, Kallan directed Astrid into his stall where she loosened the buckle on her saddle.

"The shipment of silk and alum just arrived in exchange for our soapstone, whetstone, and iron."

The gentle voice glazed over her like silk, and Kallan whipped her attention around to the well-groomed, wiry frame of her scribe, Eilif. He peered through the thin, pale brown hair that tapered to his shoulder.

"Eilif," she said and, with no qualms, leapt into his skinny arms, forcing him to catch her and knowing he would.

With a chuckle, he hugged Kallan, holding on a bit longer than was customary before letting go again.

"What news do you bring from the valley?" Eilif's thin grin creased the corners of his eyes, matching the lines at the corner of his mouth.

Kallan furrowed her brow and grinned, still holding onto his arm.

"My scout rode ahead. You know we bring the king."

Eilif shrugged.

"Rumors hardly reflect the truth. Did he say anything?" he asked, pushing the subject too often breeched by Gudrun.

"Never mind that," Kallan said. "How are Rind and Latha? And Kri? How is she?"

"As well as always," Eilif said, "and excellent evasion. What did he say?"

Kallan's face fell and she diverted her attention to Astrid, emptying her thoughts with physical work. She pulled the saddle from Astrid's back and disposed of it on the stone fence that made up Astrid's stall. Eilif whisked around the horse and, intercepting her, took her hands.

"What did he say?" Eilif asked.

Kallan did her best to look confused. "He?"

"The king," Eilif said, playing along.

"Oh." Kallan's face fell and she took back her hands to pull off the bearskin from Astrid's back.

"We haven't spoken yet," she said, heaving the load onto the fence.

Eilif blinked back surprise. "You mean to say that you finally have the King of Gunir shackled in chains, and you 'haven't spoken yet'?"

Kallan pushed a brush through Astrid's coat. She managed to get in two vigorous strokes before Eilif took the brush from her. She surrendered to his interference, knowing that a fight would be futile.

"My dearest lady," he said, placing the brush on the barrel behind her and, touching her chin, raised her face to his. Her eyes brimmed with a constant sorrow none could take from her. Eilif shook his head and forced a saddened smile. "Will you never laugh again?"

Kallan said nothing as she studied the face of her friend, unmarked from battle scars. After a moment, his brow furrowed with questions.

"Something is different about you," he said.

With a jerk, Kallan freed her chin and took up a bucket of oats she held for Astrid. If he looked at her long enough, he would reach the same conclusion that Gudrun had: that she had met someone.

"What will you do now that King Rune is here?" Eilif asked.

"My dearest Eilif..." Kallan grinned. "You always did know when to back off. I will do with the king as I've always done. The Dark One still lives. Executing the king will be just what I need to get the Dark One's attention."

"You're picking a fight," Eilif said.

Kallan shrugged.

"He picked one first," she said as memories flooded back of a raid gone bad.

Outnumbered, she had underestimated the Dark One's prowess and failed to see him double back with twice the guard. His maneuver had caught her by surprise and left him with a scar she had seared into his brow. She had barely escaped.

"I have an unfinished quarrel with that berserker," she said. "One I look to end."

"You are certain you'll win?" Eilif asked.

"I must," she said, looking up from the oats.

With a nod and shoulders slouched, the scribe started back toward the corridor.

"Eilif?"

Her crystal voice pulled him back and he stood as she mustered the strength to gather the words while biting the side of her lip.

"Tonight, when I receive my people..."

Fine lines creased the corners of Eilif's mouth as he grinned.

"When you are dressed and primped and are ordained in glistening jewels. And Gudrun has you stuffed into a gown made of the finest Eastern silks," he said, quoting a much younger Kallan from ages ago.

"Whether I am ready or not, I will be forced to receive the king," Kallan said, setting her worries aside. But it was too late, she knew Eilif had seen. Fondly, the scribe took up Kallan's hand.

"Lady Kallan." He planted a kiss on her knuckles. "You have always been and will always be my dearest lady. If you run to the ends of the world so it is there that I will follow."

Without another word, the scribe disappeared into the corridor, leaving her alone with her thoughts turning to the feasts the cooks were preparing. A tremble that began in her arms built to Kallan's shoulders until her entire body felt as if it would crumble.

Fighting to breathe, Kallan dropped the bucket of oats, passed Astrid an apple from her pouch, and took up the reins. Without a second glance, she climbed onto Astrid and steered him around, sending him into a canter down the path behind Livsvann as the apple restored the luster to his coat.

She had barely ridden the few steps out into the open before coaxing Astrid into a full gallop around the precipice where Livsvann fell.

Chapter 21

"Daggon!"

"Woman!" Daggon bellowed back at Gudrun, not bothering to look up.

He turned the smith's poker over in the orange coals as Gudrun pushed her way to the open forge tucked in the corner of Lorlenalin's courtyard that droned with excitement of the evening's festivities.

With ease, Daggon took up Thor's hind leg and held it between his knees. Briefly, he placed the hot bronze to the underside of his horse's hoof, confirming the correct shape one last time before releasing the horse's leg and submerging the metal multiple times in a bucket of hot water.

The metal hissed as Gudrun huffed, coming to stand within the smith's shop.

"Couldn't you have Uthbert take care of this?" she said as Daggon lifted Thor's leg again. She glanced at the leather bag resting on the bench beside a collection of tools.

Taking out a collection of nails, Daggon placed all but one between his lips. He pounded the first nail in, taking his time to reposition the crescent before taking up the second.

"I didn't learn the craft so another can shoe my horse," he mumbled through clenched lips, driving the nail through the hoof wall. "Besides..." Daggon flashed a knowing grimace at the stallion, who snorted. "Thor can be moody."

Daggon placed a third nail into position.

"Like his master," Gudrun said, striking Daggon's nerve.

He pulled the nails from his mouth.

"Speak, woman," Daggon said, returning the nails to his lips and bending his head down to continue.

"Have you seen Kallan?" Gudrun asked over the dull pounding.

Daggon positioned another nail over the shoe.

"I've barely had time to get Thor fitted with new crescents and already you've come to nag at my back side. Woman..." Daggon lifted his eyes, taking the nails, once more, from his mouth. "There are places where a man should never be nagged. Neither at the forge, nor the table, nor with drink in hand. Now..." He returned the last two nails to his lips and spoke from the corner of his mouth. "Go away."

"I'm not asking if you've spoken with her," Gudrun said. "I've asked if you've seen her." Mid-swing, Daggon glanced up with a curious eye. "We can't find her."

"Check the Warrens," Daggon said and continued his work.

"We did."

"Well, stop looking for Kallan and start looking for Eilif." Daggon fitted the final nail over the shoe. "No doubt he's a footfall behind her."

"We found Eilif," Gudrun said. "He said he was with her in the stables."

"Well then, there you have it." With a clang, Daggon dropped the hammer to the workbench in exchange for a metal file. Gudrun stepped closer, careful to leave him the space he needed to file the stubs of excess metal protruding from the top of the hoof.

"We can't find her," she said.

"I wouldn't fret too much. Kallan's been taking off long before she learned the cloaking spell," Daggon complained under his breath.

He inspected his work, adding an occasional swipe of the file where needed, ensuring the last of the nails were flush. "She hates to be sheltered. You know this. And putting a signet ring on her finger won't force her to stay within the boundaries she's been fighting against since she could crawl." He paused to look over the finished job. "She's probably escaped the palace again for a breath of fresh air."

"Perhaps," Gudrun said, but clearly fretted nonetheless.

"Alright." Daggon slammed down the file and released the horse's leg. With a comforted clop, Thor distributed his weight once more. "What aren't you saying, wench?"

Gudrun didn't need the nudge. "She's different."

"Hm," he grunted. "The boy."

"Daggon. It's not just the boy."

Gudrun dropped her shoulders. "He was a Ljosalfr."

"Who was?" Daggon asked.

"The boy."

Daggon shook his head. "No, he wasn't."

"He—"

"Because if he is," Daggon said, "I'll kill him."

The captain ran his large hand over his face with an exhausted sigh. For a moment, he glanced up at the beams overhead.

"Where's Kallan?" he asked, returning his gaze to the woman.

"That's what I'm trying to tell you." Gudrun stepped closer, lowering her voice as her eyes widened with worry. "She isn't anywhere, Daggon. This isn't about the boy. Forget the boy," she said when Daggon opened his mouth to speak. "Kallan isn't well."

Daggon shrugged. "Kallan hasn't been well since—"

"Her Seidr is fading."

Cocking his head, Daggon glanced to Gudrun, waiting for a better explanation than that.

"She has found a way to stop it all," Gudrun said, lowering her hurried words even more. "She was cold. She wouldn't respond."

"That's Kallan," Daggon said.

"Hear me," Gudrun said, pulling Daggon's hands together. "I felt it. I saw it. She has slowed the Seidr to numb her grief."

Daggon shook his head. "You know I have no understanding of this, Gudrun."

She released Daggon's hands.

"The Seidr must flow. Without it, the body dies. It shapes. It grows, departing its host when the body dies to join with the Seidr around us. But the Seidr itself is always there, in a constant state. As much as we must breathe, the Seidr must flow."

Daggon's brow wrinkled, understanding the urgency.

"Kallan has found a way to change its state," Gudrun said. "The grief she harbors grows and her grief rises. There is nothing left. The darkness is taking her. She empties everything into the shadows, feeling nothing just so she can breathe. But, in turn, it takes her will, and slows the Seidr." Gudrun sighed. "In silence, I saw her screaming."

Thor snorted, stomping his hind leg, and Daggon patted the horse's hindquarters.

"Have you not taught her how dependent a Seidkona is to the Seidr?" he asked.

"As dependent as we all are. She knows this, but she doesn't know she's doing it. Daggon. She's too far beyond feeling to know she's doing it."

Daggon nodded. "I'll go to her." He was on his feet. "Where is she?"

"Ugh." Gudrun threw her hands in the air. "We don't know."

"What do you mean you don't know? Ragnar," Daggon called out to the streets where a lone soldier led his horse toward the stables.

"Here," Ragnar called back.

"Find me Eilif and Aaric," Daggon ordered.

"Sir." Ragnar nodded and left to relieve his horse and carry out his orders.

Daggon took up the poker, pushing around the red and black coals in the forge. "Kallan had a page deliver the order of execution to me a day ago. When I asked to speak with her, she refused to see me."

"She's going through with it?"

Daggon nodded. "I believe so."

Gudrun grasped Daggon's forearm. "A lifetime, Daggon," she said. "All her life she has known nothing else. Her entire existence has been made of war and death. This is the first time she'll have to face life without it. She should be happy, but instead she clings to it. As much as she hates it, she depends on it. She needs it. As long as the war is on, she keeps a part of Eyolf with her."

Daggon tossed the poker into the forge with a sharp clang.

"What I can't figure out is how far she'll go to keep this war from ending," Gudrun said.

Daggon shuffled the last of the tools in order, rolling them into the leather to put away. "We can't help her anymore, Gudrun. Not until she accepts her father's death. She's gone where we can't follow." With a sigh, he returned to the forge. "She has to find her own way back now."

The sun settled behind the far reaches of the sea's horizon, streaking the sky with orange and red light. Pines hugged and shaped a clearing where Kallan looked to the sea from the edge of the precipice. There the river began the Livsvann. Content to sit alongside Astrid, who munched the assortment of wild grass, Kallan watched until the last of the rays vanished beyond the sea.

She couldn't delay much longer. Below, the city burst with excitement over the evening's apogee. Her absence would soon attract attention in which Gudrun would lead Lorlenalin's staff in an uproarious manhunt for the missing queen. Regardless, Kallan didn't move, deciding to extend her delay until they found her or the evening's cold forced her inside.

The horizon squeezed out the last of the light and extinguished the last of the day. Only the distant purples remained as night settled in. Kallan sighed, allowing an uneasy sick to churn her stomach. The end of the war, an era, and new beginning peered over the horizon and she could not stop it.

Just a while longer.

The world grew dark and winds blew cold as the clouds moved in from the sea. Kallan shivered and hugged herself against the chill. Stubbornly refusing to go back, she opened her palm in front of her.

Streams of gold emerged from the tips of her fingers. Guiding the tiny threads, she called them out and back and turned them over, twisting them about at will, watching, amused with the threads of Seidr until she forgot her cold.

The winds changed, a darkness descended and Kallan extinguished her Seidr. Whipping her attention to the shadows behind her, she stared into the trees with sharpened senses.

Kallan narrowed her eyes and grasped the hilt of her dagger. With a flick of her wrist, she summoned a flame and looked deeper into the shadows. There, a large umbra lingered separate from the winds and forests. They were there. She had no doubts about it this time. She could feel them and they were growing closer, stronger, closing in like the walls of Lorlenalin.

Chapter 22

An eerie tension settled inside the keep where Gudrun stopped at the farthest west passage of the Great Hall. The voice of seventy thousand roared with jubilation in the courtyard and carried down Lorlenalin's labyrinths. Their voices entered the keep, leaving a dulled riotous roar that prevented the silence the old Seidkona had been looking for.

The servants, having covered the four long tables in meats and pies, sugared fruits, cheeses and barrels of ale and mead, had long since returned to the kitchens, but not before lighting the oblong fire pits between each table. The scent of roast pig filled the hall with the warmth of the flames. Fresh branches and wild berries decorated each torch, adding the fall pine to the collection of scents. Suspended above each table from the ceiling, the wrought iron wheels were alight with burning candles.

Preparations were ready. The masses cried out. Formalities were in order. Everyone was dressed in their finest and waiting where they needed to be. Save for the queen, who she couldn't find anywhere.

Gudrun shifted a fatigued eye to the barren throne facing the two doublewide arches that decorated the south wall. Flanked by Lorlenalin's high seat pillars, the queen's seat waited desolate and empty. Gudrun sighed, her heart heavy with worry, and pulled her attention from the hall.

Up the backside steps, Gudrun trudged to the next floor, gathering her green silk skirts as she counted the stairs. Her foot scuffed each step until she reached the top and turned the corner toward Kallan's bower. Gudrun pushed open the door and glided into the small maze of rooms that composed Kallan's chambers. The scent of the sea forever filled the bower of white stone lavished in elegant woodwork. Today, it mingled delightfully with rose and lavender oils.

Gudrun ignored the bath and the plethora of swords and daggers strewn about with the occasional collection of bundled heather or sage, the desk overflowing with powdered spices, minced herbs, and dried rose petals resting beside the mortar and pestle, which she recognized as her own. Gudrun made mental note to come back for it later.

The private balcony doors were open wide, welcoming the view of the sea. The only gown lay carelessly on the floor. Several candles filled the room with a warm glow that ended at the bedchamber.

Gudrun pushed open the door. The decor mirrored the sitting room, save for the large bed framed in rich, elegantly carved wood centered in the room between two side tables. There, at the seaside of the room, adorned in a gown of silver and blue and crowned with a headdress that dripped through her hair, Kallan stood with her back to the door.

"You've caused quite a fright, this time," Gudrun said upon entering the room. There was no reprimand in her voice.

Kallan turned to the old woman. The white elding bracelet ordained her wrist and the scent of rose and lavender oils wafted from her skin. A circlet of silver and sapphire crowned her brow, but Gudrun's eye followed the signet ring that caught the light.

"Do they know yet?" Kallan asked, staring at the moon over the sea.

"No," Gudrun said. "They've given up looking in the most obvious places and are now searching the streets and the prisons."

Kallan shook her head. "I wouldn't be in the prisons," she whispered.

"And why is that, Kallan?" Gudrun asked and watched Kallan unfurl her fingers in angst.

A prolonged silence stretched between the women as Gudrun waited, knowing the exact moment when Kallan would move, desperate to feel anything.

As if painfully numb to the stagnant nothingness, Kallan stared into the black waters of the Kattegat.

The waves washed into the rock, beating at Lorlenalin's base like the void that Gudrun knew pushed against Kallan, wearing her down little by little, carving out the rock one wave at a time until the foundation of the city conformed to the shape of the sea.

"My goals are lost to the void that has taken me," Kallan whispered. "That void. It is there I have banished everything to the darkness...there I can place everything that reminds me of that pain."

Kallan turned from the window and Gudrun watched as Kallan tried to still her quivering lip while holding back the wall of tears Gudrun knew would never fall.

"I love this city and its people," Kallan said. "I know this. But through all the blood and the war and the hate, I fear I've lost my love for Lorlenalin. I know I love Lorlenalin. I must. But I can't *feel* it. And I don't *care* that I can't feel it." Wide-eyed, Gudrun searched Kallan's cold face. "If I go to him, if I see the king who killed my father, I fear I will lose the last of what little I still feel, even if it is hate." Kallan closed her eyes. "I am so desperate to feel what seems so far from reach, but the pain is too great and I am faltering."

Gudrun dropped an ancient hand to Kallan's shoulder, urging her to raise her eyes, but Kallan stood, visibly numbed by the weight of her burden.

The old Seidkona breathed a weighted sigh.

"I am alone in that room with no door," Kallan breathed. "I'm lost to the black that's keeping me. I can taste its foul stench. But I can not run. I can not fight. The last of my life is leaving me. I'm losing myself in the abyss. It's taking my air...and I can not breathe."

"And what of the children, Kallan?" Gudrun asked and waited for Kallan to find her words.

"I do so love those children. They alone are the last memory I have that bears me no pain or regret," Kallan said. "They alone give me no reason to withdraw into the darkness."

"Then it is there you need to find you again," Gudrun said, rising to her feet. "I will gather the men from their search." Gudrun held Kallan in a warm hug. "I will send Eilif to you. He, after all, is the calmest of the three. I can give you five minutes," Gudrun promised as she started for the door. "But Aaric's temper is as hot tonight as Daggon's patience is short. I can not keep them longer than that."

Kallan nodded, but Gudrun had already swept from the room, leaving the queen to compose herself in their wake.

Kallan hugged herself against the chill that wasn't there. For a moment, she had contemplated telling Gudrun about the Ljosalfr hunter and the Shadows that had chased her from the precipice that night. And just as quickly, she had closed the last of her heart within the cold that consumed her center.

Aaric spun on his heel as he continued his pacing along the entrance of the receiving balcony. As he walked, his polished sword clanked at his side. His dress clothes seemed only to enhance his threatening form, despite covering most of his tattoos.

"Of all the jewels of Alfheim," Aaric said, "she is our most precious. Everyone in Lorlenalin seems to know this, save for the jewel herself." He turned on his heel to Gudrun. "You had to teach her the cloaking spell."

"She is trying to cope, Aaric," Gudrun said.

"The girl's favorite pastime is running off and wreaking havoc through the city that would put her mother to shame and you teach her to vanish," Aaric said.

Daggon leaned against the arched frame of the balcony in his finest clothes, just out of sight of the crowd.

"The girl is leading her people into a new era, and she's doing it alone," Daggon said.

"She's seen little else outside of the world Eyolf had given her, you know this," Gudrun said.

"Bah," Aaric said, giving a sound as if he understood, but didn't like it.

"That girl was nearly born into war and lost a parent in each." Daggon said, staring out into the masses. "The least you can do is to empathize with her."

"I empathize," Aaric said. "But, emotions aside, she has to go forward whether she likes it or not, and we don't have the time for the apprehensions of a whimsical girl. The New Era is here, now, and the queen can't be found to welcome it." Aaric released an audible sigh and forced himself to stop. "Has she changed her mind, at least?" he asked, peering at Gudrun, who was already shaking her head in answer.

Aaric threw his arms in surrender.

"She's determined to kill him," Daggon said. "She won't budge. She plans to launch the celebrations tonight with the execution."

"It's a mistake," Aaric said. "An execution will lure the Dark One from his hole."

"I think that's what she's hoping for," Daggon said, but Aaric stood at attention, drawing Daggon's interests from the courtyard to the passage leading to Kallan's bower. There, shadowed by Eilif, Kallan glided down the corridor in her gown of silver and blue.

Daggon straightened his posture, tightened his jaw, and took her hands in his. "You look so much like your mother," he said.

Kallan weakly smiled as Aaric swept his arm around Kallan's back.

"Enough of this, there is no time. Lorlenalin is waiting," he said, leading her onto the balcony alongside him.

Seventy thousand voices rose up and engulfed Kallan as she stepped into the moonlight that bathed the courtyard in its splendor. Below, amid the masses, torches and lanterns blazed, adding to the gaiety that already infected the Dokkalfar gathered there.

They roared in jubilation, eager to welcome the end of the age-long war. At the courtyard's center, the fountain rose up from the crowd where a platform and executioner waited to receive the king.

The crowd quieted at the wave of Aaric's hand and Kallan expanded her lungs as the last of the uproar died down.

"Bring him out," Kallan called.

The Dokkalfar exploded with a tumultuous roar that filled the courtyard and rolled up Lorlenalin's high towers as the first of the guards appeared. From high in her balcony, the crowd appeared to swallow the Ljosalfar king.

Kallan's insides flipped and she averted her attention to the moon, to Daggon, to Aaric beside her, anywhere but the king who killed her father. She refused to see him, who masked his grief with the blank stare he held firm through the crowd, his head cocked high with honor as he followed his guards to the platform to welcome his death. There he would find the merciful headsman that would relieve him of his failure.

The cheering grew quieter. Although Kallan was certain the king had reached the platform, she still refused to look. An encouraging hand took hers and Aaric gave it a gentle squeeze. He nodded, urging her ahead. Only when the crowed quieted, only when Kallan was certain she could not prolong another moment's delay, she forced her gaze to the platform below.

Her spine tightened. Her breath ceased. She felt her hand go cold in Aaric's grip.

In the courtyard below, flanked by a pair of guards on the raised platform and shackled with elding, stood Rune, son of Tryggve, Lord and King of Gunir: the Ljosalfr hunter she had loved in the wood, if only for a moment.

Stripped of his bow and quiver, Rune stared, his gaze secured, unwavering on Kallan. His black hair fell to his shoulders. But his eyes, his cold, silver-blue eyes wide with relief, held hers as if he could see beyond her iron wall buried within her void.

A cold chilled her spine, but nothing could stop her head from spinning, leaving her battling to clear her mind. In the time it took for her to gasp and for the color to drain from her face, Kallan's strength left her, her legs gave out, and the world went black.

Chapter 23

What happened?

Kallan tried to speak. She tried to open her eyes, to move, and failed. She was alone in the darkness, in the void.

Gudrun? She tried to speak, but her lips wouldn't move. Her legs wouldn't obey and so Kallan lay in the dark, trying to remember.

I was on the balcony, she thought then remembered everything at once.

The crowd. The executioner. The platform. The hunter. But where was the king?

She tried to ask that too and failed.

Focus.

"What. Happened." Kallan heard Daggon's voice punch the air. The waver he always had when he was angry was there.

Why was he angry?

"She fainted," Kallan heard Aaric say.

No, I didn't, Kallan tried to say, to tell them. *I didn't faint. It was something else!*

"Kallan."

She heard Gudrun calling and Kallan felt her finger move.

"Can you hear me?" Gudrun asked.

Kallan tried to move her arm and her fist tightened. Her eyes, at last, flew open.

Peering down around her in a circle with eyes all wide as if the dead had risen, Daggon, Aaric, and Eilif stared at her stretched on the corridor floor.

"She'll be alright," Gudrun said beside her. "Help me get her up."

At once, Daggon and Aaric leapt to the instructions. With an arm to Daggon and one to Aaric, who supported her back, they lifted her to her feet.

"Easy now," Gudrun said as Kallan found her feet beneath her.

"What—" Kallan gasped. "What happened?"

"You fell," Eilif answered as Daggon said, "You fainted."

"What...happened?" Kallan had to raise her voice to be heard over the clamoring.

"You fell," Aaric said, but Kallan's thoughts were already onto the next worry.

"Where is the king?" she asked.

"The king?" Daggon raised a brow.

"She really should go to her room," Gudrun said.

"Where is he?" Kallan asked with growing irritation.

"He has been returned to his cell," Aaric said

Gudrun mumbled. "You need to rest."

"Why wasn't he brought out to the platform?" Kallan asked.

Silence encompassed the hall.

"He was, Kallan," Daggon said with apparent ever-growing worry.

"King Rune was on the platform," Aaric said.

"That was..." Kallan whispered and remembered his face. She had no doubt the hunter from the Alfheim wood had stared up at her from the platform beside the executioner.

"It's worse than I thought," Gudrun said, eager to get Kallan on the way to her chambers.

"That's why we thought you fainted," Aaric said, "because—"

"I didn't faint!" Kallan's voice filled the corridor.

Distance muted the joyous cries of hundreds of thousands of voices that carried from the courtyard. The mass had dwindled considerably. Kallan pinched the bridge of her nose.

"The man who was on the platform...is he dead?" she asked.

It was a long moment before anyone dared answer.

"King Rune was on the platform, Kallan," Daggon said finally. "He has been returned to the prisons."

Kallan released her nose. "Who—Who ordered him back to the prisons?"

"I did," Aaric said.

Kallan whirled about on her heel. "He was to be executed immediately," she said. "Why, when I've made my choice, and my decision was clear, why did you disregard my orders?"

"You fainted," Aaric said. "And without my queen conscious or present, I had to do what I felt was best for Lorlenalin."

"I didn't—" Kallan took a breath and returned her fingers to the bridge of her nose as she forced her demeanor calm and her head clear. "That man was to die today."

"And I stand by what I said days ago," Aaric said. "That killing that king forfeits our lives, and while my queen was incapacitated, I had to do what I felt was best for Lorlenalin and her people."

"And I will not have him go unpunished," Kallan bellowed. "For the massacre of Austramonath and the lives his berserker has claimed, for every drop of Dokkalfar blood and for the orphans he's made of our children. For the life of my father, the Ljosalfar king must answer. If I have to carve Odinn's Eagle into his back with his own sword myself, I will!"

Her voice rang clear through the corridor.

Aaric heaved, matching Kallan's temper. "If you do this, if you insist on this madness, I promise you, Kallan, King Rune will live through the Blood Eagle long enough to see the berserker tear down our gates and witness the start of this...this madness...as you start this war all over again."

A stab of anger quelled to a sharp pain, pushing from behind her wall, but she was too late. Hurt blanketed Kallan's face in the sheer second it took her to suppress it.

"Aaric," Gudrun said, looking to ease back his rage.

"She has to know," Aaric said.

Gudrun shook her head. "Not like this."

Kallan tightened her jaw, closing her eyes in an attempt to focus more strength on holding up her wall. Paralyzed, she prepared to stand against the torrent that was to come.

"She has forgotten what Kira taught her," Aaric said, then frowned at Kallan. "The people look to you to end this, Kallan. They trust you to deliver, and if you don't, they will abandon you. You will lose their support. Do not kill the king."

Kallan forced herself to gulp down the knot in her dry throat.

"My people—"

"Your people trust you to make this choice for them," Aaric said. "You seek to end this war, to give them what they have dreamed about for centuries, but you invite a wrath the Dark One will bring. If the king dies, his berserker will not stop until every last Dokkalfar is dead. The Dark One is loyal. He will seek vengeance. What answers will you have for your people then, Kallan, when they call your name for aid while the Dark One runs them through in his berserker rage?"

Kallan closed her eyes, desperate to feel what seemed so far from reach, but the pain was too great and she was faltering.

"I," Kallan's voice cut the tension, leaving her company suspended on bated breath, "am tired."

The simple words struck the room like a thunderous wave, giving voice to the burden they all had carried for centuries. In silence they stood, anxious for what she would decide, worried for what she wouldn't.

Kallan raised her face to Aaric's. Her color had returned, and with it, the burden she shouldered. It weighed her down heavier than ever before, but a new look glowed, and with it, a shimmer of hope she seemed unaware of. Silence hung suspended with every breath she took.

"One day," Kallan said. "I can delay his death one day. Whether or not the Dark One has made his move or not. And then I will cut Odinn's eagle into the king's back myself."

Without pause or delay, she swept from the room, and plodded all the way down to the dungeons.

Chapter 24

Beneath the city, buried deep within the mountains, the guards led Rune down into the vast caverns hewn of black earth and stone. Every footfall echoed back throughout the labyrinth to become the only sound in the darkness where the last of day's light ended and the occasional torch left large gaps of black between each orange dome.

Into the depths, they lumbered until they came to a small passage where the prison's key keeper dragged his leg with a slight gimp that followed his every left step. The keeper unlocked a door that loudly whined as he pulled it open to reveal a stone pit devoid of sound and light.

With a violent shove, a guard pushed Rune down the three stone steps into the black hole. The last of the torchlight vanished, leaving Rune buried alive in the darkness. But, before the guard with the gimp could pull the door closed behind him, a palm struck the wood, leaving it ajar as the echo dwindled.

Awed by the contrast, the key keeper followed the folds of silver and blue up the slender body of his queen who stood like a beacon amid the desolation. He gulped down the hot ball that had formed in his throat and suddenly wished he had shaved the whiskers from his face.

Kallan moved too quickly, snatching the keys from their keeper. Her eyes remained fixed on the prisoner, who noted the rise and fall of her deepened breath.

"Leave us." Her clear notes permeated the stale death of the prison.

The key keeper limped away. The last of the shuffled gimp faded into the silence where even the sharpest of hearing couldn't make out the slightest footfall, and still she remained unmoving.

Finally, pulling her hand from the door, she flicked a wrist, sending streams of white light to flood the room and suppress the darkness. The silver headdress in her hair glistened like raindrops bathed in moonlight. Enchanted by her trick, Rune watched, intrigued by her stunning presentation.

The door banged closed, leaving the echo behind as she descended the three steps into the room. Her gown swept the floor, adding a contrast that enthralled him.

Rune said nothing as Kallan's hands flew over his bonds, perhaps lingering too long on his hands while she fumbled with the keys. His attention lingered on the bits of silver in her hair glistening beneath her Seidr light. She fitted the correct key into the shackles and turned the lock with a series of metal clicks.

His gaze strayed to the delicate lines of her neck. From there he followed the fine chain down to a tri-cornered knot of black silver and elding. The simple jewel would have appeared out of place with her ensemble if it hadn't fit so naturally in the nook of her collarbone, magnifying the elegance of her slender curve.

The chains clanked as she pulled them free. They hit the floor with a metallic crunch as Rune rubbed his raw wrists. He could hear her every breath in the silence, taking in the scent of lavender as she lifted her face to his.

He had correctly remembered every dip, every curve, elated that she stood unscathed before him, her eyes as vibrant an iridescent blue lapis as he remembered. For a moment she seemed fixed on his mouth until he was certain she would close in. And just when he thought he had the right words to begin, she caught the smile on the corner of his lips and slammed her hand into his face.

"Ah! Son of a..." Rune squawked, holding his cheek.

As he regained his balance, Kallan threw back her head in defiance, daring him to slap her back. As if wishing him to strike her, she visibly braced for the impact.

Rune's hand twitched with the temptation as he heaved, pacing himself through the anger.

"Why did you come here?" Kallan whispered.

Rune cocked his jaw. He felt it pop.

"I'm pretty sure you were present when the queen gave her orders," he said, checking his fingers for blood.

Before he could regain his composure, Kallan stepped in, closing the last of the space between them, and splayed her hand upon his chest. Just as heat flooded him beneath her touch, Kallan fired a blast of wind into his body. He fell to his back, releasing a groan. As Rune fought to regain the breath she had knocked out of him, Kallan was on him, straddling him with her arm braced across his chest. In one hand, she cradled a ball of flame poised at the ready while her hair fell like a curtain around her face.

"My Seidr is only the tip of my very short temper," she said. "Answer me."

"You brought me here," he said. "Bound and blinded were your orders, princess."

Rage sparked in her eyes at the title and Rune fought back a grin.

"I am not weak," she hissed and slid her forearm up onto his neck. The cold in her eyes seethed as she stared down. The flame in her hand flickered idly, waiting to obey its enchanter's command.

"Why do your men follow me?" she asked.

"My men aren't here," he said, fighting the pressure she applied to his throat. Kallan shifted her weight and eased off his neck, sliding her arm back to his chest. With a twitch of her wrist, she extinguished her flame and sighed, sitting upright.

"I believed you once," she whispered. "I'll not make that mistake again." Her face softened as she eased on the venom she spewed. "They are here, nipping at my heels, cowering in the shadows."

"Did they attack you?" Rune asked.

"No," she said.

A gleam in his eye caught the light. "Then they weren't my men."

Appearing pensive, Kallan sat for a moment then shifted her weight and pulled herself to her feet. She hugged herself against a chill he couldn't feel as she turned her back to Rune and walked toward one of the hovering Seidr lights. Rune scuffed the ground as he stood, eyeing the keys still clutched in her hand.

"They watch me outside the city," Kallan said, clearly determined to keep her eyes on the Seidr light. "I can only assume they are your spies."

Rune took a breath, allowing his gaze to wander over her backside, before speaking.

"You would turn your back to a prisoner?" Rune asked, highly suspicious of her apparent foolish choices.

Kallan peered over her shoulder. "You are no threat to me."

Rune inhaled, forcing the offense aside. "Why?"

Dropping her arms, Kallan turned back to the light and slid a finger along the sphere as Rune circled around to stand before her.

"Why did you release my bonds?" he asked.

Her eyes glanced down at his chest and she threw back her shoulders. But the tension, the usual anger, the aggression was missing from her composure.

"It isn't right," she said, "attacking a man who can't defend himself."

A distasteful look pursed his lips as he blinked at the absurdity of her answer.

"You call an unarmed man against a Seidkona a fair fight?"

Kallan smiled mockingly.

"Your lies are not the first I've heard from the lips of a woman," Rune said. "Why did you really come here?"

"Why did you attack my people?" she asked. She glanced at his bare chest again then forced her head up in a stiff angle as if to prevent herself from gawking.

Rune narrowed his eyes, heavy with disbelief.

"You did not come here to discuss politics. If you're creating excuses, you could at least ask where Bergen is or when we plan—"

"Why did you follow me in Swann Dalr?" she asked.

Rune grinned and relaxed his shoulders.

"Any question in the world. Any at all and you want to know why I followed you. Is this why you interrupt my final hours and deprive me of my last rights, all on a woman's whim?"

"Answer my 'why,'" she said.

"You're evading," he said with a smirk.

"Why did you follow me?" she asked again. Her jaw had visibly tightened and the urge to kiss it off of her was overwhelming.

"You're shaking to burst," he taunted. "Ready to bare your claws, screaming and kicking and you want to know why I followed you."

"Answer."

"I did once," he said. "My men needed meat."

"You left the boar."

Rune's jaw fell and he smiled.

"So..." Rune folded his arms across his chest and leaned into the wall beside her. "You went back."

"Why did you follow me?" Kallan asked again. The light of her Seidr caught the blue in her eyes.

"But you know the reason," he said.

Kallan scoffed and Rune dared a step closer, closing the last of the space between them.

"That pain you horde," he whispered. "That pain you are so adamant to keep, it will devour you in its unending darkness."

"You know nothing of what you speak," she said. "Nothing of pain." Her eyes flickered to his neck.

"You're defensive for one so confident."

Kallan locked her eyes onto his.

"I am not—"

"You're shaking," he said.

"Why did you spare me?" Kallan blurted the question in a hush.

Rune's face stretched into a wide, undaunted grin and his shoulders relaxed, savoring his victory like aged mead or a well-wooed wench.

"And there she speaks," he said.

Kallan threw back her head. Her breathing had deepened visibly.

"So that's what troubles you, princess."

"Don't call me that."

Rune arched a brow.

"You knew who I was when you found me in Swann Dalr," she said. "You could have dispatched me at any moment and claim your victory. Why did you spare me?"

Rune studied the lights reflected in her eyes. "I didn't know who you were."

"Then why did you follow? Why did you stay?"

Rune shrugged.

"You looked like you had forgotten."

"Forgotten," she said.

"How to feel, how to breathe, how to smile," he said. "How to live."

"I don't—"

"You look miserable," he said and glanced at the lines of her neck long enough to let her see that he stared. "You're cold."

"You know nothing."

"I know what I've seen," Rune said. "What it does, what it will do. I've seen the shadow of what you'll become, staring back at me from those who once knew me. You will forget everything: how to think, how to feel. It will consume you until it takes you. You'll forget it all, until nothing is left and you abandon those you love the most. They'll be the first to go."

Every word came in a fluid rush, and he watched his words dig into the hate that enveloped her.

"I love my people," Kallan whispered.

"Yet already you've forgotten the danger you place on them when you signed my execution."

Kallan smiled warmly. "Is this a final plea from one so desperate?"

"Bergen will come," Rune promised. "Do not underestimate his loyalty or his lust for vengeance. There are tempers even I can not quell."

"Do not pretend to care for those who you hate," she said. "Our walls can not be breached."

"Pretend to care?" He shook his head. "I didn't know I was supposed to hate you, and I'm not sorry you want me."

"Oh!" she exclaimed and moved toward the door, but Rune leapt from the wall. His arms flew up and, slamming his palms onto the stone, he caged her in between the wall and his body, leaning in too close as he spoke.

"You have traitors who sleep among you, hidden behind these walls, but you hate too much to see your usurpers."

Kallan narrowed her eyes into snake-like slits.

"You know nothing of my people you...coward...Outlaw...*Nidingr!*"

230

Rune's hand gripped her neck, slamming her head into the wall. His nostrils flared with rage and Kallan met his eyes, seeing them for the first time steeped in a cold, crazed hate.

"There are laws for such backless accusations made," he said, the affection gone from his voice.

"You had my father killed, stabbed in the back while you rode away. You left him to bleed without a sword in his hand or the decency to take his life and finish the job. What greater dishonor is there?"

Rune eased his grip on her neck as he changed back to indifference and released her, leaving behind a cold that had not been there before. With a sigh, he lowered his arm, giving Kallan the space to push off the wall as the cold settled between the small space left between them.

Her foot pounded the stone as she returned to the door, leaving Rune at the wall.

"Tomorrow, you will die," she said as she climbed the steps.

"You'll rescind that order."

With a rebounding amount of arrogance, Kallan stopped at the top stair.

"You claim your death will summon your berserker to the very gates of this city?"

"It will," he said.

Mustering the strength, he looked to the queen gazing down at him. Her eyes glistened in the light like jewels.

"He will come," Rune promised.

Her eyes dropped to the signet ring upon his finger and the boar's head there. She returned her eyes to his before answering.

"Then you shall die." Kallan gripped the handle.

"Kallan."

The queen stopped and turned back as a flushed red coated her neck.

"Send word to Gunir," he said. "Request your peace. I guarantee it will be welcomed."

"For centuries my father offered you that peace, and you answered with arms," she said. Her body shook. "If you desire peace so badly, you should have sent your own request."

Before Rune could answer, Kallan threw open the door, flicked her wrist to extinguish the Seidr light, and slammed the door closed between them.

Enclosed in darkness, alone, Rune stood as he said aloud in his cell, "We did."

Chapter 25

Gasping, Kallan fell back against the door. With her fist clenched, she pressed her fingers against her mouth, willing herself calm as she battled back the urge to break beneath her anger. Upstairs, the festivities had begun and she cringed at the concept of joining them.

Collecting her strength, Kallan huffed and pulled herself up, not bothering to straighten her skirts. She trudged back through the prison, all the while resisting the impulse to run to the stable and Astrid. She dropped the keys to the gimping guard who she found in the armory and then shuffled into the hallway before turning down the corridor, toward the Great Hall, away from Astrid and the prisons.

The scent of pine, sweet mead, and roasted pork wafted from the hall. Song and merriment accompanied endless bouts of laughter that failed to move her. From the corridor, Kallan stood in the shadows and watched the festivities. Her war-men had gathered around the tables. There, they exchanged food and drink with endless stories of their courageous deeds while they picked clean the three roast pigs extended over the fire pits.

A year ago, she would have led them on in this merriment, being the first to boast their victory in battle. This day, it was all she could do not to run away without a glance back.

Across the hall, in the sea of heads, Gudrun's golden eyes found her. The old woman smiled warmly, and Kallan knew her grandmother had already advised the guests of the queen's absence, permitting Kallan the isolation she craved.

Flooded with gratitude, Kallan attempted a weak smile back, trudging away from the feast and down the hall. In silence, she made her way through the labyrinth of corridors, up several sets of stairs, and as far around the Great Hall and festival as possible.

At last, she reached the floor of her chambers. Even there she could smell the food and drink. As Kallan made her final turn, she stopped abruptly at the sight of Daggon, calm and patient, at the end of the hall where he waited in front of her chamber door.

Kallan glided down the corridor. Her gown swept the floor. In masquerade, she glistened, steeped in a chill that clung to her frigid complexion.

The subtle glint of Kira's pendant caught Daggon's eye and a twinge of remorse tugged at his chest.

"Kallan," he said, taking her hand as she arrived at her chamber door. He studied her empty face. The only warmth was of the lantern light glowing back at him from the wall. Beyond that, her eyes, iced from the void and weighted with the flood of grief, consumed her. Too plainly, he saw the broken queen Gudrun had spoken of: an empty vessel, chilled by a death that was taking her.

Daggon turned over her tiny palms.

"Your hands are warm," he said, half-expecting them to be as cold as the guise she wore.

She pulled her hand free, as if afraid he could sense the shadows haunting her through the touch.

"It is nothing," she said, forcing her fake grin wider.

With a sentinel's eye, Daggon followed her as she pushed her way to her chamber door.

"All is in order," she said. "Tonight, my people feast, for tomorrow the king dies."

Her words fell like snow, sending a chill that churned Daggon's stomach. He caught her hand as Kallan reached for the door handle. His armband flashed in the light as he moved.

Daggon pulled her face to his and looked at Kallan as she stared through her mask of mock joy.

"Why so cold, Kallan?" he whispered.

Tears flooded Kallan's eyes at the word. Through depleted strength, Daggon looked into the darkness holding her, binding her to its fate, just out of reach. In silence, she pleaded, begging him to reach in, to pull her from the void. And all at once, he understood and wrapped his arms around the girl. He held her, desperate to keep her there with him the more she slipped away.

"Will you never grieve?" he whispered and Kallan tightened her arms around his wide ribs.

Sighing, Daggon planted a kiss on the top of her head and released her after giving a gentle squeeze to her shoulder. Without a word, he turned to walk the length of the corridor and round the corner out of sight.

Several moments passed where Kallan stood numb in the hall. She waited until she was certain her legs would give out from exhaustion. Sighing deeply, Kallan pushed open the door of her chambers and swept inside her sitting room.

The door had barely latched closed when the hurried footsteps of a child thumped along the floor, pulling a grin across Kallan's face like a beam of starlight touching down on moonflowers.

"Kawin," Rind cried and did her best to leap the whole three inches into the air and land in Kallan's arms.

"Rind," Kallan exclaimed, scooping up the toddler in a long and tight hug. "Oh, Rind. Dearest Rind." Kallan squeezed the child, releasing her doubts, her worries, her trifles as she rocked the child in her arms. "Oh, I missed you so."

After a moment, Kallan tightened her hug. "Where is Eilif, hm?" But the child had wasted no time shoving her little thumb into her mouth and nestling her head onto Kallan's shoulder.

"Eilif?" Kallan called, glancing around her chambers once she saw that Rind wouldn't answer.

A platter of meats and cheese with a bowl of cloudberries caught her eye and Kallan grinned wider as Eilif shuffled into view on the balcony.

"I am here," Eilif said, poking his head around the corner.

With Rind still slumped against her shoulder, Kallan stepped out onto the balcony and, at once, began swaying in place beside Eilif.

"She would not go to sleep tonight after hearing you were back." Eilif grinned, looking back to the sea. "She just wouldn't have it."

"And how did she know I was back?" Kallan asked, grinning widely with an arched brow to Eilif.

"Latha," Rind said through the thumb in her mouth.

"Latha, hm," Kallan mused, and gazed again to Eilif. "How is Latha?"

"Never better."

"And Herdis and Kri?" Kallan asked, so excited she debated on heading down to the warrens almost at once.

"They all wanted to come, but I held off the rabble with promises that you would be down to see them tomorrow," Eilif said.

He gazed from the sea and shifted his brown-eyed plea to Kallan, who could only grin wider.

"Well, then, I suppose I'll have to be down first thing in the morning. Won't I? How's that sound, Rind?"

Rind was already nodding.

"Promise?" Rind asked around her thumb.

Smiling, Kallan removed the white elding bracelet from her wrist and slipped it onto Rind's.

"I promise," Kallan whispered as Rind settled back down, turning the bracelet over to study its intricate designs.

"How well did the supplies last?" Kallan asked, gazing up at the dwindling crescent moon.

"We made them last," Eilif assured her and pulled his eyes from the sky. "You've already done more than your share, Kallan."

"I can always do more," she said as the crescent vanished behind a wall of thick cloud.

Returning to the sitting room, Kallan sat herself in the chair stationed in front of her desk, ensuring she could still see the sea in the distance. Eilif followed right behind as Kallan shifted Rind into a better position on her lap.

"Kawin?" The child pulled her thumb from her mouth long enough to plop her head onto Kallan's chest. "Can you tell me a story?" Her large eyes looked up at Kallan and waited.

"A story." Kallan shifted a glance to Eilif, who could only grin in response as he made himself comfortable against the wall. "Well, only if you promise to go to sleep."

Rind nodded and stared off into nothing and listened, waiting for Kallan to begin. The fire crackled and popped against the breeze of sea air and Kallan exhaled, finding her temporary peace within.

She thought for a moment and looked to the sky looming over her balcony. The clouds shifted again, revealing the moon's crescent, and then, with a soft grin on her lips, Kallan began the children's riddle.

"Hjuki and Bil chased the moon,
With waters from Byrgir's well,
Upon their shoulders they did share,
Simul the pole and Saegr.

'Mani,' they cried and chased the sky,
'From Byrgir whence we came,
To water the earth and water your drink,
And water the seas with rain'."

Rind nestled closer into Kallan and closed her eyes, filled with dreams as Kallan continued.

"Hati looked back and Skol ahead,
But Mani gave no reply,
For Hjuki he took, and bent his crook,
And Bil was taken thereafter.

Hjuki and Bil still chase the moon,
From Byrgir whence they came,
To water the earth and water the drink,
And water the seas with rain."

The hearth fire crackled, and Kallan risked a glance down to the sleeping Rind. Her thumb hung lazily in her mouth. Without a word, they sat there, the two of them as Rind slept, listening only to the winds and waves of the sea and the crackling hearth fire as they took in the warm scent of the feast downstairs. And for that moment, for that breathless moment, everything seemed right with the world.

Chapter 26

Aaric rolled the small vial of golden liquid between his fingers. Unease settled into his nerves. Grand cheers, music, and acclaimed praise echoed in the Hall above his chambers. The celebrations would proceed all night. The end of a war and an era was much to drink to.

He threw back his head and took in the warm mead he had swiped from the Hall before descending to his bower. He had his own demons haunting him this night.

"You've had enough time," Fand had said while Aaric waited in her chambers for the ink to dry. *"Bring her in. Now!"*

"There are complications," Aaric coolly answered. He hadn't told her of Gudrun who had done well to

hide herself from Under Earth, and he had no intentions to start.

"*Then take care of it,*" Fand said. "*You have three days, then I will interfere and if I interfere, I won't be honoring our deal.*"

Aaric had long suspected that. The moment he passed Kallan into Fand's possession, her first act would be to kill Kallan. But her patience was wearing thin and his excuses were dwindling.

"*And what of Danann?*" Aaric asked with hope to dissuade her. "*Should they detect your presence in Lorlenalin—?*"

"*It's a risk I am willing to take should I be forced to take it.*" Fand had opened a small drawer from within her bureau and withdrew a small vial filled with a golden liquid. She held it out to Aaric, who eyed the small vial in question.

"*It's a tincture,*" Fand explained. "*Undetectable, strong, and will leave Kallan incapacitated. It will also block her memory. She'll awake remembering very little.*"

"*I think you underestimate Kallan's strength.*"

"*And if I am, then Danann is closer to finding her than I thought and Kallan should have been brought in years ago.*"

Aaric took the vial and turned to leave, his own thoughts reeling.

"*Aaric.*" He glanced over his shoulder and Fand recovered that smile of hers as she eyed him hungrily. "*Don't make me an enemy.*"

A sudden bellow of laughter from above broke his thoughts and Aaric studied the golden elixir contained in the small vial.

Gudrun.

He hated the idea and hoped it wouldn't come to this, but he had no choice. Fand had him backed into the wall. But Gudrun was stubborn and oblivious to Fand's existence.

Tell her, he had scolded himself too many times. But if Gudrun knew, she would put Kallan in more danger. Like her granddaughter, the old Seidkona wouldn't sit idle while greater powers moved in. She would launch a war against Fand. He wouldn't agree. Gudrun would conflict with his plans. No. It was best if Gudrun didn't know.

Aaric continued to roll the vial between his fingers and ran his hand over his face, rubbing his eyes.

No matter. In the end, he would transfer Kallan to Fand, and he was no fool. The moment his back was turned, Fand would kill her. But Kallan couldn't stay in Lorlenalin either, oblivious to Fand's pursuit...

"High Marshal?"

Aaric's thoughts were too deep to notice the knock on the door. His scout stood, worn and ragged with worry.

"What is it?"

"The Dark One has crossed our borders."

Just as expected. Aaric nodded. "When?"

"Only just."

"How many?"

"Nearly a dozen."

"Twelve?" Aaric furrowed his brow. Twelve wasn't an attack. It was an infiltration. An idea cleared his worries like a streak of sunlight parting the clouds after a storm. "Does anyone else know of this?" he asked.

The scout shook his head. "No, sir."

"Very good."

Aaric eyed the vial knowing the scout had seen. His markings were enough to keep Danann from finding him and Gudrun had her own spells in place. But the moment Fand showed up, the chances of Danann finding them...Lorlenalin was simply too dangerous for Kallan to stay any longer. He had to get her out. And she wouldn't go willingly.

"Report to Daggon," Aaric said. "Have him ready the troops."

"Yes, Marshal." The scout turned to leave.

Raising his arm, Aaric fired a bolt of Seidr through the air and into the back of the scout's head. He slumped down, dead before he touched the floor. Aaric stared at the corpse. If Kallan was to get out alive, then his plan must work. And for that to be the case, then no one else could know the Dark One had no army with him.

The Dark One would come. He must have been guaranteed help to have brought so few to his enemy's gates.

Aaric narrowed his eyes.

They won't come in through the gate, which leaves...

Aaric stepped over the body then closed the door of his chambers behind him. After taking care to lock the door, he made his way to the stables.

Kallan can't take on the Dark One alone, but as long as Gudrun and I are here, Fand can use our Seidr to mask her presence from Danann. Aaric had no doubt. Fand would come to Lorlenalin. *She will kill us, and two dead Drui offered to Danann is enough to sate her curiosity and still keep Danann ignorant of Kallan. But Gunir has no Seidr users. A presence in Gunir can not be hidden. Fand wouldn't be able to go near Gunir without Danann suspecting too much. As ironic as it all sounds, Kallan is safer in Gunir than anywhere else. But if the Dark One finds Kallan, he will kill her. Unless...*

Aaric's thoughts turned to King Rune. After studying the king's tactics and war strategies, he could almost predict Rune's next move. He was reportedly wiser, calmer, and if anyone was more likely to take Kallan alive, it would be Rune.

He just might not kill her. With the king, Kallan stands a chance. And if anyone can command the Dark One, his king can. That leaves two complications: Gudrun and the entire Dokkalfar army. The army is easy enough to take care of as I command them, but no one commands Gudrun.

Aaric rolled the vial over in his hands and redirected his path to Gudrun's chambers.

Branches stretched like brittle fingers across the black-blue sky as if the rustle in the wind was the only life left in Lorlenalin's forest. Bergen stared into

the hollowed darkness, glad to be free of the merciless sun's light. The scar above his right brow reflected the moonlight.

His large, black pupils, once silver-blue, now consumed the whole of his eyes. He looked with ease beyond the obscurity that stretched from his seat in the
dark wood to the highest visible peak of Lorlenalin.

He had seen the Mountain City only once before.
In a fit of adventure seeking, he had ignored his father's laws and hiked across the forests of Alfheim.
His journey came to a sour end at the base of Livsvann's falls where his father had been waiting.

Bergen could rarely recall a more rigid beating.

The Dark One stared at the thundering water.
From a crevice buried above the lowest cloud, the water emerged. Under common conditions, like tonight,
Livsvann appeared to flow directly from the puffs of
haze as if the clouds themselves were forever emptying their contents into the pool below.

A twinge of annoyance pricked his chest. He still
had not climbed to the summit.

Despite the long blade forged of Seidr-stone
sheathed on his back, Bergen's dark armor, heavily
bristled chin, and black, waist-length hair did well to
hide him within the shadows. On his belt, next to a
small pouch that contained his favorite pipe leaf, he
sported a collection of blades, herbs, and medicinal
leaves he found to be rather useful in a pinch.

The solid clomp of Joren's boot came from behind
and, as alert as a sparrow hawk, Bergen looked about.
Exhaustion pulled on the scout's face. If Bergen

hadn't seen Joren a thousand times like this, wraith-like from the thick dusting that covered him after a long ride, he would not have recognized him. He was as ragged and rent as his men hidden in the forest where they waited for his signal.

Always eager to skip the formalities, Bergen jumped to the only question that mattered. "Is Rune alive?"

"For now," Joren said between breaths. The thin air must have left him battling for breath all day. "The queen signed his execution yesterday. He dies under tomorrow's moon."

"That doesn't give us much time," Bergen said. He shifted his gaze to the clouds then looked again to Joren. "What of Borg? What has he decided?"

"We're waiting on him now. If he can deliver an opening into the city, he'll hang a light at Livsvann's pool." Joren stretched a finger to the base of the falls where the waters collected at the river's head. "We'll meet him there and enter through the stables behind the falls."

Bergen had been hunting for a speck of light when he looked back to the scout. "Behind Livsvann?"

Joren nodded, catching the moonlight on his brow.

"There are only two ways into the city: the stables and the main gate," Joren said.

"I supposed the main gate is out of the question," Bergen said, looking out to Lorlenalin's high walls with a bemused look as if considering the possibility.

The wind picked up, and Bergen breathed deeply, taking in the salty-sweet sea air.

"The water conceals a cave that's been converted into the palace stables," Joren said. "A worn trail leads behind the falls. If you don't know to look for it, you won't see it. Once inside, you'll have one path to follow, a corridor that will take you to the barracks, the Great Hall, and the courtyard. You'll need to enter the prison through the barracks."

Bergen nodded, taking in every word and gazing at the sea through the trees.

"And what of the army?" Bergen said.

"Most have gathered in the Great Hall. They eat and drink to the end of the war." Joren shook his head. "They have no idea."

"And the Seidkona. Where is she?" Bergen said, staring at the Kattegat stretching to the horizon.

Joren's prolonged silence forced Bergen's attention.

"I asked Borg about the queen," Joren said, uncertain how to proceed. "If she had her Seidkona with her..." Joren sighed, bringing himself to finish. "The queen is the Seidkona, Bergen."

Bergen dropped his brow.

"What do you mean?" he asked.

"The queen doesn't have a Seidkona," Joren said. "The Seidkona...the one who gave you that scar...is the queen."

The Dark One shook his head, refusing to accept Joren's claim. Too much didn't make sense.

"The princess was home," Bergen said. "Always home...she stayed in the city while the Old Seidkona from Eire's Land fought alongside Eyolf."

Joren was already shaking his head.

"Kallan never stayed home. It was she that King Eyolf sent after us."

"But...his own daughter?" Bergen sputtered.

"Wasn't exactly helpless, if you recall," Joren said with a subtle point to the scar branded on Bergen's brow.

Bergen stood, his mouth agape, as he tried to piece Joren's words together.

Everyone had remembered the wide-eyed child in Lorlenalin's courts peeking between Eyolf's high seat pillars, and it was true, no one had actually seen the princess since King Tryggve first extended a hand for peace before...

Bergen shook his head.

Regardless, the memory of a sweet little thing, too delicate to be troubled with, pacified everyone's curiosity. When news reached Gunir that she had taken the throne, everyone had imagined a frail girl, barely strong enough to lift her father's sword, sitting in a throne so large it swallowed her whole.

A vivid image of an oversized crown sinking to the shoulders of an adolescent came to everyone's mind and they had all laughed. When Queen Kallan called in her father's troops as his burial ship still burned, she had only reaffirmed their suspicions. No one had seen these attacks coming.

Bergen recalled the Seidr flame that had grazed his brow, leaving him with a permanent mark that seemed to ignite his bloodlust. Her adamant, scornful look remained forever fixed in his head. Wielding a sword in one hand and a spell in the other, a wild ambition had blazed in her lapis blue eyes. The Seidkona had sparked a curiosity in him that dangerously toggled between his interests in ripened sexuality and his fear of feminine madness.

"You're telling me that that war maiden," Bergen said, "...that...that Seidr-wielding war wench is the queen?"

"She is."

Trees bowed beneath the wind.

"That softened little princess, who sat unscathed in her daddy's citadel—" Bergen said.

"Gave you that scar," Joren finished for him. "Always there, always looking back now and then to send a bolt of fire up our asses."

"Why didn't Borg tell us of this sooner?" Bergen forced himself from crying out.

"I asked him the same thing," Joren said.

Bergen waited for a response.

"Have we ever once asked about the queen before?" Joren asked. "On the battlefront, we assumed the Seidkona was there fighting while the princess slept soundly in her bed at home. If we found the Seidkona, she would be alone without her queen, we thought."

"No one had ever seen her majesty," Bergen said.

"Save for King Tryggve when Kallan was but a child," Joren said. "Back when you were in Râ-Kedet."

The wind blew cold and Bergen shook off the chill.

"Do you think Rune knows?" Joren asked after a moment.

"We can ask him when this is over," Bergen said, forcing his composure back in place and gearing up for the task ahead.

Looking back to the dark pool of water, they paused. The winds had settled for the moment, leaving the forest unusually silent. Clouds shifted, letting in a streak of moonlight that vanished before the winds picked up again.

Bergen released a long sigh, keeping his eye on Livsvann's pool. Still, no lantern swayed in the dark.

"Joren."

The scout looked to his commander.

"If we are found and a skirmish breaks out, it will be the fight that ends this." Joren stared at Bergen, listening to every word. "Should both monarchs fight, only one will live." Bergen walked along the forest's edge to look better upon the pool.

Joren nodded in understanding of the weight of the situation. Bergen exhaled, giving his attention to an elm tree bowed beneath the wind as he counted the odds against the unknowns.

"And if we succeed?" Joren asked. "What then?"

The wind settled, easing off the trees and leaving behind the most subtle of sounds in the darkness.

"We find our own way in," Bergen said.

Together, they stared into the shadows, both heads spinning with worry. Neither spoke, leaving each to his own while they waited.

Sensing the light before he saw it, Bergen shifted his gaze north.

"There." He pointed to the speck of light that glowed like a star from the water. With a fresh wave of restored hope, he glanced to Joren, who took up his sword. Already the blood violently pumped through Bergen's veins.

"Before the sun rises?" Bergen asked, grinning with a mischievous twinkle in his black eyes.

Joren nodded.

"Before the sun rises."

Chapter 27

From the shadows, Aaric watched the stables. He expected the traitor before he saw him: the warrior whose face he didn't know. The falls thundered, filling the air with a steady hum while the horses grazed in their stalls. The army waited where he had assigned them at the front gate, cutting the evening's festivities short, but leaving the path clear from the stables to the prisons. He expected the Dark One to suspect a trap. What Aaric couldn't determine was what the Dark One would do with it. And for that, he needed to be ready to act. Whether they wanted to or not, the Ljosalfar were taking Kallan prisoner this night.

When the warrior entered the stables, Aaric hardly expected him to be the traitor he had been waiting for. He knew him when he watched the soldier sink a blade into the back of the stable master and dump the body out of sight, indifferent to the act as if he had been changing out weapons. Aaric held his place, knowing there was more for him to see.

The warrior took up a light hanging from one of the support beams and studied the area one last time before following the small path leading out to the forest and Livsvann. While Aaric debated on whether he should go or stay, the warrior returned and Aaric threw his hand to the hilt of his sword at the face he saw next coming up behind the traitor with three additional men.

"They know you're here," the traitor said and the Dark One held out a hand, stopping the handful of men behind him. "Report came in that you're here with an army so all the troops have been pulled to the front. They anticipate battle."

"But there is no army," the Dark One said.

The traitor watched the Dark One. Waiting to take orders or waiting to give them, Aaric couldn't tell.

"They know you're here," the traitor said.

The men behind the Dark One shifted slightly. Their unease was apparent only to a trained soldier, but there was unease without question and, for a moment, Aaric worried that they would withdraw.

"It's a trap," the Dark One said. "Borg, do you know who ordered this? What their reasoning was?"

Borg. So the traitor has a name after all.

An order to move the entire army could only come from the queen or the high marshal. No one else had that authority.

"Do we turn back, Captain?" one of the soldiers asked and the Dark One shook his head. "No. Rune is scheduled to die tomorrow. And I'm not leaving without him." His decisions asserted their determination and the air within the group changed. Their confidence re-established.

"The way is clear, you say?" the Dark One asked Borg, who nodded.

"Down the passage, the first door you come to on the left, that is the barracks. I just came from there. The only guard on duty has been taken care of."

"And of the prisons?"

"Empty," Borg said. "Everyone has been called to the front."

"We move on as planned," the Dark One said. "Assume we're walking into a trap and there's a good chance we'll be caught in it. Keep your guard up more than ever. Borg. If we can further count you as our ally, can you report to Joren? Let him know of the situation?"

"I can," Borg said. The Dark One nodded his thanks and led his troops into the passage leaving Borg alone with Aaric.

The stables were silent. Aaric watched as Borg turned toward the path back to the forest and Joren, Aaric didn't doubt.

With a flick of his wrist, Aaric released a spark of Seidr that struck one of the iron lanterns hanging on a beam.

Streaks of orange swayed across the stables in a display that changed dark for light. Aaric watched

Borg study the shadows through the kaleidoscope of color and his hand went to his hilt. Before Borg could doubt his imagination, Aaric fired off another spark that struck the same light. It swayed aggressively now and Aaric grinned, delighted at the beads of sweat that formed on Borg's brow as he shifted his gaze about as if on the edge of madness.

Borg withdrew his sword and poised himself to strike as soon as he determined the target.

Another spark, this one fired at the lantern at the far end of the stables. And with the angle of the second swinging lantern...

Borg turned to the shadows that concealed Aaric.

Another spark to the first lantern. Borg tightened his poise and then made his way toward Aaric. The thunder of the Livsvann pounded the air between them as the lights swayed, slower now. Aaric fired off another two sparks to the first, then the second lantern.

That's right. See me.

And Borg did. Aaric watched the traitor twist his grip, adjust the angle of his blade, and lunge. With an agility only possessed by a Seidr user, Aaric shifted and positioned himself behind Borg before Borg could recover from the missed attack. In a matter of breaths, Aaric clamped his hand to Borg's shoulder and pulled his Seidr from him, leaving only enough to keep him alive.

Borg fell to the floor immobile, with the clank of his sword.

Grimacing, Aaric stepped over the unconscious lump and strode to Astrid in his stall. Mechanically, he shifted the furs to the horse's back along with the saddle he fastened in place, then secured the bit and bridle on his head and the bit in his mouth. With a hearty pat to the horse's neck, Aaric returned to the heap that was Borg.

After kicking the blade into the shadows where he could come back for it later, he hefted Borg over his soldier and carried him from the stables, leaving them empty and cleared for Kallan.

Kallan stared blankly at the stone ceiling above her bed. Mindlessly, she turned over her mother's pendant, tracing each strip of metal with her fingers. Four floors below her, Rune sat in the filth of her prisons.

"Where he belongs," she huffed and threw herself onto her side.

Kallan sighed for what must have been the hundredth time that night.

Or was it morning already?

She glanced at the black of night. Not even the moon's crescent was visible through the heavy cloud coverage. It was barely early morning. She growled, decided not to care, and dropped her head back to the pillow. Days had been melting into each other so much now that she was losing more time than she was able to track.

Kallan looked to her pouch and dagger resting on the table beside her.

Within ten minutes, I could be cloaked and in the prison. No one would ever know.

She shook her head, shoving away the plan, and made an effort to ignore the violent tantrum her stomach was throwing. She had skipped dinner completely, save for the bowl of cloudberries she had finished off. Her abdomen rumbled.

The kitchens are always empty this time of night. There's nothing wrong with a little midnight raid, she decided, and started to play out an innocent trip to the pantry. *Cook always has barrels of fruit lying about. Rune would be hungry. A spell would allow easy access to the prisons. I could slip him something to eat and perhaps—*

Kallan growled again and flopped onto her back. Blankly, she spun the signet ring around on her finger, studying the hammer engraved within the ring with the tri-corner knot that matched her mother's pendant. No matter how she tried to justify a raid to the kitchens, she knew it would end in the prisons.

Pulling the furs over her nose with another sigh, she flipped onto her side, stared at the doors, and crossed her arms over her chest. Just as she settled into the silence, her chamber doors flew open, hitting the wall with a pair of bangs. Icy air engulfed her room and the light blackened. Wide-eyed, Kallan sat up from the bed.

Aaric looked as if he had just stumbled awake. Donned only in trousers, Kallan could make out every rune etched onto his torso. From his arms, to his shoulders, and down his spine, she followed the pre-ancient Ogham runes she had learned as a child. A handful of blacker, newer images she could not decipher appeared to be a variant of the Glagolitic runes used by the Sklavinians.

The sword at his side, unsheathed and reddened with fresh blood, told her everything she needed to know. With fluid movement, she snatched her dagger and the pouch from her bedside table and followed him out of her chambers, leaving her boots, her cloak, and her clothes behind.

"The Ljosalfar are attacking the front gate," Aaric lied as he led Kallan down the hall. "Most of the men are there now."

"So it is to the front we must go," Kallan said, securing her pouch and dagger to her waist and falling in step beside him.

"Not yet," he said. "There are reports that the enemy slipped in through the stables."

"That passage is unknown," she said. "How did they—"

"The Dark One is with them."

Aaric watched the blood drain from her face and he doubled his pace. She was taking the news as he had hoped: with a cool head pushing and, as expected, she followed with a surge of excitement that sharpened her focus. With renewed determination, she descended the stairs, taking the steps two at a time alongside him.

"We have reason to think the troops at the front gate are a diversion to buy the Dark One some time. We think he's here to get Rune."

"Rune," Kallan whispered as Aaric rounded a sharp corner. "I can not take them both, Aaric!" She pulled on Aaric's arm, bringing him to a sudden stop. "The Dark One and the king must not unite!"

As if we have the time to stop.

"I can't take them together, Aaric. We'll never defeat them."

"Which is why we need Rune," Aaric said. "We can use him to negotiate a trade with the Dark One." Aaric watched her eyes widen even more with worry. "Get to the prisons," he said. "Get Rune."

She paused as if preparing to argue, but the air had changed. Aaric held up his hand, silencing her.

"We are not alone," he whispered.

Kallan put a hand to her dagger and shifted her gaze to the corridor behind him. The Seidr was familiar, but nothing he could place.

"Go," he said. When Kallan didn't move, he took her by the arm and walked her back several paces. "Whatever is there will detain us," Aaric said. "I will take care of the front until you get back." He was certain she was picking up on the same Seidr, but she seemed unable to focus. He pulled her closer and dropped his voice. "We have no time. Circle back to the Hall and head down to the prisons."

She met his eyes, clear at the moment and as if she had no memory of what just happened.

"To the prisons," he pressed. "Get Rune."

Slightly conflicted, but convinced, Kallan nodded and fled down the hall, leaving Aaric to breathe a little easier. He tightened his grip on his sword and turned toward the corridor. The air was thick. The Seidr was strong. She was there. Aaric shifted his position so his sword covered his head and the tip dropped slightly, guarding his face and torso.

He waited, sustaining the tension, and then he pivoted, bringing down his blade right onto Gudrun's Seidr-shield.

"What in blazes—Woman!" Aaric dropped his sword.

"Don't bark at me," Gudrun said, extinguishing her Seidr shield. "You're the one who's got this place in an uproar!"

The tincture, he remembered. *The Seidr from Under Earth was sure to alter Gudrun's own Seidr until it wore off.*

"For crying out loud, Aaric! Why is the entire army stationed at the front gate?"

The tincture he had slipped her earlier certainly had done little to sedate her ornery disposition.

"There's been a siege," Aaric said, never so relieved to see Gudrun. "The Dark One's here."

Gudrun straightened her spine and pressed her thin lips together.

"You would have known that had you not fallen asleep in your chambers," he added and watched as she tried to recall the order of events.

Based on the scrunch of her face, he confirmed she had no memory of him paying her a brief visit and certainly no knowledge of the tincture she drank or of the effects it had on her own Seidr at the moment.

By Odinn. What did Fand give me?

"I don't have time for this," Aaric said and shoved his way past Gudrun, who stood puzzling over the events.

"I never..."

Aaric looked back, feigning boredom. "Hm? What's that?"

"I..." She shook her head and rubbed her temples in duress.

A twinge of guilt pinched at Aaric's chest.

Keep Kallan alive. Nothing else matters so long as Kallan lives through this night. Get Gudrun to the front with the guard, then get to the stables and meet up with Kallan...So long as Kallan lives...

In silence, Gudrun made her way to the courtyard and the front gate. Behind her, Aaric followed, cursing Fand, the tincture, and the evening that lay before him.

Chapter 28

Kallan ran down the corridor lit with torches. After descending the flight of stairs where the room widened, she slowed and approached the Great Hall. Standing just beyond the threshold, she peered around the stone doorframe.

The fire pits were cold, leaving the throne submerged in darkness. The tables laden with devoured carcasses, food remnants, and barrels and flasks of mead were empty. She could easily see where, only moments ago, most of her war-men had passed out at the table or onto the floor.

Quietly, Kallan slipped into the Hall, crossing the large room as she swept her gaze from the tables to the throne. Reaching the end of the room, she peered into the hall that would take her to the stables, the barracks, or the courtyard. Silence found her and she stopped on the threshold.

To reach the stables from the barracks, the Dark One would have to take this hall. Kallan swallowed a chill that tasted too much like fear. No matter the training—her Seidr, her spells—he managed to outfight her every time. Each of their battles ended with a close brush with death and an impasse that forced them both to bail. Tightening her grip on her dagger, Kallan forced her breath steady and left the shelter of the Great Hall, slipping into the corridor toward the barracks.

The abandoned barracks housed a constant chill that always swept in from the prisons below. The prisons had been the oldest and first mines dug ages before by the Dokkalfar. The first stones of Lorlenalin had been built from the slab pulled from the mountain. When the mines dried up, they were made into prisons. And the old counting room, the barracks.

The guard was dead. Slumped against the wall with his eyes wide open, blood stained the side of his mouth. Giving no thought to the armory, Kallan yanked open the heavy iron door, eager to secure her bartering stone.

The deafening cláng of the door and the stale silence left an uneasy sickness that twisted her insides. She wasn't alone. Kallan flicked her wrist, summoning a small ball of red flame that danced in her palm. With flame in one hand and dagger in the other, Kallan began the long descent into the black halls.

Pale orange flame from the dying torches lined the passages that snaked their way through the labyrinth. Moisture collected on the walls, and streaked the stone with minute streams of cold water. Without a guide, she forced her way through, finding her way into the impervious dark.

Adrenaline sharpened her senses as Kallan followed the path through the winding corridors. She turned a corner and descended a series of steps.

Her pace slowed, knowing they were there. She could feel it in her blood. The foreign, unmistakable scent of an earth that didn't belong to Lorlenalin sent her heart pounding. Her foot peeked from beneath her hem as she grazed the stone with her heel. Ensuring complete silence, she made her way into the bowels of the city. The usual gusts of cold rolled up the steps, chilling her bare legs beneath the chemise. Resisting the urge to shiver, she tightened her grip on her dagger.

At the base of the steps, the hall forked to the left and right. If she took the right path, it would lead her into an open room where two additional corridors branched out. Only one would take her to Rune.

Her heart beat painfully as she neared the last step, her back pressed against the damp stone. She could wait here for them to find her and counter defensively, or avoid the delay and seize the offensive before they knew she was there.

Kallan slowed her breathing. Tension twisted her insides.

One breath. Two. She knew they were there. Three.

Kallan pivoted around the corner and fired the Seidr flame before taking aim. A sharp crack echoed the thud of a body striking the stone.

Five, she assessed.

One lay unconscious behind the four still standing. The Ljosalfr warrior on her right charged.

With a graceful sweep, Kallan slashed her Seidr flame across his face. His hand flew up, grasping a cut while stumbling back several paces. Balancing her weight evenly on her bare feet, Kallan fired her Seidr flame into a second warrior charging her left, but the first rebounded, undeterred by the cauterized laceration that stretched from the right side of his mouth to his left eye.

Kallan raised her dagger and met a sword. Elding stone screamed against iron as the blade snapped in two. She fired a blast to the right, then to the left, sending both warriors to the wall unconscious just as a great sword came down from the front.

The metal's deafening scream followed a sudden silence and her body reverberated beneath the strength of her opponent. Behind him, her last opponent stood with an axe at the ready.

Sweat from her palm weakened her grip, requiring both hands on her handle. His great-sword stood strong against her elding dagger, drawing Kallan's gaze through their locked blades. Kallan froze.

Between their hilts, the cool black eyes of the Dark One stared back at her, sending a chill down to her feet. His all-too-familiar scar glistened with sweat above his right brow. He smiled, stirring a sudden irritation she couldn't explain.

"Your Majesty," he purred. His voice was like honey.

Kallan stared at her own hateful grimace reflected in his eyes.

He knows.

With a roar, Kallan pushed her dagger against the berserker. He stumbled back, raising his blade again while, behind him, the Ljosalfr raised his axe for the fatal blow, but she was ready for them both.

Pouring her Seidr flame into the elding handle, Kallan pushed the fire through the blade as she swung her dagger. The last Ljosalfr was just out of range, but the fire reached where her blade could not as she swung one steady swing from right to left. The line of Seidr flame whipped through the air. Cursing aloud, above the roar of fire, the berserker and the last standing warrior threw themselves back into the corridor where they had emerged from moments ago.

Kallan's fire growled like thunder as the orange and red flames rolled over the stone. Leaving the Dark One cowering behind her still burning wall of flame, Kallan fled down the corridor, without a look back, into the darkness to Rune's cell.

Behind the wall, Bergen and his men cowered as the stone grew hotter, but neither moved, knowing the Seidkona's skill. Sweat dripped into the

berserker's mouth as he waited for the flames to die,
all the while counting down the seconds lost.

Chapter 29

Kallan's bare feet slapped the stone. Behind her, the corridor burned. The paralyzing panic that had clouded her head with senseless worry changed to adrenaline. Finding the Dark One so soon assured her that she wasn't too late.

The wall of Seidr flame guaranteed her more than enough time to get to Rune and meet up with Aaric in the stables.

The halls twisted as Kallan sprinted, panting as her pounding chest aligned with the rhythmic patter of her feet. After descending further into the darkness, she made a sharp corner and stopped in front of the oak cell door.

Kallan stared.

The hall was quiet here. So quiet she found it too easy to let her thoughts drift.

She thought of his smugness, his arrogance, his regal confidence on the other side of the door.

Kill him, she thought. *He must die. He should die. But then what? The Dark One unleashes his rage on the city and countless more die in the process. Aaric was right. To kill this king would be to invite the Dark One's wrath.*

So she couldn't kill him. Not yet. She remembered his calloused hands as he grabbed her, challenged her, and pushed her. She had found the change refreshing and she recalled the sweet scent on his neck.

Kallan shook her head, forcing the thoughts from her mind.

She couldn't take the Dark One and the king together, but now she tasted the bitter truth of that lie. Truth was, she couldn't take on the Dark One at all. He exceeded her skills and she knew it.

Kallan placed her palm on the handle.

If I kill this king, the Dark One will come. He will wage his war on my city and none can stop him. None can control him...except his king.

Kallan released the door's handle.

No, I can't kill him. But he can't stay here either. The Dark One will find him. And if they unite...if they unite.

With a resounding blast, the oaken door burst into splinters. Stretched out on the stone floor amid the coals and glowing remnants of the door, wearing nothing but his trousers and signet ring, the King of Gunir rested comfortably, too comfortably. With his hands tucked lazily behind his head and his feet crossed at the ankles, he angled his neck to better see his guest.

Kallan's chest heaved as she sent off bits of Seidr-light into the room and descended the steps where she stopped short. A grin stretched Rune's face as he looked her over.

From the dainty bare toes peeking out from beneath her gown, he followed the folds of thin, white fabric. Her hair spilled over her shoulders and fell unceremoniously to her waist where she sported a dagger and her Seidkona's pouch. The frown she gave him was all he needed to discern her mood. Nevertheless, he couldn't help but grin all the more at her disheveled state or goad the playful dragon he saw within.

"This is hardly the place for a bit of philandering," Rune said, "but I'm willing to give it a go."

He watched with delight as fire burned in her eyes. Her hand twitched and he could only assume she meant to scorch him.

As predictable a lass as any. Rune shook his head, letting his laughter roll over her. "You're too easy to rile up, princess."

"Don't call me that," she said and Rune caught the additional flare of annoyance in her tone.

Predictable.

Marching across the cell, she leaned down, unaware of the view she granted him as she snatched his wrist from behind his head and yanked him up. "Come on," she said.

Rune let her pull him to his feet. "Alright, alright," he said lazily.

She was in a hurry to wherever it was she was taking him, so he decided to do the most sensible thing. He took his time.

He stretched his arms to the ceiling. "Give me a minute. I need to wallow," he said, not bothering to quell the half grin he formed as her eyes wandered over his chest. She blushed when she realized what she had done and, unnaturally, forced her eyes to his face.

Obtusely, he looked her over again until she crunched up her nose in disgust and he was pleased with himself. Again, her hand twitched as if to slap him.

That's right, princess. Slap me. Let's see just where your breaking point is.

"Wallow later," she said and spun on her heel back to the steps. Rune didn't move.

"Well?" she asked.

"Aren't you going to shackle me, chain me?" His eyes flashed with amusement. "Tie me up?" Rune eyed the sway in Kallan's step as she climbed the stairs back to the door. "Aren't you worried I'll stab you in the back?" he said.

Kallan assessed the corridor. "You can try," she said.

Somewhat put off by her lack of participation in his game, Rune leisurely followed her up the steps

272

where he could appreciate the generous view of her backside.

"I assume then that my transfer was not approved," he said.

Kallan peered over her shoulder as if loaded to fire a series of assaults then blinked blankly at his chest only a few inches from her face. Rune watched as anger gave way to panic, to a familiar red glow on her neck, then sheer confusion. It was all he could do not to laugh.

A moment later, after she seemed to settle on anger, Kallan grabbed Rune's wrist and pulled him into the hall.

"Come on," she said. "And try to keep up."

It was her turn to stab at his patience with her belittling tone as he bounded into the corridor after her.

Through a series of passages, twists, and turns, Kallan led Rune down a hall where the stones of Lorlenalin and light ended and earthen tunnels and darkness began. With the Dark One and the blazing corridor blocking her favored route, she had no choice but to steer Rune into the mines.

With a flick of her wrist, she summoned a palm of flame to light her path. The passage was twice as long, but guaranteed no complications, and the last thing she needed was a complication.

Intercept Rune. Get to the stables. And then what? she thought.

"Now what, princess?"

Her temper flared and she whirled on him. Only then did she wish she hadn't. The light from her Seidr-flame cast a silent dance of shadow and light that complimented the tunnel, his features, and frame. An uncomfortable heat warmed her neck and, afraid he would notice, she turned and carefully made her way over the raw earth.

"What is your plan for handling the guards?" Rune asked.

"The guards are dead." *Why am I telling him this? He shouldn't know this.*

"Why are the guards dead?" His tone was dark with a worry that satisfied her.

She couldn't tell him about the Dark One. He may be complacent now, but that may change once he realized his army is near.

"Is that why you didn't shackle me?"

There was a sense to danger, a smell to it, a certain feel that starts in the chest and spreads like a poison released in the blood. For years, she trained to detect it. It bothered her more that she had been strangely absent around Rune. If anything, she felt calm around him. She would kill him before admitting that.

"Yes," she lied. In fact, she had been so set on getting to him before the Dark One that she had forgotten the shackles.

And why is that, Kallan?

274

She breathed with relief as the tunnel's end appeared ahead and joined with the stone passage that would take her up to the barracks. It pleased her to see this passage was also empty.

"This isn't the way they led me last time," Rune said as she stepped her bare foot on cold, smooth stone.

Is that pleasure I hear? Is he actually enjoying this?

She bit her lip to hold back a retort.

"Are we lost?"

"No."

"Are you sure?"

She debated turning on him and firing her Seidr until all that remained was a shriveled corpse of a man. So why didn't she?

The Dark One. Right. He would evoke wrath. Unleash his fury, and why can't I think today?

"I think we're lost," Rune said.

That was it. Stepping into Rune, Kallan ignited her Seidr, and slammed him into the stone wall as she raised her Seidr-flame to fire.

"Too long I've hunted you," she said. "Too long I've dreamt of pouring my Seidr-flame onto you until all that is left are the charred pieces of your blackened remains." She shoved her weight into him, knowing the stone scraped his back. He didn't wince, but a twinge of guilt pierced her chest. "Do not forget this, Ljosalfr. Nothing is keeping you alive right now except my good humor."

The words were there, but she couldn't stop staring at his mouth and wondering how it tasted. With much asserted effort, she forced her attention to his eyes where she saw the lone hunter who admired the harmless peasant alone in the wood and, at once, she doubted that such a man could be responsible for all the terror beset on her kin.

"You won't," he said.

Kallan blinked, unsure what to do with his declaration.

"How do you know I won't?" she asked. She could break him. Too easily, she could break him. *Isn't that what you want? To break him?* But something was holding her back, as if a part of her was protecting him from herself.

"Because I've already pushed you," he said. Kallan eased off his chest. "If you were going to hit me with that..." He nodded to her hand filled with Seidr. "...you already would have."

There was no doubt, no worry, no hesitation in his voice. Only trust. Pure and simple, and she felt the last of her rage ebb.

"Deny it," he said as if egging her on, taunting her to fire the Seidr-flame at him and the anger he provoked flooded back.

In response, she extinguished her Seidr and dropped her arm from his chest.

"I should kill you," she said, shoving a finger into his chest.

"But you won't."

And she wouldn't. But she hated that he knew that. She hated more that he was right.

Without an answer, Kallan continued through the dark. Her fire would have ended and the Dark One would have continued to Rune's cell. If he knew where he was going, she had another ten minutes before the Dark One discovered Rune was gone. By the time the Dark One returned to the barracks, she would be at the front and Rune would be...she wasn't sure yet.

Kallan dragged Rune on through the labyrinth. At every blind corner, she verified the way was clear before picking up pace again. Taking the steps three at a time, Kallan led Rune to the barracks where she threw open the door with a bang. Empty tables and upturned chairs littered the room where she had found them earlier. The guard's corpse still sagged against the wall.

Shoving aside a chair, Kallan made her way to the armory. She felt Rune watching her and glanced over her shoulder in time to see him shift his eyes up to meet hers and he grinned. She blushed and decided instead to inspect the fuller of an iron blade too chipped and cracked to withstand another battle. The elding dagger next to it was in far better condition to take into battle, but too small to be of any use aside from a rabbit skinning. She wrapped her hand around the hilt of the sword.

"I would expect more from the legendary Dokkalfar armory," Rune said as she raised the blade then thrust to test its balance.

"The armory has been stripped," she said.

"Odd habit, don't you think?"

There was that jovial tone again that urged her to kill him. She hated herself more for not doing so. His lack of danger was disheartening. He had no sense of trouble, or hid it well. Perhaps he didn't care. His only consistent purpose seemed to be finding new ways to push her. She decided he did want to die and, the moment she had nothing better to do, she'd be sure to oblige.

"My guards have reported to the front gate to hold back the attack your precious berserker has led on Lorlenalin."

Her words wiped the jocularity from his face.

"Bergen is here?" he asked.

Kallan ignored the question and studied the sword's fuller, judging its quality before lowering the blade to her side. "They're here for you."

"Where is he? Take me to him!" Rune slammed his hands onto the table between them. "I can order him to stand down! Bergen will listen to me!"

Oh, something can bother the pompous King of Gunir.

Kallan scoffed as she scanned the armory for a suitable weapon.

"And stand by while my executioner removes your head tomorrow night?" she said, keeping her eyes on the wall that had been stripped of all axes and most of the swords. Only a handful of daggers remained aside from the mediocre sword in her hand.

Rune straightened his back.

"Do you desire my death so much?" he asked.

He seriously sounds hurt. "My people will have your head whether I give it or not."

"Then we'll negotiate a bargain," he said.

Kallan dropped the sword on the table.

"The King of Gunir for the lives of my people," he said.

Kallan mulled over his proposition.

"Am I to believe you and your...Bergen will quietly leave once you are united?" she mocked.

"You have my word."

"Your word," she repeated and the anger came flooding back. "I've seen how good your *word* is."

Rune dropped his eyes to the table between them and took up the single dagger resting there.

He turned the weapon over, examining the twelve-inch blade. Kallan watched him run his fingers along the silver-black sheen of the elding and the series of runes inscribed in the ricasso. Spinning the dagger, Rune read the inscription aloud.

"*Blakkr Ond.*"

"Black Breath," Kallan translated as Rune admired the artisanship.

"Your weapons are heavier than ours," he said.

A compliment?

"If you can't handle it, perhaps you would find the inadequate blades of Gunir more to your liking," Kallan said.

Rune peered up from the blade.

Kallan supplied a fake grin. *And there's his soft spot.* "Or, perhaps, the smaller blades on the wall behind you will better suit you." The hint of humor vanished from Rune's eye.

Silence stretched between them until she extended her hand for the blade and Rune tightened his grip on the hilt. The blade was harmless, but the point was clear. This was a standoff.

"I will take it by force," Kallan warned.

She summoned her Seidr flame and readied her hand. Rune shifted his gaze from the blade in his hand to the Seidr in hers.

"Where did you find a smith who can forge elding?" he asked. She didn't answer.

Rune placed the weapon on the table and Kallan extinguished her flame in response, scowling as she glided past him to the barracks door. None of these weapons would hold up in battle. They were wasting their time.

"Move it," she said with a nod that indicated the door and he obliged. Cautiously, Kallan poked her head into the corridor. Once she was certain the way was clear, she signaled to Rune to follow and dashed into the hall just as she heard him mutter beneath his breath, "This will be interesting."

Chapter 30

The battlement was quiet. Like sentinels, each guard stood at attention, peering into the shadows of hill and tree. Aaric walked the lines of men. He studied the worry, the anxiety, the fear held within each face. It tightened the jaw, sharpened their sights, and collected the adrenaline that would flow through them. When battle began, the surge would force them on.

But no army waited within those trees.

Not yet, he had told the troops. *But they will. Look sharp.*

And so they had done.

Kallan should be in the stables soon.

Aaric entered the small stone passage of the battlement keep. He slipped down the steps to the courtyard where the second battalion waited in the open air. The warriors shifted nervously. The night had a chill, but the tension was thick, filling each Dokkalfr with raw angst that bound the nerves. The wind passed through the city with the taste of a sweet cold as if it carried the morning dew of a distant land.

Aaric made his way across the courtyard and entered the corridor that would take him to the stables. Within the hall, the wind shifted and a thick, warm air settled around him. Aaric paused. Something wasn't right. The air was different. He reached with his Seidr, touching the threads around him and counted: *Daggon behind...He must have followed. Kallan ahead with...Ljosalfar.* His heart eased and he almost grinned when a ripple shook the strands of Seidr. There was a change in the web that he knew sent his heart hammering. *She's here.* At once, Aaric charged down the hall.

"Kallan!" he called. He felt the pull on the Seidr tighten. He turned the corner where Kallan came into sight. Beside her, the king looked as startled as she and for a moment, neither dared move.

A second ripple shook the web and, just as Aaric felt his foot leave the floor, he pulled on the Seidr around him, throwing up a shield with it. The ripple became a solid pulse that struck the floor, throwing everything in the corridor to the air moments before Aaric wrapped his Seidr around Kallan, himself, and Rune. The pulse ejected them from the corridor into the stables, where they struck the stone hard.

And then there was silence. Shaking off the stun that accompanied the blow, Aaric pulled himself to his knees and froze when his eyes found Kallan. On the ground beside Rune, she lay unmoving. Already, the Ljosalfr was up, trying to raise her from the ground. A bit of blood seeped where her head had struck the stone and Aaric lunged, dropping a hand to her brow. Her Seidr was strong, and he could heal her easily enough, but he couldn't afford to wake her. Not yet.

She won't comply. She must stay asleep until she's gone.

"Take her," Aaric said, not bothering to look up at Rune although he could feel the questions he didn't ask. "She lives. She's fine." This time, Aaric did look at Rune. "But you must get her out of here."

"Why—"

"There is no time." He was nearly done. Her wounds were closing fast, but the Ljosalfar king made no attempt to move from Kallan's side. "Take her horse," Aaric said. "The brown destrier. He rides faster than the others."

He could feel the moments slipping away.

"B—

"I'm giving her to you now go or you'll both be dead!" Aaric cried.

"She's Seidkona. When she wakes..." Rune shook his head. "I won't be able to hold her."

Aaric read the questions clear on Rune's face and stared back with a look that asserted his warning. There was no time, no choice.

Clasping his hand to Rune's wrist, Aaric poured his Seidr to the threads that slept within the Ljosalfr. There, where the energy coursed, Aaric linked his

Seidr to Rune's and pushed the lines, coaxing them awake, forcing them through until he reversed the flow of Rune's Seidr.

The Ljosalfr gasped and fell, catching himself on his palm so as to not fall on Kallan. Taking him by the shoulder, Aaric shook Rune to attention.

"It's from the shock," Aaric said. "You'll get used to it. Now go."

"What did you do to me?" Rune asked.

I tethered your sleeping Seidr to the Shadow that lies in the bottom-most depths of the abyss far below Under Earth. His heart will be pounding like a state of berserk. His strength won't ebb. If anything, he'll have a constant surge of adrenaline without end.

"Saved your life," Aaric said. "Now get."

At once, Rune moved and took Kallan up from the floor with an ease that Aaric could see came unnaturally to him. The Ljosalfr made his way to the saddled stallion and tossed Kallan onto the horse. Aaric felt the seconds slip by as if counting down the breaths to his timely death.

"I can't promise I'll be giving her back," Rune said, pulling himself into the horse.

"Don't bring her back here," Aaric said. "If she does, she'll die."

Without question, Rune steered Astrid from the stall.

"And Ljosalfr," Aaric said.

Rune pulled back on the reins and gazed at Aaric.

"Don't tell her about this," Aaric said. "She won't listen. She won't believe you."

Without a word, Rune snapped the reins and followed the path out behind Livsvann into the forest, allowing Aaric a sigh that allowed him to breathe easy.

Aaric muttered a charm. The image of Borg that had masked his true appearance from the Ljosalfar king melted away just as the air went cold. The color drained from his face. Sweat beaded upon his brow. He knew that prick to the back of his neck, the drug-like perfumes of Under Earth.

"How now, sweet Aaric." Fand's hot breath grazed his ear and his chest tightened. "She's here," Fand hissed. Her voice spilled down his back like honey. "I can feel her and you have fear."

He could hear her breathe, drawing in his scent.

"I can smell it."

Her words slithered from her mouth and Aaric cringed when he felt the tips of her fingers graze his bare shoulders.

"Stand back, witch," he growled and watched the black of her eyes dilate with prowess.

"Where is she, Drui?" Fand asked.

Aaric clenched his jaw, loathing the word and she smiled. *Delighted at her own cleverness*, he mused.

Fand repeated the word with a grin.

"Drui." It rolled off her tongue.

"She isn't here, Fand."

The Fae goddess gave a plump pout that forced all his attention to her mouth. Her spells hung heavy in the air and they worked to cloud his mind.

"Not here?" she asked, feigning disappointment. "But I feel her. She's near. She's—"

"I didn't give *her* the tincture, Fand." Aaric watched her performance change to rage as she abandoned her game. "I gave it to another. She's gone, Fand."

Hate tightened her face and her chest rose and fell with increased breath.

"Where?" she seethed.

"Gunir."

Spinning on the ball of her foot, Fand stomped toward the hidden passage.

"You can't go, Fand!" Aaric shouted as she moved her hand to transform, his words pulling her back. "The Ljosalfar have no Seidr users. Their knowledge of the Seidr is the same as Men. You step one foot near Gunir and Danann will know."

"Danann can detect the girl—"

"Danann doesn't know the girl exists," Aaric said, knowing he had her. "Unless something such as the Fae approaches Kallan, Danann won't know. You're out of options."

Venom twisted her face and she raised a hand filled with golden Seidr.

"You—"

"Lay a hand on me, Fand," Aaric shouted over her threat. "Lay one finger and then what? You have only a few more breaths before Danann finds you here!"

Fear stripped her rage and he watched with satisfaction as she glanced at the runes that lined his chest.

"You wouldn't?" she said.

"If it means Kallan will remain safe," Aaric said, "I will undo the spells that bind my Seidr all so that Danann can find me. Kill me and Danann will know. What then, Fand? What will you tell her when she finds you've killed one of her precious Drui?"

Fand twitched with the want to kill. He had her.

"Danann doesn't forgive," he said. "You have no time."

"There are other ways for me to find her," Fand said. "Others who will want what she has."

"So long as it isn't you."

"If I find her, I promise there will be no prison that awaits her," Fand said. "I will kill her. Get in my way again, Drui, and I will kill you."

Aaric felt the fight in him rebound. The battle he thought he had won, he had only postponed.

Her task having failed, she turned to leave when a step, too soft to be heard by most, earned the attention of the Drui and the goddess. There, in the shadows the Dark One stood, his longsword poised, his dark eyes fixed on Fand with such loathing as to make Aaric's blood turn cold.

Fand smiled. Her eyes glistened with amusement as if she had found a long lost toy.

"You..." Bergen snarled.

"Bergen," she purred, grinning and studying him up and down with a look that made Aaric's skin peel.

Bergen's name in her mouth seemed only to darken Bergen's temper.

"Fae whore," Bergen grumbled.

"Still burning?" she asked.

Bergen tightened his grasp on the hilt, catching a bit of light on the blade. Faint lines of gold glistened from beneath the folded, black metal where Seidr composed its core.

"Still have my sword, I see," Fand said.

"Always in my grasp, Fae whore," Bergen said.

Fand scoffed and turned her venom to Aaric. "Drui," she said, bidding farewell. With a flick of her wrist, she contorted herself into a raven and flew from the stables out through the corridor behind Bergen and back to the courtyard and the sky.

Aaric leered at Bergen, who leered back while neither moved.

"Go on then," Aaric said, indicating the passage leading back to Livsvann and the wood. "They'll be long gone from here, I imagine."

Aaric felt the tension shift as Bergen increased his guard.

"You're letting me go, just like that?"

"Just like that."

Neither man lowered his weapon.

Aaric assessed the Ljosalfr whose alertness hadn't waned.

Bergen took a step into the stables and Aaric mirrored his footwork. As Bergen shifted from the corridor, Aaric slipped into the hall to leave Bergen's path clear and both men with a safe amount of space between them. With nerves wrought high and both men armed to attack, they stepped back, ensuring their eyes never left their opponent until Aaric was deep in the shadows of the corridor and Bergen was several paces into the stables. Only then did Bergen turn and walk from the stables, back to the Livsvann, his men, and the wood.

Aaric drew a deep breath. The adrenaline still ran its course, leaving his awareness piqued.

One last end to tie up.

He made his way down the corridor, ignoring the fractures in the stone from Fand's blast. From the hall he could see the many dead that lay there, dead or dying from the force of the Seidr Fand had brought down from Under Earth. Had Gudrun not drunk the tincture, she would have Seen all of this.

Had Gudrun not drunk the tincture, she too would be dead.

Aaric stopped at the heap that was Daggon's body crumpled against the stone wall that made up the arched entrance to the Great Hall. Despite his proximity to the blast, which had thrown him into the arch, it very well saved him from the bulk of the blast, and from death.

Aaric placed a hand to his burnt brow. His Seidr was there, but faint, and Aaric at once set to work, muttering the charms he learned a lifetime ago.

Just enough to keep him alive for Gudrun and...

Aaric deepened his Seidr and muttered beneath his breath.

...all I need now is a witness.

Chapter 31

The road followed the river, twisting down the mountainside from Livsvann. Clouds filled the sky with magnificent silhouettes, while below the ocean stretched into the horizon like black glass. Countless shadows reflected the clouds that seemed to rise like billowing wraiths from the sea.

Eager to put as much distance as possible between them and Lorlenalin before sunrise, Rune had steered Astrid from the road and into the forest. The steady pound of the horse's hooves upturned the leaf litter and invaded the silence.

His hands shook. His head reeled as if the traitor had infused a drug into him. But there was so much more than that, like the drug was always there, now awakened. His heart thundered with the surge until his chest ached, and he couldn't steady his hands from shaking. Despite the changes, he felt stronger, like he was ready to charge into battle with sword and bow and knew he could win.

Rune gazed at Kallan lying limp in his arms.

What of the Seidkona?

In the heat of battle when all other lines had failed, the desire to kill her and ensure his brother's victory had been clear. But out here, like this...

Her hair had fallen to the side, leaving the lines of her slender neck exposed.

Bergen wouldn't hesitate to break your pretty, little neck.

He imagined his hands wrapped around her throat. Like this, he could snap her neck with ease.

A coward's killing.

The cut on her head was gone, leaving behind a series of questions without answers. He remembered his mother and sister. They had been Swann Maidens and shared a link to Eire's Land that he had seen from no other. Not even he and Bergen were born with that gift.

Too much of their father in them, his mother had said.

Distorted shadows splashed across the trees. Branches reached every which way like menacing limbs in the dark. The clouds shifted now and again to permit various shades of gray to spill into the wood, obscuring the night.

For half the night, he had considered killing her, but there was still too much he couldn't answer on his own. And then there was Borg. He couldn't shake the feeling that something was off about him, let alone whatever it was he had done to Rune. The first time they had met, Borg was adamant to have Kallan killed, but in the stables, Borg seemed more concerned with keeping her alive.

Don't tell her about this. She won't listen. She won't believe you.

Rune studied Kallan's face.

Serene and content when you're not trying to kill me. How much do you know, princess?

The clouds cleared and allowed bits of moonlight to spill into the forest. The first morning light peeked through the trees, dispensing the last of night's shadows.

But if I don't kill you now, how am I to defend myself when you wake?

Rune looked to the bit of sky seen through the sly. The searches would commence soon. The closer to Gunir he was by that time, the better. Bergen would be trailing him by morning. If he knew his brother, he knew the exact road on which to meet up with him. He would wait for him there.

By the gods, stop, why can't I stop shaking? A traitor with the powers of a Seidr user and a blast strong enough to throw a Seidkona to the air. Why release me, princess?

Rune leaned down onto Kallan as the lowest of branches and thorns dragged along his bare back instead of swiping Kallan's face while Astrid stomped through a brood of grouse, upsetting their roost. Guttural gobbles and harsh, woody pops filled the forest as the birds scattered. Their wings and calls drummed with the rustle of trees before the forest quieted down again.

As much distance by morning. Nothing else matters, Rune mused. *Just so long as I survive the Seidkona.*

Chapter 32

Gudrun looked over the desolation that spanned the courtyard and pulled her shawl tighter, as if able to block the horror before her. Along the battlement, the dead lay. Blood painted Gudrun's arms from the seemingly endless wounded that filled the Great Hall. There was no one left in the courtyard, no work left to be done, but she couldn't bring herself to stay away.

A cold wind swept in from the sea and caught on Lorlenalin's turrets to funnel down to the courtyard. Gudrun looked to the sky. The clouds had begun to clear. The light of the moon's crescent spilled over the white, blood-stained stone.

"Lady Gudrun?" The worry in Eilif's voice pulled Gudrun's attention from the sky.

His voice felt unnaturally alive among so much death. Like smooth rain, he glided across the courtyard. His tall, skinny frame left him looking ragged and worn in the dark.

Gudrun looked the scribe over and assessed his condition. The concoction she had given him earlier did well to ease his nerves and left him with a visible, empty hurt that reflected her own heartache.

"Have you found her yet?" he asked. His voice wavered as if it would break.

Unable to speak, Gudrun lowered her swollen eyes to the ground. She couldn't see that look on another face one more time.

"No. That was the last of them," she said. "Any sign of Daggon?"

Eilif shook his head. "I haven't seen him."

Turning her back, Gudrun crossed the vast courtyard, once more scanning the rows of dead faces for Kallan's. The wind whipped her long, silver hair across her face. Her bloodstained chemise trailed to the ground, catching on debris that pulled at her skirts as she walked. Gudrun hugged herself tighter against the chill.

"Lady Gudrun?"

The old Seidkona turned to the scribe. In another lifetime he had so eagerly embraced his studies alongside Kallan as they committed countless ancient runes to memory. Together they played, mapped the city, and collected the children from the streets. She watched the last of Eilif's youth fade before her eyes as he shouldered the same grief that haunted them all.

"Lady Kallan..." Eilif lost the words, seemingly unable to muster the strength to speak them.

The shuffling of feet carried through the courtyard and drew Gudrun's attention to the corridor.

"Oh," she gasped as Aaric emerged from the passage with Daggon, unconscious, supported over his shoulder. Burnt flesh and blood marred his face in gouges of black and red. The wild copper mop of hair matted nearest the places singed to the bloody scalp, and his grizzled beard had melted completely away in places. The burns disfigured the length of his right side to his hip and extended across his torso.

To her knees Gudrun fell, pulling Aaric to the ground with her. Eilif bent over Gudrun's shoulder as she scrambled with her Seidr pouch and withdrew a vial. With shaking hands, she poured a droplet of golden liquid into Daggon's mouth while muttering beneath her breath.

Golden sprays of Seidr light flowed from her hand as she inspected the injury, and immediately set to work to heal him.

"Will he live?" Aaric asked, panting to catch his breath beside her.

She shook her head, her brow furrowed, and submitted another drop onto the burns. Sharply, she gasped and halted the spell. Her hands shook and the blood left her face as her thoughts turned to wilder things buried in the lands beyond the sea.

"I know this Seidr," she breathed and looked at Aaric, who held his gaze hardened and cold.

"Where did you find him, Aaric?" Gudrun said.

"The stables," Aaric said, staring back with a look that revealed too little for Gudrun to read.

"Is he dead?" Eilif asked.

"No," Gudrun said, and returned her attention to Daggon. "Not yet, anyway."

"Will he live?" Aaric asked.

Gudrun tried to pull back the cloth that had fused with the skin near his waist. After a brief examination, she released the fabric and inspected the burns that extended across his chest. The exposed skin on his right side had partly melted away.

She shook her head, forcing down a sob caught in her throat.

"It's too soon."

"Was Kallan there? Did you see her?" Eilif asked.

Aaric shook his head.

"The last I saw of her was the third floor corridor. We were ambushed," he said. "I sent her on to the stables."

Gudrun listened to the regret that clung to his voice while administering another drop of liquid. Too much remained unclear, unanswered. Ever since she had fallen asleep, her mind had been clouded. Recent events flowed together and there were places where complete thoughts were missing. They had waited for an attack from the Dark One that never came.

There was...

Gudrun began the long task of siphoning her Seidr through Daggon while she tried to sort through the garbled confusion. She had tried to remember how she had come to be laying on the ground surrounded by dead and injured. Kallan was missing. Yet, not a single sword swung, not a single arrow released...that she could remember anyway.

For several minutes they stayed there, unmoving, all peering over Daggon as Gudrun worked. The scribe wrung his hands together, stopping now and again to chew on his thumbnail while he waited.

Gudrun administered another drop on his burns, and the first flinch of relief came when Daggon took in a long gasp that he released with a howl.

"Hold him down," Gudrun ordered then proceeded with the spell. Together, Eilif and Aaric pinned Daggon's arms, holding him against the stone as he bellowed and grunted from the pain.

The Seidkona continued, knitting the fibers, repairing the flesh until Daggon ceased his fight and eased up. His breath slowed as he found its regular pace.

"Ka—" he spoke, panting on the ground through the pain.

"Where is she, Daggon?" Aaric asked, shouting the words loud enough for Daggon to hear through the unconsciousness.

Gudrun and Eilif looked to Aaric.

"Kallan, Daggon," Aaric cried. "Did you see her?"

"He..." Daggon's voice cracked and scraped against his dry throat.

Gudrun administered another droplet into his mouth. Daggon gulped, licking the sweet nectar of

Idunn's apples as the Seidkona dropped a third onto his cracked lips.

Before their eyes, they watched the raw, burned splits close themselves.

"Took her," Daggon said between breaths. "He..."

Gudrun furrowed her brow, uncertain about the blanket daze in Daggon's eyes.

"No wonder the Dark One pulled out so suddenly," Aaric said.

"He took..." Daggon tried again, choked by the visible wave of guilt that overwhelmed him. "I...I..."

"Sh. Sh. Sh," Gudrun hushed, returning to work on his face. "Sleep now," she bade as she repaired his skin with her Seidr.

"Eilif," Gudrun said, still mending the wounds splayed over his body. "We'll be ready to move him soon. Go fetch help."

Without hesitation, Eilif fled down the passage to the Great Hall.

"Will he die?" Aaric asked, seeming to know she had held back with the scribe nearby.

Gudrun shook her head, her attention glazed with a newfound determination.

"It will take me the night and most of the day..." She looked up from Daggon. "...but I think I got to him in time."

Aaric nodded as Eilif returned with two men and a large fur. They moved per Gudrun's orders, shifting Daggon to the fur and carrying him back to the Great Hall.

"I'll need Uthbert's irons and the tailor's needles," Gudrun said. "Odinn knows I can do most of this on my own, but I'll need help. And I'll need water," she called to Eilif, who had almost vanished into the corridor. "Cut back his clothes so I can better see what I'm working with." She spoke these last few words to herself as Eilif slipped from sight.

"Gudrun," Aaric said, grabbing her arm as she rolled up her sleeves with shaking hands.

"I'll need my supply of apples brought down from my chambers," she said. "I'll need to use what I can to save him."

"Gudrun. If the Dark One has taken her, there will be no hope for her."

Gudrun pursed her lips as her reddened eyes filled with tears.

"We can't afford the men," Aaric said, with an empathetic tone. "With Daggon near death and Kallan gone..."

Gudrun rubbed her eyes with the back of her bloody hand.

"I don't have the men to go after her," he said.

The old woman pulled her hand from her eyes. A streak of blood smeared her face.

"What are you saying?" Gudrun asked.

"Gudrun," Aaric said. His voice cut through the silence like a cold, blunt knife. A breeze slashed against Gudrun's legs, but she didn't seem to notice. "We can't help her. Kallan is on her own."

The gold in Gudrun's eyes brightened with rage.

"Kallan has Kira's strength, no matter how dormant it may be. Do not underestimate her ability to survive this."

"The chances are slim," Aaric said, "and I can not spare the aid."

"Why do you do this?" she breathed.

"As long as the queen is missing," Aaric said, "my station requires that I put the needs of Lorlenalin first. And if that means turning my back on a queen so that her people may live, then so be it."

"You never had a place here." Gudrun spoke unusually low. "Never among these people. I told you that when you came here."

Aaric's chest rose and fell as Gudrun tested his temper. The etchings on his chest caught the streaks of moonlight.

"I know what you did to her," Gudrun said. "Do not think I don't know why you're really here."

Aaric matched the hatred in Gudrun's face.

"Those were different days, Gudrun. I did what I had to do then. I am doing what I have to do now. Do not mistake my duty to Lorlenalin as a lack of concern for that girl. I pledged my allegiance to Eyolf when I left—"

A raven cawed in the distance and Aaric clenched his jaw, refusing to say more.

" 'That girl'," Gudrun said, "is Kira's daughter. Don't think I have forgotten."

Aaric took in a long, deep breath at Kira's name. "A fact I am reminded of each time I see her eyes."

"Her blood flows from mine," Gudrun whispered. "That Seidr line stems from mine."

"I am aware."

"So are they." Gudrun's raised whisper caught the wind, and, nervously, she and Aaric looked to the sky as if waiting for the clouds to swoop down and smite them. Gudrun exhaled, still shifting a worried glance to the sea. The night had grown calm.

"I've held your secret this long, Gudrun," Aaric said. "I don't want them to find her any more than you do."

"I have done too much to let you abandon Kallan to the wolves," Gudrun said. "Nor will I stand by while you abandon our queen."

The wind rustled, funneling down to the courtyard from above.

"I will heal the men of Kallan's army," Gudrun said, turning her back to the sea. "I will heal Daggon and repair their wounds, and then let's see *you* tell Daggon he isn't going after Kira's daughter."

Pulling her shawl around her shoulders, Gudrun dragged her forlorn body to the passage, leaving Aaric staring at the single raven perched on Lorlenalin's balustrade.

Chapter 33

Kallan followed the recurring *thwit* through the endless blue and sickly silver corridor she wandered in dreaming. For hours, she had looked for the corridor's end. Twice she had doubled back in search of the beginning, but there was only ever the endless hall without windows or doors, filled with the echoing *thwit*.

The echo continued, sustaining its tempo, while a young girl sang:

> "*Through the wind the spriggans play,*
> *O'er the sea where they stay.*"

Kallan ignored the child's song and ran toward the *thwit* at the end of the hall. A brief rush of wind grazed her legs, urging her on ahead toward the wind, the *thwit*, and the end.

> "*The Faerie queen, she sits there still,*
> *Tending the earth beneath her hill.*"

Kallan followed the song around another corner and began the next corridor. Shadows billowed in the distance, rolling in on themselves, concealing the end or another corridor. And still the child sang:

> "*Where the mystical Fae King's throng,*
> *fills the earth with ancient song.*"

The rhythm of the *thwit* was wrong, too consistent for it to be random, and repeated itself too frequently to be an arrow. She tried to stir, to open her eyes, but sleep was too deep, her dreams too real. She could not wake.

> "*Where the Fae King's halls are gold,*
> *Where they sing their songs of old.*"

Foreign smells invaded her senses and she tried to find the familiar scent of sweet rose and lavender that always filled her room and mingled with sea air. Her hand brushed her gown. Kallan moved her fingers against the soft furs on her bed, and the silks brought from the east, but touched cold dew instead. Another breeze grazed her leg. The song was growing louder.

"Through the wind the spriggans play.
O'er the sea where they stay."

Through the shadows, the Dark One's black eyes
gleamed. Kallan opened her mouth to cry out, to
scream, but Seidr flame came instead, engulfing the
corridor and drowning out the song that turned to
screams. The soft mist of Livsvann's falls fell into the
fire that burned the water and Kallan glimpsed Daggon's face in the dark. The screaming continued and
Kallan called for the children, but shadows stretched
through an icy black. There, the Seidr seemed to end
and the screaming stopped.

With a gasp, Kallan awoke to the darkness and the
bit of orange light from a small campfire. Her shoulders screamed with pain at having her arms pulled
behind her and around a tree, forcing her back to
arch into the trunk. But the cold metal of her blade
pressed against the flesh of her throat robbed her of
all other concerns. At the end of the blade, inches
from her face, Rune stared.

"Good evening," he said.

Kallan tugged at her bound wrists, adding to the
fire in her joints while the bark of the tree grated the
entire length of her back through her chemise. She
assessed her bonds with her fingers.

"You and I need to have a talk, princess."

Kallan clenched her teeth at the name, and he
grinned. The firelight danced across his face, making him appear strikingly similar to the Dark One in
the night's shadow.

"That's right, you don't like 'princess' do you?"

"Untie me," Kallan said.

"Not until we have an understanding."

Kallan summoned a bit of flame from the tip of her finger and proceeded to singe the rope.

Keep him talking. "What do you want?"

"You have no reason to trust me," Rune said. "I have no reason to trust you. Ergo, I have no reason not to slit your throat and leave you dead and tied to this tree."

He's serious. "You have a point," she said. *Burn faster.*

"Now let's assume as one possible option, that I don't kill you right here and drag your body back to Gunir as a spoil of war."

Kallan crunched her face into a fake smile.

"Instead, I extend my hand in truce and offer you...call it a choice."

"A choice."

"Let's assume I lower this blade and untie you," Rune said. "You then can kill me with that Seidr of yours."

"Sounds good to me." Delight flashed in her eyes and she watched his attention shift to other matters for that moment.

"Or, you can make a choice," Rune said.

Keep him talking. "I'm listening."

"Let's say you hear what I have to say, return to Gunir as my—"

"—prisoner."

"My guest," he corrected. "We'll sit down and negotiate peace between our people. Perhaps declare a holiday in our name and we all go home and forget this misunderstanding."

A coal in the fire popped.

"Misunderstanding?"

Her binds were weakening.

"Or I can kill you now," he said.

"There is no misunderstanding," she said.

Rune narrowed his gaze.

"I've sent out hundreds of messages to your city requesting peace, imploring you to meet with me on civil ground."

"Why do you lie?" She twisted a wrist.

"You have traitors in your city, fair princess."

The smell of burning hemp reached her nose. Tension dissolved Rune's confidence and Kallan pulled her wrists free, firing as she brought them around.

Still clutching her knife, Rune jumped back and around the tree, missing Kallan's Seidr just in time.

Kallan rebounded, firing a blast that singed the trunk and Rune ran toward Astrid, who stood at the bank of a stream.

"Kallan!"

She fired a blast at Rune's feet.

"If you would just hear me out!"

She fired a second blast, striking the ground ahead of him and steering him away from her horse.

"We look for peace!" he cried.

"Peace?" she shrieked and fired the ground again.

"Come to Gunir. We c—"

"You take me for a fool?" Kallan said. "You think I would trust you? I go to Gunir and I go to my death! The Dark One would personally cut my ribs through my back!"

"Bergen woul—"

"I've seen the horrors he unleashed on my people!" Kallan cried. "The horrors you and your father ordered! The orphans he left behind!"

Rune furrowed his brow. "The massacre of Austra—"

Seidr erupted from both palms as Kallan fired her flames into Rune. Under the energy, he arched his back and screamed.

Within, the Shadow erupted. In the abyss, the Darkness thrashed. In the depths of Under Earth far beyond the Falls of Light, beneath the lakes of Seidr, there, the Darkness waited. Writhing, it twisted and took shape until like a dragon awakened, it rose: the Black Beast.

On the Seidr lines given by Aaric, the Beast found its way into Rune, where it devoured Kallan's Seidr, feasting on it, drawing it into Rune's body. There, the Beast ate of it and, unscathed, drank of the Seidr while Rune buckled beneath Kallan's fire as it passed into him, trailing down his own threads of life. There in its belly, the Beast hoarded the energy, holding onto it and storing it, preserving it until the right time when the Seidr would be called upon again.

All at once, the fire stopped and Rune fell to his knees, panting.

His hands shook. His body quaked, and Rune gasped, wide-eyed. Energy surged through him, igniting a strength that felt like it would shred his body with want to break free. He clasped his hands, but the shaking persisted.

From the ground, he raised his eyes and met Kallan's across the clearing. The lone campfire did well to reflect the horror in her gaze. Before he had a chance to breathe, she struck again.

And again, the Beast drank of its share. Again, the Seidr flame flowed. Throwing back his head, Rune roared as she poured her Seidr into him. His body twitched and just as he was certain his chest would implode, she broke the line.

This time, Rune sustained his balance. He drew up his knee and the Seidkona took a pace back.

She fired again. The Beast drank, but Rune held his ground. Her streams were growing fainter. Her endurance weakened. Rune moved toward Kallan, who stepped back and fired again, sending his body into another set of tremors. This time, when she broke the line, he remained upright, gasping for breath, but with far more strength than before.

As if his body had been jolted awake, he bounced on his heels, eager to run, eager to fight. Blood roared through his body. He saw the Seidkona—*the small, feeble princess rendered powerless*—and he grinned.

Kallan stepped back.

Rune mirrored her footwork.

She retreated two more steps, and he delighted in the nervous shift of her eyes.

No sword, no dagger, no Seidr. Just claws. He widened his grin. *I can handle claws.*

Kallan retreated, Rune lunged, and she ran into the forest.

Kallan kicked up the leaf litter as she tore through the wood. The wind stirred like Death's cold breath. A chill pricked Kallan's flesh and, all at once, the winds stilled. Darkness enclosed the forest like a black pool of bottomless water. The whispers within the shadows returned. They were there watching, waiting as they had for weeks now.

Stripped of all weapons, and without a way to outrun them, Kallan summoned her Seidr. Flames swallowed her hands, spreading up her arms as the shadows grew colder and devoured the forest around her, and Kallan relinquished her flame into the darkness.

A path of embers climbed the leaves and branches. The rush of adrenaline sharpened her senses. Not knowing if she should attack again or run, she studied the umbra for the things that drained the life from the wood.

"Kallan!" Rune called from behind. He emerged from the brush.

"Call them off," she said, already amassing another round of Seidr that snaked up her arms like sleeves. Rune looked from Kallan's Seidr to the umbra.

"They are not my men," he said.

"I have no reason to believe you," she said, eying her dagger gripped in his hand.

The dream was clear and I am a fool for ignoring the signs. "I'm going back!"

"You can't go back." Rune flexed his grip on the hilt. "You don't know what goes on there."

The gentle note in his tone only augmented her rage. With a matching flick of both wrists, Kallan expelled the Seidr through the wind and Rune stood, enduring the Seidr, taking it in as he had before. As she poured her Seidr into his chest, as he took it in until he teetered from the rush she knew it gave him, Kallan approached him and snatched the hilt. But his guard had not been so low. As she moved to take the dagger, he grabbed her and spun her about, pinning her to his chest, her blade pressed to her throat.

Kallan inhaled against the prick upon her tender flesh.

"Why the sudden interest in peace?" she asked, not daring to turn against the poised tip of the blade.

"Gunir has always, ever sought peace," Rune said.

Kallan threw back her head into Rune's face. He stumbled back as blood poured from his nose.

"I don't believe you," she replied and released a blaze that rent the air, launching Rune across the forest floor. The force slammed him into the tree with a crack while his body took in the Seidr and fire.

She broke the stream and made her way across the clearing as he lay panting.

"If I wanted this war, I would have killed you while you slept," Rune said.

A stream of Seidr roared from her hands. Like before, Rune buckled under the impact as it flowed into him until she disrupted the stream.

"I would have left you at the stables!" he shouted.

Sprinting, Kallan fired a blast to his chest. Rune's back arched beneath the Seidr as if his body devoured the surge, taking in all that she gave him.

She broke the connection and he fell forward, catching himself on his palms.

"I would have left you to the Shadow," Rune gasped as Kallan recharged her next attack.

Welcoming the rage that was taking her, she sent a discharge and another, not caring where her Seidr landed. Each discharge Rune met and drew in. When the Seidr missed, it curved into him as if pulled by something inside of him.

If only he would die, then maybe she could forget.

She marched across the forest and Rune stood, his full focus clearly on the Seidkona. The next round of Seidr pooled in her hand.

Kallan pulled back her arm emblazoned with flame when Rune's hand flew to her wrist hard enough to startle her. He wasn't weak. If anything, he was stronger. Too strong.

"I would have killed you as you lay dying in Swann Dalr," Rune's words held Kallan in place.

"You were there," she whispered, her palms still surging with Seidr.

"Free to impale you with my sword while you lay dying," he said.

"My father..." Anger held the word in her throat. Kallan condensed the Seidr into her palm, amassing the strength into a smaller surface. "My fath—"

"I never gave that order," he said between breaths.

Kallan narrowed her eyes, weighing his words for truth.

"Why should I believe you?" she asked, not yet ready to surrender her Seidr.

"Because," he said, "I wouldn't have killed a king to spare his daughter, who, I might add, has proven to be more of a pain in my ass than her predecessor."

Kallan relaxed her grip, quelling the Seidr that had pooled.

"I swear to you, Kallan," Rune said, "I am not your enemy."

Silence engulfed the forest. Within the quiet, the shadows closed in.

"We need to leave," Rune said. The darkness swelled. "Now."

Rune grasped her hand and turned from the shadows, but his feet never left the ground. A whirlwind of black engulfed him, propelling Rune through the trees.

Whether it was branches or bones that Kallan heard crack, she couldn't tell. Expanding her lungs, she opened her mouth to scream, but no sound came. The shadow dove down her throat and into her belly.

Something hard struck the back of her head and she fell into a pool of her own blood. As the world faded black, the pendant slipped from her fingers, and Kallan lost herself to the darkness.

Chapter 34

Gudrun stared into the flames, watching as the fire danced. An unnamed darkness had befallen the city. The silence left by Bergen's men lingered, plaguing Lorlenalin with stifled sobs that no one gave name to.

The old woman pulled her shawl around her shoulders, desperate to shake the chill that had crept into her core overnight.

"You can hug yourself in front of the fire all day long." The amber of Daggon's voice slid over her. "You're not going to get rid of the chill that haunts us all."

Gudrun glanced at Daggon, who wore his exhaustion in the kitchen's doorway. He had attempted to dress himself, getting as far as his muddy boots, some worn trousers, and an unkempt tunic that hung limply from his shoulders.

Armed with a large flask of mead, Daggon threw back his head and gulped down three mouthfuls. Diminishing shades of red and pink, the only evidence left of the attack, trailed from his hardened face down his neck and vanished beneath his tunic.

"So, you're awake," Gudrun said. "You don't look so bad after a night's work."

"I could say the same for you," Daggon said as Gudrun's chair scraped the floor.

Pushing off the doorway, Daggon shuffled across the room and dropped himself into a chair that creaked beneath his weight. Moments later, Gudrun returned to the table with a small kettle of boiling water she had pulled from the fireplace.

"How do you feel?" she asked, not bothering to look up as she poured the hot water into a cup of herbs.

"Don't trifle over me, woman," Daggon said from behind the flask. "Your hen-pecking belittles a man's honor."

"I'm sorry." Gudrun dropped the kettle to the table. "Turn your cheek and I'll grant you a set with which to boast your endurance."

Daggon grimaced and swallowed his mouthful, then omitted a sound like a half growl, half sigh. After a moment, he met Gudrun's eyes and furrowed his brow.

"You haven't slept," he said across the table.

"You shouldn't be up." Gudrun settled herself into the chair opposite him. His white knuckles gripped his flask as he slumped over the drink, supporting his weight on his elbows.

"Any news?" Daggon asked.

Gudrun snatched the flask from Daggon's grasp, added a liberal amount to her tea, and returned it to its owner. She rested her elbows on the table, keeping the drink just below her nose where she could breathe in the valerian root. The firelight glistened off her silver hair. The old Seidkona stared into her cup, arguing with herself over how much she should say while Daggon listened to the fire crackle.

After a long sigh and a sip, Gudrun spoke. "Nothing new since the Dark One took her."

"The Dark One didn't take her," Daggon said.

Gudrun's cup hit the table with a cold thud.

"The king took her," Daggon said.

Gudrun's golden eyes softened as if lost in distant thought, unable to find her way back. She took another sip, then lowered her cup to the table and folded her hands against her mouth.

"Alright, woman," Daggon growled. "Out with it."

Rearing up for the tempers that would fly, Gudrun sighed.

"We believed the Dark One had taken her. And with all the wounded..." Daggon shuffled uncomfortably in his chair. "Your wounds alone are too new to go off on a blood hunt."

"What are you not saying, Gudrun?"

The old woman shook her head as firelight spilled across Daggon's scars, adding black to the streaks of red that made it look as if his face blazed with flame again.

"No one has left the city," she said. "Not the war-men...not for Kallan. No one."

Daggon slammed his hand to the table and stood, shaking. With the creak of the chair beneath the pound of his boot, Daggon staggered his way to the door.

"Daggon."

The giant mop of red hair whipped about, streaking across his bearded face.

"Aaric left my queen to the whim of that...that heathen. And you sit here sipping your teas and spinning your visions."

"Daggon, be still," Gudrun said.

"I'll have his head!" Daggon roared, stomping toward the door.

"Daggon, stop." Gudrun rose to her feet, releasing a crack of Seidr that split the air.

"You can See," Daggon said. "You have the Sight! You can see where she is, if she lives...where he has her, if she's dead!"

Gudrun's chest steadily rose and fell with an ageless patience.

"The last person I know who went looking for knowledge lost an eye," she said gravely, holding his attention with a darkened gloom about her.

"I'll give both of my own if you can assure me she's safe."

"Wishes made in haste are often ill-thought," she said and settled herself back to the table.

Gudrun resumed drinking her tea as if they had said nothing between them, as if he still sat nursing his mead and wallowing in self-pity.

The fire popped as she weighed the images that played in her mind.

"Twelve, twenty, two-hundred times a day," Gudrun spoke low behind her cup. "Some pictures as clear as you standing across the room, others faded and scrambled, without placement, as if the Norns had not yet engraved them in stone."

Daggon shifted himself to better stare down in wonder at Gudrun's power.

"Yesterday the most faded of visions were as vibrant as they have ever been, forming a hardened ball of dread in the deepest, innermost reaches of my Seidr," Gudrun said.

Gudrun lowered her cup, looking past Daggon into the empty space behind him.

"Yes. I can See," she said with regret. "I can See far more than I ever wanted to See. *And some things not clearly enough.* "I see things that, once spoken, would change them. I see things I wish I didn't See. Things I can't un-see. And things better left unseen. I See enough to know that what is here is more than you or I can change."

"More than Kallan?"

Gudrun bowed her head, swirling the few dregs left floating in her tea.

"Look at me, Gudrun," Daggon pleaded, "and tell me you wouldn't beg me for the same information if I had it."

Pulling her eyes from her tea, Gudrun studied Daggon's scarred face long before she answered.

"The Dark One has a bloodlust that can not be sated," Gudrun said. "His thirst runs deep. But the king..." Gudrun shook her head. "The king will not act quickly."

Daggon heaved his breath, clearly pacifying his temper as Gudrun spoke.

"Circumstances have changed beyond the point of aiding Kallan," Gudrun said. "If we had gotten to her sooner, if we had swayed the tide before she was taken, we stood a chance. But by her leaving here with him, it solidified events." The Seidkona shook her head remorsefully. "There's nothing to be done, Daggon, but wait for events to unfold."

"Swear to me," Daggon said, his fists clenched at his side. "Promise me that if the tide changes again, we won't sit by while Kallan dies, even if it can not be helped."

A coal popped in the hearth, adding a spark of orange to the room that faded.

It will change again, but where I go, I go alone. "I swear it," Gudrun whispered.

Slightly satisfied, Daggon looked down at his flask.

Daggon let out an exhausted sigh. "I will send out my own men to look."

Gudrun nodded as Daggon swirled the mead in his flask.

"Searching the roads will, at least, postpone the madness that helplessness brings," he grumbled and threw back his head, polishing off the last of it.

Chapter 35

Rune stirred on the forest floor. Daylight poured through trees, blinding him at first as he shifted and pushed himself up from the ground. Every inch of him ached and thoughts flooded back with his memories, colliding into a state of confusion.

The birds had returned to the forest. The angle of the sun's light told him it was mid-day. Kallan was gone. Rune winced against the sharp pain that travelled up his back into his shoulders. A constant throb pulsed through the back of his head. He touched the well-formed knob and cringed, then propped himself against a tree.

Remember. The shadow had closed in. Like death, it sucked the very life from the forest. Kallan's Seidr and his...

Rune turned his hand over. Even now, he felt an energy writhing within. Unsettled, it paced as if ready to tear itself out. Kallan had thrown her Seidr and something inside of him had wanted it, drawn it, pulled it in with such a ferocious hunger that could not be sated, and there it brooded.

Rune shook the confusion from his head and forced himself to stand despite the aches that protested movement.

Astrid. The supplies. Check the horse.

Rune stopped. On his feet, he could see the beam of sunlight caress the forest floor where a bit of metal glistened. Brushing aside the debris, Rune pulled the tri-corner knot from the forest floor. Still attached to the chain that had snapped clean, Kallan's elding pendant swayed.

The Shadow.

Like a plague, it had descended and devoured the forest. Uninterested with him, its only concern seemed to have been Kallan.

"What Hel have you caught yourself in, princess?" Rune muttered scanning the forest.

Broken trees. Disrupted forest. I need a direction.

His gaze wandered to the west.

The Shadow came from the west. West.

Rune walked to where the Shadow had entered the clearing and focused his attention to where the trees were thickest. At first glance, the wood appeared undisturbed, but the restlessness that stirred within him pulled him into the foliage.

323

There, he knelt and scanned the terrain until, several paces ahead, buried deep into the trees, he saw where the earth was unsettled.

Four.

Rune raised his eyes to the faint trail that twisted a path through the forest.

To the west.

Beside Astrid, Rune cleared the leaf debris from the ground and dumped the contents of Kallan's pouch, tossing it aside.

Folded packets of powders he couldn't identify, a vile of golden liquid, multiple stones engraved with runes he couldn't decipher, round stones he assumed were bartering stones of some sort, and an apple were its only contents. But his eyes fell to the apple that glowed as if threads of gold and light had been infused into its skin.

With furrowed brow, he reached to take the apple, but the moment his fingers grazed the flesh, the Beast within him stirred. He clamped the fruit and the Beast pulled on the lines of gold that trailed up his arm and into his skin until the light had ended. An apple with red, ordinary skin remained.

Gasping, Rune dropped the fruit and fell to his hands. Sweat beaded upon his brow. Shaking, he rubbed his face while the apple lay as ordinary as any apple, and the Beast resumed its pacing.

Uncertain of the surge that encouraged his blood to flow, Rune blew a short sigh and, determined to be on his way, snagged the pouch.

Rune stopped and looked to the pouch he held, certain he had dumped all the contents. Taking it, Rune turned it upside down, and another apple, as gold as the first, hit the ground. Unease stirred the pacing Beast as Rune's heart pounded.

Cautiously, he reached out. As before, the Beast roared and pulled the light from the apple into his arm. Another ordinary, red apple fell, but it was the increased weight to the pouch in his hand, that drew his attention while the Beast settled once more.

Peering inside, Rune saw another, single apple as golden as before, nestled within. Before his hand passed into the pouch, the Beast was alert once more and the apple was drained and ordinary, lying on the ground with the first two.

And still, another apple appeared. Already the Beast was stirring, raising its interest in anticipation for its next fix. He could feel the draw to feed it, to take up the apple and sate the Beast, and all at once, the desire to control it, to tame it, to master it emerged.

Rune raised a hand to the apple, the Beast roared, and Rune withdrew his hand. He felt the anxiety, the frustration within the Beast, the Shadow, stir and he brought his hand back to the apple. The closer his hand came to the threads of light, the more unsettled the Beast became.

Rune fought the appetite, the need to draw on the threads, and moved his hand closer. The Beast reached for the light. The Shadow licked at the lines that would sate the need, and Rune pushed the

Beast back. Taking in the link, Rune found the lines and pulled them. The light from the apple drained and Rune focused his attention on breaking the link. Hungrily, the Beast drank, devouring the light and Rune bore down, determined to tame the Shadow.

The lines weakened. The Beast grew more desperate. And Rune focused all his strength on the light, the Shadow, his will, and the Beast. He battled the Beast until Rune severed the light lines that remained fixed to the apple. The Beast roared. It bucked. The Shadow grew, and Rune slammed it down, forcing the Beast to obey under his will.

In his hand, Rune held Kallan's golden apple. With a satisfied grin, Rune sank his teeth into the fruit and gasped when his shredded muscles rewove themselves, his broken nose mended itself, and the aches in his joints vanished.

The familiar weight in the pouch returned and Rune gazed inside. There, a fifth apple rested as golden as the one in his hand.

By the twelfth apple, Rune was able to take up the fruit and keep the Beast from stirring. The tension was there. He felt it wanting to fight, but Rune had maintained the strength to keep the Beast at bay, allowing him to draw the threads of light.

With the contents returned to Kallan's pouch, he made his way back to Astrid who had remained in the clearing.

Taking up the reins, Rune looked to the west.

He was under stocked and less prepared than usual for the situation. With Kallan's dagger and no shoes on his feet, he was in no position to track, let alone venture into battle. But he had only a few hours before Kallan's trail went cold and mid-day was long since passed.

I'll make weapons along the way, he decided.

The Beast raised its head. He felt it too: the draw and want of the light and much stronger than anything from the apples.

Withdrawing Kallan's dagger, Rune sank to the bushes out of sight.

One.

The Beast within paced hungrily, aching for the pull with more vigor than before.

Steady.

Rune located the primary source of the Seidr nearby. The energy it exuded riled the Beast, forcing Rune to focus his efforts on holding it back. The Seidr source shifted faster than anything Rune had seen before. But the Seidr from that single source pulled at the Seidr lines fused to the earth and the air. Where the Seidr source moved, it left a trail behind, making it difficult to track its location, and the moment he found it, it moved again.

The Beast snarled. And Rune turned, knowing his opponent was too fast long before the cold blade touched his throat and Rune held his breath, waiting as a dark voice spoke:

"From the threshold of Death's door where Raven loves the Crow,

Take his outstretched, withered hand. 'Release,' he calls. 'Come forth'."

Rune breathed and shoved the blade from his throat while laughter broke the forest's silence. "Bergen!"

"You looked like you were going to piss yourself three ways sideways," Bergen chuckled.

Rune ran a hand over his face, wiping away the beads of sweat before sheathing Kallan's blade.

"There isn't time for this," Rune said. "Where's your horse?"

"Hey!" Bergen called. "Where's the queen?"

"There's food here and flint," Bergen said, pulling the saddlebag from the black mare and handing it over to Rune. "A few swords and knives are secured to Zabbai's saddle. I picked them off a band of Men a day back."

Rune looked up at attention. "Men? In Alfheim?"

Bergen nodded. "Their weapons are forged with impure iron. They'll break, but it's something."

Rune ignored him and fastened the sword to his side.

"What are you doing, Brother?" Bergen asked.

"I'm going after her." Rune said, looking over the Dokkalfar blade and securing another set of knives on his belt. "Let me have your boots."

Without question, Bergen pulled off his boots and tossed them to Rune.

"Do you even know where they've taken her?" Bergen asked.

"By the few tracks they left, they went west."

"Midgard," Bergen said.

"It shouldn't take more than a moon." Rune pulled on Bergen's boots as he spoke. "Not sure yet what I'm dealing with. They're on foot, but..." Rune's thoughts trailed off. "Ride back to Gunir. Take the throne in my stead, and here."

Rune pulled off his signet ring and thrust it at Bergen, who threw his hands into the air.

"Whoa," Bergen exclaimed. "You know I can't afford to tarnish the disrespectful reputation I've been honing for centuries. What would Torunn think if she caught me being responsible with that?"

"Fine." Rune jammed the ring back on his finger and studied the longsword on Bergen's back.

The Seidr source that had awakened the Beast with such hunger, the Seidr source that drew from all other lines around them as it moved with its keeper, came from the blade on Bergen's back. Until now, he had never detected the amount of energy stored in its core. When Bergen arrived ages ago, dismissing the longsword as something he had picked of the Dokkalfar, no one had questioned it. But not even the Dokkalfar make blades like that.

"Give me your Firstborn," Rune said.

Bergen's eyes were set aflame. "You can have the boots off my feet..."

Rune frowned.

"...the shirt off my back..."

329

"You never wear shirts."

"...the pants off my hide," Bergen offered.

"No, thanks."

"You are not taking my Firstborn," Bergen declared.

Rune scoffed. "You didn't pick that off a Dokkalfar, did you?"

Bergen went pale.

"Later," Rune said. "I have no time. Give me your bow."

Bergen gave him the bow without objection.

"The quiver," Rune said.

Bergen obliged.

"And your pipe," Rune said.

Bergen made a sound like he had swallowed a cat. "You're killing me here," he said, but handed over his pipe and some leaf.

"If I'm not back by the next new moon, come find me," Rune said while he fastened Bergen's quiver to his belt. "Tell no one that you've seen me."

Rune pulled himself onto Astrid and steered the stallion west.

"Hey!" Bergen called once Rune had eased Astrid into a cantor. "What am I supposed to tell Torunn?"

"Do what you always do!" Rune called not bothering to look back. "Compose one of your stories."

Chapter 36

A void encompassed Kallan. Distant voices faded in the dark. What pain there was, she didn't feel. Not yet anyway, but she would. The darkness devours everything. Light does what it can to fight it off, producing endless energy to do so.

Endless energy. Endless Seidr. Light has to try so hard. Darkness just is, there, suspended in the Great, waiting for when the light goes out, when there can be nothing but the Great Void to welcome it.

Such stories emerge from the Black. Some of them true, some seeded by a variant of truth. Most are just ludicrous lies.

Every child grew up hearing the stories of the Shadows where figures brood with long, menacing fingers, sharpened to fine tips, and pallid, sickly skin stretched over a skeletal frame. Their hair was wild and wiry, and as black as their horrible eyes. Those eyes, those dreadful, lifeless eyes, bulbous and bulging like polished, black stones that could pierce through any darkness. It was those eyes that gave rise to the rumors of the Shadows, for it was long said that they could extract the light from anything, and with it, life.

They drank blood and ate children. The sun was their only bane. Their breath brought the winter. Their voices, death. They never slept and lived to devour. Over the years, rumors evolved, dramatizing their weaknesses: pendants and charms worn to daunt them, herbs and spices woven and hung over thresholds. Waters stolen from Mimir's Well, all to deter the Shadows. All were just ludicrous lies.

In truth, they were the Dvergar, the Alfar race whose artisanship and forge drew them into the mountains long ago, before the ancient stories were ancient stories, before the forgotten war of the Aesir and the Vanir forced Odinn to recoil into his halls in Asgard and accumulate the Dead Riders for his Great Hunt.

For three ages, the Dvergar worked and honed and molded their jewels, melting metals, and casting stones with a beauty that, ages later, none could surpass. Many once believed that the Dvergar learned their art from the Vanir. But that was ages before the war and the Schism, and much longer before Kallan had walked their halls with her mother.

Kallan curled her fingers, dragging the tips along the cold, rough stone. Every breath expanded her lungs against her chest wall, pushing on every broken rib. She counted three and knew there were more.

She tried to think, and wished her mind alert, but her thoughts didn't obey. They stirred, curiously glanced about, and dozed back to sleep where they stayed heavily weighted with a dense cloud that dampened all emotion.

She tried to breathe through her nose, but it was swollen, smashed closed and clogged with dried blood. The sudden, sharp intake of breath through her mouth was a mistake. An unrecognizable bitter tang bit her throat, and Kallan gasped then coughed.

Thousands of minute explosions burst like pops of flame through every joint. The constant hum of agony awoke like a dragon, thrashing and roaring throughout her body, ripping and renting the fibers of her being. Stone sliced her back with every movement, adding a layer of fire that managed to split through the carefree cloud that dulled her senses, weakening the haze enough to arouse emotion, but only for brief moments at a time.

The spasm subsided and, with it, the dragon, leaving her in a numbed state of consciousness. The throbbing was slow to subside and she tried to move.

Bitter copper coated her mouth and Kallan licked the split in her fattened lip. She moved her hand to assess the damage, but a dead weight pulled on her wrists. A sharp, cold staccato scraped the ground, and a grotesque sick moved in. Panic fought to scream, but the looming cloud persisted. The surge of worry died away to the iron wall in the back of her mind where fear and care dissipated.

Curiously, Kallan felt for the weight and found links of metal. Blindly, she rolled it over and followed the rows of redundant links that climbed to her wrists. There, a set of thick, heavy shackles secured her in place. She continued her investigation down the links of two separate chains that joined a single run and ended at the final link burrowed into a cold, jagged, stone floor.

Kallan opened her eyes, blinked and closed them again to allow her sight to adjust. Endless and thick, the black enveloped her. Behind her, a single monotonous drip echoed from deep within the cave. She lay there, listening, unconcerned with the drip, the dark, or the chains.

A soft, orange light shifted in the distance. Uncertain at first as to what it was, Kallan fought her eyes to work. She identified the glimmering black-orange sphere in the distance as a torch or lantern light. In the silhouette of its flame, barely an arm's reach away, Kallan deciphered the outline of a bowl that held the source of a rancid, bitter tang.

From the bowl, smoke wafted into the air in a single stream and lofted beautifully around her. Kallan lifted her eyes, more curious than concerned, and studied the shapes that rose from the floor. She dragged her hand through the fumes, mesmerized as they rolled and billowed around her shackled wrists.

Through the smoke, she made out the crude outline of rock and stone.

"Walls," Kallan said.

The sound scraped her throat, its melody clawing the raw flesh, and she coughed, sending her into another fit of convulsions that added a new collection of lacerations to her back, shoulders, and legs.

When, at last, her body stilled, she breathed in the air thick with vapor. Her head flopped about on the ground and she stared stupidly at the bowl. She gazed for a long while and contemplated moving it away, but with every second, it became harder to think and a thick, dense cloud pushed down against her thoughts.

Kallan shook her head, which proved to be the worst idea yet. Thoughts jumbled, colliding into one another until her mind was plunged into disarray and she lay, panting on the floor and waiting for the clutter to settle.

Her breath slowed and she tried to think again, but nothing came. A familiar gleam caught her eye and she reached, taking up one of the links of the chain.

Smooth, silver-black metal shimmered in the distant light. Abrupt panic leapt and her heart jumped, breaking through the daze that suppressed her. All at once, she was on her knees, clawing at the floor, panting through nervous huffs of breath until dizziness pulled her head to the side and she wavered, falling to the jagged stone that mercilessly dug at her flesh.

"Dvergar," she breathed.

Her hand flew to her neck and Kallan remembered. The back of her throat burned with want to cry. Her precious pendant was lost to the earth.

With a desperation that pushed her beyond the haze, Kallan wiped the sting from her eyes. The chain was bulky and heavy in her stiff, swollen fingers. With as much strength as she could muster, Kallan pulled.

The metal didn't give.

After two more feeble attempts that left her drained of energy and dizzy, she remembered the Seidr. Finding the energy within her core was almost impossible. Collecting it through the miasma was harder. Sporadic gusts of Seidr pulsed through her bonds. The metal shook and whined, protesting the abuse it endured, but remained fastened hard to the floor.

Despair increased with every failed attempt, and Kallan blasted the chain again and again. She fought back the fog, but with the bulk of her Seidr so far out of reach, she could not weaken the forged craft of the Dvergar.

A final pulse through the metal took the last of her motivation, and, exhausted, Kallan dropped her palms to the stone, inviting fresh cuts to her hands. Her head spun with a nausea that swayed back and forth like the sea tosses a ship in a storm. A cold, shallow chuckle crept through her blood, increasing until it became a sadistic laugh. The sound stirred a rage that soon vanished. Lacking the coordination to move and the interest to try, Kallan listened to the gritty sound of the laughter.

An inner voice beneath the cloud screamed for her to look, to move, to fight, but a greater part of her, most of her, ignored it despite knowing the voice inside her head was right. Stones clicked together and a fired roared to life, pushing back the shadows.

Kallan winced against the sudden stab that gouged her eyes as a fragrant fog of orange and red wafted into the air. From tangy to sweet, the stench pummeled her mouth. Each flavor took its turn at dominance, never fully mingling into a single odor strong with flavor. It burned and she shook her head. Pain seemed to be the only thing that could permeate the cloud. Pain alone seemed to motivate her.

A variety of cuts and blood, both dried and fresh, covered her hands. The white chemise she had donned for bed two nights ago was shredded and smudged. Streaks of red and black blotted the fabric to match her legs. Kallan gulped in the hopes of easing the nausea and closed her eyes against the swaying floor. Deep voices rose from the shadows, passing between a sharp staccato and a guttural drawl. She knew the sound, but it hurt to remember why.

The heavy clod of a boot thundered through the cave and dropped. Once. Twice. Thrice to the floor, then slammed hard into her side. Shards exploded in her torso, accompanying several cracks as she fell against the cave wall and back to the floor, held in place by the chains. Her head rebounded against the stone, imploding a wave through her head that spun like a whirlwind, urging nausea.

Fresh cuts sliced her shoulders as she fell, adding to the myriad of pain.

Get up, a small voice from behind her iron wall shouted.

But I don't want to, she said back.

The dragon awakened, roared with every breath Kallan pushed through her chest. Something warm and wet fell onto her face, suffocating her, choking her. She knew she should move, but not caring enough to listen to the voice, Kallan stayed, not bothering to budge from the floor.

The guttural growls of foreign syllables barked at her. She attempted to decipher each sound, picking them apart a grunt at a time, and was surprised at how easy it was. But after a few seconds, she became disinterested, too heavy with fatigue to try, and abandoned her efforts.

The syllables changed to something familiar and, with an added tinge of resentment, the voice belonging to the boot barked.

"Where is it?"

Kallan heaved through the heat that smothered her, trying to understand the spoken words. Cold, hard fingers clamped around her neck and pulled her from the ground, freeing her from the stifling heat. It took her a moment to realize the heat was her own hot breath caught beneath a sheet of hair that had fallen onto her face.

"The pouch, Drui," it barked. "Where?"

The chains scraped the floor as he jostled her.

True to the stories, his eyes were large and black. A pale complexion, much like her own, was buried somewhere beneath a wild, black mane of beard and hair. He wore a thick tunic fashioned of heavy, brown wool over his large chest.

Skeletal was the farthest thing from her mind as a pair of wide shoulders, spanning a hefty frame, secured his thick neck. Muscle toned his arms and torso with the kind of brawn a worker could only get from the mines or the forge.

He coldly dropped her to the ground and Kallan winced against the new wave of lacerations before his boot found her gut. Again, she gasped, losing the muscle control to regain breath against the second explosion of ribs cracking.

"Blainn."

The boot stopped mid-swing.

"That's enough." There was a growl in that command.

Through the haze, Kallan lifted her eyes for a chance to look upon her savior.

Though as muscular and brawny as the first, he was taller and wider by comparison. He had the same fair skin and round, black eyes, but his left cheek was marked with a scar that spanned his left cheekbone, from the corner of his mouth to the side of his eye. His grotesque appearance churned her nausea.

He uttered something in their native tongue, dismissing the one called Blainn and crouching down beside her.

What do you want? she thought, too weak to speak.

"Your pouch," he said with an unkindness that crawled up Kallan's back. "Where is it?"

Where am I? she tried to ask, but her throat had swollen shut and it was all she could do to breathe.

He crouched closer, bringing his wide nose inches from hers. She could taste the stale earth and putrid sulfur on his clothes. She knew that flavor...that smell, but struggled to remember why. The memory was too old to place.

"The only reason why you still breathe," he said, "is because we can't find it. Cooperate. Blainn can only be controlled for a short time, before even I lose status."

Kallan shifted a swollen eye to Blainn, who hungrily waited for the go-ahead to continue kicking.

"I say again," he repeated. "Where is the pouch?"

I don't have it, she tried to say, but her voice failed to obey. She tried something else, something easier.

"Tak'n," Kallan croaked and coughed.

Fire shook her body, and a tear slipped from her eye.

"Who?" The firelight caught his scar.

Kallan thought to answer, but choked on the fear that they would hunt Rune next. The voice in her head screamed in objection, but only a whisper reached her. She could not speak. She could not move and, instead, waited for Blainn's judgment. Within that suspended moment, her mind passed in and out of worry. She thought of Rune and wondered if he had taken Astrid and ridden on without her.

He would be in Gunir by now, she pondered, then wondered if he lived.

The cloud from the bowl seemed to thicken as it settled down closer, heavier, determined to bury her alive in its bitter tang. It was growing harder to think again. Memory vanished with the voice in her head. Blainn roared, and she stopped caring again.

Another explosion erupted in her side.

Gasping, Kallan rolled, clutching her torso. Her heartbeat drummed, pushing the blood through her as if desperately pumping the life back into her. Each beat made her acutely aware of every ache, every bruise, every break.

The room spun. Her stomach violently leapt in time to the pulsing of her blood. She convulsed and vomited, closing her eyes against the spasms that returned again and again.

A sudden, searing chill burned her back, following the length of her spine, and splitting her skin in two. She gasped, holding back a violent scream. Her hand flew to her back and she sobbed, relieved to feel that her skin had not really split in two.

Nerves. She remembered her lessons with Gudrun in the Southeastern Deserts. *Just nerves. The skin hadn't split at all.*

Kallan touched something hot and wet and recognized her own vomit. Another wave of nausea rose. Shuddering, she fell back to her side, hoping to ease the vertigo. A fire crackled in the distance, filling her with a desire, a need, to look upon the light in the darkness.

She winced and shifted her gaze to the light, fixing her eyes on the lively fire that roared in the center of the cave. Blainn was gone, but the Scarred One now stood beside the fire with a third.

This one was different. With a smaller frame, he was slightly shorter, and thinner. He looked younger. Considerably younger. They spoke in the Common Tongue. She strained to hear over the incessant pulse as her heart worked to move the blood through every cut and bruise.

"Did you find him, Nordri?"

"We found the trail several paces off where we think he landed. From there, he headed north. We tracked him to the main road of Gunir, but didn't follow further. Any closer and we'd have the Ljosalfar war-men on us."

"And the pouch?" the Scarred One asked.

Nordri shook his head.

"No sign of it anywhere. She may have stashed it somewhere. Durin thinks she left it back in Lorlenalin."

"Durin would think that," the Scarred One said. His eyes glazed over with thought as the clod of a boot, heavier than Blainn's, resonated through the cave. Another Dvergr as wide as Blainn and almost identical in stature joined Nordri and the Scarred One beside the fire. His eyes were significantly smaller, appearing beady, and were set deeper than what seemed natural. Kallan could only assume this was Durin.

"Report," came the Scarred One's order.

Durin took his cue from the commander and answered in Common Tongue.

"Their current state has left them vulnerable. An attack now would assure a win." His voice carried as if he wanted Kallan to hear. "Wipe them out, I say. Extinct."

The bowl's cloud muted any protests she would have had, so she lay submissively instead, listening to the discussion.

The Scarred One silently mulled over the proposition. There was a long silence before anyone spoke again.

"Motsognir?" Nordri pressed.

Motsognir, Kallan mused.

A forgotten name surfaced from the depths of her ancient memory then fizzled, failing to push through.

"Bring her."

The words rang through like a death sentence and the last of her worry fell numb. Throwing a spiteful look to the broken heap that was Kallan, Motsognir stepped into obscurity beyond the light. The plod of heavy boots returned and, just as Blainn came into view, everything went dark.

Chapter 37

A bowl struck the ground with a clang like a poorly tuned bell, waking Kallan with a startled jerk. Her pulse pounded her temple with a merciless hammer that twisted its way into her writhing stomach.

Pulling her legs to her chest, Kallan hugged herself against the pain that flipped between nausea and indifference. The bitter tang in the air lingered along with the dull throbbing, the sharp stabbing, and the hot, searing bursts that ripped her body apart. Her chains scraped the floor with every miniscule movement. She tried to move, but cringed instead, then groaned.

The monotonous drip was gone. Through the corner of her eye, Kallan caught the faint light of the Dvergar's fire. A bit of cave wall jutted out a ways between her and the fire, blocking most of the Dvergar from view. It was enough to outline a pillar of limestone that had not been there before and, at once, she saw it and understood. While she slept, they had relocated.

It didn't take long for her to decide she didn't care, and her head slumped to the side.

Boot, she thought as she stared at a large, square-ish boot, coated with mud. She made an effort to lift her head, following the brown trousers up to the tunic worn loosely over a pair of shoulders beneath a long, black overcoat.

It was a fine overcoat, beautifully made with black leather and lined with thick, black rabbit fur. It was an overcoat only one of importance would wear. She twitched at the face peering down at her. She was half expecting Motsognir, with his regal commands and the mannerisms taught only to those of the king's high court.

This Dvergr, like the others, was as tall as the Alfar, as tall as the tallest of Men and just as burly as his comrades. They all had beards, wild, black, scruffy things, the way some men let grow where nature takes it.

His beard was shorter, tamer, and calmer than the rest. His clothes were a bit cleaner. He had the build and strength honed by the mines, but the astuteness of a scholar. A cold, silent shadow lingered in his eye somewhere between pensive and calculative. Kallan wasn't sure if it was his well-groomed appearance or the lack of cruelty in his round, black eyes. Regardless, something about this Dvergr eased her.

He held her gaze as easily as she held his and they studied each other in turn, each of them captivated, neither of them moving, until a grim voice called from the fire.

"Ori."

Ori didn't move at the sound of his name.

The shuffle of a boot and a heavy plod soon followed. Still, Ori kept his eyes locked on hers. A heavy hand fell onto Ori's shoulder, pulling him out of his trance, and, without a word, he walked back to the fire, leaving the other Dvergr there with her.

Kallan diverted her attention to the new guard and her heart fell, catching Nordri's eerie gaze. He crouched down until his face was a breath away.

"Eat or don't." Nordri brushed a too-gentle hand against her cheek. Her stomach churned and she gave a startled jerk, but failed to pull away, keeping his pale hand on her face.

"Truth is, if we were going to kill you, we wouldn't have waited until now to do it." He grinned with a wide, malicious look to his eye. "And we wouldn't have used poison."

Kallan jerked away too weak and too wounded to throw him a glower.

Nordri flashed a smile that upturned her nerves, and, slowly, he scraped her body with his eyes. After ensuring he had a good long stare at her exposed flesh, he returned to the fire. There, he settled and shifted himself into place, and flourished another grin that seemed to linger there in the dark long after it was gone.

Kallan glanced at the bowl Ori had left her. It didn't take her long to muster up the nerve to eat the unidentifiable slop. It hit her stomach like a hammer and stirred up her nausea again. When she was done, she fell back to the floor, letting her head strike the stone.

In the dark, she lay awake, straining to hear a familiar word among them. Within minutes, on a less-than-empty belly, the gruff voices and guttural sounds lulled her into a deadened sleep.

Five Dvergar dragged her to the depths of the caves. Motsognir, Nordri, Ori, Durin, and Blainn. Blainn was the muscle. He was first to kick and last to think and had a talent for cruelty. Kallan decided she liked him the least.

It didn't take long to realize Durin was his older brother. Having the advantage of being a few years older, he also had the advantage of having a few years more sense. It added up to nothing really, though it did make him less reckless, which meant he was less likely to kick, but more creative when he did.

In other ways, Nordri's cruelty far exceeded Blainn and Durin put together in ways that neither dared go. His specialty was mental. He wondered aloud why they fed her, why they took her, why they clothed her, and made too many hints and gestures that set her into a quelled panic every time.

It didn't take her long to realize Motsognir was there to keep them all in check. Being the leader of their assorted assembly, he was usually successful, but only when he was around to step in.

Ori, on the other hand, eluded her. She couldn't determine if he was there to learn, or there to record the events. He spoke less than she did and, seemed to disappear altogether for hours at a time. When he was around, she often caught him staring, watching her, engrossed so deeply it took a jab from Motsognir to bring him out of it. There was only one thing she was able to determine about Ori. Of all of them, he was the least of her worries.

Blainn's boot regularly woke her and she frequently passed into sleep with Durin's fist. Aside from the beatings and the occasional bowl of slop, they kept their distance. They always spoke Dvergar unless there was something specific they wanted her to hear, which always involved a slew of suggestions from Nordri that ended with a sickening glint in his eye.

Day and night didn't exist in the caves. Time blended into one long, endless night where there was only the darkness, the Dvergar, and nothing. The haze and the bitter tang always wafted nearby with displays of red and orange, keeping Kallan drugged, dizzy, and daft. When she thought anything at all, she thought of Lorlenalin and Daggon, of Eilif and

Aaric, and of Gudrun and the children. Once, she thought of Rune and of how she would gut him first chance she had to take Astrid back. But mostly, she didn't think.

She slept often, said nothing, and never cried. She was too numb to cry. Too frequently, she passed between sleep and awake. There were times she entered dreams she was awake for, and woke to nightmares she knew were real. Every time she woke, she lay, silently willing herself to sleep.

She wanted to sleep. She longed for it. Sleep was her sanctuary, an invisible hole where she could crawl into and vanish for stretches at a time. Only in sleep could Kallan avoid the beatings, the darkness, and Nordri's tawdry stares.

When she was awake, she longed for sleep, and when she slept, she welcomed it, desiring nothing more than to curl back up to sleep so that she might return to the world of dreaming where the pain was non-existent. She rarely woke on her own.

Kallan rolled onto her back, taking note of every new bruise and break and the level of stiffness the old ones had developed. It took her awhile to realize the unidentified concoction of slop they'd doled out was an assortment of medicines and herbs combined with something, she could only assume, that was nutritious enough to keep her alive, along with something for the fever, something for infection, and something to keep her daft and her Seidr out of reach of her consciousness. It was the only explanation she could find as to why she wasn't dead yet. It also allowed them to exercise little restraint in their beatings.

A fresh new assortment of rock and stone accompanied a new collection of cuts and bruises that covered her from head to heel. The dizziness was stronger than usual, and the orange blaze that had cast the images in an outline of black had returned.

She studied the ceiling. The majority of jagged stalactites hung overhead like countless knives at the ready if she dared attempt anything. Her throat was dry and she suddenly found herself wishing she had more of the slop-deemed-food to wet her lips.

Kallan sighed as she tried to sort through her disconnected and jumbled thoughts. Her movements were stiff and jerky. She rolled her head to the side and gazed at the bowl that always wafted with red and orange, but all that was there was a cold, damp sick that plunged down her throat at Nordri's leering eyes.

The usual campfire and muffled chatter were gone. Fear gripped her around the throat, inside the chest, and twisted her belly, wriggling and writhing in worry. There are things done only when alone, and the hollow silence of the cave confirmed they were very much alone.

Slouching, and hungry, as still as a bird fixed on its kill, Nordri sat on a chair-sized boulder. Beatings she could take. This was something else. His eyes gawked with a silence that spoke much more than words.

In a single glimpse, Kallan saw his thoughts played out in detail. Her heart pounded in her chest as she forced her broken body to move, to obey. The floor sliced her back, but Kallan continued to move.

With a careless thud, Nordri dropped a foot and stood, holding the lever used to pry up her chains. He swaggered to the spike that secured her bonds and pried it up from the floor. It was not until then that Kallan realized exactly how much chain bound her.

Five paces of elding chain scraped the floor as Nordri bundled it affectionately into his hands, cradling it lovingly like a leash. With a wide grin, he crouched to the floor, holding his eyes even to hers. His breath reeked of a bitter, root brew known only to the Dvergar.

He was too close. Even in the poor light, she could see every crevice and dip of his face as smooth and white as wax.

"I've had Dvergar and Svartálfar," he said with a grin. "Lots of Svartálfar. I've had my fair share of Man—their women are quite an unusual breed—even Ljosalfr once. But I've never had Dokkalfr." He shrugged. "They remember too much. Can't get close enough."

He dropped his voice even lower.

"But to have Drui..." There was his sick smile again. "...now that is a rare privilege."

Kallan didn't dare move. Silent and still, she lay as if any movement would encourage him to leap. He raised a large, white hand and lightly grazed her face.

Her skin burned where he touched her and her stomach flipped as a cold crawled up her back like a giant spider, and Kallan shuddered. The motion was enough to ignite his excitement.

"Go on." Nordri nodded. "Get!"

He opened his hands, released the weight that pulled the chains through his grip, and relinquished Kallan's bonds.

She didn't have to be told twice.

In a breath, Kallan was off, scrambling to stand and run on a swollen leg. The floor sliced the bottoms of her bare feet. Kallan stumbled, but scrambled, battling to keep her body moving.

The chain clawed the floor behind her, sending a deafening scream through the cave. Surely, someone would hear, someone was there, somewhere.

Nordri moved.

Quicker than a fox, he was on her, letting her run and standing a stride behind her as he watched her stumble. The race was ludicrous, no match at all. Still he let the wounded rabbit run. After a moment, he opened his voice and chatted in time to a ditty of his own making.

> "Pretty 'ole thing can have your tart,
> But cruel as is, she'll eat your heart."

Kallan clambered through the dark, pulling the chain over the stones of the cave floor, desperate to find the door. The deafening clank of elding on stone ended when Nordri stomped the end of the chain and stopped Kallan short. She fell to the ground, splitting her elbow open and making it run hot with blood.

> "Pretty 'ole thing. She wants to run,
> But cruel as is, you won't be done."

His sickening grin revealed his teeth in the dark as he took up the chain, pulling Kallan with it, reeling her in like a fish. Kallan grabbed her end of the chain and pulled back, but she was too weak, the drugs too deep.

> "Pretty 'ole thing you'll want to bed,
> But cruel as is, she'll want you dead."

Nordri yanked the chain. With nothing to brace her, she fell, face forward, tripping foot over stone, but he was ready for her.

Into his chest, she landed and, as if he had practiced a dozen times, Nordri shifted and slithered behind her. His massive arms wrapped around her waist and he held her, possessed her, crushing her into him, and he grinned, relishing the struggle.

A cruel, wretched heat, like that of a violent fever you know will take your life after the delirium hits, rolled off his body. As he chanted the next couplet, his hot breath burned her ear.

> "Pretty 'ole thing can hear my sighs,
> But cruel as is, I'll want her thighs."

Kallan fought, digging her bloody fingers into his arm. Amused, he held up his hand in offering and, desperate, she sank her teeth into it. And when she tasted blood, she bit harder. When he chuckled, she bit deeper, and he groaned with pleasure.

> "Pretty 'ole thing could make you moan,
> But cruel as is, she'll make you groan."

He licked the side of her neck as she bucked, holding her with the same vile grin still frozen on his face.

"Nordri."

Ori's voice cut through the cave, ending the limerick immediately. Like warm sap, Ori's voice ignited a flicker of hope in Kallan, but she didn't dare release her teeth from Nordri's hand.

"Let her go."

There was calm in the order, but it wasn't without urgency or threat. Nordri grinned wider and began a new couplet.

> "Easy leave her, love her, want her,
> Sleazy lover, let her wander," he chided.

"Nordri," Ori said, but Nordri chuckled.

The taste of his blood had reached her nerve and Kallan released his hand. Too weak to spit the blood from her mouth, she hung limp in Nordri's clutches.

"She has that look about her." Nordri nodded slightly. "The same look they all get. They want it.

I'll hold her if you'd like a turn." And as quick as that he began again.

"Calling, crying, cursing canter,
Screaming Scryer, can't deflow—"

"Nordri!"

Ori's voice boomed through the black cavern. He fell silent as if Ori's voice had swallowed his song. Kallan heaved against Nordri, panting, desperate for breath. A tear slipped from her eye and fell down her nose to the tip.

"I see," Nordri's slimy voice hissed. Kallan could hear that wretched grin in his words, but it was fading. "You want her for yourself. Just yourself," he yipped. "The king's son always wants for himself!"

His grip tightened, refusing to give her up. Any tighter and he would crush her.

"The giants are about," Ori said darkly, "and we're a long way behind the others."

Nordri froze, holding onto each word expectantly.

"There are worse things than sunlight and snow out here," Ori continued in a heavy voice dripping with boredom. "If someone were to get lost..." He let the word echo. "Damn near impossible for anyone to go back for him." Ori shrugged. "I'm just saying...Damn near impossible."

And as quietly as he had appeared, Ori turned his back, and left Kallan to Nordri's judgment, taking the light with him.

Chapter 38

Olaf, King of the North, gazed from the banks of the sea of the Northern Way tucked away in the fjord. All along this land, the water cut into the coast like an outstretched finger that bent the earth. Throughout the North, mountains rose from the water from nearly every bank and tree, shaping and forming the realm of his forbearers, making a settlement difficult at best with limited farming land. But this village was different.

Within the Throendr Fjord, the wide river Nid snaked around the small settlement of Nidaros, transforming the peninsula into a natural fortress carved out by the river's flow. Flames climbed the early morning sky, rolling over thatch and clay, consuming the village as it spread. Despite skies as clear as the ice, blue water below, a dark cloud had fallen over Nidaros.

Along the docks that lined the beaches at the water's edge, a handful of longboats creaked as they broke beneath their own weight, weakened by the flames that consumed them. Their masts reached toward the sky like outstretched fingers, clawing the air as if desperate to live.

Amid the thatch-roofed houses, screams of women and children mingled with the ringing blades of his men. The fire worm within him purred and he exchanged a satisfied look with Thorer, who nodded toward the village.

Olaf shifted his gaze and saw what exactly Thorer had signaled to. A plump woman, bleeding and spirited, jiggled as she shuffled. She stepped lively, with a bounce he would not have expected from someone of her years. She had tied back her long, blond hair streaked with thick lines of gray and hoisted the skirts of her apron dress higher than what was necessary to walk up the hill where Olaf and Thorer stood.

She pushed her way past the soldiers, ignoring the dying and dead as a large ring of keys tinkled at her waist. Before she could reach them, before she could unleash her temper, Olaf and Thorer turned their backs and started for the small tent pitched a few spans away.

"I am Olga!"

Olaf spun back around on display and pretended to be vaguely curious about the Throendr.

"Wife of Halvard, Son of Sigurd, daughter of the land of Dofrar." Olaf grinned at the tightness in her voice. Olga had clearly done her best to harden the gentle lilt in her voice, but failed.

"Your Majesty." Olaf bowed low, sweeping the ground with the tips of his fingers. He was unusually tall for a son born to the race of a Man. So much so that the point of his domed helmet almost grazed the earth before lifting his eyes back to Olga.

"End your slaughter at once," Olga shouted, unable to mask the waver in her voice.

With a flourish of his scarlet cloak, Olaf looked back to Thorer, who had patiently waited.

"Kill them all," Olaf said with a boredom he was sure Olga heard. "Acts of kindness won't reach the ears of Forkbeard on his high throne in Jutland. And when you find Jarl Hakon, cowering in his corner like the dog he is, bring me his head."

He spoke loudly, ensuring the peasant heard every word over the ocean's waves and the sudden creak of a longboat as it split in two. She needed to understand. They all needed to understand.

Olaf disappeared into his tent with Thorer and grinned at the swishing of Olga's skirts and her haughty steps as she followed.

So predictable, he thought as Olga slapped back the tent's hide flap. Olaf pulled the helmet off his shimmering, blond head: as blond as the legends of Fairhair and Olga gasped. Many often had that reaction, but it never ceased to amuse him.

Olaf passed his helmet to Thorer, who added it to the rest of the armor ornately displayed in the corner between a table of fruits and a desk of maps. In the center of the room, a fire burned.

"Daughter of Dofrar," Olaf said, greeting the Throendr with an air of boredom as he removed his cloak with a flourish and handed it to Thorer.

The warmth of the tent, the glamour of the rich silks and rare, exotic furs did little to deter Olga as she snarled through a guttural hiss.

"Word of your exploits has travelled far," she said, "reaching as far north as Hordaland. They say you seek to force the Empire's god on us!"

An impressed glimmer shone in Olaf's eye.

"That you look to rid us of Odinn and Thor," Olga said. "But we've learned quickly here. You don't seek to take a birthright back from Hakon or impose the Empire's beliefs. Throendalog belongs to Dan's Reach. You target Forkbeard's land."

Olaf studied the woman, surprised at her boldness and her accuracy. He looked long and hard, taking care to examine the woman before him. With the right wording, the right timing, he could pass on the very message he hoped would reach Forkbeard.

It was all he could do not to grin.

"Forkbeard's land *is* my land," Olaf corrected and slid into a wide, wooden chair, intricately hand carved with the finest of details. "His father usurped my throne long before the North was ripped apart to find me."

Olga blushed.

"You're so quick to blame him for the death of your wife," she said, letting on more than she knew.

Olaf stiffened in his chair, not bothering to keep the darkness within from rising as the woman's words cut through the old wound that had never healed.

The woman was right, he thought. *Word has spread.*

Olaf hardened his gaze and forced himself to show no pain at the woman's words. What doubts he had of using her as a messenger vanished as he set his eyes on his target.

"I know my wife," Olaf said, letting the most of his bottled temper show a bit. "Geira was strong and the last of the bloodline to the throne of Vendland. She didn't weaken so suddenly, lacking the will or the strength to deliver our firstborn."

He held his breath.

Olga gasped. "She was with child?"

Olaf shifted an approving glance to Thorer.

"News of her pregnancy reached the ears of Fork-beard," Olaf said. "A month later, Geira died and the throne of Vendland passed to Forkbeard along with Jutland."

"Forkbeard," Olga said. "Then why not declare war on Jutland?" she asked once she recovered her voice. "Why rape the land of your own people?"

Olaf furrowed his face in disapproval.

"Rape is harsh. As your new king, the subjects here are eager to contribute to my campaign if only to ensure their protection from foreign affairs."

"You call murder and scorched earth in the name of your gods a contribution?" Olga asked.

"God," Olaf corrected. "And by forcing my hand with the imperial god, I'll have won the favor of Otto III and the Empire. They pay their endowed well. Svenn Forkbeard won't see this coming. He will lead Jutland into war against Throendalog. I'll have the backing of the Seat. And when Svenn dies, my marriage to Tyra will ensure that the land—"

"—falls to you," Olga said. "You would seek to rule all of the North and Dan's Reach."

The peasant's understanding confirmed the solidity in his plan. He couldn't help but smile.

"One conquest at a time," he said. "Where is the Jarl? What hole does Jarl Hakon cower in?"

"Forkbeard won't stand for this." Olga's voice shook. "He'll draw his attention from Ethelred."

Olaf grinned.

"I do hope so," he said. "But Forkbeard is slow to anger. Even now he sits idle while I'm kept warm between the legs of his sister."

"The people will know," Olga shrieked. "The people will learn."

"I am your rightful king!" Olaf's voice boomed back. "I declare the food you eat, the gods you praise, and the bed-fellows you keep. Now..." He rose to his feet. "Where is your Jarl?"

Olga kept her silence.

"Thorer." Olaf's eyes never left her. "Ready the men for departure."

"In what direction are we heading?" Thorer asked.

361

"Dofrar," Olaf growled and watched the blood drain from Olga's face, leaving her a sickly shade of white beneath the web of aging lines.

With a nod, Thorer conceded, then stopped before carrying out the order.

"And the Seidkonas we found?"

Olaf released Olga from his gaze as he shifted his full attention to Thorer.

"Do any of them carry the pouch?"

Thorer shook his head.

"Not the one you seek."

Olaf's face fell with discouragement.

"Tie them to the banks of the Nid at low tide," Olaf said. "As long as there is breath in me, I will not suffer the Seidr users to live."

Thorer nodded and, in silence, left Olga, wife of Halvard, son of Sigurd, daughter of Dofrar, to the mercy of Olaf.

Chapter 39

Kallan lay listening to her own breath wheeze within her chest somewhere, beyond the world painted black.

"Spriggans sing, across the sea," Kallan breathed and dropped her head to the side. The light was dim.

"And orange," Kallan mused. "And far away."

She shifted her glossy gaze to Nordri.

By the fire, he sat, watching, eagerly waiting for the moment when Ori would walk away. Ori never walked away, not since the night he had found him chanting his rhyme. Occasionally, a verse or two of the dreadful ditty carried through the caves to wake Kallan or lull her to sleep. Always Nordri stared.

Kallan rolled her head away and peered up at the black ceiling. She no longer noticed the bitter tang or the weight of the elding chains or the endless fire that scorched her broken ribs. She was too broken to feel anymore. Deep, thick scabs formed where she laid on the stone the most, and she was always thirsty.

"Forever thirsty."

Kallan watched a drip of water desperately cling to a stalactite overhead.

Her parched lips—swollen, cracked, and bleeding—left her face numb to the beatings Durin and Blainn eagerly provided. Only after her senses shut down to preserve her sanity, after she surrendered all likelihood of survival, did the Dvergar beat the last of the hope from Kallan.

The voices behind the haze were silent. Eventually, they too abandoned Kallan, despite their best efforts. The haze of silver, blue, and white clouded Kallan's mind. There, shapes waxed and waned as they came and went, spilling through the empty, endless room of smooth, silver stone. There, behind the iron wall, images of forgotten memories and ancient voices stirred. It was there Kallan went when she slept, when she slipped into the shadows to hide.

Here, no pain could reach her. Here, Dvergar eyes couldn't find her.

The haze billowed as Kallan moved with ease through the mist. Distorted shadows of forgotten faces peered from a distance where they were the most obscure. Their voices carried through the silver blue like an endless echo, repeating words they once uttered long ago. Like eternal darkness into the endless moonlight, the haze stretched on.

Aimlessly, Kallan wandered wherever the impulse drove her. She passed many hours like this. Never looking back, she roamed the great Void behind her ironclad wall, drifting about, desperate to lose herself in the haze.

For if I were to lose my way, Kallan reasoned, *perhaps I should not return at all to the other side of dreaming.*

It was like this, roaming about as it pleased her, that a glint of silver caught her eye in the shadows ahead where the mist was thinnest. Curious, Kallan glided toward the pale, silver light that glistened through the ice blue white.

Through the mist, Kallan slipped over the cold, polished floors following the gray figure in the distant shadow. What began as an ambiguous shade became a woman standing alone in a beam of pale moonlight where the haze diminished.

Solitary and alone, she stood. A lilac gown hugged her form and flowed to her feet without a blemish or ornament to distract from the subject. Her hair hung in long russet ringlets, as dark as clove flowers, past her waist. Simple elegance encompassed the woman whose high cheekbones and slender figure matched Kallan's perfectly, all but the eyes. Almond eyes with bright rings of gold enclosed black pupils.

Hot, unfallen tears burned Kallan's eyes and clamped her throat closed. The end of her smashed nose burned and she lowered her gaze to the woman's left hand. Black characters encircled the base of the woman's index finger in a ring of Ogham runes. The lines and dashes flowed like webbing, down the back of her hand to and around a tri-corner knot intertwined with a circle. Like a climbing vine, it wove runes around her wrist until an intricate, black bracelet, etched in ancient letterings, had formed.

Kira gave Kallan a soft smile, displaying her perfect, pale face. With burning cheeks, Kallan dropped her eyes to her own bare feet, maimed and calloused from the cave floor. She scrutinized the shredded remnants of her chemise.

"Here she stands," Kallan whispered. "Lorlenalin's queen, Dokkalfr and daughter of Eyolf. Here in my glory, my filth, and rags."

"Kallan."

Her mother's voice, so soft, so clear, as she had heard it long ago, lanced her, choking the breath from her, and only then did Kallan realize she had spoken aloud.

Despite the cuts and bruising, her tangled hair matted with filth from the caves, her blood and vomit, the red, black, and broken limbs that made up her body, Kallan raised her eyes to her mother.

And Kira smiled.

They stared at one another, neither speaking for a long time as Kira studied the woman her child had become and Kallan relearned every strand of hair, every curve, and every movement her mother made.

After a while, Kira furrowed her brow.

"Where is the pendant?" she asked without a hint of a reprimand.

The question weighted Kallan's chest.

"I lost it," Kallan said, lowering her eyes, and every bit of Kallan ached to fall through the mist and hug her. Her mother's golden eyes were as sharp as ever. They had never been any other way.

"And the hunter?" Kira asked, adamant and sincere.

Kallan's shoulders slumped lower. Twice she would disappoint her mother within a single breath.

"I lost him too," Kallan said and looked at her feet.

A tuft of wind blew, spinning a bit of the haze into a mini tornado at her mangled feet.

"Where is it?"

The deep amber voice rolled over Kallan like warm, sweet sap and Kallan looked back to her mother, but all that remained was the pale moonlight beating down at the empty silver-blue shimmering in the mist.

Behind the haze, Ori sat on a slope of flowstone that had poured and hardened from the stalagmite that fastened her chains. He sported his usual leather overcoat and casually, comfortably, rested an arm loosely on one knee. He stayed in the shadows, seemingly indifferent to her appearance.

"My mother's gone," she said, forcing the words from her throat.

If Ori was put off, he didn't show it. Kallan lay where they had dumped her on the floor of the cave, believing she still stood in the haze.

"This will all end if you give them the pouch," Ori said.

Kallan cocked her head, unsure if pity clung to his words. An audible grunt of disbelief escaped her throat. It sounded too much like Gudrun and she made a mental note never to do it again.

"I don't believe that," she said, "and I'd be the greater fool for thinking it."

"You look like you don't believe anyone."

He didn't move, but sat quietly as if waiting for an opportunity to come.

"I shouldn't," Kallan said and looked back to the pale moonlight. The disappointment was visible on her face. From the corner of her eye, Ori stood from his seat on the flowstone. Having learned to associate any movement with pain, she twitched and Ori froze, allowing her security in his distance.

"You don't trust me, do you?" Ori asked.

His large figure in the shadow loomed where the last of the mist swirled and diminished around his boots. She met his black, round eyes, unable to see past the smooth, pale skin and black beard.

"You're one of them," she said. "You're the same."

It was the first time he showed any emotion and the cold, hard calculative stare vanished. Ori held Kallan's gaze for a long time. She pondered the whys and wherefores of his visit and cursed herself for not seeing it sooner.

"Why are you here?" Kallan asked, irate that she hadn't asked this first.

Ori shrugged, closing his eyes briefly as he did so. It stirred a distant memory behind her wall.

"We collect trinkets."

"Lie," she said, suddenly aware that she had been slurring through the entire conversation and immediately made the effort to stop.

Ori studied Kallan's eyes.

"It doesn't suit you."

"Lie again." Kallan spoke more boldly. The haze was clearing.

"No." Ori shook his head and pointed to the shackles she had forgotten were there. At once, her wrists were heavy again.

"The chains," he said. "They don't suit you."

"Don't you have someone else's dreams to invade?" Kallan asked, growing more irritated with his presence.

"You think this is a dream?"

"I know it is," she said.

Anger was flooding back as energy surged through her. It engulfed her as if taking in a long, deep breath of fresh air. On suspicion alone, she reached her consciousness down to her core, and, like the dragons of lore, the Seidr sparked to life.

"Why are you here?" she whispered, realizing he had evaded her question. Her voice was strong, though raw from disuse.

A grin was his answer, a kind grin that stretched the face beneath his beard.

"You haven't changed at all, Kallan," he said with a deep sigh. "And you were right." He pointed to the chains and solemnly added before walking away, "Sometimes, the dragons are real."

"*Kallan!*" A voice called through the mist somewhere behind her iron wall. "*The dragons are real!*"

It came from far away.

The high, soft twitters of a girlish giggle mingled with forgotten squeals and laughter.

"*There he is, Ori! There the dragon is!*"

"Ori," Kallan whispered as the voices faded with the haze.

One last time, Ori gazed at the elding chains. The two links that trailed from Kallan's wrists were free from the single run. The bowl that burned with the bitter tang lay upturned on the floor.

In the darkest corner, at the root of despair, a fire erupted to life. Long abandoned hope awakened, flooding Kallan with a bloodlust only Dvergar blood could sate.

Ori, Nordri, Durin, Blainn, and Motsognir.

If she was going to make a run for it, they would all have to be down, and once she started running, she would not be able to stop, not for a while, at least.

Kallan stood on shaking legs, reminding her that the drug was still clearing her system. She collected the chains in her hand and charged for Ori. Swinging the links down, she smashed them into the back of his head. He was down before she had time to study the room.

Vindictiveness in its rarest form exploded to life as Kallan located Nordri, who sat by the fire alone. She imagined that sick smile of his and fired a double shot of pent-up Seidr from both palms. He fell before he had time to reach for his axe.

Not bothering to watch Nordri fall, Kallan ran in a direction she guessed would take her to the mouth of the cave, already pooling the next ball of Seidr in both palms as Blainn came at her with his axe, but her inhibitions were gone.

Lunging ahead, Kallan threw herself toward Blainn, stopping so close they could have touched. Before his axe came down, Kallan grabbed his face with her left hand, his chest with her right, and fired her Seidr through him.

The blast propelled his body back. He was dead before he hit the wall behind him. With the mouth of the cave in sight, Kallan collected her next round of Seidr and grabbed the chains at her wrists.

So close to the end, Kallan sprinted, battling back the urge to vomit. With every step, pain gored her gut. Fire ate her legs and burned her chest. From the mouth of the cave, Durin emerged, each hand gripping an axe.

While channeling the Seidr through the links, Kallan whipped the elding chains and Durin dropped beneath the lash. Infused with Seidr, the metal whips lashed the air. Swinging the axes toward her feet, Durin lunged. Kallan leapt back, snapping her chains as Seidr flowed from her palms down into the links.

She grazed his back and Durin howled. Her final lash flogged his chest, and Durin fell. At the cave's end, the clear night sky beckoned her. A breeze blew and the Nordic wind swept her face as she stepped from the stifling Hel of the caves.

Hope engulfed her, easing every fire with the cold, sweet air and the fresh winds, but before she could feel soft grass beneath her bleeding, broken feet, the handle of an axe splintered the back of her head and sent pricks of light through her vision.

Before Kallan hit the ground unconscious, she knew she was no longer in Alfheim.

Chapter 40

Darkness clung to Kallan's skin. Like a disease, it devoured her, suffocating her and sucking out the light a lifetime of laughing beneath the sun had soaked in. It weakened her as she lay dying in the darkness.

A distant beat drummed the silence. One. Two. One. Two. Kallan counted as she lay as still as her breath would allow. The agony rang in her shattered nose and she realized the drumming was her own pulse pounding her face.

She tried to open her eyes, but the swelling had forced them shut, keeping her submerged in the darkness. Unable to shudder, she remained paralyzed by the pain, taking in every ache that spread from the tips of each finger to the core where her Seidr recoiled. And in every breath, she wished for death when the darkness would take her.

Fire poured through her insides. Kallan didn't wince. She didn't shudder. She didn't flinch. Her body was too broken.

A boot kicked her over, forcing the stale, stagnant air to rush into her lungs as the cave floor scraped her back. With much effort, she managed to open a single eye. A sliver of orange pulled back the black, and Durin stood, cursing, in what she could only imagine was a slew of guttural slurs that suggested he had been hitting the black root brew hard.

She saw his mouth move, but heard nothing. Her eye wandered to the stalactites clinging to the roof of the cave.

Durin landed another kick.

Kallan gasped this time and studied the limestone tips above her as her body shook against the pain she could no longer feel. Color flowed through the stalactites glistening in the fire light.

Durin's foot stomped her hand. She felt a snap and he ground his heel into her smallest finger. A tear rolled from her eye. The orange light gleamed off the minerals embedded in the cave wall. Durin's boot slammed into the side of her head. She felt nothing.

Shadows danced against the stone, awakening her to the hidden treasures buried within the earth. It breathed and moved with the land, its heart concealing a Seidr of its own, forever dormant, waiting forgotten in the bowels of the world. All who knew of it had passed on to become part of it. All who lived had forgotten generations ago.

This was the Seidr Gudrun had spoken of, the Seidr that mingles and flows, the Seidr that is there. Living and breathing, it moves. Until now, Kallan had failed to see.

Durin had stopped. Over her, he stood seething with drunken breath. Curious, Kallan lolled her head to the side where she could see. His face twisted as he screamed words she could not hear. Kallan relaxed and took in each breath. No longer fighting to breathe, she welcomed her death.

His lips moved and he spat, but Kallan didn't hear. She watched Motsognir pull on Durin's shoulder. They were shouting for a long while before they stopped. With flask in hand, Durin took a swig. Droplets of liquid—so dark a red they looked black—dripped into his beard, where he left them.

Behind him, Nordri watched with the same sick grin, now mingled with darker thoughts. His shredded tunic hung from his shoulder, revealing his chest she had seared with her flame.

In the shadows, at a distance, Ori stood silent. His eyes, as pensive as ever, fixed on hers, blanketed and empty, unreadable, as always. If he heard what Motsognir was saying, he didn't acknowledge it, engrossed instead with Kallan's mangled body dumped carelessly on the ground.

She didn't move to communicate. She didn't try. She didn't care. She rolled her head back to the stalactites that greeted her where the Seidr glittered and danced in the Dvergar's fire light.

Cruel, cold hands clutched her wrists, forcing her gaze from the rivers of Seidr. Desiring her final breath, she watched as Nordri pulled a ring of keys from his leather belt. He located a silver-black elding key, and fumbled with the chain that bound her to the floor.

With indifference for her broken, bleeding body, he violently shoved his arms beneath her. Each jolt sent splinters screaming through her and, when he stood to lift her, he jostled her harshly. Pain surged through her and the world fell dark once more.

Silence.

Kallan lay, unmoving on the floor. Her breathing rasped against her dry throat. She tried to remember time and failed. Pain reared its merciless claws, digging its way as it burrowed through her, but she didn't move.

Tears flowed in their stead and Kallan stayed in the darkness, waiting to die.

A hand brushed her face. She tried to flinch and failed. Long fingers, gentle fingers, cupped her head and she relaxed, accepting the pain that followed.

Cold and wet flowed over her dry, cracked lips. They parted with relief, and she gasped. Water sloshed mercifully into her mouth, quenching the fire burning there and she gulped hungrily for the drink given to her.

The water stopped, allowing her a chance to breathe. The moment she stopped to catch her breath, the thirst returned stronger than before. Whoever showed her mercy saw her need, and again allowed the water to enter her mouth.

She drank, but not enough to have her fill.

The water ceased and a gentle hand lifted her from the hard stone. She needed to know. Forcing her one good eye open, she saw the faint, orange light of Ori's lantern. Relief flooded his eyes, and he smiled.

"W—Where," she said.

It was the first sound she had uttered in days. The word ripped her dry throat, sending her body into a fit of convulsions. Ori tightened his grip, holding her body still. He waited until the coughing subsided before he answered.

"Sleeping," Ori said. "They all are sleeping now."

"Why?"

"You really don't remember," Ori said. "Do you?"

Knowing she couldn't answer, he didn't pry further.

He released a deep sigh and once more submitted the water, letting the few droplets run from the cup he held to her lips. Kallan gasped and he gave her a moment to catch her breath again.

"Motsognir makes no plans to feed you until Svartálfaheim. I know how long it's been since last you ate, since you drank." He shook his head. "You won't make it that long."

She didn't answer, but studied the gentle eyes the others lacked. Only after her vision wandered did he speak again, this time in a hurried tone, quieter than before.

"Kallan."

She returned her attention to him.

"I can not help you again," he said. "They credit your escape to your skills. But a second attempt won't wield such luck. They've abandoned your health to the generosity of Durin, whose brother you've killed, and are no longer making use of the drug. There is talk of letting Nordri..." Ori couldn't finish the thought.

"If you make it alive to Svartálfaheim," he said, "Motsognir plans to kill you there. If you die on the road to Svartálfaheim..." Ori shook his head again and gulped. "It's all the same to him."

"Why...tell." The two words clawed their way through her throat and she stifled another cough.

Ori laid her back to the cave floor and took up his lantern before standing.

"Because," he said. "Sometimes the dragons are real."

The last of the lantern's light faded, swaying with each step he took, and left her alone in the darkness.

Lost and broken, Kallan laid alone on the empty floor of the cave, abandoned to the mercy of a vengeful hate turned berserk that brewed inside of Durin. She saw the hatred with every inebriated fit of anger he exercised.

378

Ori had been right. There was no need for the drug anymore. The pain supplied by Durin's rage was her new drug, and he was more than eager to administer it.

Shadows from their lanterns came and went, but the darkness was constant. Each cave she woke in looked like the last, unique only by the assortment of stalactites and stalagmites and stench that ate her skin. Pain and shadow remained her only companions, pushing her deeper into obscurity. And when the voice had long abandoned her, when Kallan decided to succumb to their wishes, she closed her eyes and surrendered to death.

It was there, in the darkest shadows of the deepest caverns, that his voice found her.

"What have they done to you, princess?"

Chapter 41

Blood caked Kallan's hair, gluing chunks to her battered face. What little covered her body was as shredded and black as the rest of her. Fighting to keep his arm steady, Rune slid a hand behind her head and attempted to pull back a clump of hair that had dried to her shattered eye. She breathed, but barely, and moved, jerking as if too broken to utter the screams inside. Tenderly, he took her mangled hand in his and, although she turned her head to see, he doubt she saw anything at all.

Biting down on his finger, Rune held back a wave of screams, biting until he tasted blood. And the rage, it boiled, and the hate, it consumed. Gently, he laid Kallan back to the cave floor. Too near death to cry out, Kallan omitted a feeble breath he could only assume was a cry.

Rune moved a hand to his hilt, and raised his gaze from the shadows. The Beast was up and pacing within him despite no Seidr on which to feed. Three, he saw as he made his way into the cave.

Two by the fire. One by the exit.

With movement like water, he notched an arrow, inhaled, took aim. He released his breath and then the arrow.

In the time it took the larger of the two to fall back with an arrow secured in his skull, the second stood with a sick smile that fueled the Beast in Rune. Before the Sick One could take up his axe, Rune's bow met his face, knocking him end over end.

From the exit, the largest, who Rune could only assume was the leader, shouted something that sent the Sick One scrambling from the fire toward the exit. Already, Rune had the next arrow notched. Inhale. Breathe. Release. The arrow pierced the thigh of the Sick One, who screamed while the Leader charged.

Unsheathing his sword, Rune raised the blade and met the axe, shattering his weapon in two. On the downswing, the Dvergr fell into the weight, and Rune brought up the broken stub, goring the Leader in the gut where he left it in time to notch another arrow. He took aim and released. This one speared the Sick One's spine.

Howling, the Sick One arched against the shaft. Before Rune could ready another arrow, a hand fell to his shoulder and Rune met the Leader's stare. The Beast bellowed as lines of Shadow siphoned through him. Like venom, it seeped into Rune's flesh, ripped through his Seidr, and tethered itself to the light stored within the Beast.

The Shadow pulled from Rune's core, drawing out the Seidr the Beast had devoured. With it, Rune felt his own strength ebb. He buckled beneath the Dvergr's hand as if the Leader sucked the very life from him.

The bow slid from his fingers as Rune's legs slowly gave out. Still, the Leader maintained his hold as the Shadow rose up and engulfed him.

Move.

The Beast roared and thrashed. The Shadow enclosed the fire and light, taking all life around it. Until, upon his knees, Rune found the hilt of the daggers he had picked off Bergen. Fighting back the Shadow, Rune lunged. With a dagger in each hand, he sank the blades into the Leader's sides.

The Dvergr coughed. The stub of the sword still hung from his gut. Rune gave another shove, burying the daggers deeper into the Leader's sides until the hand slid from his shoulder and the Shadow retracted, severing the ties to the Seidr.

Gasping, Rune fell to his knees.

Nausea accompanied the spinning room. The Beast within him lay, heaving on the ground as if drained its life. Rune forced a knee up and waited for the wave of sick to pass. The Sick One whimpered and Rune looked up. Still alive, the Dvergr dragged himself toward the door, his body too wounded to work.

With the back of his hand, Rune wiped the sweat from his brow and found his feet under him. The Sick One groaned.

The distant plink of dripping water carried through the cave as if counting down the steps to death's door.

One. Two.

Rune pulled Kallan's dagger from his belt.

Drip. The Sick One whimpered.

Rune's boots crunched the cave floor.

With a hand fisted into the Dvergr's hair, Rune slid the blade across the Sick One's throat, leaving the sickly smile forever frozen in his eyes.

Distant roars of the giants merged with the howling winds as Rune's breath punched the cold night air, forming puffs of clouds in the storm. Specks of snow obstructed his view.

He afforded a glance to Kallan. Unconscious, she hung limp in his arms as she swayed with each step that crunched through the thin slate of ice on the snow. Her swollen eyes and broken nose distorted her face. The rags she wore did little to cover most of her, leaving her dangerously exposed to the elements.

Over sheets of sleet and snow, the cold burned his lungs, adding a chill, he feared, that would stay with him for days. He attempted to alternate breathing from his nose to mouth, but the cold coated his

383

insides, freezing his air passages as the snow swallowed his shins.

The winds sliced Rune's arms as if the snowflakes were blades. Desperate to shield her from the storm, he hugged Kallan tighter. The wind screamed and, with a start, Rune stumbled, mistaking the shriek of the wind for memories he heard in his head.

The Sickly One crawling for the door who never made it. The blood still covered Rune's hands. He hadn't bothered wiping it off. There had been no time.

Rune tightened his hold on Kallan, hugging her closer to his own thin tunic in hopes of shielding her from the storm. She wouldn't survive the cold. He narrowed his eyes against the sharp sting of the snow, but saw nothing for miles but black.

"Ljosalfr!"

The command cut through the wind, stopping Rune in the snow. Slowly, he turned back toward the cave where he had just emerged, carrying the Dokkalfar's queen.

Tall and pale and buried beneath a mesh of beard, a lone Dvergr stood. His large, leather overcoat fell to his knees where it settled onto the surface of the snow. Rune's heart pounded his chest, increasing the amount of breaths he drew as he calculated the distance between he and the Dvergr. Kallan's dagger hung out of reach at his waist.

"I'm not here for you," the Dvergr spoke over the screaming wind that forced him to push out every breath against the gale. "I'm here for her."

Rune tightened his hold onto Kallan.

"I can kill you just as quic—" Rune said.

"She'll die up here like that," the Dvergr shouted over Rune's threat.

"Based on her condition," Rune said, "I doubt very much you care."

The storm was worsening, but neither moved.

"Here," the Dvergr said and extended a large bundle wrapped in leather.

The wind cut the air between them, filling that space with groans. Rune looked him over. The Dvergr could be hiding anything within the folds of the overcoat.

"If I was going to kill you," the Dvergr said, "I would have done so when your back was turned."

Without the luxury to stand in the cold and weigh his options, Rune decided to move. With long, cautious strides, he closed the space between them, stopping just out of a sword's reach.

The bundle hit the snow with a muffled slump and the Dvergr shifted his arm, startling Rune into a retreat.

Cursing himself for being so foolish, Rune moved to run, but before he could take a step, the Dvergr pulled off his large, black overcoat lined with thick, black fur, and dropped it over Kallan's near naked, frozen body.

With a second flourish, the Dvergr brandished a sword, sheath and all. Silver filigree and black opals, the largest of which was a pommel, encrusted a black elding steel hilt. The retracted light reflected off the

385

snow, adding a magnificent shimmer, the likes of which Rune had never seen before.

"I'll start them on the roads toward Vestfold," the Dvergr said. The warning pulled Rune's ear. "I'll keep them there for as long as I can. That should clear the southern roads to Viken for you."

Rune forced his gaze from the sword and studied the deep black of the Dvergr's eyes.

So much like Bergen's, he thought.

"Please," the Dvergr said. "Keep her alive."

Waves of relief and gratitude filled Rune, mingling with a hatred that boiled over at the sight of Kallan's condition.

Before Rune could spit in his eye or thank him, the Dvergr placed the sword on Kallan and, without coat or weapon, the Dvergr backed away several paces then turned.

In silence, he vanished into the darkness, leaving the bundle where it lay in the mountain's snow.

Chapter 42

Kallan stirred at the unmistakable hush of rain. The rancid stench of the Dvergar was gone. In its place, the soft, sweet scent of lightly chilled earth engulfed her senses. The fire popped and Kallan jerked awake, opening a single eye.

A dilapidated shack suspended the remains of a low ceiling that barely provided rudimentary shelter. One full wall and half of a second had rotted away, leaving much of the bowed ceiling suspended by derelict corner posts and weathered wall planks secured to the floorboards where she lay.

Kallan curled the tips of her fingers against the grains of a wooden, weathered plank. A fire in all its wonderful collection of smells of smoke, dry earth, and charred wood mingled with the delicious scent of roasted grouse.

Her belly tightened with hunger and a cool breeze hit the ground rolling. It swept up and over her body, sending a gentle chill through her. Light of the mid-day sun shone through the rains.

She had to work to focus her one eye on the clear, white rain that fell like sheets onto a variety of wild ferns peppered with hardened tundra. It rolled like the sea, blanketed in crimson, orange, and yellow. The foliage had grown, spreading wild into the shelter through the mostly missing walls. An arm's length away, a single tundra flower grew and she stared, mesmerized by its simplicity.

The fire crackled, drawing Kallan's attention to Rune, who sat studying her with eyes too dark to read. He didn't falter when she glanced at him or when she looked back to the light, lost in thought to the caves.

The bitter tang that had dulled her senses and made her indifferent to the beatings was gone. She could feel everything now, and began to assess the damage. More ribs were cracked, fractured, and shattered than were whole. Her nose had been broken and recently reset. Crushed into powder, the smallest finger of her left hand distended into her signet ring. Swelling forced her right eye closed, significantly limiting her vision. She could hardly breathe, but, as much as it hurt to move, it hurt more to be still.

Attempting to stand, Kallan shifted her stiff legs, but something thick and heavy restricted her movement. She glanced down and hot anger devoured her insides. Splayed over her body, on top of a blanket, the leather overcoat lined with fur lay.

Ori.

Kallan twisted her face. Something between hate and rage grew and she bit the corner of her bottom lip as she fought back the urge to cry. Upon careful inspection, she discovered that her new warden had taken the liberty of stripping off the remnants of her chemise and replaced her clothes with a heavy, green woolen tunic that loosely hung from her shoulders to her knees. A pair of plain trousers, too large for any woman, extended well past her ankles and Rune had obviously washed the first layer of grime from her skin.

Despite her battered body, overall, she was comfortable and warm.

Kallan shifted again to stand, forcing Rune to emit a syllable that sounded too much like a botched protest. She stumbled and fell, breaking her fall on her crushed finger. Like a curtain, her hair fell, shielding her face from Rune.

Anger sent tremors through her.

Each bruise that covered her, each cut that burned, sent wave after wave of agony that seemed to start at the side of her hand. She bit her lip, quelling her anger and arousing the hate the Dvergar had seeded.

Memories clawed at her head, of the pain, of the darkness, of the nightmare she had endured for so long. Tears burned her eyes as a giant wave of hate washed over her, dragging her into the darkest-most fathoms of abhorrence where vengeance brewed.

Kallan's body shook against the silent screams, making her aware of every ache the Dvergar had inflicted. A greater loathing settled as she ached to scream, to lash out, and cry, but no Dvergar sat before her. Only Rune who sat silently with her, oblivious of the desecration she endured.

Kallan waited to speak until she could slow her breath and ease her rage.

"Where am I?" she gasped, careful to keep her face hidden behind her hair.

Sound scraped her throat and she shook, coughing on the words. Worry enclosed her mind as she drew in long, deep breaths, forcing herself at ease.

"Where," she growled again, and lifted her eyes to Rune. Tears burned the back of her throat.

"Upplond," Rune said. "As of yesterday."

His voice was like sweet honey and assured her the last of the caves were behind her, and she hated him for it.

Kallan gasped and her good eye widened at the rising sick.

"Midgard?"

Rune nodded. "Drink this," he said shoving a tankard at her before she could speak further.

Too weak to object, Kallan accepted the tankard of hot tea that soothed while she drank. It flowed down her throat, coating the muscle with the familiar sweetness of black currant tea. She coughed.

"Where is Astrid?" she asked.

"Safe," he answered. "Again."

Kallan drank.

The liquid hit her belly, immediately flipping it in on itself. She fought back the rising nausea as Rune rotated the multiple skewers of roasted grouse over the fire and her stomach clenched for food.

"Before yesterday..." Her throat clamped shut against the words. "Where was I?"

The pause that followed confirmed Rune didn't want to tell her.

"Jotunheim," he replied.

The single word dowsed her back with a chill. Kallan shuddered and forced the next words out.

"You went to Gunir." The words dripped with resentment. "Why did you come back?" she asked, lifting her eyes from her curtain of hair.

"Bergen went to Gunir," Rune corrected. "It was he the Dvergar followed."

He removed a spear of meat and passed her the smallest one, which she devoured within moments, easing one cramp in her stomach as another, more prominent, cramp doubled in objection.

"By the time I caught up to you, they were preparing for their descent into Svartálfaheim," Rune said through a mouthwatering slice of grouse. "You've been unconscious since."

While she attempted to process his story, Rune took a moment to look over her condition.

"I reset your nose and bound your ribs," he said. "Several of them are broken. Most are cracked. Your eye..." Rune trailed off. "I am no healer and Geirolf isn't here. I did what I could."

Kallan dabbed at the swollen flesh around her eye that felt strangely empty.

"Your finger was smashed," he said. "I did my best to splint it, but found nothing in the bags or your pouch to help much."

Kallan looked to the smallest finger of her left hand and raised the bandaged mess. After inspecting it, she knelt back on her makeshift bed. Her thoughts drifted and Rune gave her a moment of silence before beginning the plethora of questions he must have waited days to ask.

"Did they tell you what they wanted?" Rune asked.

"Repeatedly," she whispered. "Where is my pouch?"

She could see the reservation stay his hand. After a moment, Rune turned to the leather bag behind him, exposing the hilt of an elding blade encrusted with fine jewels that drew her attention.

"Where did you get that?" Kallan said. Her voice was barely a breath.

Rune didn't answer.

She tightened her jaw, repressing the countless questions that came as Rune pulled the pouch of amadou from the bag of supplies. With her good hand, Kallan snatched the pouch.

"I already emptied it of whatever herbs I could identify," Rune said. "There wasn't much."

Kallan shook as she shuffled the contents, pushing her way past potion packets and herbs until her fingers clasped Idunn's apple. The shimmering fruit with golden skin glistened like the opals in the sword behind Rune.

Sinking her teeth into its flesh, Kallan ravished the apple in a few mouthfuls. After the smooth fruit slid down her throat, Kallan focused and muttered a charm as she reached for her Seidr. She was elated to find it there, intact, eager, and readily waiting. The Seidr flowed and mingled with the Seidr from the apple, repairing the damage done as it moved through her.

Muscle fibers re-wove themselves and bones re-calcified, returning to their original state. Bruises vanished as the clots broke down, urging her blood to flow. Her heart pounded her chest with a zealous vigor. As Kallan took her fifth bite, the ligaments and nerves in her finger re-knitted themselves, and fluids restored her eye.

Free of the pain that had limited each breath, Kallan fell to her hands as the last rib mended itself. She gasped against the sudden rush of air and drew in long, deep breaths that fully expanded her unbruised lungs, leaving her lightheaded.

When she found her breath again, the only evidence that remained of her captivity was the filth of the cave that still clung to her iridescent skin.

"How?" Rune asked.

Kallan looked up. Silence and cold confirmation stared from behind Rune's eyes.

Kallan scoffed.

"You brought me here. You took me from my city. Were it not for you, I would still be in Lorlenalin.

393

Were it not for you, my father would still be alive. And you want me to answer how."

The rain fell in a constant sheet. Striking the ground with a persistent patter that did well to drown out unwanted thoughts. Free of the incessant pain, Kallan turned her eyes to the elements and scrambled to her feet, taking care to secure the pouch around her waist while she did so. Eager for the taste of her restored freedom, Kallan leapt from the blanket and overcoat, scrambled her way out of the dilapidated lean-to, and stepped into the clean, cool rain.

She pulled each breath deep in her lungs and lifted her face to the sky, welcoming the shower as it washed the filth from her skin. Like tiny red rivers, blood and black streamed from her hair and face and pooled, down her body to her bare feet, free of the lacerations, calluses, and scabs from the cave floors.

The soft earth beneath her feet was kinder than any night she had spent among the Dvergar. The winds of Midgard blew colder than she ever remembered in Alfheim and the rain seemed tainted somehow, weighted with a grief she couldn't place.

Closing her eyes, Kallan pulled from her core. The Seidr flooded to each limb, mingling with each fiber as it twisted and wove its way through her, restoring her very cells to their beginnings. The last of the pain vanished, nurturing the life that shone with renewed energy in its stead. When Kallan opened her eyes, her plans were clear, her path decided.

"I won't stay here," Kallan called through the rain.

Rune stood. She was more than vaguely aware of his heightened guard, alert and ready to leap the moment she moved.

"Where is Astrid?" she called over the rushing rain not bothering to lower her face from the skies. She expected him not to answer at all and jumped when he spoke.

"There's a lake at the base of this hillside," he answered. "He waits by the river that flows from the north."

Inexplicable anger surged, and Kallan shook with the effort it took to contain it.

"You left him?"

"You had a fever," Rune answered. "I couldn't afford to keep you in the rain and there are no shelters by the river, nor could Astrid make the climb. He's hidden and safe. I checked on him not an hour ago."

Kallan trembled with rage that pulsed through her. She felt her Seidr pooling, and clutched her fists at her sides.

"How many days from Alfheim?" she asked, indifferent to the rain.

"Come out of the rain, Kallan," Rune bade coldly.

Kallan dropped her face from the sky. Rune's hand rested casually on the hilt of her dagger buried in the waist of his trousers. His face, forever hardened on hers, was as unreadable as always.

"How many days?" she repeated.

"Fourteen."

A sudden sick tightened her stomach.

"H—H— how long was I—?"

"Twelve days."

Her head spun as it tried to find a way to understand that her endless captivity had lasted only twelve days.

"Twelve days," she breathed.

Twelve days without sunlight. Twelve days without rain. It felt like twelve months.

"Come out of the rain, Kallan."

"I'm leaving," she said, overwhelmed with the want to run.

"And where will you go?" Rune asked. "The Dvergar will suspect the road to Alfheim. They'll swarm those roads, hunting you. We go north, through the Dofrarfjell," he said.

He wasn't asking.

"To Nidaros?" she asked.

"Hakon is Jarl there," Rune explained. "My brother and I traveled this road decades ago and formed alliances with Lade. We can get a boat in Nidaros and sail around the fjords. We'll be in Alfheim in eight days."

Kallan didn't move.

"I'm going south."

"You won't make it," Rune said.

"I am not your prisoner!" Her rage swelled with the Seidr in her hands, holding back as she remembered the last time she hit him with Seidr. "I'll go where I like!"

Rune drew in a deep breath as if pacing his irritation. "The land is different here," he said. "The tundra is littered with jagged rocks. For miles, large, white stones are scattered throughout the land. The terrain is rough. The forests are thick and if we venture too far west, the land will drop into the sea...sometimes without warning. The wrong path could leave us doubling back for weeks. There are marshlands in the east that make it impossible for a horse. It will be slow moving, slower with a horse."

"You don't know what Astrid can do."

"You don't know the area, Kallan," Rune said.

"I've traveled Midgard before. I will go alone."

In that instant, Rune was on her, slamming her into a tree and pinning her back with an arm across her collar as he clamped her wrist.

"You don't know what you are up against here, Seidkona," he said. "The monsters here are nothing like our own."

"I've been gone too long," she said.

"We both have." He gave a look that dared her to argue that point. "But Midgard has its own wars and we are currently standing in the middle of them. An unwanted king has seized this land. He comes with a law he enforces in the name of his own gods. He seeks to challenge Asgard, hunting the Seidkona as he goes."

Kallan stopped fighting for the moment, frozen by his words.

"He hunts Seidkona?" she whispered. She shuddered against the tree, eager to break Rune's neck.

"Your Seidr is not a weapon here," he said. "It will betray you and if they find you, if they know you are here, they will not let you live long enough to make it to Alfheim. They will follow you to the borders and will not stop until you're dead."

The rain fell down their faces, coating them in the drab gray that blended them into the surrounding wood.

Rune sighed. For the moment, he had her attention.

"All roads leading south to Viken are crawling with his men," Rune said.

Kallan's face twisted back, sending her into a fit that impelled her to attack. She wanted to run, to scream, to cry, and hated Rune all the more for taking her from Lorlenalin.

"We must head north...across the Dofrarfjell."

All at once, Kallan slammed her knee up into Rune, who gasped through the piercing anguish of electrical pulses that radiated up to his lower back. Unable to breathe, he clutched his groin and fell to the ground on his knees. Yanking her wrist free, Kallan snagged her dagger from his belt and stepped around the heap that was Rune.

"I follow no enemies," Kallan said, brandishing her blade. After snatching the blanket from her bed and doubling back for one of the bags, she began the descent down the mountain's side.

A fire burned in Rune's silver-blue eyes. Grumbling beneath his breath, he forced himself to his feet. It was slow going as he released a series of short breaths and waited for the majority of the sharp pain to subside to the dull throb that would follow him for hours.

"It's going to be like this, is it," he grunted and, taking in a long breath, he gazed at the trail where Kallan had ventured. Her head cocked high with confidence only confirmed she would be harder to take down than he thought.

"Alright then," he said and, following suit, bounded down the mountain path behind her.

Chapter 43

Kallan plodded through the rain, down the mountain's side with little thought to the road ahead. Anger stifled her most reasonable thoughts as the steep slope forced Kallan along faster than she had intended. Each jarring footfall barely gripped the ground as she clomped about in trousers too big for her.

She slipped twice, caught her foot on a sharp stone more than once, and kicked up a roost of willow grouse that drummed off. At the base of the mountain, Kallan scuffed to a pre-mature halt and gasped.

Within a fortnight, the warmest of summer days had ended in Alfheim and the late summer harvests had rolled in. Bold reds and gold painted the land and stretched from the end of her path to a river that drained from a wide, blue lake. The wide waters curved with the land and vanished in the distance behind the mountains. The mountains seemed to rise out of the land at every turn and pulled the valley floor.

Rune had been right to leave Astrid. White jagged rocks covered the terrain, contrasting the reds, yellows, and greens of the tundra grasses as if someone had randomly dumped them there. Some stones were small enough to fill the palm of her hand, while others were magnificent in size, nearly twice as tall as Rune.

The ground was like one giant sheet of stone that stretched beyond the mountains. Barren tundra grass blanketed the rocky earth in places, giving the illusion that the ground was soft beneath the red tundra willow and reindeer lichen. White tundra cotton and pink arctic bell heather provided frequent patches of color to the various moss and grass and stone. Lush greens of the tundra had thickened, welcoming the harvest with vibrant reds and vivid oranges. Sunset yellows and white stone painted the tundra in an overall striking display against the gray of endless rain.

Behind Kallan, thick clouds pushed between the mountain's peaks and spilled into the valleys like a vast suspended waterfall, wrapping the land in a wet chill she took in with every breath. Beside the river's bend, along the harsh tundra, Astrid grazed peaceably alongside a large span of purple mountain saxifrage. The red and black of his coat greatly contrasted the scene.

"Hardly hidden," she muttered, but grinned nevertheless.

At the sight of her dearest friend, anxiety lifted from her shoulders. She wiped the rain from her face and continued down the path to Astrid's pasture.

Beside him, Kallan buried her face into Astrid's black mane and brushed her hand down his long neck, breathing in the sweet, lingering scent of Alfheim and hay. The scent of home was almost gone and she swiped at her eyes, irritated at the tears that burned there as Astrid nudged her pouch.

Moments later, the stallion happily crunched the apple as Kallan gazed up the mountain. Following along her path through the throbbing handicap she had bestowed upon him, Rune trudged in the rain down to meet her and came to stand before her, both soaked in the rain. Rune extended his hand.

"What?" she asked.

"The dagger," he said over the downpour.

Making her intentions clear, Kallan flicked her wrist and summoned a flame that danced undaunted by the weather in her palm. "Not a chance."

"I don't suppose you'd be open to a truce," he suggested, a smile cocked on the corner of his mouth.

A burst of flame left her hand. Rune reached out and snatched the flame, drawing it in as he had before.

Kallan's mouth fell agape as she watched Rune draw on her Seidr with ease until she severed the Seidr, leaving Rune unscathed.

"No, then," he said and, as if with all his might, he launched himself at Kallan, plowing into her stomach and sending them both to the ground in the rain and the wet and the mud.

He was on her, restraining her arms at the wrists over her head as she fought.

"Get off," she howled, firing off another stream of Seidr that Rune caught with his hand and drew in.

"You want to go home?" Rune shouted.

Kallan twisted and squirmed.

"You want to get out of this forsaken land the Dvergar dragged you into?" Rune said as Kallan bucked beneath him.

"I will not follow," Kallan said. "My home is south and to the south I will go and I'll not let a spoiled, Ljosalfr prince stop me."

"If we travel apart, we risk not making it back to Alfheim at all," Rune said.

"I'll go my own way, to the south and Viken," Kallan said.

"The Dvergar are on that road, Kallan," Rune said, silencing her tantrum.

Kallan stopped moving, unable to mask the horror splayed upon her face.

"If you take the southern roads, you will place yourself right where they want you: right where they expect you to go," he shouted over the pouring rain.

His grip remained adamant, ensuring she wouldn't move until he had his say.

"Come with me to Nidaros," Rune said. "I will speak to the Jarl there and escort you home myself."

The rain splattered the ground.

"To Lorlenalin," she said.

"To Alfheim," he said.

Kallan stiffened in protest beneath him, but she didn't dare press her luck just yet.

"And you'll show me the way?" she asked.

"I will show you the way." He nodded.

"And I will ride alongside you through the land of Men and their wars?" Kallan asked, the fear clear in her eyes. "To sail with you on to Alfheim and away from the Dvergar?"

"As far as I can take you away from them, for as long as it takes to get home," Rune vowed.

"Until Alfheim," Kallan said, making it clear she had no intentions of following him one-step further toward Gunir.

"Until Alfheim," he said tightly.

Kallan relaxed and, the moment her guard dropped, Rune grabbed the dagger, wrestling it with ease from her grip, before he stood and pulled her to her feet.

He shifted to move and return to Astrid, but Kallan tightened her grip, refusing to relinquish his hand. Through the rain, Rune held her gaze.

"Give me my dagger," Kallan said.

Rune chuckled, and tightened his grip on her soft hand in reply.

"Not a chance in Hel."

404

First Midgard, then Alfheim, Rune thought. *After that, we can bark, bicker, and bite over which road to take.*

The Beast that had awakened hungrily for Kallan's Seidr now purred contentedly, sated for the moment. Alone, Rune started back up the path in the rain. Ten minutes to collect the camp, extinguish the fire, and erase the trail. Ten minutes was too long to leave any Dokkalfr alone.

"If you make me have to hunt you, princess," he called through the rain. "I will bind you when I find you."

Rune grinned as Kallan stiffened her spine and crinkled her nose, taking extra care to ensure he saw it before he turned.

"And grab the saxifrage for the road, the purple flowers at your feet," he said, bounding up the rest of the path. "It's edible."

Kallan burrowed her eyes into the back of his head before staring at the large span of purple flowers balanced on tall, leafy stalks at her feet. She pulled at the tundra plant, snapping some off too easily midstems while others came up properly by their roots from between the stones. She collected the plant until she had gathered several handfuls.

After dumping the pile of wildflower on the ground beside Astrid, Kallan looked back to the path. Although he was out of sight, Rune's dry threat still carried on the wind. She waited a moment, ensuring her complete solitude, before feeling bold enough to trot off to the lake.

The cold water pricked her skin like dozens of stinging nettles. Every muscle tightened and contracted as she scrubbed the mud from her legs. Dipping her head into the cool lake, Kallan closed her eyes and attempted to ease her anxiety, but the memories closed in, and the bombardment of voices, the darkness, and the weight of her chains all flooded back.

Gasping, Kallan opened her eyes wide. At once, the images vanished and left the lake, the rain, the tundra, and Astrid. Her hands shook as she ran them over her face, patting her eyes and clasping her hands multiple times to ensure herself that the wounds they had inflicted were gone. Kallan still trembled when she climbed out of the lake and pulled the clothes back on.

While Kallan pulled her long, sodden hair out of her tunic, Rune bounded down the mountain with a large leather pack thrown over his shoulder. A quiver hung at his waist matching an elegant, black bow etched with foreign runes he clutched with an affection any passer-by could see. Over one arm, he draped the black, leather overcoat, but Kallan's eyes flashed red and her temper flared at the sword encrusted with jewels, strapped to his waist in possession.

Kallan tightened her jaw as she battled the slew of questions and it was with envy that her eyes grazed the elding handle of her dagger still tucked into his waist.

With one hand grasping his bow, Rune stopped in front of her, shuffled the overcoat and then draped it over Kallan's shoulders. The coat was thick, heavy and hung to the ground. Despite belonging to a Dvergr, it smelled wonderfully of earth and pine.

Regardless, Kallan shrugged her shoulders in disgust, letting the coat fall to the ground.

"The nights are getting longer," Rune said, not moving yet to retrieve the coat from the ground. "You'll be grateful you have it at night when the temperature drops."

"I don't care," Kallan said. "I'll not wear their clothes."

"Alright," Rune said. "Take off your clothes."

Kallan threw back her shoulders and her neck flushed red.

"That's Dvergar clothing you're wearing," Rune said with a smug look that seemed to savor the look of horror splayed on her face.

"We don't have the conditions to be choosy." Rune said with indifference. "Wear it, or don't. Freeze, or take the coat. Walk through Midgard naked for all I care." And Rune stood, waiting, ready, and watching to see what choice she would make.

After a heavy pause, Kallan grabbed the coat from the ground and pulled it back over her shoulders. The soft furs engulfed her in warmth, immediately ridding her of the chill in the air. She slid her tiny arms through the large sleeves that extended well past her hands. After she snuggled her body into the thick furs, Rune moved to the horse and fastened the pack to Astrid's saddle.

Kallan frowned over a tuft of black fur that tickled her nose and whipped about with each spoken word.

"You have a sword." She was too angry to hide the resentment in her tone. Rune shifted a bored look then fastened the satchel.

"I'm travelling with a Dokkalfr," he said. "I have to protect myself."

Kallan's eyes flashed with hot rage.

"And a bow," she added doing her best not to shriek. "And my dagger."

Without a word, Rune gave a final jerk of the strap.

"Take it," he dared.

Kallan clenched her fist and fought the ache to curl up there on the ground and die.

After an exchange of matching glowers, Rune collected the bundle of saxifrage and led them north.

The terrain widened the farther north Kallan and Rune traveled. It stretched on all day, without change to the vast clusters of cotton grass that mingled with patches of tundra willow glowing crimson like a sea of fire. Treeless hills rolled over valleys and stretched into wide plains that rose into cold, gray mountains, cradling them on either side while vast clouds covered what little skies peeked beyond the towering peaks.

The river was a sight in itself. Torrential rapids flowed into calm waters as it twisted through the land, winding around the mountain's base. Its supply of fish was abundant. There seemed to be no end to the lakes and streams that met the water's path. They stopped only to replenish their water supply, spear fresh salmon from the river, or pluck a grouse from the sky during takeoff.

The rains continued well into the evening, long after the afternoon sun settled behind the mountains. In darkness, Kallan and Rune walked, saying nothing as they made their way across the endless tundra. Kallan threw a frequent glance to *Blod Tonn* tucked at the waist of Rune's trousers and spent much of her time brooding on how to take it back, while Rune threw her an occasional glance blanketed in vague expressions she couldn't read.

The rains ended long before they rested, and it was with heavy eyes, weighted with exhaustion, that Rune finally stopped.

"What are you doing?" Kallan asked with the reins still clutched in her hand.

"It's not safe to go any further tonight," Rune said. "We'll set up camp here and head out tomorrow before the rising sun." Rune was already busy untying a run of salmon from Astrid's saddle.

"We can't stop," Kallan said. "We have to keep going."

"The roads are too dangerous to risk travel at night."

Too exhausted to argue further, Rune turned his back and disappeared into the forest before Kallan could object. "I'm going for wood."

Kallan listened to his footsteps die away, leaving her alone with Astrid. Desperate to catch a glimpse of light, she scanned the forest for a bit of light then turned her eyes to the sky. The cloud cover was still too thick to see what moon was out. Disgruntled, she released her Seidr light with a wave of her hand and set to work removing Astrid's saddle and furs.

Wearily, she dumped the last of the furs onto the saddle and patted Astrid's forehead. He nudged her pouch, but before Kallan could move to withdraw an apple, a branch popped and she fired a haphazard shot in the general direction of the disruption.

Leaves sizzled and wood splintered beneath the trail of Seidr. A young tree, charred in half by Kallan's flame, creaked as it fell behind Rune, who stood, hand raised, his palm still smoking from where he drew the Seidr into him. A pile of broken twigs, branches, and small logs lay scattered at his feet.

"It's me," he said beside a tall shrub that sizzled black and orange with smoldering flames.

"I know," she said and returned to Astrid, leaving Rune to recollect the branches and twigs from the ground. Over her shoulder, she stole a glance and watched the swiftness of his hands as he gathered the timber, engrossed in his work.

She recalled the arch of his back as his body took in her Seidr. Her eyes followed the curve of his back and she bit her bottom lip.

410

"How do you do it?" she asked.

"Do what?" he asked, not bothering to raise his eyes.

"Catch it."

Rune stood, his arms loaded down with the fixings to build a fire. His eyes bore into her with a conviction that made her want to look away. Instead, she matched his stare and waited while he approached her.

"I don't know," he said and proceeded to a small clearing where he dumped the branches on the ground. He broke the wet sticks and loudly shuffled the little bit of dried wood through damp dead leaves and pine needles.

"I was hoping you could tell me," he said.

Kallan scoffed.

Stones clicked over and over, tweaking Kallan's nerves with each *click, click, click*. She dropped herself before Rune's pile of brush.

Click, click.

Kallan pulled the overcoat around her and Rune struck the stones.

Another *click* and Kallan fired an angry blast into the woodpile, sending Rune falling back from the sudden explosion as he dropped his rocks.

Partially singed, Rune sat up cursing. The wood already hissed from the day's deluge and burned hot as Rune settled himself back down, void of objection.

Rune took up a stick and poked at the fire. "Where'd you learn your tricks?" he said.

"Where'd you learn yours?" she asked.

Rune looked up from the flames as the corner of Kallan's mouth twitched and she leaned forward.

"Would you mind if I...?" Kallan said, splaying a palm on the wet ground as Rune straightened his back.

Golden threads of Seidr flowed from her fingertips and snaked their way over the earth to Rune. Her Seidr threaded his, following his lines and plunging deeper into this core where the heart of his Seidr gave him life. There, the darkness began and the lines of Seidr ended. There, Kallan could go no further.

She stretched her limits, pushed her Seidr against the Shadow. But frustration overcame her curiosity and she withdrew quite suddenly, allowing his body to fall limp and leaving him gasping for breath on all fours.

Rune gasped. Kallan could hear his heart racing. "I want to stand," Rune said between breaths. "I want to arm myself and fight."

Kallan tensed, preparing herself for battle, but Rune remained kneeling on all fours while he caught his breath.

"What is it?" he asked, still visibly shaken from the surge of adrenaline.

Kallan shook her head and sank back into the large, leather coat.

"I don't know," she said, pulling in a long, deep breath and, despite sharing a fire with her enemy—despite the war, her hate, and her company—she slipped into the stories planted there by

Gudrun ages ago. Anything to escape the fresh memories of the Dvergar caves.

"The earth grows wild in Midgard," Kallan said. Her eyes shone with love for the lore. "We received the Seidr as a gift from Freyja. A gift she infused in us all. The Seidr is in you. The Seidr that nurtures Alfheim grows with our use of it, wielding it, honing it, allowing it to flourish. The air drips with it. Carried on the wind as Alfheim breathes, it moves. It lives."

Kallan listened and remembered the streams of gold that passed through the walls of the caves. She shivered despite the warm night air.

"The Seidr is also here in Midgard," she continued, "buried beneath the soil and forgotten by Man, dormant and ready, waiting to be released from its prison."

Rune remained seemingly enraptured, as if he hung on every word she muttered and it lulled him into repose.

"Ages ago, I trekked these lands. The earth was different then," she said. "There are those who found the Seidr and harbored its growth. During those years, they tamed it. That was when the sons of Man still wielded its power, granting them the long life that now comes naturally to the Alfar."

"What happened?" Rune asked. "How did the race of Men forget?"

Kallan smiled.

"Gudrun spoke of a king whose hand stretched across the lands. He uttered spells and the sun turned grass to dust. There, the snows no longer fell. For nearly six hundred years, his followers destroyed all who opposed him. Like a plague, they annihilated any who dared defy the Desert King."

Kallan tucked her legs to her chest, resting her chin into the crook of her knees. She stared into the fire, beyond the flames, and remembered.

"The followers of the Desert King declared that he alone was the high king and sought to destroy all who opposed that claim. The Seidkona's very existence proved Freyja lived, that there were others who had, and the Seidkona were hunted."

Kallan gazed at Rune across the fire. Orange shadows spilled over Rune's face making him appear more threatening than usual as he sat enraptured.

"This is not the Midgard I knew so long ago when the Dokkalfar journeyed from Svartálfaheim."

"Why did your people leave?" Rune asked.

"I'm sure in all this time, the Ljosalfar have composed some explanation." She added a bitter grin.

Rune shrugged.

"Biased speculation," he said. "Random stories buried now in legends twisted with so many versions it's hard to see which parts are truth anymore."

Kallan rested her chin back to her knees as she tugged at the overcoat, pulling it down against a breeze. She flicked back a lock of her hair that had dried into ringlets and spilled to the ground.

"Why did the Dokkalfar come to Alfheim?" he asked again.

Kallan shifted her gaze back to Rune, studying him.

"We warred with another, who had been our kinsmen," she said, "and a schism divided us: the Svartálfar. That is what Aaric said."

"So your father sought to revisit an insatiable bloodlust," Rune surmised aloud, but before the last word left his mouth, Kallan was on him, pulling her dagger from his waist and pressing the tip to his throat.

"Do not speak of what you don't know," she hissed. "Heartbroken, my father forfeited that war, abandoning that realm to his foe."

Sweat beaded on Rune's brow and he gulped down the knot that grazed the tip of her blade.

"But not all the Svartálfar saw things his way, did they?" Rune said.

Kallan lowered the dagger and sank back on her knees.

"Half stayed behind," she said.

"What became of them?"

Kallan shrugged.

Wonder suspended in the air as Kallan took the time to pull the overcoat back around her shoulders. He waited until she had snuggled back into its fur before asking.

"What would make a king abandon half his people and his kingdom?" Rune asked.

Kallan stared into the flames. A bright red log broke in two and fell, releasing a spray of red embers that floated into the air between them.

Kallan peered up from the flames.

"The death of my mother at the hand of an old friend: the Dvergar king, Motsognir."

Chapter 44

"Aaric!"

Daggon slammed the doors of the war room open and strode toward the high marshal, who was hunched over a vellum scroll between the grand hearth filled with flame and a table strewn in maps. Aaric lifted his eyes. He had tied his hair back, revealing the ancient runes etched at the base of his neck. Like the runes trailing up his fingers, wrists, and arms, these continued to his shoulders and down his back beneath his tunic.

"What is the meaning of this?" Daggon said.

He hastened across the floor, passing through strips of moonlight that spanned the stone from the high windows. His sword, sheathed at his side, swayed in time with the chinks from chainmail stretched across his chest as he marched.

"You'll have to be more specific," Aaric said, straightening his back.

"My men tell me you called them back!" Daggon's face was as red as his hair, save for his scars, stretching across the side of his face like the white branches of a birch tree. "My men, my war-men, who I personally trained, command, and sent out for Kallan!"

"That's right," Aaric said as calm as ever as Daggon planted his fists on the top of the table and leaned in.

The captain's copper eyes flashed with murder.

"What are you doing?" he asked.

There was a cold calm in Aaric's demeanor as he studied Daggon whose tunic, cloak, and trousers looked travel worn. Filth from the road covered him from his wild, red hair to his muddy boots.

"I'm bringing them in," Aaric answered.

"Kallan is still out there!" Daggon extended a finger to the door behind him.

"We can't afford the troops," Aaric said.

"But those are *my* men!" Daggon pounded his fist on the table.

With a sigh, Aaric rechecked his composure and surrendered the last of his attention to the seething captain. As he circled around the table, the firelight caught the strange runic markings on his wrists.

"Lorlenalin is vulnerable," Aaric said, doing his best to look interested. "The more men we have dispersed in search, the less we have here on hand in Lorlenalin's defense." Aaric stopped at the table's end, leaving at least three arm lengths between him and Daggon.

Daggon's hard stare darkened.

"Gunir hasn't moved since the king and Kallan vanished," Daggon said. "You know this. The Dark One sits, preening himself on the throne, and you're worried of an attack? Gunir knows we are without queen. They know we are vulnerable. If they were going to make a move, they would have done so by now, a fortnight ago."

"Lorlenalin has lost its fountainhead," Aaric said. "I am left with few resources to keep this city running. If Gunir does decide to move, Lorlenalin will fall."

Daggon's wide chest heaved with each breath. "You would turn your back to Kallan?"

"I do not have the luxury to grieve," Aaric said. "I have a responsibility. While your place is on the battlefield fighting alongside our queen, my work is here among the scribes. And as much as I want to ride out and find her, as much as it pains me to say it, I must stay here and order what only is best for Kallan's city and her people and not for Kallan herself. Regardless of how much I hate it, I must do this."

"Need I remind you that I am captain," Daggon spoke through his teeth. "I oversee decisions made in regards to Kallan's war-men—"

"And it will do you well to remember that I am high marshal!" Aaric's voice boomed to the high-vaulted ceiling. "I oversee decisions made in regards to Kallan's court. My duty, first and foremost, is to draw up the inventory and account for all the men, Kallan's war-men. And, in times of crisis, am I not free to reassign them where I feel they are needed the most?"

The fire crackled as Daggon appeared to search for a rebuttal to gain the upper hand.

"Are we not in a time of crisis, Captain?" Aaric asked.

"We are." Daggon seemingly shoved the words from his mouth.

"I did not override your war-men, your position, or your orders," Aaric said. "As high marshal, I reassigned."

"Kallan needs us."

"Her people need us," Aaric said. "Her people come first."

Daggon tightened his already whitened fists.

"The people you seek to protect adored Kallan long before she ascended the throne. Wherever she goes, they will loyally, eagerly follow and they have a right to go." Daggon exhaled. "We all do."

Aaric narrowed his eyes. "You sound like someone who already has lives lined up."

"Ten thousand citizens wait for Kallan's return," Daggon said. "Many of whom would be willing to ride out for her at the word."

Aaric shook his head, exhaling his frustration. It was with a calm voice that he spoke again.

"As high marshal, I have no choice but to act on the best interests of the people. Nor will I waste what few resources we have hunting for one girl."

"Queen," Daggon corrected.

A flash of anger passed through Aaric's eyes before settling again.

"I will go after her myself," Daggon said and marched from the table.

"Daggon."

"That's Kira's daughter out there!" Daggon spun about on his heel.

Aaric's blood drained as memories of Kira smiling, Kira laughing, and Kira dying flashed and faded, leaving him pale. He forced down a gulp that seemed to stir up his blood again.

"It will do you well to remember, Captain, that your duty, first and foremost, is to protect the people of Lorlenalin. Not one girl," Aaric said, forcing the words through a stiff bottom jaw.

Both wills unbending, both decisions made, a suspended silence hung between them.

"My queen is in need of my services," Daggon said, dismissing himself. His boots clomped with every stride toward the door while Aaric forced his head clear. He couldn't risk a rogue captain leading Fand to Kallan and battled the urge to raise his hand in arms.

"If you leave this city, I will have no choice but to record that you abandoned your post." Aaric's voice filled the room up to the crossbeams as Daggon stood, not moving. "I will have no choice but to find you insubordinate and charge you thus," Aaric said.

The fire popped.

"Traitor," Aaric said, leaving the word to sit in the air between them.

Without a word, Daggon passed through each strip of moonlight splayed upon the stone floor. He didn't bother closing the doors behind him.

Daggon pulled Thor's saddle strap taut before looping it back through the metal clasp as ancient memories passed through his thoughts. The horse master and stable-hands bustled about, paying him no mind as his fingers moved, pulling back the leather.

"In so many ways, you are just like her father," Gudrun said.

Daggon held his eyes on the saddle.

"Be gone with you, hag," he grumbled.

Ignoring his insults, the old woman joined him at his horse's side.

"Your station commands you stay," she said.

"My loyalty demands I go." Daggon tugged the saddle's belt before grabbing the bit and bridle from the wall.

"And where will you go, Daggon, that you haven't already looked?" she asked.

"I can't do nothing," Daggon said.

The lantern light caught the worry in Gudrun's eye.

"I promised him, Gudrun."

He slid the bit into Thor's mouth and fastened the bridle in place.

"The tide has not yet changed, Daggon," Gudrun said.

"How can you know that?" Daggon said. "How can you possibly know? With your Sight blinded for nearly a fortnight now—"

"Only parts," Gudrun kindly corrected.

"All you have seen is the Dark One perched patiently on the throne," he said. "He isn't even looking for his king."

A loud bang filled the grotto, followed by a series of shouting stable-hands in a corner.

Gudrun dropped her voice beneath the ruckus.

"Daggon, I assure you. If I could see her...if I knew where she was, I would ride out with you myself."

With a grunt, he shook his head heavy with doubt.

"The road ahead is unchanged regardless of whether we go or stay," Gudrun said. "Stay...until I at least see a change in the tides."

Exhaustion and wear visibly pulled on Daggon's face, bearing down on his back. With a sigh, he pushed his hand through his hair then rubbed his face wrought with worry.

"Where is she?"

The embers glowed red in Rune's pipe as he turned the hilt of her dagger over in his hand. Taking it back from her while she slept had been too easy.

He shifted his eyes over her body, half hidden beneath the overcoat. She slept, undisturbed beside the dying fire, content and unaware of the pawns aligned, oblivious to the part she played.

Streams of smoke billowed from his mouth then rolled into the air as he watched. The last of the fire smoldered. Kallan's words played over in his head as Rune examined each word, each sigh.

Kallan stirred and uttered a name.

"Ori."

Heat clawed Rune's chest as insurmountable waves of hate toward the Dvergar burned his insides raw. The urge to kill was agonizing. He brooded as he counted the players.

A Dvergar king, who murdered a queen.

Rune pulled a long draw from his pipe.

A dead Dokkalfr king.

He released the smoke as he exhaled.

The Seidkona, Queen Kallan, Rune lowered his pipe, resting his arm loosely on a knee, *and Borg, the mercenary.*

He recalled Borg's face as the mercenary pleaded with him to take Kallan from the stables. The exact moment he dropped his hand to his shoulder and felt the lines of Seidr within him awaken followed the rage, the vile contempt reserved in the Shadow that had lurked in his core since. The Beast.

Rune blew the smoke and watched it billow, then looked again to Kallan. Her slender, pale face reflected the light of the moon. It was full tonight.

A message of peace that has failed, time and again, to reach the ears of the queen and a pouch with mystical apples.

"What do you grieve?" he whispered to the sleeping Dokkalfr.

The fire that burned in her eyes did well to mask the grief she had buried in the shadows of her mind. She seemed content to ignore the pain that ate its way through her, hollowing her out, consuming her, until the empty shell of a woman driven mad would remain.

Rune exhaled and watched the smoke rising as it twisted into the air above him.

Eyolf. Kallan. Borg.

She was breathtaking bathed in moonlight.

The Dvergar king, Motsognir.

He took another long draw.

The dead Queen Mother.

The smoke billowed.

The abduction of the Dokkalfar queen, all for the want of a pouch.

Rune's gut churned with intuition that would leave him sleepless that night.

Ori.

He gazed upon her serene face.

The unease between them would spread, but certain questions needed answers, though certain words would increase hostilities. With every question asked, he knew he would be closer to evoking her rage. Time would not be on his side, but necessity pushed caution aside.

He planned the order, the balance, the tension, the gradual move to the one topic he dared not breech, lest her guard be raised and her Seidr fly.

And the apples. He would have to coax her into telling him about the apples. *Yes, let's see how well you lie, princess. Let's see how stubborn you really are.*

Rune sighed and took a long draw on the pipe. What he needed was for her to trust him.

Before she wakes, I'll give back the dagger.

The light of Alfheim's moon gleamed brightly in the deep black of Bergen's eyes, reflected there like bottomless, black pools of water. Throwing his head back, he took a long drink from his flask then wiped his mouth with his hand.

Moonlight bathed the city in shadows of blue and white. Gunir's stone houses twisted around the streets, creating a maze of thatch and stone. They hugged the base of the keep's battlement perched atop the motte. This night, the silence seemed to reach to the ends of Alfheim.

The wench asleep in his bed released a groan that became a sigh, drawing Bergen's attention from the window. His eyes grazed her bare flesh, lingering for a moment on the exposed skin soaked in moonbeam.

With a gleam in his eye, Bergen gulped down another swig and, dressed only in trousers, quietly made his way into his sitting room, leaving Gretchen...or Gertrude...undisturbed by his restlessness.

While smiling to himself for a job well done, Bergen stepped out onto the landing between the war room and his chambers and closed the door behind him. His stomach growled and he washed back another gulp, content with the solitude he rarely found. After fixing his thoughts on Cook's kitchens, he sauntered down the steps to the Great Hall.

The silence from the late summer night permeated the castle's keep as the sleeping servants dowsed Gunir in a peace they could never accomplish awake with their eagerness to serve. He had made it as far as the stairwell window, halfway down the steps, before recalling the last time he had picked at the unguarded assortment of salted meats hanging in the larder.

A night that had begun with innocent pilfering had turned into a severe tongue-lashing that ended with a wooden spoon across his hide. After a lowdown threat to tell Torunn, Cook had made him promise never to touch the kitchen's larders again. Though odious, the blackmail had earned his respect, and ended the night, in much the same position as Gertrude...or Gretchen...asleep in his chambers to compensate for his late night thievery, of course.

Abandoning any thoughts of a late night lunch, Bergen veered widely away from the kitchens at the base of the steps and, instead, swaggered into the Great Hall, throwing his head back for another swig.

It was with a guilty eye that he shifted a gaze to the empty throne and chugged down another gulp of mead, replaying his last conversation with Rune until the words echoed back on themselves.

"*I need to go after her...if I'm not back by the next new moon, come find me. Tell no one that you've seen me.*"

And Bergen had done just that, much to the chagrin of Torunn. The castle's old keeper had been like a mother to them, and had squawked and clucked as loud as a hen when Bergen refused to speak.

Rune had ridden off on the Seidkona's dark steed, leaving behind more questions than he had answered, and more responsibility than Bergen cared for.

That was fourteen nights ago.

With careless grace, Bergen stomped up the five steps to the empty throne sequestered between a pair of pillars etched with animals and runes, and dropped himself into the chair. As he threw back another gulp of mead, Bergen eyed the pair of grand iron wheels suspended from the trusses over two long tables. A thick layer of hardened wax had melted and molded around the iron and fallen to drip on the tables. Bergen looked past the pillars to the double oak doors of the Great Hall.

"In all my years, I didn't think I'd ever see you seated on your father's throne," came a familiar gruff voice.

Geirolf's large, bear-like frame emerged from behind the wooden screens passage set behind the throne. With a glint of mischief in the old codger's eye, he stopped short at the base of the throne steps.

"The weight of a crown is heavy," Bergen said. "I like living without the burden, and besides..." He shrugged. "...such a life would never permit me the freedom to frolic as much as I do."

Bergen grinned, tipping the mouth of the flask to his lips as Geirolf grunted at the man-child seated on the throne.

"A throne doesn't suit you," Geirolf grumbled. "If I recall, you always were a stubborn child, quick to strike and eager to ignore."

With a grin that flashed in his round, black eyes, Bergen proudly chugged back another gulp and released a flatulent-sounding grunt in his brother's chair. Geirolf pretended not to notice, learning long ago that it was never good to encourage the mischievous sparkle in Bergen's eyes.

"I find it implausible that you know nothing of the disappearance of Queen Kallan or your brother," the old man grunted at the youth. "Where is he?"

Geirolf waited for Bergen to speak.

Instead, the Dark One grinned again from behind the flask, catching a bit of light with the scar on his right brow.

Geirolf brought his voice down with a bit more severity than before. "Rune is nowhere to be found. The Dokkalfar queen is unaccounted for, and you haven't sent a single party to locate either monarch in more than a fortnight."

"I don't want to."

Geirolf sighed, long and low.

"Where is your brother?"

"I don't know." Bergen's words were dry, as if over-rehearsed.

Geirolf expanded his chest, inhaling a large helping of patience, and climbed the steps to the throne. His wide frame towered over Bergen, barely dwarfing the berserker. He braced each hand on the armrests, and bent low until his nose stopped inches from Bergen's.

"You show up a fortnight ago stripped of your bow, your boots, and reeking of imported Thash Grape Ale with nothing more than a grin and some story about a rose, a goat, and a ring."

"It was a great night." Bergen beamed. "One I will never forget," he added with a dazed look as though in a mist.

A small vein on Geirolf's forehead pulsed.

"For the sake of an old man who desperately looks to end the ceaseless nagging of Torunn's maternal woes, please," he said, "tell me where your brother is."

Bergen sympathetically dropped a hand to Geirolf's shoulder.

"As much of my pity as you may have," Bergen said with feigned devoutness, "I have been sworn to secrecy under the command of my king."

Geirolf stared at the twinkle in Bergen's eyes.

"How noble," Geirolf grumbled at the wide smile pasted upon Bergen's face. "When will he be back?"

"I don't know."

"Is the Dokkalfr with him?"

"I don't know."

"Is she dead?"

"I don't know."

Geirolf released the chair, exhaling a patient breath. As he straightened his spine, he locked his ice-blue eyes on Bergen, who returned the glare Bergen had learned from him.

"Before the new moon?" he guessed.

"Before the new moon," Bergen agreed.

Geirolf nodded, giving his consent to the plan the boys had designed without him.

"And if your brother has not returned before the next moon?" Geirolf asked unpleasantly.

"I have orders to find him."

The answer was sufficient to allow Geirolf to drop his shoulders, and he descended the throne. He took a single step and peered over his shoulder. Bergen had resumed his drinking.

"What am I going to tell Torunn for the next fort-night?"

Gulping down the last of the mead, Bergen flashed a grin that glowed in his eyes long after Geirolf closed the grand doors behind him.

Chapter 45

The darkness had returned with the thick, acidic stench that clung to Kallan's skin. The red smoke wafted from the bowl with its bitter tang. Kallan tried to stand, to fight, to run, but the chains of elding held her bound. She could not move or open her mouth to scream. There was only night, the shadows, and darkness.

Blainn stood over her, staring down with the black that filled all the white of his eyes. Behind him, donned in the leather overcoat, Ori watched, unmoving and indifferent as Blainn drew back his foot. His kick landed against the side of her head and Kallan awoke.

Crimson willow greeted her with the scent of grouse sizzling over the fire instead of the bitter taste. Her stomach churned for want of food. She tried to stand, but found herself still weighted down. She glowered with vile contempt at Ori's coat covering her body, and, with great force, angrily flung it away as if it had been a blanket crawling with spiders.

Above, the sun spilled its late morning light onto her like a warm, yellow blanket that filled the cloudless sky. Without a word, she ran her hands over her face and battled back the nightmare with a slew of silent curses to Mara.

"Good morning," Rune said as he flipped the skewers on the fire. "I felt it best to let you sleep."

Firing off a miserable frown at her warden, Kallan rose to her feet. Her hair tumbled past her waist, and she fumbled her way to the fire in the oversized tunic that slid off a shoulder. The pants, which she had tightened with a strip of twine, added a distinct frumpy look to her morning muddle and seemed to evoke a smile from Rune, who kept his face low as if trying to obscure her view.

Tucking her knees to her chest, Kallan crouched beside the fire as Rune nudged at the charred wood beneath four skewered grouse breasts propped beside the flames. The day was sickeningly happy and bright, the exact contradiction of her mood.

Birds twittered as Kallan flashed a gaze to Astrid, who grazed peaceably at the river. Rune promptly passed her a helping of grouse while she twitched nervously at each critter hidden away in the surrounding forest.

Kallan ate in silence, unable to ignore Rune's scrutiny. She was all too aware of the tension. Her breath remained steady, her fingers curled with unease, and her back was forever taut as if ready for battle. Once she finished her second helping, she picked at the ashes with the skewer then surrendered the empty stick to the flame and reached a hand behind her.

Blindly, she fished for the woolen blanket she had used as a bed the night before and pulled it over her shoulders against the absent chill in the thick warmth of the sun. With a muffled thump, her dagger struck the ground. Kallan widened her eyes as she stared at the sleek, slender sheen of *Blod Tonn* in the grass. She raised her eyes to Rune while the dagger lay, unclaimed.

Sunlight glistened off the blade as Kallan wondered when he had taken it. She turned her attention back to *Blod Tonn*.

"I've found you," Rune said. "I've healed you. I've fed you. I've guarded you. For three nights, you've slept beside me."

Kallan blushed red with embarrassment.

"If I sought to kill you, I would have let the Dvergar to do it for me," Rune said.

Blood rushed from Kallan's face, leaving her skin an unnatural white as Nordri's words came rushing back.

Truth is, if we were going to kill you, we wouldn't have waited until now to do it. And we wouldn't have used poison.

"I wouldn't have waited for you to annoy me," Rune said and Kallan knew he saw the sudden tremor in her hand and the increase of her breath at the mere mention of the Dvergar. "Or tolerate you kicking me in my—"

He stopped there.

Kallan stared at the blade and waited for Rune to swipe *Blod Tonn* back. Slowly, she reached out and took up the elding hilt.

"What do you want to know?" she asked, her back stiff with tension.

"Tell me why the Dvergar took you." Rune's words bit the air. More than eagerness audibly snipped his tone.

Kallan waited until she had finished securing the dagger at her waist before answering.

"They said they wanted my pouch," Kallan said.

"Did they say why?" Rune asked. She noted the urgency in his voice that had picked up again.

She bit her bottom lip and shook her head.

"Most of the time they spoke Dvergar," she said.

Rune glanced at her hand still holding the dagger's hilt as a long silence settled between them.

"Why would they want a pouch?" he said.

Kallan looked at Astrid grazing along the river before turning back to Rune.

"There are spells and enchantments associated with a Seidkona's pouch as unique as the Seidkona carrying it."

"And what spells lay dormant within that pouch?" he asked.

Kallan tensed and he was on to the next question.

"Why didn't they kill you once they knew you didn't have it?" he asked.

Kallan shrugged. "I don't know."

"Who is Ori?"

Kallan sharpened her alertness. Her knuckles were white on the hilt.

"You talk in your sleep," Rune said. "Who is he?"

Kallan shrugged again, passing off an urge to wield her Seidr and pull her dagger on him. The fire tickled the air. Pursing her lips, she gulped.

"He was one of them," she said, knowing her answer left Rune with a distinct feeling that there was more to the story than she told.

"There was one in a cave," Rune said. "Dead. From the looks of it, a Seidkona had stormed the place with all the ash, fire, and brimstone that forms in Muspell-sheim."

A sudden sick settled, making Kallan regret eating her fill of grouse.

"How did you get free?" Rune asked, not giving her the chance to deny she had.

Kallan shook her head and pressed her mouth to her knees.

"When I woke, my chains were gone," she said, lifting her head and keeping her eyes on the fire.

"Why did Motsognir kill your mother?" Runes asked.

Calm caution drained from Kallan's face.

"We were at war," she said. "I was six. I know very little."

A shadow fell over Rune, no longer masked in passive inattentiveness.

"I am my father's heir," he said. "I was trained and groomed to inherit the kingdom my father left to me. I do not doubt your father did the same for you. He would not have hoarded Lorlenalin's secrets. Not from its heir."

Kallan gave a small pshaw, abandoning her pleasantries. At last, she released the dagger's handle and pulled the blanket closer, hugging her legs tighter into her chest.

"And you think I would hand them over to you so freely?" she asked.

Rune narrowed his eyes. "Who honed your Seidr skills?"

"Gudrun." Kallan was already snipping.

"Who taught you the sword?" he asked.

Kallan's hands shook against her legs. She didn't answer.

"I've seen you in battle," Rune said. "I know a skilled swordsman when I see it. "Who. Taught. You."

"Daggon." She released the name reluctantly.

Flames between them flicked their tips, whipping the air as the wind carried them.

"The Dokkalfar you charged with diplomatic exchanges with Gunir, who was he?" Rune asked.

Kallan's knuckles were white, numbed from the death grip she had on her legs. She felt her cooperation waning.

"Aaric."

"What station does he hold in your court?" he said.

Kallan remained tight-lipped.

"Indulge me," he said. "Let's assume for one moment that I did send a letter requesting peace. If I were to send such a letter, who would see to it that it reached your hands?" Rune asked.

"My high marshal," Kallan answered between her teeth.

"Who is—?"

"Why do you ask so much?"

"How did you your father die?"

Kallan's eyes widened with memory. She parted her lips. Fear and madness swelled behind her eyes.

"Months passed before I stopped seeing his blood on my hands," Kallan said.

"What did you see?" Rune said.

"You should know. You were there."

Rune released a long sigh. "You've managed to expend the last of my patience with your vague answers and half lies. What did you see?"

A guttural cry rolled from Kallan's throat.

"Through the back, he was stabbed, through the back without sword or honor. That," she spat, "is what I saw."

Rune drew a deep breath.

"On that day you fought at the Dokkalfar outpost," Rune asked, "who rode with you? Whose face did you see as your father lay dying at your feet?"

"Enough," Kallan said, punching the ground. The fight had left her. The color drained from her face, and his words ripped down her wall. With choreographed precision, Kallan stood and stomped to Astrid. After snatching the reins, she hoisted herself into the saddle, and sent Astrid trotting along the river's edge.

In the light, Kallan's eyes were clear and vibrant, responding to each shade and hue, which reassured Rune that the drug had finally passed through her system. Her complexion, no longer grayed with the decay of malnourishment and abuse, radiated beneath the sun.

Rune stared after her, annoyed at her sudden flight. He had pushed her beyond the line of tolerance, risking her rage, but timing was everything. If he jumped too soon, he would lose her. A part of him knew she was not ready, but he had flouted an air of indifference and played his part too well.

As long as she evaded, he would not get his answers. As long as she brooded, denying the abuse she had endured from the Dvergar, as long as she harbored her hatred and avoided the true core to her rage, she would not trust him to speak. If she insisted on burying her grief with avoidance, then anger would be just the thing to force the grief to the surface.

Her anger just might save her yet.

And, at long last, Rune knew what he would have to do.

Uneven tundra sliced Astrid's hooves, forcing Kallan to dismount almost immediately while the camp was still in view. Kallan crossed her arms over her chest and watched as her warden stood, stretched, belched, and aimlessly strolled about the camp, collecting their possessions and extinguishing the fire at his leisure.

After a long ten minutes, and a longer trip into the forest to relieve himself, Rune swaggered along the bank to Kallan. The sunlight caught the fire opal poised at the end of the hilt as he sauntered, holding the sword steady at his side.

"You forgot this, princess," he said, dumping the overcoat into her chest, considerably rougher than needed and holding it where she couldn't shrug him off or drop the coat.

"Don't call me that," she said. "And I don't want it."

"You mistake me for someone who cares," Rune said, releasing the coat unto Kallan. "Keep it or freeze, princess." With a cold shoulder, he tied the bags to the saddle. "You could always bunk up with me at night."

An egotistical grin pulled the corner of his mouth taut and Kallan seethed while holding back a stream of Seidr.

Their slow start cost them half a day's light spent at the bank of the river, until the water veered east. Required to abandon their water supply and reliable fish stock for the journey north, Rune caught as much salmon as they could carry and refilled the bladders he found in Ori's pack.

The cold, harsh winds whipped mercilessly across the frozen plains, slicing their exposed skin. Grouse were abundant among the crimson carpet, the burnt browns, and mild mustards of the tundra grass. The change in the landscape was welcomed and allowed them to increase their pace, but only slightly. They finished the last of the purple saxifrage, nibbling it as they walked, and, much to Kallan's delight, replaced it with the occasional batch of cloudberries where they could get them. By late afternoon, a deep thunder moved in, not from the clouds but the barren plains ahead.

Reindeer, no fewer than eight hundred, speckled the land, blended with the white tufts of cotton grass. Their endless barks and grunts mingled with the constant clicks of their knees, enclosing the region in a deafening collection of sounds that mingled with the steady pound of their hooves.

Forced to keep their distance from the danger of the rut, the Alfar watched from afar, stunned at the occasional skirmish between bulls. Nearly an hour had passed before the herd had moved on like a flowing river of brown and white through the valley.

The once frequent white stones dwindled with the increase of trees as the sporadic clusters of birch continued to pepper the horizon. They moved through the trees, pushing past smaller rocks and thick, abundant mosses that pleasantly cushioned their feet.

The sun threw oranges and reds across the sky, casting a golden glow overhead. As they walked, dusk added shadows of purple and blue to the landscape until the last of the day's light vanished behind the mountains. Beneath the barely waning moon, they walked until they stood at the brink of open ground cradled between far-reaching mountains on either side.

Rune was the first to stop, his gaze fixed on the distance through the darkness where fire's light beckoned to them like a beacon.

"What's wrong?" Kallan asked.

"Stay back," Rune said as he moved into a large cluster of shrubs.

From behind the foliage, he looked to where the base of three mountains joined into a single valley.

The path they had followed into the north, cut through the valley before them. Like a grand basin of green, the land expanded to the west and the east, continuing through the base of the mountains. There, the land leveled out, reaching like a hand that invited them.

Rune kept his voice unusually low. "Years ago, this was a route used by merchants and traders. The glade was vacant then, with a single farm tucked to the corner of the valley."

Kallan said nothing as she peered through the valley of which he spoke. The spacious glen was gone, filled instead with an endless number of tents crammed into every opening as far as they could see. A myriad of campfires filled the valley in light.

And in their midst, mingled with mead, laughter, and song, a king's army sat exchanging swords, swapping food, and hoarding drink. Their numbers exceeded well over ten thousand. They had scattered their armaments about, leaning spears against tents, and splayed out bows and swords on dried hides. Carved into shields, molded into the hilts of their swords, and painted haphazardly onto tunics and tents, was a thin, sickly rune painted red on white.

Behind him, the warmth of Kallan's breath grazed his neck.

"I told you to stay back," Rune said in a hushed whisper. Her face was inches from his.

"*Naudr*," she whispered, eying each rune emblazoned by the fire's light. "They need help."

"That is not a *naudr*," Rune said, looking back to the camp.

"But it is. They've written it there." Kallan pointed. "*Naudr* means 'need'. We must help them."

Kallan pushed herself past Rune, who managed to grab her by the waist before she plowed on into the encampment. He pulled her back harder than expected and she fell back into him.

"They do not need help," he whispered. "That is not the rune of our kin, nor are they born of this land."

"Then their mark is of Asgard and that is Mjolnir," Kallan argued, pointing to the nearest soldier whose shield bore the mark. "They must be riders of Thor."

"No," Rune said, shaking his head. "That is no hammer."

Kallan looked through the shrubs that hid them, clearly not entirely sure of the problem that presented itself.

"That is the valley we need to cross if we are to continue this trail north," Rune said.

"So, we'll go around," Kallan said, determined to not linger over such petty things.

"We are surrounded," Rune said. "To the west, cliffs plunge to the sea. They are impassable without a ship. To the east, the mountains climb as high as Jotunheim."

"We'll go south, then, back toward Viken," she said.

"Where the Dvergar hunt you?" Rune asked. "Our only path is here, away from the mountains and the cliffs that fall to the sea."

Kallan studied the nearest tent.

"Then we go on," she said and, with her mind apparently made up, she gave Rune a shove and tightened her grip on Astrid's reins.

"Be still, woman," Rune said.

"We can't sit still and we can't go back," she whispered.

"Do you see how many there are? There are thousands." Rune shook his head and looked back to the tents. "We'll wait. By morning, they should be gone and then we ca—Kallan."

Kallan stepped from the cover of the brush, leading Astrid into the camp as Gudrun's words merged to the forefront of her thoughts.

"The race of Men is different. Like the Ljosalfar, they know nothing of the Seidr that flows through the land. Their women, sickly and weak, are nothing at all like the slender grace of the Alfar whose long, hardened torsos, tapered ears, and strength match the gods. There are those who will stop at nothing to look upon the grace of the Alfar. Even those who would seek to take one as their own."

The first of the soldiers froze, captivated by the sheer wonder of the Alfr. Standing just a head higher than most, her skin, as luminescent and as pure as moonlight, radiated with a permanent youth that did not fade. Her eyes glowed clear with a brilliance unparalleled by any beauty beheld by the race of Man.

Rune came to stand behind Kallan, with a look like he was holding in a lecture.

Passing like a stifled breeze through the camp, Kallan, Rune, and Astrid walked on without a word. Silence followed them as they moved, taking with them a trail of bystanders. Soldiers dropped swords, lowered drinks, and stilled their tongues, all for a chance to gape at the Alfar. Most had heard the legends that tradesmen and raiders carried to the islands in the west. With awe they gathered, eager to steal a single look from the woman's eye.

They moved as if in a dream. Some pondered which side of sleep they were on. Though the Alfar heard the clang of dropped swords followed by the murmurs of onlookers, they saw only their end. The tents dispersed and the light from the camps grew dim as the crowd behind them grew.

445

When the darkest black of the distant road was in sight, Rune dared to take his eyes from the goal and glanced at Kallan, who seemed entirely indifferent to the danger. With her head high, she displayed her regality through her confidence.

Her stupid, arrogant confidence, Rune mused. *Bergen will laugh himself mad over this.*

The tents finally vanished and the Alfar returned to the sanctuary of the forest, slipping into the darkness like white wraiths whose corporeal presence had materialized before human eyes for a moment's breath.

At the edge of the forest, eager for a second glimpse of the female, a group of soldiers peered into the shadows where the enthralling mystic had vanished with her horse and guardian. Among them, unable to ignore the diminishing doubt, Thorer focused his stare on the Dokkalfr.

"Follow them."

Chapter 46

The campfires burned like glowworms in the distance, leaving them in shadows and moonlight before Rune allowed his rage to take him. Shaking with a fury, he grabbed Kallan, bruising her arm as he pulled her back.

"Are you trying to get us killed?" he said.

Kallan shrugged, urging the twitch in Rune's hand to fly off and strike her.

"We survived."

Enraged that she cared so little about the risk, Rune snarled, pausing for the words to get through to her.

"Flaunting our presence and taunting the enemy is not my idea of survival," he said.

With a twist of her arm, Kallan broke free from his grip and tugged Astrid's reins, leaving Rune to seethe.

"You'll have saved us nothing if we don't arrive at all," Rune said, refusing to follow.

Kallan gave a quiet nicker, encouraging Astrid along.

"I didn't just spend a fortnight tracking the Dvergar to get you back so you could risk my life and yours," Rune said.

Kallan stopped and Rune waited for her to turn, to spit, to scream, to argue...something...anything.

She didn't.

"There are conflicts here in Midgard that will soon demand the attention of the Alfar," he said, "In the meantime, the Alfar must lay low."

"Lorlenalin has no dealings with Midgard, the wars of Men, or Gunir," Kallan said, turning on her heel and leaving Astrid to graze.

Rune took a step closer.

"You must understand the stakes at risk and the lives threatened."

"Is there something about this king that you have not told me?"

Kallan waited for an answer while Rune stared blankly. Kallan scoffed and returned to Astrid.

"The king who has come from Eire's Land," Rune said, "who claims rights to these lands, is the great elder son of Harald Fairhair."

Kallan turned about, eyes wide as she stared with disbelief.

"You do remember Fairhair, don't you?" Rune said. "And the claim to our land he made when he killed Lodewuk?"

Kallan frowned.

"Lodewuk," Kallan said. "News of Gunir's high king, reached all four corners of the world when Fairhair slew him. But the wars that scoured the lands of Midgard two hundred winters ago have no bearings on us now. Besides, Lodewuk was *your* High King. Not mine, the Dokkalfar's, nor Lorlenalin's. Ownership of the land died with him."

She managed only a single step back to Astrid as Rune felt his control leaving him.

"This king of Eire Land has revived them," Rune said, desperate to reach her. "Already he has laid claim to the kingdoms his great grandfather united when he killed Lodewuk. He is moving through all of Midgard, taking what land he desires. What's to say he won't breech Alfheim next?" Kallan clenched her fists and the Beast within Rune awakened. It felt the Seidr pool in Kallan's palm as if she ached to take aim and fire.

"Dan's Reach already contests our rights to Freyr's land, *our* land," Rune continued. "Too long, my vassal has guarded the southern borders of Alfheim ensuring that Forkbeard remains in Dan's Reach. A third contester could push Gunir into a war with Men. What side will Lorlenalin take when Alfheim is overrun and Men unite against us?"

"What concerns do I have if Gunir declares war on Midgard?" Kallan said.

"This war will belong to us all," Rune said.

Kallan narrowed her eyes. "I have more than enough dealings with the stubborn, irascible, erroneous King of Gunir, without worrying about a rampaging king from Eire's Land and the king from Dan's Reach or the ki—"

An arrow grazed Kallan's arm. She clutched the cut and fell to one knee in the time that it took Rune to draw his bow, aim, and release an arrow into the shadows behind them. Blood seeped from between her fingers as five men bearing the *naudr* rune on their tunics emerged from the wood.

An archer fell to the ground impaled by the precision of Rune's arrow, and Kallan threw her dagger into the heart of a second man. Rune unsheathed his sword and speared the third war-man, sliding the corpse off his blade while Kallan slammed the base of her palm into a face with hazel eyes, filling her hand with blood. He fell limply to the ground as the last war-man stared, stunned stupid, his eyes wide with fear as he read his fate moments before it came.

With hand glowing red, Kallan seized his throat and fired a blast through his neck. His lifeless body hit the ground with a thud.

"Erroneous?" Rune said. "Really?"

Kallan and Rune's breaths punched the air, neither aware of the single set of hazel eyes still watching from the ground.

Thick red flowed down Kallan's arm, mingling with the blood that covered her hands. After wiping the blade of his sword, Rune sheathed the weapon and came to stand before Kallan.

"Are you hurt?" Rune asked, taking her arm and inspecting the shallow wound from the arrow.

"I'm fine," she said, taking back her arm before he could inspect the wound further. "I don't even require a spell."

Rune scowled.

"Great," he said, bending down to a corpse and pulling off a pair of boots. "Then you'll have no trouble keeping up. Here." Rune tossed the boots into Kallan's chest. "And don't use your Seidr here. The last thing we need is more attention, princess."

While hopping about on one foot, Kallan slipped on the boots. An accompaniment of grumbles followed Rune as he kicked about the corpses and gathered up as many of the swords and daggers as he could find. After looking over each sword, he selected the best of the bunch and bundled the rest in the time it took Kallan to lace up the boots.

"Here," he said, extending an iron sword to Kallan.

She snatched the weapon as Rune took up the reins, pulling Astrid into the forest.

After looking over the mediocre sheath and its blade, Kallan fastened the weapon to her belt. Once the sword was in place, she shuffled the contents in her pouch and withdrew the golden fruit. Kallan sank her teeth into its flesh, and, after a quick examination to ensure her cut was on the mend, she scrambled along over stump and stone in the shadow of Rune's footsteps.

"Where are we going?" she asked as they bounded away from the road.

"Off the trail," Rune said. "When these men don't return, more will come looking for them."

Kallan added a skip to her step and ate through the apple as Rune grumbled from within the darkness.

"It's a fine pickled mess you've gotten us into."

"I've gotten—" Kallan said, oblivious to the pair of hazel eyes that dilated at the shimmering apple. "You're the one who feels the closest route to Alfheim lies in the opposite direction!"

"And put that coat on," Rune said. "I'm tired of seeing you shivering. You're making me cold."

"I won't—"

The coat landed in her face.

"Hurry along, princess." Rune resumed leading Astrid through the dark, not bothering to see if she followed. "I don't have time to compensate for your feminine weaknesses."

"I am not—" Kallan released a high-pitched growl.

Breathing steadily through a pair of swollen eyes already blackened from a shattered nose, Olaf's warman focused on the fruit clutched in Kallan's hand as he watched their figures fade into the darkness.

Olaf burrowed his gaze into Tarn. A fire rolled between them, casting shadows over the spacious tent, illuminating the dried blood that covered the whole of the warrior's chest.

A table and chair served as a prop for the several swords and shields strewn about with the finest armor of Eire's Land. Fine furs and feathered pillows buried the makeshift bed. Polished trays of fruits and meats, breads and meads, stretched along the far side of Olaf's tent.

The cast iron fire pit rolled with flames in the center of the room where Olaf sat, his fingers woven and his elbows propped on the armrests of his chair. Sitting beside him, a large elkhound rested its head on Olaf's knee, his dark brown eyes half closed with drowsiness.

"She's Seidkona," Tarn said. His eyes remained steadfast with certainty. "I have no doubt she's the one you've been looking for."

"And you're sure of this?" Olaf asked.

He unfolded his fingers, allowing his hand to fall onto the top of the elkhound. The large dog lifted his eyes in adoration as Olaf ruffled the top of Vige's head.

"She fired the Seidr through Varg's neck," Tarn assured him. "I watched her mend the wound from Njord's arrow with an apple as gold as the flakes sprinkled into your imported wines. She is the one you seek."

"And she's an Alfr peasant, you say?" Olaf peered from the hound, his hand resting immobile on Vige's head, his attention captivated by Tarn's report. "It seems you were right," he muttered to Thorer standing in the shadows behind him. "Did you happen to catch of what clan?"

Tarn shook his head. "They didn't make mention of it. Only that they journey to Alfheim."

"By passing through the Dofrarfjell?" Thorer said.

"It's entirely possible they journey to Nidaros." Olaf rewove his fingers and returned his elbows to the armrests. "All roads lead to Nidaros."

A suspended silence thickened the air within the tent.

"So she's Alfr." Olaf turned a curious eye to Tarn. "What of her companion?"

Tarn nodded.

"He is also. At first I thought him to be a guide, but he spoke too boldly to be a servant and she was dressed too poorly to own a slave." Tarn recalled the Seidkona's objections as she followed through with her companion's directions.

"Thorer." Olaf turned to his shoulder and Thorer straightened his back at attention.

"Sir."

"How many days are we from Nidaros?"

"Four."

"We risk losing their trail if we delay." Olaf gave the dog's head another gruff mauling. "Send a scout and twelve armed men. They are to take her alive. I want the scout to report on their whereabouts as soon as we have them within sight. I will lead a group of my men and provide aid once they have her in custody."

"And the men here?" Thorer asked.

"Have them break camp, but lead them on as planned to Viken. We can not divert our road to Aeslo. I have messages meant for Dan's Reach that can not be delayed."

"Rest here." Rune shoved Kallan onto a large rock within a small clearing. The long day was visibly wearing on them as the midnight hour crept steadily by.

Without argument, Kallan shifted her weight on the stone before pulling off the boots too big for her feet. At once, she set to work tearing off strips from her pant legs and fashioning herself foot wrappings as Rune gave her a discreet once-over from the corner of his eye.

Her bloodied, bare feet had been sliced and healed again. A layer of dried blood, caked and crusted, clung to her neck, her hands, parts of her face, and most of her arms, and, although the large, leather overcoat kept her shielded from the dropping temperatures, its constant weight had to burden her.

Whether she admitted it or not, the journey was taking its toll.

Exhausted, Rune settled himself down on the boulder beside Kallan.

"We can't stop to sleep," he said, exhaling some of the weariness. "Not until we can guarantee a few hours between us and the locals."

"Then what?" Kallan said.

Rune shrugged.

"Then you'll sleep." Rune stared at the night sky.

"What about you?" she asked.

Detecting a touch of concern that eased his irate mood, Rune studied the placated Dokkalfr. Her eyes glistened beneath sleepiness.

She was exhausted, and, if he pressed her, provoked her to lash at him, even rile her up a bit, he knew he stood a better chance at making her talk now than ever before. The situation was too readily available for him.

I'd be a fool if I didn't take advantage of this.

A brief concern for her sanity came and went as he resolved to push her to anger. If she was strong enough to survive a full blunt attack from Bergen, she could handle far more than what he had planned for her.

"I'm not foolish enough to mistake deceitfulness for empathy," he said, easing into the role and pouring on the disdain.

For a moment, Kallan appeared hurt, then grimaced.

"Perhaps I suspect deceit in you," Kallan said. "Besides...I'm not tired."

Rune frowned at the blatant lie.

"Good," Rune said and crossed his arms, ensuring he looked the part. "Then you have enough energy now to tell me why so many people are interested in you."

Kallan furrowed her brow. "I don't know."

There was the cue he had hoped would come. Before she could reach for her dagger, Rune had her by the arm, pulling her into him and holding her inches from his face.

456

"I know too much about the players involved to believe you know nothing about what's going on here. What's so interesting about that pouch of yours that the Dvergar would keep you alive?"

Kallan's eyes glistened in the moonlight, wide and clear like glass. He could see the turmoil spinning within.

"Abductors don't make murderers," she whispered. *Still lying.*

"I know the Dvergar," Rune said. "They don't take hostages alive unless you have proven to be more valuable alive than dead in their mines. And you hardly look like you'd survive a day."

Kallan pursed her lips in question. He was losing her anger and he knew it.

Rune gave her a shake and released her, letting her fall to the boulder.

"How does a Ljosalfr know anything about the Dvergar?" she said.

Rune scoffed, milking her temper. "I know a lot more than you give me credit for, princess."

Kallan dug her fingers into the rock. "Stop calling me that."

"Why does the Dvergar want your pouch?"

"What's to say I know anything about the madness of Motsognir?" she said.

Her exhaustion was making her slow to anger. If he wanted the answers, he would have to push her harder. Rune shrugged, and pulled his mouth into a smirk he knew she wanted to slap off his face.

"What's to say you don't?" he said. "You've driven me to bouts of madness numerous times in the past few weeks." He widened his smile, intending this one to hurt. It would have to hurt. "And I like you. It's no wonder you were almost dead when I found you."

Insult bathed her eyes, and Kallan hugged herself against the chill. A twinge of guilt stabbed Rune's chest.

"Why did you come here?" Kallan said. She was recoiling and the fight was leaving her. Rune held his hateful stare.

"Nothing more than personal interests," he said and waited until she showed a glimmer of flattery before ripping it out of her. "The Dokkalfar will raze my city if I step one foot in Alfheim without their queen."

"They'll do that regardless. Without me to command them, they will lead my army to Gunir and rend the walls." Kallan met his eyes. "Your precious Dark One, your berserker will be the first to die."

Rune was on her. With his hand to her throat, he shoved her down into the boulder before she could even realize he had moved. He held her pinned to the stone, seething with a sudden rage that flooded back as she dug at his hand. His breath grazed her ear as he hissed, indifferent to her claws.

"Your games grow tiring. My patience is gone. You fail to see the greater threat while you play with my people to sate your blood lust."

Even beneath the filth from the road, she smelled of lavender and rose. "The pouch, princess," he said, pushing aside the perfumes that fought to cloud his mind. "What do they want with the pouch?"

Her eyes glazed behind a wall of unfallen tears.

"It's just a pouch," she whispered, clutching his forearm.

He could see her walls weakening beneath the strain he put on her. She was no longer able to withhold the angst that was dangerously close to tearing down the walls she had built.

More prominent than before, her grief reached him from the shadows. Within the depths of her eyes, he saw his mother's anguish peering back at him, images of his mother lying dead, his father howling with rage, and Bergen maddened with the wrath of the berserker.

"Please." A wall of unshed tears held in Kallan's eyes.

Rune awakened from his memories, surprised to see that he still held her by the neck against the stone. He forced himself to hold the position a while longer.

"What pain do you so preciously harbor?" he whispered, remembering his plan, his act, and his feigned rage. "What complacency do you hide behind?" he asked and wondered why he cared at all.

"Why did you come for me?" she breathed, studying him through the strands of hair that had spilled over her face.

"I can't return to Alfheim without the queen." He spoke his half lie and watched the hurt blanket her face. "What did Motsognir want from you?"

"Nothing."

"Nothing," Rune said. "They beat you. They broke you. They battered you...and you insist they wanted nothing. I'll ask again until you utter the words yourself. What did Motsognir want with you?"

"Nothing." Kallan shook her head. "Nothing"

"Then why did they take you?" he asked. "What reason?"

"Reason?" Kallan scoffed. "The Dvergar are *trols*. They have no reason. They abandon reason. It is what makes them *trols*."

A subtle grin pulled at Rune's mouth, and the moonlight caught the gleam in his eye. He knew he had her.

"Then why do you grieve what they took from you, princess?"

"Leave me," she said and, with a surge of the Seidr, fired a pulse of energy that Rune felt building within her. He caught the flame with his hand, but the movement forced him to release Kallan, who pushed herself up from the boulder and wasted no time collecting Astrid's reins.

Back to the beginning and with no answers as before.

Rune sighed and ran a hand over his face as Kallan led Astrid through the trees. He followed a fair distance behind her while maintaining his grim mood and entertaining thoughts of abandoning Kallan in the forests of Midgard.

Chapter 47

Night changed the forests of Midgard, boldly blanketing everything in countless shades of black. Light blues, cold and distant like the light that encircles the moon, mingled with the shadow's umbra. There were places where greens so dark as to look black reached into every crevice, while others, distant and darker took the shape of trees.

The mountains appeared as nothing more than vast clouds that closed in around them from all directions forcing Kallan and Rune to commit to the winding paths that shaped the valleys with flowing rivers. The rivers were a splendor all their own, flowing like quicksilver, as black and as smooth as slick strips of elding. Their sheen rippled the reflected moonlight.

Kallan and Rune heard the running waters long before they saw them. Tattered and worn with exhaustion, they trudged on. Weariness pulled their muscles and rent their nerves until their eyes burned for want of sleep. Too tired to speak, they walked in silence, saying nothing beyond the spiteful glances they permanently wore through the long night.

In darkness, they left behind the last reds of the tundra, unaware that the world had faded to a lush green dappled with various shades of yellow. Beneath their feet, the earth softened and their spirits lifted for a short time.

Clusters of pine, peppered with birch and ash, became more frequent until it widened into vast forests that stretched up the mountains' sides. Black peaks, silhouetted against the night, obscured the horizon and seemed to forever block their path ahead while enclosing them on all sides. When, at last, they rounded the final mountain, the valley widened and stretched on ahead for miles, allowing them the first clear view since Jotunheim, but only as far as the night allowed.

The gentle pull of the leather reins and soft plod of Astrid's hooves lulled them into a monotonous drawl so that when Rune stopped, Kallan walked into his outstretched arm.

"What is it?" she asked, glancing about with the precision of a bird as she grasped the hilt of the sword bound at her side. "Is it them?"

The unmistakable scent of freshly turned earth hung in the air as Rune peered through the trees, fighting to make out the shapes in the shadows. He stepped to the edge of the forest and, all at once, she understood what he saw just beyond the wood.

"No," he said. "They're graves."

An infinite number of stones, arranged to outline a fleet of longboats sent out to sea, glowed white in the moonlight. Rows upon rows of stone ships, each one a grave, stretched beyond the mountain's end and spanned the valley. Some, of impressive stature, had been made of rocks that required the aid of a dozen men to move, while others—most—were small enough to move by hand. But one, the grandest, located in the farthest corner of the field, had been shaped with boulders five times the height of a tall man and etched with ancient runes.

For several minutes Rune and Kallan gaped, neither speaking as they beheld the magnitude of stone.

"There must be hundreds," Kallan breathed as she gazed, stunned at their sheer size.

"At least," Rune said.

With a muffled thump, Rune's satchel struck the ground, averting Kallan's attention from the field.

"What are you doing?" she asked.

Rune pulled the saddle from Astrid's back.

"We've been walking for hours," he explained, dumping the saddle on the ground. "We could be walking for hours more without shelter when we pass through that valley."

Rune pulled the furs from Astrid's back. "I want to catch some rest now while we have the trees for cover."

"What about them?" Kallan nodded back to the forest behind her and Rune shrugged.

"We've put enough distance behind us that we should be able to steal an hour or two without interruption."

"I don't like it," she said.

"Good." Rune dumped his armload into a pile. "Once we've rested up and have the strength to argue, we'll have something to discuss."

The door of Gudrun's chambers struck the wall, jolting her awake at the table.

Through a glassy-sheen, and with his hand held to the door, Daggon threw back his head and downed a large mouthful of mead. He drank until his cheeks bulged, holding the mead in his mouth for several moments as his amber eyes peered through the dark glow of the room.

The countless nights spent awake, dragged his posture down with a weary slump. Only when he released the door, did Gudrun realize he had been holding his inebriated self up from the floor. Pink and red gouges scored his face.

The hearth popped behind Gudrun where a large, black cauldron brewed something that smelled wonderfully like stew. A small bed shoved up beside the side of the hearth filled the darkest corner. The rose, heather, and mint hanging from the ceiling to dry mixed pleasantly, almost hypnotically, with the aroma of fire, sage, and food.

Daggon swaggered then stumbled, catching himself on the wall as he attempted to stand upright. By the degree of his sway, Gudrun concluded he had been drinking for a while, and the second stage of inebriated babbling was about to begin.

"Well, you look like a right mess," she said, sitting back in her chair.

Daggon gulped down a mouthful of mead with a lavish swig from his flask. With a drunken stupor, he staggered across the room with a sway as Gudrun eyed his arm ring. Daggon fell against the wall beside her table reeking strongly of black currants, spices, and unwashed man.

"Aaric's called off the shearches," he slurred. "The sholders have been called back to Lorlilalin...Lorlela...the city..."

Daggon threw back another gulp and heaved a rank breath. Round, amber eyes weakened and widened with sorrow. Releasing a long sigh, he let fall his head against the cold stone and watched the fire in Gudrun's hearth beneath the cauldron.

"He's leaving her t'die out there." Before his eyes could water, he threw back another mouthful then exhaled. "If she's dead," he said, raising his glassy-eyed gaze to Gudrun. "If she's alive, you would know, wouldn't you?"

Desperation clung to every word, mercilessly pulling at Gudrun's heartstrings. His nerves were wrought raw with a pain he couldn't dull in a flask of mead, no matter how many times he tried.

"Some things are not so easy to answer," she said through a sigh. "What I see now can be just as easily changed with a simple choice or cha—"

"Oh, shtuff it, wench," Daggon said. "You'd know if Kallan's Seidr goes out."

Gudrun studied the inebriate propped against her wall. The back of her throat burned as she gulped down a knot.

"You know Kallan passed from my vision a day after leaving Lorlenalin," Gudrun said. "That I haven't Seen anything since."

Unable to answer, they shared the silence for a moment before she continued. "If you've come here for answers, then I have none. I know as much as you."

"As much's Aaric?" Daggon asked.

Gudrun raised a brow in question, wondering exactly how much Daggon knew.

"He says she's dead," he said. "He prepares a ship."

The bite in his words thrust a gloom through Gudrun's bower and he shook his head and added, "He wants my arm ring."

A sting bit the tip of Gudrun's nose and she gulped down the unexpected wave of tears.

After another gulp of mead, Daggon pushed against the wall and forced himself into a somewhat upright position. With an added stumble, he shuffled around the table and crouched down beside her. The stench of mead wafted into the air as he breathed, but beneath the mead-glazed stare, a sober desperation stared into the gold of Gudrun's eyes.

"Can you really look at me and tell me she's dead?" he asked.

Forced to abandon the path of the Seidr, Gudrun mulled her intuition over as she followed the streaks and lines of scarring on Daggon's grizzled face. It was a long wait before she could answer.

"No." Gudrun shook her head. "I can't."

"Then ride with me." A spark of hope revived itself in Daggon's voice. "We'll go where the army didn't."

Gudrun chuckled at Daggon's spirit and cupped his scarred cheek.

"And I supposed we'll ride together to the ends of the earth and on to Ginnungagap?"

Daggon shrugged with a grin.

"If you like."

"When was the last time you slept, Daggon?" Gudrun said, weary with grief.

The captain dropped his eyes to his flask, seemingly unable to think back that far. His hesitation was all the answer she needed.

Rising to her feet, Gudrun pushed off the table and listened to the legs of her little, wooden chair scrape the stone floor and the shuffle of her own feet. Throwing back his head, he washed down another helping of mead and stood. Dragging his drunken self around the hearth, the captain plopped down at the foot of Gudrun's bed.

He didn't move when the frail, thin hands whipped away his flask and shoved a bowl of thick, heavy stew in its place. Another scrape of wood on stone ended with the strong scent of mint as she pulled her chair around and seated herself in front of him.

"What of Gunir?" she asked, tugging at her shawl.

Daggon didn't budge as he stared into his bowl at the vegetables, chunks of meat, and herbs soaked in a brown, thick broth.

"There has been no word," Daggon said.

"And the Dark One," Gudrun asked. "Has he started looking for his king yet?"

Daggon's eyes beamed through the disarray of red hair as he looked up.

"No." Daggon shook his head.

Nodding, Gudrun sat back in her chair, and watched the flames whip the air as Daggon downed the stew in one, continuous gulp.

Rune took a long draw from his pipe. He released the stream of smoke as he listened to the subtle movement of the war-men watching from the forest around them. Tension rose and he waited, but none of them had made their move.

Ten. Rune took another draw. *They're waiting for something.*

Silence followed a faint rustling of leaves.

Perhaps eleven.

He released another stream of smoke, and slid an eye over Kallan's body.

If I go through with this, it must look convincing.

Kallan's chest rose and fell with the steady pace of her breathing.

If she doesn't kill me in the process, he thought.

A rather convincing birdcall broke the silence, but Rune didn't move. A reaction now would trigger an ambush.

As if it was only he and Kallan alone in the middle of the wood, Rune snuffed out his pipe and tucked it away in the satchel beside him as he did any other night. He sat back and tapped a finger on one knee.

For the first time since he had pulled Kallan from the caves, she slept without the accompaniment of nightmares. He had allowed her as much time as he could to let her sleep and hated himself now for having to wake her, but he had already lingered too long.

May Odinn send them all to Hel.

Pretending he heard no spies, Rune shuffled up onto his knees and crawled to Kallan's side. Taking great care not to wake her prematurely, he moved and silently, carefully, positioned himself over the Dokkalfr until his body covered hers. He could only hope the image he created would keep them fooled until Kallan woke.

Please. Rune held his breath. *Have the sense enough to listen before lighting my ass on fire.*

The heat from her body hit him hard and his chest tightened. He leaned closer and fought to keep his head clear as he balanced his weight over her. He could not afford to restrict her movement. She would need the use of her hands.

His hair fell forward, blocking their faces from view. He brushed his cheek against hers and found her ear with his lips.

"Kallan," Rune whispered.

She smelled of sweet rose and lavender, and he felt his reasoning waning.

"Kallan," he breathed, louder than before.

He watched as sleep faded and Kallan regained consciousness. As she visibly tried to make sense of the situation, Rune pulled his mouth from her ear and the clouded haze in her eyes passed from exhaustion to bewilderment to panic. The last of confusion cleared and Kallan slammed her palms against his bare chest.

"Kallan," Rune whispered again, desperate to draw her attention and fast.

He could feel her heart thundering and watched her face flush red. Panic was taking her. Desperate to shock her into listening, Rune slid his hand over her thigh. As he had hoped, Kallan locked her eyes with his.

"They're here."

His voice was barely a whisper, but he could see she understood.

"They're watching." He mouthed the words, barely breathing.

"Where?" she asked, matching his whisper. Rune drew himself closer where he could hear the pounding in her chest.

"In the trees behind me," he answered, "and more near the oak in front of me."

Kallan's eyes didn't waver.

"How many?" she asked.

"At least ten," Rune said. "Maybe more."

With a look that confirmed she understood, Kallan amassed the Seidr in her palm, and the Beast stirred hungrily. As if to kiss her, Rune moved and Kallan reached up and fired a blast over his shoulder into the trees behind him.

Before the bodies hit the ground, Rune rolled and snatched his bow too late. An arrow impaled Kallan's shoulder and she fell to her knees as a soldier landed a blow to the back of Rune's head. Like a swarm, four men were on Kallan. Grabbing her wrists and arms, they pinned her to the ground, shoving her face into the dirt while Rune tried to stand, but stumbled when a strike to his back forced him down and they bound his hands before he could stand. Kallan had gone still. A glazed stare blanketed her eyes and Rune, with the relentless hunger of the Beast within, felt for Kallan's Seidr.

It slowly drained, not from the core where the Seidr began, but from the wound in her shoulder from the arrow's head. Along her Seidr lines, he felt her energy fading as if a poison was spreading.

"Kallan," Rune called.

Another blow to the head silenced him. All went black for a moment then color and light returned. The Beast stirred, pacing with great unease, and Rune stretched his senses to Kallan.

Despite the dull gaze on her face, within her a mass had formed. Rune felt her push her energy out and force her Seidr through the earth. Like a single strand in a tapestry, she wove her energy around the threads inside her captors. Reversing the flow of her Seidr, she pulled, drawing the Seidr inward and taking with it the Seidr around her.

Energy from her captors filled her as she drew their Seidr from them, pulling on the golden threads only she and Rune could see. Their strength abandoned them, and, one by one, they weakened their grips, freed her wrists, and fell. Kallan moved to lift herself from the ground, but as the last of the soldiers dropped, Kallan collapsed, caught herself, and tried again to pick herself out of the dirt.

The poison was spreading.

Wrapping her hand around the shaft, Kallan ripped the arrow from her shoulder with a scream. At once, the line of poison that was draining her Seidr stopped. Sweat beaded upon her brow and her hand shook as she withdrew an apple, provoking a new wave of excitement within Rune's Beast. The fruit's skin had barely grazed her lips when a set of fingers twisted into her hair and pulled her head back. A blade cupped her throat, and Kallan dropped the apple.

"Tarn! Get the apple!" a warrior cried and another obediently scooped up the fruit, cradling it like his firstborn.

Grabbing the face of the soldier who held her, Kallan fired the Seidr, propelling his body back. She caught his knife as he fell and threw the blade into the throat of the soldier holding Rune on his knees

472

and, extending her arms, she blasted the Seidr from both palms.

Two of the last three soldiers fell before either could land another blow and all was silent.

Kallan stood and pulled her dagger from her waist. Heaving, she approached Rune and unsheathed his sword. Nerves unsettled him and he watched as she flicked her wrist and cut his bonds with her dagger, leaving him to rise to his feet as the Dokkalfar queen turned to Tarn, who kneeled, cradling the apple, oblivious to the fate of his comrades, ignorant of the Seidkona who tightened her grip on the sword and dagger. Death warmed Kallan's lifeless stare.

In three long strides, she raised the sword and, as cold as a Nordic winter, thrust the blade up and through Tarn's back, lifting him off the ground. With a twist of the hilt, Tarn's body slid from the sword. Only when he hit the ground did he surrender the apple.

Blood dripped from the tip of Kallan's blade and pooled on the earth. Ignoring Rune, Kallan retrieved the apple and sank her teeth into its flesh and Rune watched as the fibers re-knitted themselves and exhaustion vanished. The poison receded, leaving her lines strong once more.

The forest was quiet. The sunlight had finally come, casting its light from the horizon. Picking himself off the ground, Rune took up an idle sword and calmly brushed the dirt from his trousers. The first of the earliest morning blue spilled into the forest and he gazed upon Kallan as she finished her apple.

With the back of his hand, Rune wiped the blood from his nose, assessed it then returned his attention to Kallan, who made her way to Astrid and gave of the apple.

Rune's eyes glossed with the sheen of a bruise that had already begun to turn the flesh around his eyes black and red. While clutching his stomach, he ambled toward Kallan. He stumbled once and caught himself before continuing on to the Seidkona who stared across the field in thought.

She didn't see the draw back of his arm as he closed in or his open, raised hand seconds before it connected with her face.

Seething, Kallan stared through the strands of hair as the red of Rune's palm on her white face vanished almost immediately.

"You lied to me," Rune said, clutching his side where someone's boot had landed. His voice carried through the field. "You knew they were after the apples. Why didn't you tell me?"

Kallan stared, but preserved her silence and Rune slammed his hand into her face again. Again, her white complexion healed at once, leaving no red, no markings, no sign at all that he had struck her or even felt it. Before she could turn back, Rune swung his sword. Kallan raised *Gramm* and met Rune's blow inches from her face.

"Why do they want the apples, Kallan?" Rune asked.

Saying nothing, she stared between the blades locked at the hilts. With a surge of strength, he pushed their swords down, and Kallan raised her dagger to his throat.

Cold emanated from the iridescent blue rings of her eyes, and just as quickly as he felt her Seidr ignite in fury, it ebbed and indifference moved in and took the fight from her. She lowered her dagger, succumbing to the impassive walls he felt her put up.

No sooner had she returned to her dispassionate haze than Rune swung his sword. Kallan sidestepped his attack, but, this time, he was ready. Closing his hand around hers that clutched the dagger, he shoved her back into the oak and drove her blade into the trunk as he stepped in, pinning her against the tree.

"Why did the Dvergar take you?" Rune asked, keeping his hand on hers that clutched the dagger.

He felt her Seidr rebound with the fight in her eyes, and she pushed against him. He laughed, encouraging her wrath, and freed her. She pulled the dagger from the tree, poised for battle, but her Seidr ebbed once more. Again, she lowered her dagger and the sword to her side.

Rune swung and Kallan stepped aside.

"I killed your father," he said. "Now hate me!"

He swung and Kallan blocked his blade.

"Hate me, Kallan!" The metal rang as she diverted his blade. "Stop blocking my blows," he shouted. "And hate me!"

He struck the blade of her sword, goading her, but she remained impassive and lowered her weapons again. Her indifference only drove him to pursue. Swinging the blade back around, he aimed for

Kallan's head and, forced to defend, she caught his blow on the hilt. With a spark in his eye, Rune leaned across their blades and closed his mouth over hers. He felt the Seidr erupt within her. It awakened the Beast that stood and paced hungrily. He bit her lip. Her Seidr surged, the Beast roared, and Rune released her and laughed.

Kallan lunged with an ignited frenzy, evoking a second boisterous laugh from Rune, who dodged her offense with a smile. With his sword, he forced her weapon to the ground and added a hearty chuckle.

He felt her temper spark and, undaunted, Rune slipped behind her, sliding an arm around her waist. Aggravating her fury further, he brushed his lips over the back of her neck, ensuring to keep her wrath awakened now that he had it.

Rune felt her shudder with ire and he pushed himself closer, holding her tighter. With a growl, Kallan turned and, as Rune emitted a third laugh, she threw the blades to the ground, ending their game, and pooled her Seidr. Rune braced to accepted the hit and absorb her Seidr while the Beast roared hungrily in anticipation.

A sob rose from the distance.

Kallan extinguished her Seidr as Rune stood straight, lowering his blade, and they listened.

A second cry confirmed their suspicion. Exchanging a quick set of glances, they forgot their quarrel, abandoned their differences, and, after Rune snagged up his bow and quiver, they sprinted out of the wood together. Over the fresh turned earth they ran side by side into the grave field, slipping in and out of the stone ships, drawn by a woman's cry. At the far most end of the field at the edge of a lake. Over the graves, they saw a lone soldier and a maiden. There, clad in a tunic adorned with Kallan's *naudr*, a soldier sat grinding the girl beneath him.

Rage inflamed Rune. Craze awoke the berserker. With his wrath ignited, he pulled, drew, and aimed an arrow, releasing it all before Kallan could summon her Seidr. Howling, the soldier arched into the arrow that impaled his back, and, taking three long strides, Rune raised his sword and swung the blade through the soldier's neck.

With a bloody thud, his head fell to the ground, leaving the whimpers of a pale, blond-haired woman, half stripped and trembling on the ground beneath the headless corpse.

Chapter 48

Sunlight poured over the earth and stone, contrasting the rising haze of black clouds that loomed over the mountains in the south. Kallan sat, propped against a lone birch tree, staring at the sky and the storm behind them.

Bound to the earth with the poison in her arm, she had recalled the deluge of images that flooded back of the damp caves and the orange light constantly battling back the darkness and a memory of the bitter tang wafting from a bowl. Through the darkness that enclosed her while the Men pinned her to the ground, she had seen it once again: the golden light of the Seidr that flowed, and she remembered. Wakening her senses, she cleared her mind and concentrated, and finally she found the Seidr beyond her own as Gudrun had tried teaching her ages ago.

Kallan's gaze shifted to the headless corpse Rune had kicked to the side moments earlier.

The blood pooled onto the ground and steam rose to the sky in a disorderly stream of white, which added a blackish-red melancholy to the terrain. Kallan averted her eyes from the corpse to the lake where she could make out the peasant's golden hair. The distant sound of splashing water assured Kallan that the girl they found beneath the soldier was still bathing in the lake. She had been bathing for nearly half an hour, desperately working to scrub the filth that had penetrated her flesh. Kallan hugged herself against the memory of Nordri's hands, his mouth, and his ditty sung in the dark.

Blanketed in an empty shadow Kallan hadn't been able to place, Rune walked around the grave field, inspecting the stones and runes, leaving Kallan alone to brood. After a while spent exploring, Rune returned and dropped a pile of small salmon to the ground along with an armload of sticks and branches. He busied himself with the fire as Kallan leaned into her tree.

"What did you do to them?" Rune asked.

Kallan looked to Rune, who nursed a small stream of smoke from beneath the brushwood. The morning sun dowsed him in various shades of yellow that contrasted the drab gray clouds looming behind them. He kept his attention on the kindling.

"You were pinned to the ground by four men," he said. "All four of whom are now dead." He watched his fire as he spoke. "No burns. No scorch marks. No blood."

Rune blew at the base of the smoke as it flowed in a steady stream until the fire erupted from the ball of tinder, slowly at first then faster as it settled onto the branches and twigs. Rune looked up from his work. "What did you do?" he asked again.

Kallan gazed out at the lake. The waters had settled, unbroken by any disturbance, confirming the girl had finished bathing.

"I took their Seidr from them," she answered. "The Seidr is energy produced by all living things. Most can't sense it and when they do, they often dismiss it."

The fire crackled as she let the tension between them brew. She remembered their quarrel, his mouth closed over hers, and the manner in which he had awakened her that morning. His striking her hadn't hurt with the Seidr from Idunn's apple still healing her. She suspected he knew this somehow and bit her lip, refusing to allow herself to ask the question.

"Seidkonas believe we exist because we borrow that energy." Kallan rested her head back against the trunk of the tree and stared off in the distance as she thought of such things as spells, the Seidr, and an energy that harbors its own life force. "When the body dies, the Seidr passes from it and joins the Seidr around us."

"Can you live without your Seidr?" Rune asked.

"All life comes from the Seidr," she answered gravely. "What do you think?"

Rune didn't answer.

Kallan pushed her fingers through her hair, desperate to rid herself of the impervious sense that she was sitting there naked and vulnerable. She fought the urge to take up a weapon, but stayed where she sat for fear any movement would further reveal her weakness. Content to be discussing something so natural to her, she continued without provocation.

"The Seidr within is always there, holding only as much as it can produce. Seidkona learn to recognize the energy. They learn how to use it within others and how to block it. An enemy can tap into a Seidkona caught unaware and draw the Seidr out of her." Kallan studied the clouds again.

"Like them." Rune nodded toward the forest where they had left the bodies behind.

Kallan nodded. "Like them."

Rune propped the skewered fish over the flames.

"You said all living things produce it," he said. "Animals? Reindeer? Elk?"

Kallan smiled.

"The trees, the water, the salmon we eat," she said, "everything. The earth provides an endless supply we can tap into."

"So why use your own? Why not borrow from the Earth's Seidr?"

She could see his hardened eyes taking in every one of her words with careful thought.

"Unlike the Seidr within, the Earth's Seidr is not harnessed, and is harder to control."

Rune nodded thoughtfully.

"So you're weak," he said and grinned as Kallan battled back the urge to launch into a full-scale demonstration of the Seidr's power.

Kallan crunched her nose. "As weak as you trying to divert a river's flow with your bare hands."

"And what of me?" Rune asked and Kallan dropped her shoulders as her anger ebbed.

"I don't know what you are," Kallan said. "Why you..."

She remembered the Seidr entering his body through his hands, travelling down his Seidr lines to where his core should have been, and vanishing where a great shadow enclosed it instead.

Exhaling, Kallan looked back to the sky as Rune dropped his attention to the fish.

Finished with her bath, the peasant girl walked, weak and frightened out of her senses, over the freshly turned earth and entrenched stones. She had tucked her long, plain hair behind her ears, which dripped water down the front of her hangeroc. As she walked, she hugged herself, which did little to cease her violent shaking. High cheekbones protruded sharply, pulling her pallid, grayish skin taut, and emphasizing her lack of nourishment. The gray of her round, sunken eyes matched the mountain's sky, giving her the appearance of the headless corpse nearby.

The girl came to stop several feet from the fire, doing her best to not look at the bloody mass behind her as she shifted her gaze uneasily between the Alfar.

"Thank you." Her voice lilted with an unexpected brogue that forced Rune to look up from the fire.

The woman-child appeared dwarfed at two heads shorter than Kallan. Perhaps too long, she admired Kallan's tapered ears and flawless, luminescent skin glistening in the sunlight.

"You are of the Elven race from the south beyond Viken."

In reply, Kallan fished through the contents of her pouch, withdrew a small stoppered bottle, and extended it to the girl.

Brewing with inquisitiveness Kallan saw in his eyes, Rune stared at the bottle in Kallan's hand. With hesitation, the girl reached it and swiftly, Kallan grabbed the girl's wrist and held her. Before the girl could gasp, golden threads of Seidr flowed from Kallan's hand and snaked up the girl's arm to her shoulder.

Enraptured, Rune watched the workings of Kallan's Seidr as the girl's face filled out. Her bruises faded from her pale complexion and her eyes glowed with radiance, replacing the shallow, pallid color that haunted her. The golden sheen of her hair returned as the strands thickened.

As the last of the Seidr threads ended, Kallan released the girl's hand, leaving the human free to gape with widened eyes, first at her own hand, which she turned over twice, then at the Seidkona.

"You're a witch," the girl said. "One of the *hagtesse.*"

Kallan smiled.

Her sudden lightheartedness plunged the whole of her disposition in a warm glow that noticeably drew Rune's attention.

"Witch. *Hagtesse,*" Kallan said, blushing at the additional attention from Rune. "I haven't heard those words since I studied abroad in Jorvik. I am Seidkona," Kallan said, still glowing. "You're from the lands north of the Humbre River. What do you call yourself?"

Shame weighed heavily on the girl's shoulders, bearing down the visible doubt that rested there. Her shyness made her seem shorter than she already appeared. She lowered her eyes, as if inhibited by her error, and softly answered.

"Emma of Lothen."

Emma risked a glance up, alternating from Rune to Kallan, seemingly unsure which of the two she should address. Deciding to stay silent, she forced her eyes back to the ground.

"Emma of Lothen, join us," Rune said.

He nodded to the ground between himself and Kallan, and waited for the girl to take her place beside them.

Tucking her knees beneath her with an efficiency that confirmed she was used to obeying orders, Emma kneeled where Rune indicated.

"How did come you come to be here in the North?" he asked.

Emma shifted her eye to Rune then back again to the fire before answering.

"Last summer, I and my husband, Ivann of Dofrar, left Engla. Ivann wished to return to Dofrar. He has a farm there...had a farm," she corrected herself. "I was on my way to Nidaros when..."

Emma afforded another glance to the headless body and shrunk down closer to the fire.

"Dofrar is a day's walk from here." Rune's eyes hardened with pensiveness. "How did you come to be this far east of the Dofrarfjell alone?"

"Ivann and I were working on the farm when Olaf arrived with his troops," she said, gazing back to Rune. "They killed everyone. I hid among the dead. When I came out, I was alone. Ivann..." Her voice cracked and she lowered her eyes again, unable to continue.

Saying no more, the girl hugged her legs to her chest and settled her chin in the crook of her knees. She barely moved when Rune handed her a skewered fish from the fire.

"We are heading to Nidaros ourselves," Rune said once Emma's fish was half-gone. "The roads aren't safe for anyone, and we can ensure your safety along the road there."

"Thank you," Emma mumbled and devoured the last of her meal.

Rune handed her another skewer off the fire and jabbed at the coals within the flames.

"Within an hour, Olaf's troops will swarm these lands," he said. "We need to put as much distance as possible between us and these corpses before night-fall. After we've filled our stomachs, we'll head out.

We'll have to move fast. Emma." The girl turned her clear eyes up to Rune. "You can ride Astrid."

As Emma devoured the last of the fish, Kallan looked to the south where they had journeyed down from the mountains of Jotunheim. Like a plague that stretched over all of Midgard, black clouds annexed the sky. A chill prickled her back and darkness moved in over the Dofrarfjell carried on the wind as if Olaf himself was leading the storm that was coming for them.

Within the hour, the rains began peppering their small caravan with pellets that left them drenched. Kallan was more than willing to lend Emma the overcoat along with what blankets they had obtained from Ori, sheltering her somewhat from the elements as they moved out of Upplond into Throendalog.

There, the mountains stretched on with endless greens of pine that complimented the drab blue-gray of the clouds overhead. Their road strayed from the river, abandoning them to the generosity of the land and fortune.

Kallan stumbled alongside Astrid appearing to be permanently peeved at Rune as she shifted a suspicious eye to every unusual shadow lingering in the trees.

The constant anxious glance from Kallan did little to ease the Ljosalfr's mood. Aside from the elation of picking off a pair of rabbits, Rune doled out a good portion of his own foul mood back to Kallan. Oblivious to their threatening charades and grateful for their company, Emma rode along, too weary and miserable to say much of anything.

The rains persisted into the evening, coming to a slow end an hour after the sun settled beyond the mountains. In the russet and gold of overgrown foliage, long after the deluge ended, they found an abandoned lean-to tucked away.

Rune pulled Emma's stiff body from atop the horse. Her frame seemed delicate and too easily broken, like a child's, in comparison to the Alfar women he had known. Taking care not to drop her, Rune held Emma by the waist as he waited until she found her horse-legs beneath her.

After regaining her balance, the Englian bounced along the clearing, restoring the blood flow to her legs. Exhausted, hungry, wet, and cold and eager for supper, a pipe, and a mead, Rune turned back for the rabbits and stopped short. Kallan's menacing gaze met him there as she scrutinized, trialed, assessed, and condemned him all within a glance.

After a moment, Kallan left him alone to the pair of rabbits as she hugged herself against the chill that wasn't there. The opportunity was too ripe, and the circumstances, irresistible. With a wide grin, Rune made up his mind to play the game, eager to keep the simmering fire inside Kallan well stoked lest she withdraw to her lies behind her iron wall.

Although...

Rune mused as he gutted the rabbit. Appealing greatly to the sadist within, his imagination flourished with the thought of having to provoke her all over again.

Exchanging sneers, Kallan and Rune sashayed and danced as they settled into their routine around Emma. He collected firewood. She tethered Astrid and removed the saddle and furs. A fire roared and soon the scent of roasted rabbit filled the air.

Claiming a small area beside the fire, Emma took the liberty of drying herself in its warmth. Still awed over the difference Kallan's Seidr had made, Rune, not so discreetly, dragged his eyes over the woman from Lothen. The wear and abuse from her life had vanished and she glowed with the radiance of the Vanir.

A flash of gold caught Rune's eye as Kallan passed an apple to Astrid. She planted a kiss on his velvet nose and, bored, hungry, and exhausted, Rune remembered their morning. His eyes lingered on the soft lines of Kallan's neck and soon his eyes wandered with his imagination.

Mid-fantasy, Kallan spun about and met Rune's gaze in a way that suggested a sudden urge to ignite the Ljosalfr in flame. Through the Beast, Rune felt a ball of Seidr manifest inside Kallan's palm. Rune cocked his head and grinned, egging Kallan on. Her Seidr built.

"I walked these roads with Ivann once." The sudden lilt of Emma's voice broke the tension, Rune's amusement, and Kallan's focus and her Seidr dissipated.

"He told me these shelters were built years ago by the Jarls of Lade to encourage merchants and traders over the Dofrarfjell."

Making her way to the fire, Kallan settled herself opposite Rune, who rotated the skewers. Emma watched the flames lick the air.

"I overheard Olaf talking to his captain about building more shelters along the trade routes and mapping the ones that are here," Emma said.

Rune and Kallan exchanged glances, their petty issues forgotten for the moment.

"What else did you hear?" Rune asked, passing Emma a stick of roasted rabbit.

Emma stifled a yawn as sleep settled in.

"More than I wanted of the dying," she said. "Nothing of Olaf."

Emma stared into the flames.

"I remember the cries of children and the growing pile of tiny hands." A tear rolled down her cheek and, with a trembling hand, she roughly brushed it away. "I wish I could forget," she said, her eyes deep and sullen as if she hadn't slept in days.

Unable to eat, Emma gazed instead at the rabbit then looked again to Rune. The orange firelight danced over her face.

"I remember seeing Olaf when we passed through Engla last year."

Rune froze.

"Olaf was in Engla?" he asked.

Emma nodded. "For a little more than four winters. He stayed and terrorized the people after winning the Battle of Maeldun. Everyone feared drawing his interests. He caused a lot of heartache to Ethelred, from what Ivann said."

"Why were you and Ivann looking to leave Lothen at all?" Kallan asked.

Emma's cheeks flooded with red.

"Ethelred wasn't ready to give up Bebbanburgh to Alba." Emma lowered her voice. "And King Kenneth was moving in to take it by force. After the wars with Dan's Reach and the wars with Miercna," Emma counted, "and the wars with Alba, Northumbria, and the conflict growing in Eire's Land between the high king and Boru..." Emma shook her head. "Ivann wanted to settle down and return to Dofrar. Take up his father's farm...try for a family without fear of—"

Emma dropped her head and swiped at another tear.

"We only arrived last summer," she said. "We stopped off in Bjorgvin then made port in Nidaros. Ivann has family there. We had just started to get things going on the farm..." Emma's voice trailed off. "It feels like Olaf followed us here straight from Dubh Linn."

"Do you know why Olaf left Dubh Linn?" Rune asked, eager to keep her talking.

Emma shook her head. "No one knows, really. Many just talk of mindless speculation. Some say he was growing restless in the shadows of Sigtrygg—"

"Sigtrygg?" Rune interrupted. "Sigtrygg Silkbeard?"

Emma nodded.

"How does Olaf know Silkbeard?" he asked, paying no mind to Emma's sudden wariness.

"A few years back, Olaf married Sigtrygg's sister," she said.

Rune sat up, his mouth agape.

"He married Gyda?"

"What's wrong?" Kallan asked as Emma nodded.

Sighing, Rune rubbed his hand over his face repeatedly before answering.

"Gyda and Silkbeard are two of Amlaib Cuaran's children." Rune dropped his shoulders when Kallan blankly stared at him.

"Who is Amlaib Cuaran?" she asked.

"Was," Rune corrected before Emma could speak. "He was the greatest king of the Ui Imair: the Dynasty of Ivar the Boneless, son of Lodbrok. Their family spanned Eire's Land, Alba, Strathclyde, Northumbria, Jorvik, even Miercna. Blodox and Cuaran warred for the land. Cuaran's skill in battle exceeds the songs of bards. It is still one of the strongest families in Dubh Linn."

"And Olaf married into this line through Gyda," Kallan said.

"It's more than that," Rune said. "Amlaib Cuaran's oldest daughter married Mael Sechnaill mac Domnaill."

Kallan stared, oblivious to the name as Rune waited, expecting her to react.

"Mael Sechnaill mac Domnaill," Emma answered for Rune, "is the High King of Eire's Land."

"Husband to Gyda's sister," Rune said.

Kallan's eyes widened with understanding. "And her brother—"

"Silkbeard." Rune nodded.

"—is king of Dubh Linn," Kallan concluded.

"To anger Olaf would be to arouse the 'attention' of the greatest family known to Eire's Land since Conchobar mac Nessa and Eire herself," Rune said. "It wouldn't be a small fight we'd be picking."

Kallan smiled with a twinge of delight in her eye. "Do you have plans to go picking?" she asked of Rune, who had a sudden urge to kiss her.

"What about you?" Emma asked. "What king do you serve?"

A smile split Rune's face as he realized they had not yet given their names. The girl had been so eager to not speak that they had welcomed the chance to get on their way.

"I serve the Ljosalfar," Rune replied. "I am Rune Tryggveson, King of Gunir." He nodded politely, earning himself a snort and an eye roll from Kallan.

Emma blushed and lowered her eyes to the ground as if suddenly conscious of the company she kept.

"You must be a great king to bring only a thrall through Midgard," she said.

Rune threw his head back and openly laughed loud and long. He felt the Seidr in Kallan collect.

"Kallan," she said with a gentle smile. "Daughter of Eyolf, Lady of Lorlenalin and Queen of the Dokkalfar."

Emma eyed Kallan's rags.

"It's a long story," Rune whispered to Emma, leaning in closer than necessary. Kallan clamped her teeth and her pool of amassed Seidr grew.

"His adversary." Kallan forced a kind smile and nodded at Rune.

"My prisoner." Rune grinned mischievously.

"His warden," Kallan snarled at Rune.

"My nag." Rune beamed.

Emitting a girlish growl, Kallan stood as Rune widened his smile, holding his full attention on Emma while Kallan marched off through the trees, slapping back the leaves and foliage as she went.

Emma hid her mouth behind her knees and flushed a brighter shade of red that glowed on her pale Englian skin. Strands of her long, golden hair fell to her face. "I'm sorry," she said.

Rune shrugged.

"Don't be. Kallan is over-sensitive and under-emotional. It's why I brought her along. So, you have kin in Nidaros?"

Holding her breath, Kallan dunked her head beneath the water's surface and rose again, sleeking her hair down her bare back. It was easy to forget her troubles in the middle of a vast Nordic lake surrounded by tall pines and clean water in the silence.

The light of the waning moon danced on the black water. The storm clouds had passed, taking with it the fog and leaving behind the vibrant, green waves of Odinn's lights that painted the clear, open sky.

The sharp pain that stabbed at her chest every time she thought of Rune smiling at Emma had dissipated to a dull nuisance she cursed beneath her breath. Free of the fierce panic that no longer provoked her worries, Kallan's thoughts wandered back to Daggon, Gudrun, Aaric, Eyolf, and the children left behind in the warrens.

She stared at the lights for a long while then dipped her head beneath the icy waters, purging the worries from her consciousness and forcing herself to forget. She forgot Rune's face when he sliced through the neck of the soldier seated on top of Emma.

Kallan wiped the water from her face, gasped, and dunked beneath the surface again. She forgot the wretched morning that began with Rune splayed over her and his words, his kiss, and the burn of his hand as he struck her. Raging ripples broke the water's surface and Kallan dove again with a gasp. She abandoned all thoughts of the Dvergar, and the pungent taste of their drug that robbed her of her senses, sanity, and her Seidr.

Kallan surfaced for air and plunged again into the lake, silencing the countless nightmares of Daggon's screams as she watched him consumed by Seidr flame. She recalled Rind's wide, clear eyes and the curl of Latha's bottom lip as Kallan waited for her body to adjust to the cold. Pain pinched her chest and she battled to breathe as she recalled a certain promise.

"I'll be down first thing in the morning."

The children had been expecting her. The children were waiting.

Kallan surfaced, releasing a gasp, and cleared her mind until all that remained was a single hunter deep in the forest of Alfheim, holding the tips of her fingers. Her insides warmed as they twisted with discomfort. Engulfed in memory, she swam to the bank of the lake, holding her eyes on the lights, the lights where shadow couldn't go, the lights that were free of Dvergar.

Kallan walked to the patch of brush where she had left her clothes well over an hour ago. She shivered against the damp, cold cloth as she pulled the woolen tunic over her head. Her attempt at scrubbing the filth from her clothes left them stiff and cold against her skin. The hem stopped mid-thigh.

One leg after the other, Kallan pulled on her trousers, reminding herself of the shredded chemise Rune had stripped from her only days ago. Another wave of warmth rolled through her, and she cursed her stupidity as she fastened the twine at her waist.

"It's too easy to forget everything here in Midgard, miles away from Lorlenalin and Gunir," Rune said.

Startled, Kallan jumped, hugging her front protectively.

There, leaning too comfortably against a birch in the shadows, Rune stood, arms crossed and wearing only his trousers, his boots, and a grin.

Heat burned every inch of her body as she felt her face flush red. Shaking, Kallan tied the twine at her waist.

"None of us should wander off alone," Rune said as Kallan sat down on the ground, where she wrapped her feet and crammed them back into her boots.

"How long have you been there?" she said, releasing her second foot.

Rune grinned, matching the mischievous sparkle in his eye.

"Long enough to know you haven't traveled north to see the lights like this before."

Another wave of heat and blood rushed to Kallan's face then poured down her neck and Kallan reached for her sword before remembering she had left it back by the fire.

"You—"

"They shine differently here in Throendalog," Rune said, raising his eyes to the sky.

Stunned by his impassiveness, Kallan stared, forgetting her anger almost immediately.

"We should visit Lofot and Vargfot up north in the winter sometime, although I recommend going by boat," he said. "The cliffs and mountains are merciless in the winter."

The ribbons rippled.

"They are beautiful," he whispered. "Some nights I would lie awake wondering why the spectacle isn't accompanied by a battle cry. I would spend hours, walking all night beneath them, straining to hear their horses' hooves beat the skies and Heimdallr's horn leading them on. But they are silent." Rune shook his head, still staring at the sky. "They shouldn't be silent."

Trembling, Kallan closed her eyes, ignoring every word, save one.

"*We?*"

Rune dropped his attention from the lights as she peered through the dark, hating him.

"Why would I ever...travel anywhere...with you ever again?" Kallan seethed.

Rune gave a look that feigned hurt.

"You act as if we're enemies. You know, if things had been different between our people, our families would have married us off to each other ages ago. You would be my wife right now, broken into obedience."

Flames consumed Kallan's hand, and Rune only grinned.

"You killed my father!" she screamed.

Her words echoed over the lake as all joviality fell from Rune's face.

Kallan forced each breath, panting as she shook with rage while the silence returned and she extinguished her flames.

"Why are you here?" she whispered.

Rune arched a brow.

"The Dvergar took you and dragged you across Midgard—"

497

"No! Here! The lake! Now!"

A single strand of wet hair caught in Kallan's breath.

"Where's Emma?" Kallan said, desperate to change the subject.

"She's fast asleep," Rune said. "I had to be sure her bed was warm before dragging myself away to find you."

His answer punched her stomach like dagger dipped in dragon bile. Nausea churned her insides and Kallan clenched her fists for want of her sword.

"I can take care of myself," Kallan said through clenched teeth.

"You always act so tough," Rune said, not bothering to hold back the amusement that dripped in his voice. "Like you're something I should fear."

"Bold words for someone whose neck was lingering beneath my executioner's axe a moon ago."

"You always have to be so spiteful." Rune pushed off the tree then widened his eyes with a sudden ingenuity. "This is because you're weak."

"What is it with you?" Kallan shrieked. "Constantly pushing me, saying whatever pops into your head, knowing it will drive me to kill you! Do you want me to kill you?"

"You must be exhausted brooding as much as you do all the time," Rune replied. "I am curious. Did the Dvergar find you to be this much trouble?"

Hurt flashed in her eyes and Kallan spun on her heel eager to return to her bedroll and sword, but

Rune was on her from behind, wrapping his arms around her so tight, he might have crushed her.

"It's still there." The heat of his breath grazed her ear. "Every bone they broke, every beating, every day you spent chained to the floor like a dog, lingering beneath the surface of that wall you have up."

The memories flooded in and Kallan thrashed, trying to break Rune's grip.

"Release me!"

Rune tightened his hold.

"You will remember their filth," he said, "every bruise, every break, every sound that stifled your senses."

All at once, the Dvergar stench flooded back: Nordri's voice, his smile, the bitter-tang and the darkness. She wouldn't remember and falter. Not where *he* could see, not he who was to blame for her capture in the first place.

Kallan released a shrill cry and Rune pulled her around to face him, pinning her arms to his chest before she could regain the sense enough to run.

"Tell me," he said, "are you elated for what they did to you, eager to thank them, or do you deny what they did to you completely?"

"Where's my sword? Where's my sword?" Kallan searched the ground, desperate for the blade she left behind.

"Your hands aren't good enough for the likes of me?" Rune said, riling her further. "You have to resort to cold steel?"

"I want to feel you writhing on the end of my sword as I run you through!" Her voice carried across the lake, filling the night beneath the lights.

Rune smiled through his retort. "I could say the same to you."

Like a Bean Si, Kallan screamed and flailed about. Rune flexed his arms to keep her in place, squeezing as her anger flowed like magma.

"You're a spoiled Ljosalfar prince," Kallan cried. "Thinking you can bend a woman if you ruffle her skirts the moment she swoons!"

Rune held his grin. "And that's only half the offenses I've shown you. Perhaps I should have been kinder. Broken your nose..."

Kallan growled, refusing to remember, not here, not now, not with him.

"...beaten your sides until your bones broke under my fists..."

Kallan swung her foot, but Rune crushed the fight out of her before she could land a kick.

"...kicked you in the face," he said.

Kallan turned her claws to his chest and he took her claws. He let her draw his blood and held his feet planted firmly into the ground, balancing their weight as she thrashed about.

"...crushed your hand into powder," he hollered against the strips of blood she dug out of him. "But, no," Rune purred. "I really showed you, didn't I?" He added a laugh and tightened his grip. "I *beguiled* you!"

Kallan's scream permeated the valley, leaving behind the echoes as she sunk her teeth into his chest. Rune roared and took the bite, tightening his hold as Kallan bit harder, until she tasted blood.

Nordri's sick smile beamed through the dark and Kallan battled back the memory as his laughter pierced the shadows. The sick stench came back to her with that laugh.

Forget...Forget...

And still Rune held her, unbending beneath her tantrum until her strength waned and she released him.

"You barely allow grief let alone the pain you harbor," Rune spoke hurriedly into her ear. "If you won't thrash and scream at them, then come at me." Rune shook her. "Come at me!" He shook her again, but Kallan had fallen limp. "Or should I kiss you? Maybe then you'll feel *something*!"

Kallan lay flaccid in his arms, saying nothing as she panted for breath.

Forget.

"You are weak, unable to confront even the slightest reality," he said. "Or did you enjoy the company of the Dvergar? Should I hand you back to them now?"

Kallan didn't move as she shook with unrelenting venom reserved just for Rune, for the Dvergar, for the clothes on her back that came from the caves...all because of the King of Gunir.

"What they did to you," Rune whispered. "That doesn't get to you even a little?"

"What they did to me," she whispered, hating the Ljosalfr holding her. "What they did..."

But the words wouldn't form without tearing down the wall that had secured her sanity.

"Yes, Kallan," Rune said. "What they did to you. What they took from you..."

"What they..."

Exhausted, Kallan slumped down into his arms and dropped her brow to his chest.

Forget...or you'll break. Not here. Not with him.

"They're not here, Kallan," Rune said. "They're miles away. Say it."

But in silence she slumped, her forehead resting against his chest, defeated, as she breathed in his scent of spiced earth and wished her death would come swiftly.

The green lights rippled across the sky in silence as Rune wondered, once more, why he couldn't hear the hooves of the horses and their battle cries. Sighing, he wrapped his arms around her waiting for the moment in which Kallan would break beneath her grief, when she would acknowledge the abuse she had endured from the Dvergar, her father's death...anything.

Rune listened to her huff.

"Will you never break, princess?" he whispered and touched his lips to her brow, unaware of the steady streams of hot tears that flowed down her face.

Chapter 49

Kallan slogged back to camp as Rune lingered behind her. With a cold shoulder, she crawled beneath the blankets, welcoming the cold over Ori's overcoat as she settled herself beside the fire. Within moments, fitful, dream-filled sleep eased Kallan's rage, leaving Rune to spend the night alone on guard.

It felt like minutes later, when he shook her and Emma awake. The sun's light barely spilled through the mountains. All evidence of the storm from the night before had vanished, leaving behind blue skies untainted by the blemish of cloud coverage and a comfortable nip in the air that encouraged movement.

They ate, said little, and broke camp half an hour later.

Sleep did Emma well and left her in a spry mood that bounced her every step. Oblivious to the silence suspended between Rune and Kallan, she plodded about through the open valley with an unnatural gaiety.

The lush pines thickened, and before the sun found the sky, they were buried in the depths of Throendalog's forest speckled with yellowing orange trees that had just started to turn from summer's green.

Whenever the impulse struck him, and it was often, Rune shifted an anxious glance to Kallan, who kept her head down, her mouth shut, and her eyes forward. Passing tufts of shrubs and lichen, their motley crew trudged along through Throendalog: the Dokkalfr, Ljosalfr, an Englian, and a horse.

By mid-day, when they stopped to finish the last of the lake trout, Rune tried again to provoke Kallan.

He sat. She scowled. He shifted. She sneered. Rune sighed and Kallan glared.

"You can't ignore me forever," he said with a soft grin.

Kallan stared into the north beyond the trees, the forests, and mountains. Her chest tightened as she thought of the open, endless horizons of Alfheim. A hollow void settled itself within, filling her with an ache that pulled her home.

Rune settled himself down beside her, pulling Kallan from her daydreams. Calmly, she met his gaze then turned back to the mountains before speaking.

"The mountains here remind me of home," she said.

"You worry often," Rune said, drawing an alarmed look from Kallan. "About Lorlenalin, I mean," he clarified and she returned her eyes to the horizon and mountain peaks.

"Surely you have your captain and high marshal to maintain order in your absence," Rune said, forcing Kallan's critical eye. She studied him as he spoke. "What impending problem demands the constant vigilance of Lorlenalin's queen?" Rune asked. "What is so fragile that you neglected to secure someone to oversee the issue in your absence?"

Taking in a breath and releasing it through her nose, Kallan gazed out among the mountains. Their white tips reached to the sky. There were places where she couldn't tell cloud from snow tipped peaks.

"The children," she answered.

Rune raised his brow when a series of sudden, sharp snaps averted his attention to Emma. Gripping a stick too tightly, Emma whacked away at the trunk of a defenseless, lone birch, forced to take her beatings.

Staring blankly at the skies, Kallan paid the human little mind. Her thoughts filled instead with white stone halls and cloudberry jams served with warm breads from Lorlenalin's kitchens.

Rune picked himself up from the ground.

"Here," he said, pulling the Dvergar sword from his waist.

Curious, Emma lowered her stick and blushed at the attention drawn from the Alfr king, who offered her the hilt of his blade.

"Like this," Rune said, coming to stand behind her.

The weight of the sword pulled Emma's body forward and her arm dropped to the ground with the blade. Long strands of golden hair fell like a shimmering curtain, catching the sun as the sword pulled her off balance.

Rune relinquished a huff that drew Kallan's eyes just as he stepped in closer behind Emma to help her lift the sword with both hands. Kallan's nostrils flared at the sudden awareness of how petite and pretty the peasant was.

"It's meant for two hands," Rune said, guiding her delicate left hand to the hilt. She dropped the sword again, forcing him to hold the unsupported weight with her. "Raise it up and draw it down, against the edge on an angle."

He followed through with a set of strokes, left then right then left, before leaving her to her own. Almost at once, Emma lost her balance again and fell forward, digging the fine point of the blade into the earth.

Kallan cringed.

Unable to watch any more, the Dokkalfr emitted a grunt and jumped to her feet. "Oh, here," Kallan said, making her way to Emma.

The girl blushed again, uncertain of the concealed rage of the Dokkalfar queen swaddled in woolen rags two sizes too big for her frame.

With a rigid flick of her wrist, Kallan yanked her dagger from her waist and tossed it to Rune, forcing him to catch the blade mid-air before it struck him in the face.

"I want it back," she said, extending a finger to Rune and relieving Emma of the sword.

Its jewels and black blade caught the sunlight and encouraged Kallan to twist her wrist around, gaining a solid feel for the sword as the Englian skipped out of the way, clearing the area for Kallan.

The sword's balance was perfect, too perfect. It was dead on. A twinge of jealousy pricked her chest. Intricate gem work featuring black opals, black hematite, and silver filigree adorned the elding hilt. The pommel itself flashed in the sun with the reds, black, blues, and greens of a black fire opal. But the runes, the elegant, lavish runes, caught her eye and Kallan read aloud.

"*Gramm.*"

Her palms grew moist as she recalled the stories Daggon told from an age nearly forgotten. She raised a widened gaze to Rune.

"This is *Gramm.*"

Grinning proudly, as if he himself had forged it, Rune extended a hand for the blade.

"Give it back," he said, still smiling.

With another turn of her wrist, Kallan spun the blade, poised at the ready for battle.

"Take it back," she dared, with the slightest hint of a grin.

Rune glanced at the eighteen-inch blade in his hand and then to the thirty-five inch blade pointed at him as if inadequacy suddenly weighed heavily on his consciousness.

"You could at least loan me one of the man-made swords," Rune said.

Kallan shook her head.

"They're iron," she said. "An elding blade would break them." Kallan raised *Gramm* at the ready.

"How convenient." He thrust the blade to test its balance. "No Seidr."

Kallan grinned, adding a malicious ambience to the air.

"No...whatever it is you have in you."

Flicking *Blod Tonn* at the ready, Rune waited and Kallan lunged. The sword collided with the dagger and Rune pushed back, parting their blades. Again, Kallan channeled her energy, bringing the sword into Rune. He swung the dagger around, catching Kallan on the upswing, recovered, and swung again, forcing the Dokkalfr to dodge.

Mirroring Kallan's footwork, Rune parried and provoked, guiding her next offense to his liking. He shifted opposite Kallan, brushing alongside her as he guided her dagger into each block, but Kallan was somewhere else, lost to the swordplay.

Spellbound in musings, she relived the sparring she once rehearsed with her father. Up again, Kallan spun, pacing her breath and balancing her footwork as her father talked her through the motions.

And again, she heard her father say as she swept the blade, bringing it down onto *Blod Tonn.*

First and foremost, hold your balance. You'll never win a fight with poor balance. But she was unbalanced and losing her footing there with Rune. Too quickly, Kallan felt herself slipping. She spun, bringing *Gramm* back around as she had done with her own sword so many times before.

Use your weight to anchor the swing. Let the sword do the work for you, her father had coached.

Guiding *Gramm's* blade up, Kallan swung the sword to her shoulder, following through with her father's advice, but she was reaching and falling.

Reach with the blade, not with your arms. Never overextend. Remember, the blade is an extension of you.

The sun had caught the pride in Eyolf's gentle eyes as he had looked down at his daughter. Desperate to hear his praise once more, Kallan lunged, forgetting it was Rune standing in front of her. *Gramm* slammed down into *Blod Tonn,* sending waves through her. Her voice faded, his smile vanished, and her father was gone all over again.

"Kallan?"

The sunlight flashed and the leaves whispered in the wind. Astrid snorted nearby, nuzzling the grass beside Emma.

Beads of sweat poured down Kallan's face as her minute gasps of breath hit the air. A memory flashed of black blood covering her hands and she flinched, her hatred rebounding. From between the blades,

Rune watched with a concerned look that baffled Kallan. She recalled Rune riding in the distance from the Dokkalfar keep, leaving his men to do his bidding. A dark desire to pull back the blade and summon her Seidr surged through her, but she would be lost without him, here in Midgard.

"I don't know the way," Kallan whispered between their locked hilts.

Forced to ignore the hate that stirred her rage, Kallan lowered *Gramm* and passed the sword to Rune. She accepted *Blod Tonn* without a word. Alone, Kallan returned to her place on the stones beside the trees where she resumed her silent brood.

Through forest and valleys, they continued their march, stopping to water the horse when the opportunity presented itself and doing their best to keep a steady pace. Within hours, they found their progress lagging, and frequent breaks at streams did little to lift their spirits. At last, as day's light succumbed to the void of night's darkness, Kallan, Rune, and Emma settled down around a fire and roasted game, happy to see most of their journey behind them.

Locked joints and shredded muscles numbed them to a dull, constant ache they could not ignore. Without a word, they ate their share, and, when Rune moved to goad Kallan's temper, she coldly dismissed herself for the night. It was with a heavy mind that his plans of rumpling her emotions came to an abrupt end.

Miffed with a mood, Rune bid Emma good night and begrudgingly sent himself to bed.

The early night made for an early morning blanketed in gray. Low clouds lingered, suggesting a constant drizzle that never came. They headed out through a heavy, morning mist that thickened as the day dragged on.

Ignoring every pass and short-handed comment Rune made, Kallan kept her tongue stilled and her eyes set on the path encircling the base of the mountains. Streams and rivers flowed together around the land, leading them on through the forests of Midgard.

For long stretches at a time, the forest remained thin, allowing them a glimpse ahead to the next mountain. Other times, they walked, unaware of the world outside the trees enclosing them. By late day, their steady pace came to a sudden halt at the banks of a wide, thunderous river that obstructed their path.

Emma slid from Astrid's high back, hitting the ground hard before joining Kallan and Rune on the river banks. They stared upstream and down then out across the torrents flowing north through the trees.

After a moment, Rune nodded downstream.

"We'll have to cross there," he shouted, pointing toward a wide region. "It should be shallow enough that we can wade through without too much trouble."

"Couldn't we follow it?" Kallan asked as Rune took up Astrid's reins.

Rune shook his head.

"We need to get to the Nid." He looked to the southeast. "The river is too wide and the current too swift. Its end will take us to the sea and there is no telling how far back it starts."

"How do you know this isn't the Nid?" Kallan asked as Rune pulled Astrid along the edge.

"Because," he said after finding a reasonable place to cross and easing his feet into the icy water. "We haven't crossed the Gaulelfr yet."

He was too busy watching his footing to look her way.

"When will we cross the Gaulelfr?" she asked as he eased further into the waters.

"Now."

Together, Kallan and Emma scanned the banks where rocks clustered along the edge. Pulling Astrid onto the shoals, Rune signaled to Emma, who obediently followed.

By the second step, she misplaced her footing and slipped, forcing Rune to catch her mid-fall. Up and around, he flung her onto Astrid's back as Kallan inched her way into the water behind them. Already the relentless roar of the deafening rapids needled its way into their nerves.

"Is it deep?" Kallan asked.

Rune looked out, examining the disrupted grays and white of the current.

"We won't have to swim," he said.

The further they walked, the more the surface rose until it stopped at the top of their thighs where the cold bit the most. They made their way over large, white rocks that had washed downstream.

Half way, Rune stopped, forcing Kallan to call from behind.

"What is it?" she asked over the roaring rapids.

"Salmon." Rune eyed the multiple streaks of silver that swam past. "Big ones." He felt one brush his leg. It was so close that he contemplated reaching down and grabbing it. A smile burst across his face. "We'll have to come back here for a few days with a net or some line. It'll make for a—"

A flash of fire grazed his leg and a large, steel colored salmon, nearly three stones in weight, floated to the surface and swept into Rune's thigh. With her palm raised, Kallan cradled a tiny flame. Her eyes seared the air.

"Move!"

Stunned, Rune lifted the fish by the base of its tail. His smile didn't falter as he slogged on, leading the way through the current to the other side with horse and fish in tow.

Sharp splatters of water slapped the ground as Kallan and Rune took turns wringing out their clothes. After fastening the fish to the saddlebag, they continued through the forests of pine.

For hours they trekked through the thick foliage of Throendalog where the yellows dissipated, leaving behind the last lush green of summer. At the mountains' end, the forest cleared and, for the first time since arriving in Midgard, they could see on ahead to a clear horizon and the sea.

"There." Rune pointed ahead to where a river twisted with the land. "That is the Nid and there..." He shifted his finger out to the inlet. "...is where she bends to the east."

For a brief moment, they studied the end of their road, entirely too aware of their throbbing joints and stiff muscles.

"Come along," Rune said. "We'll continue north, and follow the Nid to the sea. From there, we follow the beach to the village."

Down into the valley they continued, plodding on as the foliage thickened. Pines gave way to large clusters of white birch speckled with the occasional ash and pine.

By early afternoon, they joined with the Nid, whose wide, calm waters cut into the land, carving a path they followed through the trees. As the last of the forest cleared, the land sloped down to the shores where the gulls cried and the river veered east.

"Nidaros is named for the Nid that flows around it," Rune said. "There is only one road into Nidaros and that is the land bridge here."

A mere three hundred paces of land spanned the area between Nid and the sea. So close to their end, they walked along the beach, weary and ready to rest. In the distance, across the water inlet, rows of rounded mountains blended with hills that lined the fjord, seeming like one continuous mountain.

"The Throendir have established a fishing settlement that flourishes on trade," Rune continued. "Already they have secured routes to Bjorgvin and the Faer Islands."

The waves lapped the sands as they made their way down the gray shore.

"And the Throendir themselves?" Kallan asked, sounding worried.

"Eager to help," Rune assured her, flashing his grin. "Mostly because it will annoy Forkbeard."

The last of the trees thinned, revealing a barren plain barely visible through a thick fog that had rolled in from the sea.

"I thought Forkbeard was their king," Kallan said as Emma, too tired to comment, listened atop Astrid.

"Forkbeard thinks he is," Rune said. "The Throendir prefer the rule of their own people and the Jarls of Lade Northeast of here. When last I was here with my brother, Hakon was complaining about the tribute Forkbeard forces him to pay to keep his ships at bay. Nothing a king hates more than having to pay tribute."

The first of the homes appeared through the haze.

"Why?" Emma asked.

"How much can you drain a kingdom's economy all to secure your throne and buy peace for your people?" Rune asked and watched Emma flush. "At that time, when last I was here, Hakon Jarl was talking about putting an end to his levy. In fact, that was the reason for our visit."

Rune remembered the ornery, old man mulling over a mead. "He called upon Gunir for aid in hopes that we would form an alliance based on our mutual tension with Dan's Reach."

They drummed along to the rhythmic clomps of Astrid's hooves, allowing the silence to rise up between them before Kallan spoke again.

"Did it work?"

Rune held his face unchanged as he looked on to the village ahead. It was a long wait before he answered.

"Gunir accepted the alliance, but..." Rune glanced at Kallan, unsure if this was the time or place to test her temper. "...without assistance against Lorlenalin, we could not lend resources against Forkbeard."

Visibly taken aback, Kallan flushed as they neared the village.

The fog mingled with a lackadaisical dreariness over Nidaros. The distant plink of a blacksmith's hammer coldly welcomed them. A dog barked. A lone child cried. The happy buzz that usually accompanied a trader's port had fizzled to a low drum that dropped every merchant's spirits to a drudge set to the rhythm of the smithy's hammer.

Upon closer inspection, a number of the houses, blackened from fire, had fallen in on themselves, and the infamous ports of Nidaros, always stocked with the grandest of ships, were barren. Only a number of smaller vessels lay in the harbor, their keels broken like the back of a once grand berserker. And in the town's center, amidst the lingering gloom and despair, the main posts had been placed and the floors laid for the makings of what, it could be assumed, would be a mead hall grander than the one behind it.

It was a moment before the Alfar realized they had drawn more than a few inquisitive glances as the crowd around them grew. Emma slid down from the horse, hitting the ground hard as the mutterings of countless faces kept their safe distance.

Stepping closer to Rune, Kallan gripped her dagger unseen. He too shifted his eyes to each blank stare all marked with the distinct, deadened look everyone wears following a catastrophe.

"Who are you?" The gruff voice of an old woman carried over the anxious compilation of curious on-lookers, commanding a hush that the Throendir heeded. Pushing her way through the crowd, a short, stout woman emerged. A ring of keys rattled at her side.

"What business do you have here?" she barked, undaunted by their grand appearances that glistened and gleamed in contrast to the drab, gray village. Anger lined her face. A bit of leather held her long, silver-streaked, blond hair, accenting her thin cheek-bones.

Though clearly exhausted, Rune flashed a smile at the woman.

"Hello, Olga."

The gentleness of his voice seemed to soothe the lines of rage from her face and relaxed her shoulders. Gasping, her entire physique warmed.

"Rune."

"This is Kallan Eyolfdottir of the Dokkalfar, Queen of Lorlenalin," Rune said slipping a hand behind the small of Kallan's back, encouraging her to give a warm smile. "Kallan, this is Olga, wife of Halvard. She runs the place." When he spoke again, he returned his full attention to the stout woman before him. "We need to see Hakon. Is he here?"

The name seemed to pierce Olga like a twisted blade and she dropped her shoulders, swallowing a visible lump in her throat as her clear, blue eyes swelled.

"I'm afraid you've come for nothing," she said. "Hakon Jarl is dead."

The heavy burden carried from Jotunheim, doubled as Rune's head spun for answers.

"Olga?" Emma's small voice cut through the crowd. As she pushed her way to the forefront, Rune watched the color drain from the old woman and her eyes met Emma's.

Olga gasped.

"Emma." With eyes filling with tears, Olga met Rune's gaze then looked to Kallan. Worry filled her eyes as if she scanned their small group for another. "Dofrar," she muttered and the tears fell. "Olaf said...he would send troops to Dofrar..."

Her thin bottom lip quivered as Emma spoke.

"Olaf came...we didn't have a chance. There was no warning. The blood...the rivers were red. Piles of children' hands...Ivann didn't make it...Ivann didn't...And then one of his men...they...he was still in me when his head hit the ground."

And Emma fell into Olga's arms and sobbed, quietly at first, then louder, giving voice to the grief of Nidaros.

Chapter 50

Earth-green fabric trimmed with gold fell from Kallan's shoulders. Gold cords laced the dress beneath Kallan's arms, allowing the fabric to yield where needed and exposing more of her bosom than she was accustomed to. Aside from the skirts stopping mid-shin and the dress being snug in places, it fit perfectly.

"I'm sorry we don't have anything longer." Emma flushed as she poured a bucket of the bath water outside the Throendalog bathhouse on the down slope toward the sea.

"It'll keep the hem out of the mud," Kallan said as she admired the fine leather boots that hugged her delicate, raw feet and shins.

Preening every which way, Kallan studied the fine embroidery of the fabric and exhaled.

"We don't usually make much use of the bath house between Laugardagr," Olga said as she threw Kallan's old clothes into the fire. "I don't care what day Halvard says it is. Nothing refreshes a weary traveler more than a hot bath." She watched the black smoke billow through the ceiling then looked to Kallan. "How do you feel?" she asked as Kallan twisted and turned before the glass, catching the fire and candle light with the gold cords.

Kallan smiled.

"Better," she said. "I prefer the trousers and tunics for sparring, and avoid the gowns Gudrun insists I wear." She pulled at a handful of waist-length hair, curled into ringlets over her shoulders, and began positioning them strategically over her front. "But the stench of the Dvergar is embedded into that set and besides..." Kallan sighed, still fussing with her final results. "...it's nice to look like a woman again."

"I bet Rune will approve," Olga said, repositioning the clothes in the fire with a stick.

Kallan's blood stilled and her face drained before flushing red. Without a word, Kallan looked back to the glass, turning her profile to chance a glance at her rear while she mumbled something akin to 'not caring what Rune thinks.'

Olga released a bark of laughter that startled Kallan.

"That's the boldest lie I've ever heard." She shook as she chuckled and tore her eyes away from the fire. "Fool yourself all you like, my dear. I know what I see when I see it, and you have no need to fret. You look as stunning from behind as you do in the front. He'll approve if he's not dead or without package."

Blushing, Kallan ran her hands over her stomach, unnecessarily smoothing the fabric, and repositioning her ringlets one more time.

Buried in the dark corner of the mead hall, Halvard dropped the tankard carved of cattle horn onto the table in front of Rune. With a nod of thanks, Rune took up the tankard and examined the lopsided horn that generously filled his grip. The end of the horn had been cut and discarded, leaving two spans in height, which had been hollowed out and fastened with a plate of soapstone, allowing it to stand upright on the table. Brimming with black mead, its contents smelled strongly of honey, mulled spices, and currants.

"Why the second mead hall?" Rune asked with a nod toward the door as Halvard settled himself into a chair across the table from him. His own drinking horn carved mug clutched in his hand.

"It's a house for Olaf's gods," Halvard said, peering into his mead. "Olaf invaded this land barely a fortnight ago and demanded Hakon's head for reward. His thrall obliged. He found him cowering in a fallout shelter south of here in Odinssalr."

Rune found Halvard's eyes in the dark. The wrought iron circlet suspended over the hall's center and a fire tucked away into a small hearth provided the only light.

"It doesn't make sense," Rune said, shaking his head. "Hakon shared Olaf's disdain toward the Dani and posed no threat for his throne. He could have used him," Rune said. "Why would Olaf want Hakon's head?"

Halvard gulped down a mouthful of mead.

"Long questions deserve long answers," he said and tipped his tankard to his mouth again.

"Where is Olaf now?" Rune asked, his face hardened with thought.

Halvard returned his tankard to the table.

"After declaring himself king and throwing Hakon's head to the sea," Halvard said, "he started work on that house of his. There was talk of them heading south to Aeslo. The market there in Viken has drawn his eye." Halvard washed down a large mouthful then dropped the weight of the mug back to the table before he continued. "But what of you, Rune Tryggveson? What brings the Alfar to Midgard?"

Rune smiled.

"Long questions deserve long answers," Rune said and took his first gulp of Throendalog honey mead. The sweet and smooth mingled with a full body that enchanted his pallet with a myriad of spices.

"I've never heard of a king traveling alone without a guard before," Halvard said. "There is the occasion where a man seeks to roam free from the constant eyes of his peers and the burdens of responsibility known only to a man. I understand the need for a man's solitude. Hel, even a romp with a wench is needed once in a while, but you've selected the monarch of your enemy." Halvard grinned across the table. "A situation like yours demands answers."

Rune took another swig.

"I took her."

"Took her?"

"Yes." Rune folded his arms across the table. "I saved her from herself. I took her from Lorlenalin to save her from a traitor, who seeks to kill her. While on the road to Gunir, the Dvergar intercepted her and I tracked them to the mountains of Jotunheim."

Mead dripped from Halvard's black beard. Too stunned to drink, Halvard slowly lowered his tankard.

"I managed to get her out of there before their descent into Svartálfaheim," Rune said. "With the Dvergar scouring the obvious routes back to Viken, we had no choice but to head north from Jotunheim."

Halvard gasped.

"You traveled by way of the Dofrarfjell?"

Rune nodded.

"Across the Dofrarfjell," Rune said.

"Are you mad?"

Sitting back in his chair, Rune released the mug. There would be no more drinking until he had concluded his business.

"I came here expecting to call upon a favor from Hakon Jarl owed to my brother and I," Rune said. "We are grateful for the lodgings, food, and drink you've provided us. It is with a heavy heart that I must ask for more."

Halvard peered from behind his tankard with brown eyes that matched the golden glow of the mead hall.

The sharp clank of soapstone plates dropped to the floor accompanied a bellow of laughter from an inebriate nearby. Rune and Halvard examined a neighboring fool, who had stumbled to the floor and taken half the table with him. The uproar settled and his comrades helped him to his feet as the men returned to their conversation.

"We need a ship," Rune said. "Our cities are at war. Bergen holds the throne in my absence, and a rogue hides too close to Lorlenalin's throne."

"Your fair maiden, she—" Halvard stammered. "Does she know?"

Rune shook his head.

"She suspects nothing."

"Tell me, Ljosalfr," Halvard rasped. "How did a king of Gunir come by this information?"

Rune shifted his gaze to the table of comrades as the cold, blue eyes of one Dokkalfr blazed in the forefront of his memory. After much contemplation, he decided to disclose his findings.

"Nearly a moon ago," Rune said, "I was captured by the Dokkalfar. Upon my imprisonment, I was approached by one of Kallan's men, who offered my freedom and an alliance with Gunir."

Halvard tightened his lips.

"That's a hefty offer," he admired. "What did he ask in return?"

Rune shook his head.

"Nothing," Rune said, "but my word that, when I rode from Lorlenalin a free man, I would take Kallan with me...and kill her."

A rise of laughter carried through the hall, briefly diverting their attention.

Halvard leaned closer, lowering his voice.

"Does she know?" Halvard asked.

Rune grinned as he turned the tankard over in his hands.

"That girl would slit my throat if she ever learned I made that deal."

"Will you go through with it?" Halvard asked. "Will you kill her?"

Rune shrugged.

"Too often I've asked myself that question." A memory of Kallan's knee landing his manhood came to mind. "I can't deny that the thought has tempted me once or twice." He shook his head. "But no. A dead queen would produce more questions than it would answer."

Halvard threw his head back and took a long swig.

"The problem is," Rune said after Halvard returned the tankard to the table, "if she returns to Lorlenalin, that Dokkalfr will see that the job that I didn't do is done. I've no idea how long he'll sit quietly in Kallan's absence. For all I know, he believes I've upheld my end and has set his own workings in motion.

As you can see, it's imperative that we get back to Alfheim immediately."

Halvard frowned, clearly realizing the full scale of Rune's problem. He clutched the mug in front of him as his large frame slumped over the table.

"Olaf won't make the journey easy for you," he said. "He seeks to drag Alfheim into it."

"This isn't our war," Rune said. "We have our own in Alfheim. We can't be dealing with the troubles of Men when we lack the ability to settle our own differences."

Halvard peered down into his mead with a bit of admiration.

"The troubles of Men may be coming for you sooner than you think," Halvard said as he took a drink.

Rune eased back into his chair.

"You Alfar have always been void of our rule." Halvard looked up from his drink. "You are content to remain ignored by our *Thing*. With your own politics and your own laws, you—for the most part—stay to your business while we stay to ours."

"You're saying it may not be long before even we are forced to adhere to the rule of your king?" Rune's accusation raised Halvard's attention from the table.

Halvard grunted.

"Not my king," he said. "But there are few who share my hatred for a king who doesn't look to protect his people, and abandons them to the mercy of one who seeks to usurp him."

Exasperated, Halvard lowered his eyes and took another gulp before continuing.

"I can spare no ships," he said. "But it is not for a lack of want. Olaf claimed every water vessel in port and burned what he had no use for, or what he deemed too weathered to repair. We have nothing left beyond a *feraeringr* and four oars is too small to transport a horse or take out to sea. It'll be another two moons before a ship can be built that is sea-ready. Another three before one is scheduled to dock. You're welcome to stay until then, but from what you've told me, you don't have the time to sit around here in Nidaros."

Rune shook his head.

"Olaf knows we're here," Rune said. Halvard was mid-drink again when he stopped and lowered his mug to the table. "He's been tailing us for three days now. His troops swarm the Dofrarfjell. We can't go back the way we came."

Nodding, Halvard fixed his eyes on a blackened knot in the table. With pursed lips, he answered, "If you came over the Dofrarfjell, you must have crossed the Gaulelfr."

Rune nodded.

"You'll need to follow the Nid south to the lake in Selabu," Halvard said. "That lake feeds the Nid. Stay to the shores and head east. When the lake veers south, follow it until you come to a river. That river will lead you more than half way to Aursund."

Halvard leaned back in his chair.

"Follow the Nid to the lake," Rune repeated, committing the directions to memory. "Then follow the shores to the river."

"And on to Aursund and the lake there where the Raumelfr flows," Halvard said.

Rune jerked to attention.

"The Raumelfr," he said. "She marks the western borders of Alfheim."

Halvard nodded. "She starts there, giving you a straight road away from the mountains through the valleys to Viken."

"The Dvergar aren't likely to follow so far east," Rune said aloud.

"And with good reason," Halvard warned. "Too far east will land you in the Wetlands. The land there is bog-plagued and stretches far beyond what the eye can see. It will add several days to your journey if you don't stay to the Raumelfr."

The light glistened in Halvard's eye.

"Of course, if you look to challenge yourself," Halvard said, "you're welcome to leave that prized stallion here. I assure you, he'll be kept in good care."

Rune smiled at the offer.

"I want to reach Alfheim *alive*. If I propose leaving that horse, I won't make it out of Nidaros."

"The lady loves her horse, huh," Halvard said with a grin.

"Suspiciously so," Rune said, logging another slew of questions aside for Kallan when next he had an inkling to prod her temper.

Halvard shrugged, indifferent to the will of an Alfr, and surrendered with a swig of his mead. With the clunk of his tankard and a heavy sigh, he returned his attention to his guest.

"If you're determined to take your horse," Halvard said, "we have a mare we can spare for your journey."

In thought, Rune bit the tip of his thumb as he plotted the new road home. A sick churned his stomach at the thought of telling Kallan there were no boats, and he held back a groan.

"Thank you," Rune said to Halvard, who was in-between gulps. "And Halvard," he added. The Throendr paused mid-drink. "You can count Gunir among your allies."

All hint of humor was gone from Rune's face, replaced by genuine sincerity.

"Careful," Halvard said with droplets of mead tracing his beard. "With the way things are going, we'll call upon that favor sooner than you think. Now..." Halvard stretched, pulling his arms up over his head. "A favor granted requires payment."

Rune shook his head, holding his expression blank.

"I have nothing with me."

"It isn't silver I seek," Halvard said, hunched over his tankard.

Rune furrowed his brow.

"What is it you desire?"

With two final gulps, Halvard slammed the empty mug to the table.

"Kallan."

Rune shook his head.

"She's not available."

"Oh, she's yours then?" Halvard said, grinning with his crooked mouth.

"Not mine," Rune recovered, peering down into his mead. "She's just...not...have-able." Rune raised the tankard to his mouth and added, "Or logical or reasonable."

Halvard bit his bottom lip as Rune avoided eye contact.

"This war of yours in Alfheim is infamous throughout Midgard," Halvard said. "You've been at war since before Raum ruled as king over these lands. We don't ask why, we don't know why, we don't care why. It isn't our problem to ponder, and a war like yours is enough to ensure your business stays your business."

Halvard washed back another mouthful of mead

"In turn," he continued, "we ask nothing of the Alfar. You speak of rogues and the masked *fjándinn* in Lorlenalin's bowels. You speak of the Dvergar who hunt her, who steal her, and the blood money paid by a mercenary. But one thing still eludes me, Rune Tryggveson. One thing you still have not answered."

Rune stared with furrowed brow across the table.

"That is my payment."

"All right, old man," Rune said. "Ask your question already."

Halvard widened his grin, delighted at his upper hand.

"Why would the Ljosalfar king care at all about a Dokkalfr, let alone their queen? One would think it would be in your favor to let the traitor kill her. Why save her from this rogue? Why follow her into Midgard to save her from the Dvergar when they would have neatly, nicely, cleaned up this mess for you?"

The blood ran cold down Rune's neck. He knew the question asked of him. He shrugged, pretending indifference.

"This war is our fathers' war," Rune said without missing a beat. "Not ours. I seek to end this."

Halvard snorted, dismissing Rune's tidy answer.

"So quick to reply," he said, shaking his head, "as if you had expected this question and had the answer tucked away for when it would be asked of you. No. Don't feed me the dribble you've stored away for your mother or fishwife back home. That isn't the answer I seek."

Rune watched as the inebriate at the neighboring table chugged back another mead. His comrades gave him a jovial shove. Each had a smile stretched across his face as they raised a drink and threw back their heads, downing another round.

The fire light flickered, casting red and black shadows across Halvard's old face as he waited for Rune's answer.

"The Dokkalfar were not born to Alfheim as the Ljosalfar," Rune said. "They came from Svartálfaheim. They were once part of the Svartálfar, who they left in the city neighboring Nidavellir."

Halvard's eyes widened with horror.

"Nidavellir. The Dvergar city?"

Rune nodded.

"The Dokkalfar arrived as one great wave. Though great were their numbers, they didn't compare to the legions of Gunir." Rune shook his head, lost to the memories he summoned. "Gunir made their masses seem like a harmless flock of elk birds. Their culture was so unlike ours. Their language and clothes...even their skin..." Rune's voice trailed off. "...as white and as cold as the mid-winter moon. The king's Seidkona evoked a curiosity among the Ljosalfar that soon became fear."

Rune pulled his attention from his mental wanderings and continued. "Their close friendship with the Dvergar allowed them to inherit secrets of forging that Gunir's own smiths still can't fathom," Rune said. "But what we lacked in metallurgy, we made up for in our vast numbers."

A sudden sorrow washed over Rune's eyes as he recalled the lives all lost to war.

"When war broke out, the only thing that sustained us against our formidable foe was our sheer numbers. There used to be so many more of us," he said. "Warriors have come and gone. We've all been forced to watch our brothers fall. Sagas and songs have recorded our heroics. Those who sing them today, lived them, but there is one that stays with us. One story above all others."

Lost in thought, Rune stared as he watched the inebriate slam down the mug of mead to take up another. The sound died away although he could see the laughter from their eyes.

"In death we vanquished enemies,
In death, we slew our foes.
Blood soaked rage engulfed our blades,
When blood lust took its hold."

Halvard lowered his tankard as Rune continued,
his eyes never leaving the merry comrades nearby.

"In death, a darkness troubled one,
In death, concealed, undone.
Deep in darkness dragons wait,
When blood would set the sun.

In death, we glorified his name.
In death, we saw too late,
When drink, to him, we raised in praise,
The dragon sealed his fate.

In death, we lived. In death, we fought.
In death, we grew to hate.
In death, the blackened wraith released,
The blinded shade beneath.

In death, his darkened eyes grew dim.
In death, his mind was lost within.
With blackened eyes, he slew his kin,
In death, we lost to him.

In death, I took up sword and slew.
In death, the dragon's wrath ensued.
We had no choice. The dragon fumed.
In death, he was consumed.

In death, our brother's blood deplored,
In death, our brother, did I gore,
When I rose up and killed one more.
His blood ensconced my sword.

From death, his mutterings are weak.
From death, his voice, to me, it speaks.
Entombed within my brother's keep,
Revived in death, he sleeps."

Rune raised his eyes to Halvard, who sat frozen by each word. White knuckles clutched his mug. The jovial nature from moments ago was gone.

"He saw the Berserk," Rune said, forcing his hand to relax his grip. "Stories of Odinn's sons possessed by the sudden blood lust."

Rune took up his mug and chugged down another mouthful before continuing.

"This war has plagued more lives than I care to count," Rune said, staring into his mead. "I watched my mother die consumed by the internal grief she refused to accept. My brother and I watched my father fight to save her from the Shadow that suffocated her in sorrow until all that remained was the shell of a body that lived and moved for naught but to forget the pain she harbored."

A knot had formed in Rune's throat.

"That same shadow that consumed my mother and plagued my father almost took my brother. That same shadow looked back at me when I ran my sword through my comrade's heart, when I vowed to rid this world of that darkness. That same shadow I now see in Kallan's eyes."

Rune paused, lost in thought as if deciding to add something. He instead released a sigh that carried his exhaustion with it before he continued.

"It is that shadow that is my enemy. It drives vengeance and blood lust and spreads like a disease that passes on to the living with every breath. It will take Kallan as it did my comrade, my father, my mother, and countless more before them, and now regardless of any station, I am bound by a vow I took centuries ago to destroy it."

Halvard looked as if Rune had dumped lake water down his back. Visibly captivated by Rune's words, he watched the Alfr take a long gulp from his tankard.

Chapter 51

It was a long while before either Halvard or Rune spoke again.

"You can count your debt as paid," he said, sitting forward to slump over the empty tankard. "My men can provide you with food and arms," he offered. "We invite you to stay and sleep in some proper beds. Drink, eat, and before you go, you are welcome to a mare, and any armament you find in the barracks."

A sudden pair of thuds jarred their attention to Kallan, pulling Rune's eye over the two tankards brimming with the tans of freshly brewed mead. Curves of green lined with gold traced the line of her bosom. Soft, brown ringlets of hair fell down her front, their tips brushing the table.

The bathhouse had done as much for her as the tankard of mead had done for him. She was relaxed and at ease, more than she had been in weeks. The blue of her eyes glistened, and the lingering exhaustion that had followed her since Jotunheim had washed away with the bath water. Kallan stared, not bothering to mask her gaze when Rune found her eyes.

"We're grateful for the offer." Kallan smiled, forcing her attention to Halvard. "But I doubt you can provide a better sword than *Gramm*."

Her voice chimed over the table as Halvard flashed a wide-eyed look to Rune. When Rune answered with an impassive shrug, Halvard looked back to Kallan.

"He carries the elding sword of the Dvergar king forged by Volundr himself," Kallan explained with a hint of jealousy.

The jingle of keys accompanied the sighs of Olga as she plopped her sturdy frame into a chair beside Halvard. At the end of the table, Emma settled herself on the other side of the Throendr. Blushing red at the wide smile Rune flashed her, Emma looked away, holding back a smile.

"You are a swordsman, Kallan Eyolfdottir," Halvard said.

"Volundr has forged many swords," Kallan said, thrusting aside her contempt for Rune, "but there were only a few whose fame exceeded their maker. A swordsman unable to recognize *Gramm* would be an abomination among swordsmen."

"You are a swordsman, and yet you carry a dagger?" Halvard used the opportunity to look Kallan up and down, eyeing her curves for the iron sword that wasn't there. "Surely you have a need for more."

Kallan's blood burned and, with a flick of her wrists, fire burst to life in her palm she held at eye level.

Halvard's eyes hardened with secrets unspoken.

"You are Seidkona," he said.

Kallan nodded, proudly.

"I am," she said and extinguished her flame.

"It is you Olaf hunts," Halvard said, bringing the mead to his mouth.

Kallan shrugged.

"Perhaps." Supporting her weight on her knuckles, she leaned forward onto the table. "But one must ask why."

Halvard shifted a solemn eye from his tankard.

"Long questions deserve long answers," he said, running his hand over his beard in thought. With a pensive eye, he looked to Rune. After taking a gulp of mead from his fresh tankard, he slammed the drink back to the table. There was a delayed moment before he answered.

"Olaf seeks to avenge his father's death by killing Forkbeard," Halvard said. "He desires to reclaim the throne his grandfather's father left him in death."

Kallan stood upright, unsure where to begin with Halvard's news.

"Forkbeard?" Rune repeated and shook his head. "Forkbeard didn't kill Olaf's father."

"No, he didn't," Halvard said. "Bloodaxe's son, Greycloak, did. To understand Olaf, you must be familiar with Dan's Reach, The woodland realm of King Dan for which the Dani were named. And Fairhair." Halvard spoke the name like a dark, distant memory surfaced. He looked to Rune. "You would be familiar with Fairhair." Darkness that shadowed an unspoken memory fell upon Rune's face. Without an answer, Halvard continued. "In a way, I guess all of this really stems from him."

The wooden chairs groaned as everyone shifted and settled themselves in for Halvard's tale.

"Fairhair, his sons, and their pursuit of the throne of Midgard," Halvard began. "Let's see now. Of the sons, there was Erik Bloodaxe, Hakon the Good, and Olaf, King of Viken." Halvard paused at this last name and looked to each face, anticipating their reactions. When four blank faces stared back at him, Halvard dropped his shoulders and explained. "Olaf, King of Viken, was elder father to Olaf."

"His elder father?" Kallan asked with piqued interests.

"Aye." Halvard brooded and took a large mouthful from his drink. He placed the tankard to the table and looked at each face in turn, ensuring he held their attention before continuing.

"Before Fairhair, the land was made up of several smaller kingdoms that spanned all the land. There were constant wars between the kingdoms back then, exchanging out new kings for old. Blood watered the same fields that kings killed hundreds for. The rivalry and wars ended when Fairhair united them under one rule and assigned his three sons as vassals. But to

Bloodaxe, Fairhair gave all of Midgard, crowning him high king."

"Erik Bloodaxe," Rune mused.

"His cruelty surpassed anything I care to recall. The people rose up against him and exiled him. But Bloodaxe left behind a son who would avenge him. Greycloak executed all the lesser kings of Midgard, including the King of Viken, whose wife and heir escaped."

A long silence passed over the table.

"King Tryggvi of Viken." Rune coldly stared at a knot in the center of the table.

"Tryggvi, son of Olaf, son of Fairhair, was father to Olaf." Halvard brought his mead to his lips. "*He* was the heir who escaped."

"It was Greycloak who ran Olaf out of Midgard," Kallan said.

Halvard gulped his drink. "And Hakon Jarl with the help of Blatonn killed Greycloak."

"The Blood Oath," Rune concluded.

Halvard grinned. "Olaf believes the murder of Greycloak belonged to him. And that Hakon and Blatonn stole the Blood Oath meant for him." Pushing his tankard aside, Halvard leaned his weight onto his arms crossed over the table. "After Blatonn and Hakon Jarl killed Greycloak, Blatonn appointed Hakon as Jarl and sent him here as his vassal. And now Olaf is back."

Halvard shrugged. "He killed the Jarl to regain his throne. And Forkbeard killed Blatonn."

"His own father?" Kallan asked.

"Forkbeard inherited two things that day: all of Dan's Land and Olaf's blood oath. Dan's Reach and Swealand united," Halvard said.

"And now both seek Olaf's death," Emma said.

Halvard downed the last of the mead allowing the silence to settle around the table. Before the mead flowed down his throat, Emma asked the one question he had failed to answer. "But why is Olaf after the Seidkonas?"

Halvard dropped the empty tankard on the table and altered his full attention to the Englian. Her blue eyes, brimming with questions, glistened in the fire light.

"Word is, he seeks a pouch that one of them carries," Halvard said.

Kallan's face flushed red as she dropped her eyes to the table.

"Why?" Rune exclaimed.

Afraid the words would escape her, Kallan pursed her lips and frowned at Rune. Rune threw her a look that dared her to intervene.

"I've known Olaf and his superstitions now for years," Halvard said. "I have never seen him this obsessed, or this consumed with bloodlust. Olaf believes that pouch will gain him an advantage over Forkbeard, one that will ensure his victory."

"What kind of advantage?" Rune asked, clutching his tankard.

Halvard shook his head.

"I don't know."

A silence settled over the table. In deep, distant thought, Halvard brooded, clearly overwhelmed with the need to give voice to his own notions.

"There is talk about Olaf spanning the kingdoms of Midgard and reclaiming the land Fairhair once united. Those same rumors have secured a fear throughout the land, but I know Olaf," Halvard finished, shaking his head in doubt. "His visions are not so narrow. That summer, Olaf married Fork-beard's sister and secured himself a line for the throne of Dan's Reach right alongside Forkbeard," Halvard said. "Rumors of vengeance and blood debts have circled the trade routes. The way I see it, last man standing gets Danelaw. And Danelaw spans all of Northumbria, Vendland, Viken, and the Dan's Reach along with support from Otto III and, possibly, the Empire. But Olaf has Dubh Linn, and the land of Eire and Alba on his side and this..." Halvard shook his head. "This is little more than a race."

"Last man standing gets the throne," Rune surmised.

A laugh barked and a slap to Halvard's back broke the tension that had descended over the table. With a toothy grin and an untamed mop of red hair, a face pinned by a crooked nose peered over their table.

"Brand! You startled me, whelp," Olga said, adding a firm slap to the youth's arm that only seemed to encourage his wide, flashy grin.

"Why are you back so soon? I thought you were headed to Lofot?"

"We made port in Maere and I jumped ship." He pushed back his wide shoulders, not bothering to look at Olga as he answered. "Egil told me I'd find you here with Halvard. Where'd the dark stallion come from?"

After a nod that began with Halvard passed around the table, Brand smiled, holding his full attention on Kallan.

"Where'd the lady come from?"

"What in Odinn's name would persuade you to jump ship in Maere?" Olga said.

Brand shrugged.

"There was a girl," he said. He adjusted his position to better look at Kallan.

"There are days I can't believe you're my kin," Olga grumbled to deaf ears then waved a limp hand toward Brand. "This is my brother's son, Brand."

Only Emma bothered with a polite nod that Brand ignored.

"And this..." Olga slapped Brand, in hopes to draw his attention from Kallan. "This here is Rune Tryggveson, King of Gunir."

Slouched in his seat with his legs stretched out beneath the table, Rune stared at the tip of his boots. He didn't bother to acknowledge the lad, whose interests remained fixed on Kallan.

"And the lady," Olga said, "is Kallan Eyolfdottir, *Queen* of Lorlenalin." Olga's emphasis on 'queen' did little to discourage Brand's motivation. "The horse belongs to her."

"The lady is..." Brand said, dragging his eyes over Kallan with a stupid grin.

"Alright, be off with you," Olga said, giving a shove that slid Brand from her chair.

He pulled himself up, boasting his full height that matched Rune's and leaned his weight onto the back of Kallan's chair so that he remained suspended, holding his face inches from hers where her perfumes reached his nose.

"He's yours?" he said, holding his voice just above a whisper.

"He?" Kallan asked.

"The stallion," Brand clarified.

Rune scoffed.

"Yes," she recovered, throwing her full attention into Brand.

"You bought him?"

"Bred him."

"Parentage?"

"Mixed."

"With?"

"A line from the desert sands and my father's courser."

Something of an impressed whistle escaped Brand's lips as he slanted his eyes in envy.

"Show me," he whispered, holding a hand to Kallan, who beamed.

A stifled hic-cough from Rune's chair was all the urging she needed to slide her hand into Brand's out-stretched palm. Returning the wide smile, she stood from the table, casting a subtle glance to Rune, who appeared indifferent to the scrape of her chair on the floor.

Pushed to the point where her irritation surpassed her intent, Kallan looped her arm into the crook of the youth's elbow and permitted him to pull her toward the door.

As one, Olga, Emma, and Halvard turned to Rune who still studied the tip of his boot.

"Well?" Olga pressed impatiently.

Rune glanced up from the floor.

"What?" he asked.

"Aren't you going to do something?" Olga asked.

Rune shrugged. "About what?"

"About that." Olga gestured to the dainty swag of Kallan's rear as she vanished out the door, her arm still hooked on Brand's.

Rune cocked his head toward Kallan's backside and, complacently, returned his eyes to his boot, indifferent by anything the woman said or Kallan did.

"The woman brought us mead," Halvard held back from booming over a half-attempted whisper. "Are you daft or dead?"

Rune raised his eyes from the floor, a grin stretched across his face with a known mischievous look to his eye.

"They deserve each other." Rune shrugged. "He's slimy and she's ornery. Besides, he'll be begging to bring her back before the night's end."

Chapter 52

The scent of sweet hay rolled from the stables as Brand pulled open the doors. Orange light from his swaying lantern streaked the stalls and Kallan swaggered several steps ahead past the rows of horses.

"How old is he?" Brand asked, eager to pull her back to him.

"Well," Kallan said with a grin, peering over her shoulder. "How old are you?"

Brand flashed his wide grin.

"Does my age change your answer?" he asked.

"How old do you think?" she asked.

Brand shrugged.

"Three, maybe four."

Kallan shrugged back.

"Let's call Astrid three, then."

"Let's," Brand said, dropping the lantern onto a hook.

With a hearty pat to Astrid's neck, Kallan snatched up a brush beside her.

"And 'Astrid'," Brand threw his hands to the air, with a half chuckle lost to his grin. "What is that?"

Kallan pushed the brush through his coat as Brand followed her long locks down her back where they stopped at her backside.

"He was born when I was a child," she said. "I insisted he was a girl and named him Astrid."

With every stroke of the brush, her ringlets bounced lightly, holding Brand's attention there at their tips.

"A child?" he whispered. "That would make you..."

Kallan smiled.

"Yeah, let's say Astrid's three," Brand agreed.

With every stroke, the gold cords laced at Kallan's side caught the light, and he followed the lacing in and out through Kallan's gown.

"How is it you know of Palfrey and Courser when the draw horse is all that's found north of the empire?" Brand asked pulling his eyes from the gold.

Kallan cocked a single brow as she pushed the brush through Astrid's coat then abandoned it to a barrel.

"Should I not?"

Brand eyed the hem of her dress. His attention lingered on her feet wrapped in leather then dragged his eyes up.

"Most in the area have never seen anything beyond the creams of the fjord horse," he said. "Let alone own one that looks so much like the horses found along the desert markets south of Volga."

He watched as Kallan opened her palm for Astrid to snuffle with his wet nose as if sniffing for a treat. After a gentle stroke to his face, Kallan planted a kiss. A lump caught in Brand's throat as he studied the fine lines of her jaw down to her neck.

"You should come with me," he whispered.

Kallan looked up, hooking him on the lapis blue rings of her eyes.

"With you?" She kindly grinned.

"When next we go out," he clarified. He gulped. His hands were cold and damp.

"We?" She snickered. "And when would that be?" Her voice lilted with an eagerness that encouraged more from him.

"Leif has another expedition planned next summer," Brand rambled on, uncertain why he couldn't shut up. "He looks to go west."

"To the islands of Englia?" she asked, pulling herself from Astrid's face. A single ringlet fell to her eyes.

"Further." He lowered his voice.

Aching to pull back the ringlet, he dared a step closer, carefully, as if she was a fledgling that would take flight.

"To Groen Land?" Kallan widened her grin. She was shaking her head before Brand could stop her. "False promises of a land rolling with green." She repeated the stories aloud. "And farmland enough to feed an entire country. Hopeful settlers have returned, laden with stories of fields of ice and barren rock."

Brand shrugged.

"Well, how else would Leif and Erik draw settlers if not by calling it Groen Land?"

Kallan laughed and his chest tightened.

"It's an ice block," she managed to say between chuckles. "Even the Northern Passage is warmer."

Brand shrugged with a smile.

"Either way." He shook his head, letting his face fall to severity. "No."

Kallan stopped laughing as the joviality fell from Brand's face, leaving behind her grin.

"No?" she asked.

Brand shook his head. "Not Groen Land," Brand whispered. "Beyond."

"Beyond."

The light of his lantern caught her eye.

"There is nothing beyond," she whispered. "But Ginnungagap and the tips of the ash branches that stretch into the endless sea made black by the sea worms that fill those waters."

"There is more," Brand insisted. "I've been there."

Her eyes widened with clear fascination. Now that he held her captivated, he kept her and wouldn't let go.

"Fields of green and pastures lined with berries in so much abundance that wine flows right out of the ground," he said.

Kallan shook her head, her grin recovering.

"More false promises of sheets of ice?"

"No." He lowered his voice, forcing her closer to hear. She smelled of roses and lavender. "This is real."

"Green ice," she whispered.

He exploded into a laugh, encouraging her smile that launched him into his travels.

"The Empire is building a cathedral in Mainz," he said. "Books containing the newest innovations are flowing from Râ-Kedet."

"Books," she said with intrigue.

"Books bound and made with silks and mesh fibers they call paper. The Arabi have been doing this for two centuries." His eyes brightened with excitement. "Ideas are written and sold right there in the markets. Innovations and knowledge brimming with possibilities that are moving along the Volga trade roads in exchange for spices. Explorers bring gods from the lands beyond. They say the scholars have found maps in the stars."

"Maps in the stars," she said.

"Too easily you could forget home," he said. "We can travel farther than anyone before us. There's a world, twenty years ago, we didn't even know was there. And there's something there, beyond that one."

"And how far will you go?" Kallan whispered. "Until the branches of Yggdrasill reach beyond the stars?"

Brand paused, coming down from his maps in the stars to meet Kallan's mystical eyes beaming with the worlds he spoke.

"Come with me," Brand bade just above a whisper.

"To the stars?" Her eyes glistened with excitement. His words brushed her lips.

"Come with me," he whispered.

"Unfortunately..." Rune's voice cut through the stables like an ugly horn sounding from the North. "...Her Highness has other commitments requiring her immediate attention in Gunir."

Kallan snarled at Rune as Brand straightened his back. Hate filled Kallan's head at the sight of Rune, pushing aside thoughts of stars, books, and worlds carved with green ice. On the other side of the lantern, Rune rested a large arm on the stall. His hair tied back made him appear older, wiser, and angrier than usual.

"Olga has asked me to fetch you." Rune's voice rolled through the stall like venom.

"Olga has," Brand answered, not sounding entirely convinced the Ljosalfr told the truth.

"Yes," Rune insisted. "She's in the Mead Hall, saying something about Halvard needing some-thing...with...something..."

Rune handed the words to Brand, not bothering to make his improvisation sound convincing.

Brand exchanged Kallan's apologetic glance for a remorseful one and, with gross hesitation, walked to the end of the stall. Pulling the lantern from its hook, Brand stopped long enough to gaze at Rune.

With chests puffed out, they sized each other and, after an eternal second, Brand moved on his way.

"What is wrong with you?" Kallan hissed once Brand's footfalls faded.

"Wrong? Wrong?" Rune said, feigning innocence. "I was delivering a message."

"There is no message," she said.

"There could be."

Kallan gave a girlish growl. "What are you doing here, anyway?" she asked.

"Rescuing him," Rune said.

"Rescuing."

"From you," he clarified before he could catch the huff from her lips. In silence, Rune strolled from the stables with Kallan cursing beneath her breath behind him.

The night had settled, mingling with the orange lights that poured from the Mead Hall. In the distance, muffled laughter of the Throendir carried on the wind as Rune plodded down to the beach with Kallan in tow.

"We were enjoying a pleasant conversation," she said just as Rune stopped short.

Slamming her shoulder into his, Kallan stomped on ahead, taking the lead. Her skirts rustled as she pushed her way onto the beach.

"*You* were enjoying a pleasant conversation," he corrected. "That boy was hopping on the verge of madness."

The weight of his eyes bore into her back and she whipped about on her heel. His arms hung at his side.

"I was," she said.

"You had him strung along tighter than a mast line," Rune said.

"I did?"

Rune shrugged. "You're cruel."

Kallan whipped back around.

"I am not cruel," she said.

"Were you going to sleep with him?" Rune asked. A bite in his tone replaced his impassiveness. Kallan flushed white then red as she clutched her fists with the want to summon her Seidr. "Because he thought you were," he said, not bothering to wait for an answer. "And you let him."

He gave her the moment to flash her finest glare.

"See." Rune shrugged. "Cruel."

He sauntered down to the water's surface, ensuring he slammed his shoulder into her along the way.

"Why are you here?" she asked.

Rune held his gaze on the black sea. Another huff escaped her lips before he bothered to answer.

"Why do they want your pouch, Kallan?"

Kallan threw back her head.

"Not in all my days," she said, "for as long as I reign, will I ever concede to your twisted..."

Rune gazed into the cold hate that met his eyes.

"I am not your ally!" she shouted.

Holding up his arm in answer, Rune let slide a single, black tri-corner knot that stopped short at the end of a chain.

Kallan gasped, turning as pale as the moonlight that glistened off the silver-black sheen of the elding steel.

"Where did you...?" she breathed.

With trembling hands, Kallan reached for the pendant.

"It was all I could find," Rune said as Kallan took the tri-knot.

Too stunned to speak, Kallan cradled the charm until she collected the strength to tear her eyes away from the boon.

"My mother..." Kallan tried to speak, but caught her words on a breath as she caressed the lines of elding with her finger. "This is all I have left."

Dark days flooded back of the bitter tang buried beneath Dvergar caves, and the hopelessness she had found there as the sea air rushed in and over her, clearing her thoughts and allowing questions that hadn't surfaced before. With a gulp, Kallan found her voice.

"In the caves...how did you know where to find me?"

Rune looked to the clear sky. The moon was almost gone now.

Rune breathed in the sea air.

"My brother spent some time in Nidavellir," Rune said with a subtle grin. "He managed to bring some knowledge back with him."

"Your brother," Kallan whispered, holding her eyes on the pendant again.

The moonlight glistened off the elding as she turned the metal over. Distant laughter rolled through the silence of the evening's festivities and the impenetrable walls of Kallan's grief began to weaken.

"You often speak of your brother," she said, running her finger along the lines of elding. "Earth. Air. Wind," she muttered and looked to Rune. He stood gazing at the black sea.

The black sea.

Kallan watched each wave twist, roll, and contort itself like the black, sleek bodies of the sea worms. Any moment now, a flat, snake-like head with metallic, beady eyes would rise up and peer out from the ocean waters.

Kallan watched and waited, but the sea worms no longer swam to the shores of Men. All at once, she took a long, deep breath as if surrendering her defiance.

"The Dvergar seek the pouch I carry," Kallan said. "They made no mention of its contents."

Rune turned around. His eyes were wide from the thoughts that had drifted as Kallan examined the charm in silence. His carefree nature was gone, replaced with the composure of the cold, methodical king he was. Free of her inhibitions, the information Rune desired now poured from Kallan.

"Why would they want a Seidkona's pouch?" he asked.

"I would imagine..." Kallan sighed, staring out to sea still looking, still hoping for the sea worms to come. "...because it was Odinn's."

Rune blinked stupidly.

"Odinn," he said, with a drawl of doubt.

But she didn't smile. She didn't flinch. She didn't move.

"*The* Odinn," he said.

"Yes," Kallan said, tearing her eyes from the sea. "That Odinn."

Rune battled incredulity as Kallan went on, not bothering to wait for his senses to catch up with what she was about to say.

"The pouch was crafted by Freyja as a gift to Odinn while he journeyed Yggdrasill for the wisdom he sought." She paused, giving Rune a chance to speak. When he said nothing, she continued. "Freyja infused the pouch with an enchantment, making it forever replenish the single apple Idunn bestowed as a gift, and Odinn was free to wander Yggdrasill with an eternal supply of Idunn's apples."

Rune lost his breath, unable to think while he tried to sort out five single words.

"Eternal supply of Idunn's apples." He spoke the words slowly.

Kallan nodded and waited.

"Those apples then," Rune said, remembering every time she ate one, each time she passed one to Astrid, the glow of her skin and how quickly she had healed.

"Are Idunn's apples," Rune finished.

"They are," she said.

"The apples of Asgard that give eternal youth to any who eat of them." Rune's voice was straining with tension.

Kallan nodded.

557

"And your pouch provides an eternal supply of them?"

"It does," Kallan said.

Desperate to understand, Rune shook his head.

"But Idunn's apples provide youth to the gods," he said, "and I've seen you heal with them."

Kallan sighed.

"Gudrun isn't just a Seidkona. She's a healer and studied extensively on this matter, leading her to discover the healing properties of the body. When a person is born, the body restores itself. As a person gets older, the body's ability to heal and restore itself slows down until it stops, as if the body is too tired to heal or just...forgets."

"Old age," Rune said of Olga and Halvard in the Mead Hall, laughing, living, and dying. In the longhouse, with Ori's overcoat, Kallan possessed the ability to save them.

Kallan nodded.

"Exactly. It's why children heal so much faster than an elder and why some elders never heal at all. It's why an elder can die from a break or a fall."

"Because their bodies have stopped," Rune thought aloud.

"With an adjustment to an enhanced healing spell, Gudrun was able to use the apples to rejuvenate the healing process. She uses the body's memory." Rune nodded, saying nothing as she spoke. "She's reminding the body of what it once knew as a child then re-teaching or reminding it to heal itself. She refined it so well that Gudrun can renew life in the dead."

Kallan amended, "To an extent."

"The youth it gives to the gods..." Rune assessed.

"—and the healing properties it gives the Alfar—"

"...would make men immortal."

Kallan nodded.

"For as long as they eat of the fruit."

Awe blanketed Rune's face as his head raced for something to grasp that he could understand. After a moment, Kallan returned to the sea and her silent ponderings.

"And what of...this?"

Kallan looked back at him and studied the subtle shifts in his composure and unnatural stillness. She admired the cool control in his words. "This thing inside of me," Rune said. "How does that fit into your Seidr?"

Kallan shook her head. "I don't know. I've never seen anything like it."

"How..." he asked. "How did you get Odinn's pouch?"

The moonlight formed a clear, perfect crescent on the water's surface.

"It was a gift from Gudrun," she said.

Rune shook his head.

"But where did she get it?"

Kallan flushed red, knowing she had said too much. Regardless, she spouted forth the answers.

"Odinn gave it to her in exchange for a favor," she answered.

Rune crinkled his brow. "What could Gudrun possibly have that Odinn would want from an old hag?"

Gudrun would kill her. Kallan decided this. She had said too much, but somehow, she trusted him and she was no fool. After all they had been through, after all he had done for her, she owed him these answers.

"A prophecy," Kallan said and watched Rune's eyes widened and she knew: he understood. Kallan gazed up at the moon.

"She—she—" he stuttered. "She—"

"Yes. Gudrun is a Seer," Kallan said. "You've heard of the Volva's Prophecy."

Rune's eyes widened further, his mouth fell open and Kallan turned her gaze to the sea.

She continued without his answer.

"After he placed his eye into Mimir's Well and drank of the water, Odinn learned he needed to speak to a Volva. The Volva Odinn sought for eternal wisdom—"

"Was Gudrun," Rune finished for her.

"Yes."

With mouth agape, he waved a finger at Kallan.

"You know what she said," he breathed.

Kallan shook her head with an admirable grin. "Not a chance. I've spent years trying to extract that knowledge from Gudrun."

Rune looked to the sea, watching the waves rush to the shore.

"Olaf seeks Idunn's apples to regenerate the strength and power of his troops," Rune said.

"I assume so."

"Halvard said Olaf had spoken to a Seidkona," he mused. "Could she have known about the apples?"

Kallan dropped her shoulders. "I don't know."

"And the Dvergar for that matter," Rune asked, but Kallan shook her head.

"I still don't know."

Rune sighed and pushed his hand through his hair as Kallan bit the corner of her bottom lip. Almost immediately, his eyes widened and he straightened his back.

"Someone was helping them," he said.

Kallan pulled back her shoulders as if ready to attack.

"A human king is looking for you, killing every Seidkona along the way," Rune said. "The Dvergar traveled as far south as Alfheim after pinning the pouch's location to you. Without help, they never would have been able to track the pouch to you."

Rune paused as if gathering his thoughts as Kallan stared wide-eyed at him.

"Who else knows about the pouch?" Rune asked. "Really knows?"

"Gudrun, my father, Eilif, Daggon, and Aaric."

"Any others?" he asked. "Any at all?"

Kallan shook her head as she reviewed the list again. "No. It's just a pouch. All Seidkona have them."

"No. Not all Seidkona have a pouch that produces Idunn's apples. Gudrun," Rune said. "She's the Seer."

"My elder mother," Kallan clarified, nodding.

"Elder mother," Rune repeated.

"It is she who gave me the pouch," Kallan said. "She who taught me."

Rune nodded. "Your father is dead, which rules him out."

A distasteful sick stirred Kallan's gut as Rune passed over the statement with indifference.

"What about Eilif, Daggon, and Aaric?" he asked.

"Eilif is my scribe," Kallan said with a renewed twinge of malcontent. "We've been friends since we were children. Together we rounded up the orphans in the warrens."

"And he's just a scribe?"

Kallan shrugged.

"My bard," she specified. "He maintains our libraries, our records, and our history. He can read and write and recite centuries worth of dissertations."

"And Daggon?"

"Daggon is my captain, my keeper. My sentinel," she said. "My father left me in his care before the Dokkalfar even came to Alfheim."

"And Aaric?" Rune asked, concluding her list.

"My high marshal?" Kallan tightened her mouth.

Rune nodded. Kallan's face was stern as Rune waited for her to begin.

"Aaric was dearest friend to my father long before we came to Alfheim. Father stationed him in Lorlenalin to build alliances with the Ljosalfar."

Rune arched a brow, riling her further.

"Build alliances?" Rune asked.

Kallan nodded.

"And yet we are at war," he said, with a tone that suggested she reconsider.

"Well, you didn't exactly welcome us when we got here."

Rune didn't answer.

"Father trusted no other to that station," Kallan snipped. "Aaric oversaw my education and still works to bring peace to Alfheim."

Rune said nothing encouraging her anger.

"Aaric even argued in your favor," she said, unable to hold back the rising bout of rage, "speaking highly of you while I ordered your execution. At one point, Father was going to appoint him captain."

Rune ended his brooding.

"What happened?" he asked.

Kallan shrugged.

"Daggon was chosen instead."

"Why?" Rune asked.

Kallan blinked, uncertain of the answer herself.

"And he holds no resentment?" Rune asked.

"Aaric has lived among the Dokkalfar for centuries," Kallan said as if this cleared Aaric's name and finalized her argument.

"You mean he wasn't always one of you?" Rune asked.

"He was not born Dokkalfar, no," she said cautiously. "But he is one of us."

"You sent him to build friendships with my people and yet we are at war," Rune said.

On the balls of her feet, Kallan turned with a huff. Her arms held stiff at her side, ended in balls of fists.

"Aaric has proven his loyalty beyond question," she said.

"You have demons sleeping in the bowels of your city," Rune said, his voice rising in urgency. "Someone is looking to usurp you, and until you find out who it is, everyone is suspect."

With a scoff, Kallan gathered her skirts and stomped from the beach, forcing her head down as she made her way back to the Mead Hall.

"There are no ships, Kallan."

The words slammed into her like a wave, taking her senses and draining her head of blood flow. Suddenly dizzy, she stopped and looked back to Rune and the sea. He waited until she made her way back to the beach where she had left him.

"Olaf took everything the Throendir had," he said. "What he did leave them was a couple of *feraeringr* for fishing and the few ships out on route."

Kallan swayed on her feet.

"How will we get home?" she breathed.

Her eyes stared frozen to the distance as if hearing nothing at all.

"We have to move east," he said. "There's a river, which will lead us south as far as Viken. From there we can make passage around the mountains, through Midgard, and take the road to Guni—Oh..."

Rune clamped his mouth shut too late as Kallan's temper rebounded.

"I'll not go to Gunir," she said before Rune could cringe. "I promised the children. They need me. Gudrun and Eilif are alone. And Aaric—"

"You can argue the details once we're in Alfheim!" Rune's voice boomed over hers, forcing her to swallow her tongue as he spoke.

"I want to go home!"

The waves washed upon the shore as Kallan huffed, near tears. Rearing up for the battle, Rune raised his voice to match the sea.

"We have a raging king on our tails with an eye for your head. The Dvergar are adamant to have you and avenge their kin. We're a fortnight away from home and the only company you have to look forward to until then..." Rune exhaled. "...is me!"

"What do you propose?" Kallan asked, glaring at her new comrade.

"Peace talks! Right now!"

Kallan scoffed, ignoring the rage that flared in Rune's eyes. "All that matters is that we get to Alfheim at all. Once we are there, we can haggle, bicker, and bitch all you want over which city to go to, but for now, the only chance of survival we have is to stick together. Now you can come along quietly..." Rune huffed. "Or I can fashion up some rope before we leave."

Kallan glanced to the orange light over the distant houses where the Mead Hall's lights glowed. The muted laughter carried over the village, filling everyone with a merriment that matched their warmth.

"I'll go with you," she said at last, gazing back to Rune. "I'll travel and hunt and follow the river to Viken."

"That's all I ask," Rune said with a nod. "We leave at dawn. We can't afford to sit still for too long, and while we're on the road, try...try not to draw any attention to yourself."

Still obviously seething, he turned leaving Kallan alone on the beach.

With the same spitfire she reserved for him, Kallan called to his back.

"But my blade will pierce your gut with the first foot fall that touches down on Alfheim!"

Rune flashed her grin. "I'm looking forward to it," he said and marched back to the village.

Chapter 53

"Harald carved this stone after his father Gorm and his mother Thyra. Harald, who won for himself all of Dan's Reach..."

Through the darkness, Svenn Forkbeard peered at the runes etched in stone. The fraction of moonlight permitted by the crescent was barely enough to read the lettering. Countless times, he had spent his youth reading the inscription carved there by his father. He had repeated the words until the sounds had burned themselves into his memory. Each time, his hatred grew.

This night, his eye held fixed to one part of the inscription.

"...Harald, who won for himself all of Dan's Reach..."

The small, silver disc Forkbeard turned over in his hand passed through his fingers as he followed the lines of runes stamped into the coin. His eye lingered, caught on the words and, once more, he debated having the stone torn down altogether. The temple Blatonn had erected was easy enough to burn to the ground, but this...

A twinge of hesitation pulled at his chest as he re-read the names again.

Gorm and Thyra.

His gaze shifted to his left, and the great southern mound of Thyra's grave. Those names alone were what saved it.

Forkbeard stared at his father's stone again. Its size dwarfed Gorm's stone, which was twice the grandeur. From this angle, it completely hid the second stone from view.

Another reason to tear it down, he thought.

"My king?"

Forkbeard looked up from the stone. Along the side of his Mead Hall, looking closer to thirty than he did to twenty, Vagn, son of Akes, stood.

Releasing a sigh, Forkbeard straightened his back as the young captain peered through the dark.

"Speak," Forkbeard said, annoyed at the disturbance.

"The Alfr is here."

The darkened halls of the Mead Hall carried a lingering gloom that moved through the whole of the room where Queen Sigrid paced the floor. Forkbeard eyed her blue silk gown. It rustled as she moved, adding to the chill of the deep blacks of the Hall. Despite her wide, sturdy frame, there was a feminine delicacy about his wife's composure. Her freckled complexion appeared almost untainted and misplaced by the black walls of the Hall.

Tonight, she had sleeked her blond hair into a braided bun that accented her high cheekbones, drawing his eye to the sleek curve of her slender neck. With her chin high and shoulders relaxed, she moved with an air of command, keeping her arms to her sides.

"You're proposing we lay waste to Alfheim," the queen spouted.

Forkbeard's boot struck the floor following each step with a noticeable offset gimp that dragged his every left step. If the king's arrival daunted their dark guest, he gave no indication.

"As of right now, the Ljosalfar have no king," the Alfr said. "Gunir looks to Bergen Tryggveson, who sits restless on the throne. Gunir has lost great numbers. The city is weak and leaderless."

"And without aid, you lack the power to move in and take Gunir for yourself," Sigrid said. "But what guarantee can you give that Lorlenalin will side with us once battle is at hand?"

Svenn stifled a smile he hid well within his forked beard and said nothing as he climbed the steps to the throne, positioned between a set of high seat pillars.

"All Dokkalfar have felt the queen's disappearance," the Alfr said, impervious to the regality of Dan's Reach's queen. "Her people are shaken. Vulnerable, they are desperate for leadership. The city is on the brink of chaos. I assure you, the Dokkalfar will unite against Gunir. If you were to move now against the Ljosalfar, no one would stand in your way."

Forkbeard pushed a fist to his mouth, the coin in his grip.

"There are others you could request for aid," Sigrid said. "Why Dan's Reach? Why not Englia, Lade, or the Rod Men of Gardaríki?"

The Alfr beamed, knowing their position.

"No other alliance has as much to gain." His answer was as honest as it was simple.

While pondering her reply, Sigrid settled herself into her throne positioned beside the pillars.

"Gunir has long since battled against your stance," the Alfr said. "Since Blatonn's reign, the southern keep has held you at bay. Even now, though Danelaw spans all of Dan's Reach and Northumbria, you can't gain the position for Alfheim, which would give you a great advantage unmatched by any other location."

"We've spent our rule content to leave the Alfar to their own...uninterested in the politics of ancient wars," Sigrid said, tired of the Alfr's evasion. "Above all, the Alfar know this. Yet, you came here confident we would accept your offer. What boon do you bring that would win our favor?"

The Alfr peered at the woman, knowing the weight his words would carry.

"Olaf has claimed the Northern Realms."

Svenn looked at Sigrid in time to witness the blood drain from her face before she flushed red with hate.

"The sting of his hand still burns my cheek," she said and the Alfr knew he had her. He continued, giving little pause for her to regain composure.

"He's already laid claim to Throendalog and Opplandene. His troops now march to Viken and Vestfold. Nothing stands in his way from Lade to Agdir. He moves to take Aeslo where his hand will move freely into the Silver Road and the Eastern trades from Volga to the Khvalis Sea. A hold in Alfheim will gain you the advantage to move troops into Viken and everything west of the Raumelfr without resistance. From there, you could reclaim the North."

Lowering his fist, Svenn spoke with a deep lull that boomed from his seat on the throne.

"Where is the queen?" Forkbeard asked. "Where is Kallan Eyolfdottir?"

The Alfr shifted his attention to the king, leaving Sigrid to brood.

"Arrangements have been made with Gunir's king," he assured Forkbeard. "Kallan Eyolfdottir, is dead."

Svenn threw Sigrid an impassive glance, allowing a chance for her to speak. When she didn't, he stared down at his guest.

"Return to the White Opal," he said. "My scouts will follow. They will watch. And when Lorlenalin is ready, we will answer."

With a silent bow, Borg turned from the feet of the monarchs and took his leave of the Dani's king.

Kallan shifted and stretched her legs out along the flat planks of Olga's longhouse. Movement amplified every ache, leaving her painfully stiff that morning. Instead of the usual bustle around the central fire pit, boiling over with the midday's meal, the longhouse was empty.

Grateful for the absence of Olga's kin buzzing about to wash and dress for the day, she forced her sore joints back into the gown of green and gold, wincing with every stretch. With her pouch secured to her waist, and her dagger sheathed at her side, Kallan fluffed her hair, preened before the glass, and stepped into the crisp, morning haze that had moved in from the Northern Sea.

She allowed a moment for her eyes to adjust and grimaced at the late hour of the day. A lone pile of cindered ash smoldered in the square where a single strip of smoke rose into the sky, mingling with the fog. Workers had all but abandoned their progress on Olaf's house. Without a second glance, Kallan trudged along to the Mead Hall, concluding it to be the most reasonable place for a certain king to be.

Kallan's mood was lighter by the time she entered the hall. Almost immediately, she located Rune at the same table where the inebriate and his comrades had indulged the night before.

He downed a morning mead next to Halvard and exchanged a chuckle, taking turns devouring strips of dried meat from the pile on the table between their tankards. She was pleased to see he too had secured a fresh change of clothes, boots, and, from the looks of it, a bath. A weathered, but well-made, leather belt firmly secured a quiver of arrows on one hip and *Gramm* on the other. He wore his hair loose, which blocked her gawking from his peripheral vision.

Pulling herself out of complacency, Kallan straightened her skirts, fluffed her hair, and proceeded to the table. Before either could voice their objection, she snatched up a strip of salted reindeer and settled herself down beside Rune.

Flashing a quick smile, Halvard downed the last of his mead and, dismissing himself, gave a firm pat to Rune's shoulder. Day's light engulfed his wide frame in the doorway before Kallan snatched up a second strip.

"I thought we were leaving at dawn?" Kallan asked, biting into the venison.

"You needed the sleep and we needed time to get the provisions together." Rune watched from behind his tankard as he gulped down another helping and dropped the drink to the table.

"Where's your bow?" she asked, eyeing his back a bit longer than she needed.

"Halvard is having a new string put on," Rune said, shoving the end of a strip into his mouth. "The last one was looking threadbare."

The mood of the Mead Hall was nothing as it had been the night before. With most benches empty and the fire in the center of the hall extinguished, a fresh air had settled over the room.

"Astrid will be saddled and ready as soon as you put something in your belly," Rune said, shifting a glance to Kallan, who was delicately prying apart the individual strips like cheese curds.

"Halvard has gifted us with a second horse," he said. "Olga and Emma are preparing salted and sugared foods that will keep well on the road and should last us a few days."

Kallan finished the last of the strip and snatched up another.

"How many days before we meet the river?" Kallan asked, pulling this one apart as she had the first.

"Raumelfr," Rune clarified.

"What?" she asked between coughs on a mouthful of meat.

"It's the River Raumelfr." He gave her no time to recover. "If we keep the same pace, ten hour days of steady stride, in five days we should see Alfheim."

Kallan gasped.

"Ten hours? Are you mad? A horse, on that pace will be dead in three!"

"You have your apples, don't you?"

Kallan frowned and bit back her bottom lip.

"At Lake Aursund, the river starts," Rune continued. "From there, she will lead us down into Heidmork, then Raumariki, and into Vingulmork, the first fylke of Viken. We'll need to be sure to catch the east side of the river when leaving Aursund or we'll have to cross the Raumelfr in Viken."

Pausing to drink, he passed a discrete glance to Kallan, who seemed only engrossed with her meal.

"The frequent rivers and streams will keep our water and fish supply well stocked," he said, giving her time to comment or question.

Kallan bit another helping in two while she eyed Rune over the venison.

"Halvard has invited us to look through the armory," he said. "You should see if anything holds your appeal before we leave."

"What happened to the swords you picked up?" Kallan asked before dropping a bit of meat between her teeth.

"I gave them to Halvard's smith, who thinks he can re-forge the metal into something half decent."

"It will weaken the metal," Kallan said, speaking between a venison strip.

"They know that," Rune said.

With a loud smack, Kallan finished off the strip and stood from the bench then snatched up Rune's tankard. She drank his mead, and, with a wide grin, dropped the drink to the table. With a flourish, she made for the door.

In the sun, Kallan frowned at the strip of meat lodged between Rune's teeth as he joined her and sorted the strips clutched in his fist.

"You're the King of Gunir," she reminded him with a tone that suggested this would improve his etiquette.

"I'm a man," Rune professed through the chunk animal clamped between his teeth. He gave a hearty chomp and a swallow before continuing. "I like my meat. This way," he said, looping his arm into hers and steering her to the right.

"Where are we going?" Kallan asked, cocking a brow at his jovial mood.

Pointing to the barracks ahead, Rune declared in a booming voice, "To the stars!"

With their arms still linked, Kallan furrowed her gaze as Rune walked her past the center square, around the barracks to the back where a smith plinked away on an anvil.

Polished weapons honed into fine precision, lined the walls of the armory. Bows splayed about covered every surface beside quivers of arrows and a wide variety of daggers. Eagerly, Kallan untwisted her arm from Rune's and bolted for the nearest table strewn with doubled edged swords.

"I thought Olaf laid waste to this land?" Kallan asked while judging the spine of a particular blade.

She checked the balance before giving a few practice thrusts and down swings.

"I asked Halvard the same thing," Rune said, shoving the last of the strips into his mouth. "Apparently, the land's seclusion has won his favor. He plans to make Nidaros his base here in Midgard and wants to get into good standing with the Throendir."

Kallan paid no mind as she poured all her focus into the blade, guiding each swing through to pull on her stiff joints.

"The villagers said he's calling it Kaupangen," he said, "and plans to station his own *prestr* or *priast* here at the house he's having them build. They couldn't remember what he called it."

Kallan heaved, aligning her arm with the spine as she peered down the blade.

"And now he marches south to Aeslo?" she asked.

With a final swing up and around then down to the table, she returned the sword and switched it out for a second blade. Again, Kallan assessed the spine and balance before guiding the blade through the air with a fluidity she carried through to the next position.

"There's rumor he's looking to expand and join the Silk Road and the Volga Route in Aeslo," Rune said.

He said nothing more for a moment, and she continued testing the blade until he spoke in a sudden rush.

"Why did you leave with Brand last night?"

Through the air, Kallan moved the sword, cutting the wind with her blade.

"I fail to see how the selection of my...companions....concerns you," she answered.

"I asked why you left with him. Not why you slept with him," Rune said. "And standing you up does not a *companion* make."

Kallan raised the sword to thrust, and froze. Her stomach twisted with ire. After a silent glance, she returned to sparring and lunged as she stabbed the air with her blade.

"He did not stand me up," she said. "You ran him off."

"Saved him," Rune corrected.

Returning to form, Kallan lowered the sword to the table and ran her fingers over a series of daggers, eyeing each for their balance.

"And what matters, if I did?" she asked.

Taking up a pair of matching blades, Kallan wielded the daggers through a series of turns, slashing at the empty air where she imagined Rune to be standing with his smug smirk smeared on his face.

"None," Rune said as Kallan slashed the air and sparred with the imaginary Rune. "Unless your actions were conducted to provoke me."

Kallan returned the weapons to the table and lifted a double-headed axe.

"Were they?" he asked.

She gave it a wide swing up and over her head, stopping mid-air as she carried it down before deciding to answer.

"Perhaps I was fond of the youth," Kallan said, giving a second swing of the axe. "Stamina counts, you know."

Rune heaved a single breath, but his composure remained.

"Perhaps you found a way to aggravate me," Rune said.

"Did I?" With a wide swing overhead, Kallan brought the axe down toward Rune forcing him to unsheathe *Gramm* and meet her advance. He blocked her.

"And why would that aggravate you," she said glaring from behind the axe.

This time, Rune cocked a brow.

"For the same reason my warming Emma's bed last night would aggravate you."

Flushing with anger, Kallan pushed against his blade with the axe.

"Did you?" she asked, seething.

Rune said with a grin, "Now who's prying?"

Swinging the blade, Kallan lunged, forcing him to pivot.

Before she could recover from the weight of her missed swing, Rune pinned her and slammed her against the wall with his body.

"I'm beginning to think you're angry," he goaded, his grin never waning. "Has your jealousy finally clouded your judgment?"

Tightening her grip on the handle, Kallan pushed against him, and Rune released her, allowing her the space to swing at the air, her blade missing every time.

"Thoughts of me with Emma getting the better of you?" he asked, widening his grin.

With a shrill exclamation, Kallan took up the daggers from the table and threw the blades at Rune.

"*Uskit!*" Rune exclaimed and dove through the door, hitting the ground hard just as Kallan flicked both wrists, ignited her hands, and fired.

A pillar of fire roared, grazing Rune's back as he lay with Kallan's rage rolling over him.

The confidence was gone, replaced by a blanket of white that coated Rune's face. Afraid to breathe, unable to move, he waited, motionless until the fire died and the smoking, charred door of the armory groaned as it swayed closed. The smith's rhythmic plink carried on the wind without missing a beat.

"Don't you have enough sense to not anger a Seid-kona?" Halvard's boisterous voice quelled a chuckle. Rune raised his face from the dirt.

With mead in one hand and bow slung over a shoulder, Halvard lifted Rune to his feet.

"Stubborn wench doesn't know how to admit when something's eating away at her," he said as he slapped the dirt from his trousers.

"Let me give you some advice, lad," Halvard said, still chuckling. "If it can throw fire at you, don't make it angry." The last bit of his words slurred into a chuckle that brought tears to the old man's eyes.

Rune's smile had recovered.

Studying the door, he watched as the last of the Seidr flame whispered out.

"Could be worse, I suppose." His grinned widened. "She could be incessantly weepy."

Snatching the flask from Halvard, Rune headed for the stables as he took a drink.

"Astrid and Freyja are saddled," Halvard said. "Olga and Emma are stocking the horses now with the last bit of provisions."

Rune nodded. "As soon as I've collected my wench, we'll be off," he said and downed another gulp.

"Your wench?"

Halvard grabbed Rune's shoulder, stopping him where he stood and snatching back the mead. "So, you did plug her. Is that why she set fire to your arse?"

"Not yet," Rune answered, grinning boldly, and the old man released another bout of laughter. "But if I don't, somebody has to, or one of us won't be making it to Gunir alive."

And before Halvard could object, Rune grabbed the mead back from the Throendr and downed the last of it as he sauntered on into the stables.

Within the armory, Kallan heaved, gasping between breaths. Oblivious to the fire that rolled from her palms and the hot tears that fell down her face, Kallan stoked her temper as endless images filled her head of Rune and Emma.

Chapter 54

Nidaros buzzed with an air of excitement as Emma and Olga scurried with the last of the provisions. With unchecked enthusiasm, the women took turns stuffing an assortment of food and drink into the satchels. Lured by the enthusiasm of the Alfar, a small crowd had started to form and on-lookers extended their parting wishes to Rune wherever they found the chance in between Olga's orders.

It was not long before Halvard joined him armed with three flasks of mead, two of which he crammed into the saddle of a short, cream horse deemed Freyja. With long, strands of the finest fur, Rune curiously ran his hand down the pony's thick neck.

"Freyja is from the north in Gasdalr," Halvard said. "Brand arrived two winters ago with her on board."

Rune intricately examined the strands of wavy, cream fur as soft and as thick as rabbit hide and twice as long as his arm in length.

"She isn't much for riding," Halvard said, heaving a roll of blankets onto her back, "but her wide girth can handle the mountain air during the coldest of winters, and her stout legs will ensure an easier climb through the forest in Heidmork."

Halvard gave Freyja a final pat and unstopped his flask.

"Avoid the lake to the south of Aursund or you'll find yourself trudging through days of bog."

"Bog," Rune said with a hint of concern.

"Aye." Halvard tugged the leather strap. "Bogs. The kind that stretch for days on end. You'll be forced to double back countless times before you manage to find the right path through."

"Days," Rune said, "in a bog...with Kallan."

The thought alone made him shudder.

"Once you cross into Heidmork," Halvard continued, "stay to the river. Always stay to the river. There's a gorge there, that will cause you more headache than its worth with a pony, a horse, and a lady."

With interests piqued, Rune shifted a brow.

"A gorge?"

Halvard nodded, pulling back the mead from his mouth.

"Aye, nearly two thousand paces from the river at one point. Don't let the lady wander." His eyes were cold and severe. "And keep a sharp eye for yourself if you veer from the river."

Rune shook his head.

"The lady won't like it," he said.

Halvard stared at the ground in thought.

"The lady won't."

"I won't like it," Rune said, glancing to Halvard who grinned and threw back another mouthful of mead. "Speaking of the Venom Queen, where is she?"

The mead sloshed about in the flask as Halvard dropped it again and gulped.

"She was with the horses when I grabbed Freyja here." Halvard patted the horse's rump then added, "She might still be there."

But Rune was already gone.

Kallan's hand poked through the fur of Ori's overcoat as she gave a vigorous rub down the neck of one of the fjord ponies. Happily munching away at Idunn's apple, she planted a kiss on its head. Already, its coat glistened with the sheen of a newborn colt.

Once more, her thoughts strayed to Rune's final words. Her stomach tightened with a hurt that clamped her chest and stung her nose. She dug a hand into her eyes, forcing away the fire that burned there.

"I was hoping you'd be here."

Startled, Kallan jumped and heaved an audible sigh with relief at the sight of Brand, and not Rune, leaning over the stall gate.

"You're getting ready to head out?" he asked, coming to stand beside her. The wide grin Brand frequently sported was gone, replaced with a somber smile.

"Yes," she said with a single nod.

"Will you be back?" he asked with wide eyes.

She did not miss the hopeful tone rounding each word.

"No," she said.

Brand's shoulders dropped, pulling Kallan's pity with him and she let it, happy to feel anything other than bitter rage for Rune.

Silently, Brand nodded and extended his hand to hers.

Within his outstretched palm, a pair of tiny discs stamped with a profiled face and crowned with a dome glistening with silver. Around the edges, foreign runes encircled the image. On the back, a cross divided the discs into quarters. Each had been dotted in the center. Runes on the back also lined the edges.

"What are these?" Kallan asked, turning the pieces over, intrigued by the foreign markings.

"Coins," Brand said, his flashy smile somewhat revived, "from Eire's Land, stamped by the finest horse trader in all of Dubh Linn. King Sigtrygg just started making them."

"They're beautiful," she said, encouraging Brand to speak.

"We picked them off a monastery on our way through."

Kallan looked up, suddenly aware of how very close he stood.

She dropped her voice to almost a whisper.

"Where are you headed to next?"

"Well..." Brand said. "...I'll have to wait for the ship to come around for port, which will be around next moon."

The horse shook its head, snapping the reins against the wooden beam, as Kallan looked the coins over, unaware that Rune lingered several stalls over.

"But after the snows, I'll probably take to Eire's Land again," Brand said.

Kallan shook her head, still mesmerized by her new trinkets.

"I've never seen her land." Kallan looked to Brand. "Eire's Land. I've been to Northumbria, but Gudrun left no time in my schedule to make a trip to Eire's Land." Her eyes glistened with intrigue, urging him on, begging him to speak without saying a word.

"Eire's Land is as beautiful and as green as the sea is blue," Brand said. "Endless green. There's something in the air in Eire's Land as if the gods are still there breathing life into it."

Kallan's eyes glazed with wonder as her chest rose and fell with each breath.

"There are scholars there who produce pictures," he said, "hundreds of pictures on vellum with the most intricate of art work, some made out of gold.

They'd fetch a high price on the trade roads. If you can get to them, that is."

The fine strands of rabbit fur grazed Kallan's cheek. Her hair bunched up around the collar, spilling out and over the black fur, down to her waist where Brand's eyes lingered.

"Kallan?" He stared at her lips. "Come with me." The words came fast.

She grinned.

"Over your sea through the land of green to your world flowing over with wine?" Kallan said, remembering and allowing her words to carry her through to the ends of the earth.

"Where we'll find the maps in the stars and sail home again," he said, daring at last to brush her face with the back of his fingers, and she let him. Brand split his face with his wide grin, both oblivious to the Ljosalfr who slipped from the stables, unseen, unheard, unknown.

"Home," she whispered, and remembered, her smile falling with her memories. "I must go home."

Releasing his breath, Brand nodded and dropped his hand.

"I know."

As if his accord was the cue she had been waiting for, Kallan swept past Brand, leaving him alone in the stall.

"Kallan."

His voice pulled her back, as keen to hear his words as he was to speak them. "If ever you're done

587

being queen, and there's ever a day when you're looking for a somewhere..."

Kallan grinned.

"Come find me," he bade.

Her eyes beamed.

"And where shall I look?" she asked, still grinning.

"To the sea."

With a nod that shook her hair into her face, she turned, leaving the memory of her smile behind.

Rune's insides twisted, igniting his rage with a maddening lack of sense. Thoughts of impaling Brand entertained his wrath for only a moment, before shifting his thoughts to Kallan. Too angry to growl, Rune marched back to Halvard still nursing the mead. With a second run of curses, he ripped the drink from Halvard's hand.

"That bad?" Halvard asked as Rune threw back a gulp.

"Why would anything be bad?" Rune asked. "Can't a man be thirsty without being prodded with questions?"

"Brand got to your wench, didn't he?" Halvard asked.

"Not my wench. Never my wench." Rune shoved the empty flask back to Halvard as he collected Astrid's reins. "She's the damn Dokkalfr who I wouldn't touch with all the blessings from Freyr."

Still grumbling, Rune hoisted himself into the saddle and froze when he spotted a black, leather overcoat swallowing a certain Dokkalfr emerge from the stables. With a tug of the reins, Rune veered Astrid, giving him a gentle nick.

"What of the lass?" Halvard asked as Rune rode off.

"She'll follow," he said, picking up speed.

"Are you sure?" Halvard called from beside Freyja.

"Yep," Rune said and encouraged Kallan's horse into a light canter down the beach.

Along the banks of the river Nid, Rune grimaced beside Astrid as Kallan and Halvard joined him with Freyja.

Two weeks. Rune deepened the furrows on his brow. *Two weeks enduring a sniveling, spoiled, palace brat.*

Too sour to notice the off-hand quips and glowers from the Dokkalfr, Rune greeted Halvard, extending his thanks with a cold shoulder facing Kallan.

"That's including the two you have packed," Halvard said, passing a mead to Rune.

With another run through the directions, they exchanged their good wishes and bid farewell, then watched as the Throendr made his way back to Nidaros alone.

With a distinct squeak of the flask's stopper, Kallan seemed to catch the darkness blanketing Rune's face. Eyeing her with callousness, from her leather boots, to the piercing, cold iridescent blue of her eyes, Rune threw back his head and began the first of three flasks. Without a reprimand or word, he took up Astrid's reins, and began the long trek home.

Rune gritted his teeth until he was certain they would crack. Kallan's melancholy was no better, though he didn't give much thought to what inspired hers.

By the time Rune polished off the last of the first flask, her blatant sneers had become vile glares that accompanied them down the River Nid.

The river differed from that of the harsh, barren region of the Dofrarfjell. Endless pines mingled with the reds and oranges of autumn that had settled in with the impertinent cold of the harvest.

After half a day's walk, the lake of Selabu greeted them with an air of dread that added to their bitter temperaments. Steep slopes plunged the land into the lake, making the journey difficult, at best. For hours, they walked without rest, the ground fixed at a near permanent incline. Whenever the opportunity arose, they led the horses away from the persistent drop of the terrain.

The sporadic flat stretches of land that would allow them to rest came too infrequently, adding to the hostile strain between them. On occasion, a misplaced step sent them sliding into the water. Only once did Rune extend a hand to Kallan, who slapped it away mumbling something akin to 'murderer.'

Tension brewed as the impending argument thickened, leaving them both bitter and vile when they arrived at a wide, but shallow, river that interrupted their path.

Rune looked to the sun suspended over the lake then to the northeast where the river flowed. Ahead, the water spanned seventy-five paces, though appearing shallow enough to cross. Without a word, he tugged on Astrid's reins.

"What are you doing?" Kallan asked behind him.

"Halvard said the river would lead south," Rune said, still making his way toward the water.

"But he didn't say anything about there being a river before then," Kallan said, clutching Freyja's bridle.

"I don't know how you'd know that, seeing as how you were too busy making plans with the whelp."

"What difference does it make what I do with my whelp?" Kallan asked.

"It doesn't." Rune returned his eyes to the slippery stones submerged in the water. "But it does matter what that whelp does with my prisoner."

"I am not your prisoner."

"Well, I'm not yours," Rune said, spinning around in time to see Kallan heave like a dragon ready to scorch the earth.

"I will not follow you blindly," she said.

"Blindly?" Rune barked an unstable laugh. "You have done nothing *blindly* since we started this, princess."

"Stop calling me that."

"Foolishly, weakly, loudly maybe, but never *blindly*," Rune said.

"It's because of you we're here at all," Kallan said. "I won't follow you!"

"How is that?" Rune asked, too angry to stop pushing his way through the river.

"You killed my father." Rune turned to her. "You took me from Lorlenalin, and I'll not follow you all the way to Gunir!"

Rune arched a brow as the river's babble filled the silence.

"Alfheim," Kallan corrected.

Rune heaved a patient breath, his grimace holding strong.

"I am going south," he said, "and Astrid is coming with me."

Without another word, he guided Kallan's horse across the river, leaving Kallan to stay or follow. A moment later, with her slew of curses mumbled under her breath, Kallan entered the river behind him.

The flat plain on the other side of the river was more than enough to convince them to stop. They watered the horses and rested their feet while eating a quick meal composed of apples, flat bread, and mead. After a handful of silent sneers, they continued with only the whine of the third flask stopper to break their silence.

Around the water with the curve of the lake, Kallan and Rune made their slow way south then west along the shores. When, at last, the water glistened with the light of the setting sun, the forest ended, and the southern river flowed like glass. Exhausted, their path veered from the lake and Kallan and Rune began putting distance between them and the lake in Selabu.

Long after the day's end, and too tired to grimace, they, at last, settled along the bank of the river and made camp, without so much as an insult.

Empty and forgotten, the third flask lay among their bags as Kallan stared up at the crescent moon. With every image that plagued her imagination, her sanity slipped further from rational. Huffing, she flipped to her side. From across the fire, light spread up and over Rune, spilling over his back.

Just like Emma, she thought and again sorted through endless variations of Rune and his Englian strumpet.

Hatred swelled, clawing her insides with a maddening rage that urged her to march back to Nidaros and kill the wench while he slept peaceably, free of the demons he beset upon her.

How dare you sleep while I lay tormented?

The words rent all thoughts, stirring awake other memories—barely forgotten memories—of her father as he lay dying and her blood-soaked hands. A wave of hate washed over her, abating all thoughts of Emma, and Kallan gazed at the Ljosalfr asleep beside her. A new darkness consumed her and the eye of the dragon awakened.

Dead men breed no pain.

Her eye settled on the black and reds of *Gramm's* pommel.

While he sleeps...he wouldn't even know...and I could return and conquer Gunir.

Throwing off the blankets, Kallan grabbed the nearest saddlebag and rose to her feet. With full force, she threw the satchel into the back of Rune's head, jerking him awake.

Before he could turn and assess, before he could comprehend, Kallan took up his sword and unsheathed *Gramm*, its blade ringing out as if sounding off the opening note to his dirge.

Within two long strides, she came to stand over the Ljosalfar king and gave her battle cry. Seeing the blade turned down, Rune visibly braced for the sword to penetrate his heart as Kallan dropped all her weight onto him and plunged *Gramm* into the earth.

Blocking her face in shadow, her hair hung free as she heaved. Blood flowed where the blade nicked Rune's ear. Against the black of *Gramm's* hilt, Kallan's white fists shook. The fire popped as Rune watched.

"Far too long I've dreamt of my sword stained with the blood of your people." Kallan said. "Too long I've sought your death. Too long I've moved to strike. Even as you pulled me from the rancid darkness and I lay dying, did I plan to kill you and avenge my father's death. Even now, all I have to do is strike. At the end of it all, I must decide. Should I kill you? Should you die?"

Rune watched, ready for whatever choice she made next.

"I should kill you," Kallan whispered, "and watch your blood run with the blood of my people. If I kill you, all my troubles end. And I go home to Lorlenalin, my father's death avenged."

"And if you're wrong," Rune said, "if it was another who stole your father's life, leaving him to die dishonorably upon the fields of Alfheim, whose life then will you have avenged by wrongfully killing me?"

The heavy burden of understanding weighted down her eyes, and, all at once, there was doubt.

"What wars may come by staining your hands with my blood?" Rune's hush swept through her. "What lies then will you tell yourself once you've lied to your people? Can you risk being wrong, Kallan? Can you risk all the lives that will die and mine, all from your mistake?"

"Why did you save me?" she breathed. "Why did you kill my father only to save me?"

"I didn't kill him," he whispered.

"I can't believe you." Her voice wavered as the words caught in her throat.

"A king's head is worth its weight in gold," Rune said. Her eyes widened with unshed tears as she recalled Aaric's words to her. "Name your price," Rune said.

The back of her throat burned as she forced all other thoughts aside.

"Crawl through Svartálfaheim," she said, "into the depths of Hel, beyond the roots of Yggdrasill, and bring him home to me." Kallan stifled a sob. "That is my price."

The chill from Rune's eyes was gone, replaced instead with a pity that reached down into her and shook the walls she had built on anguish.

"Find the father you took from me," Kallan bade, "and restore him unto me."

"I can't," he whispered thickly.

Kallan's dagger was suddenly unsheathed and pressed against his throat.

"Please." The word tripped on a gasp. A tear slipped from her eye. "If I let you live," she said, "please give my father back to me."

He visibly swallowed against the blade.

"Please," she said.

With a *thwit* of an arrow, Kallan and Rune stared at a shaft protruding from the ground beside them.

"Don't move," came the aged, gruff voice of a man from behind. "The next one is aimed for your heart."

Kallan shifted her weight.

"Don't move," he said again, but his voice wavered with doubt and Kallan rose to her feet. Rune stood beside Kallan where the fire's light bathed them in orange and gold.

Hunched before them, the beaten, aged frame of an old man stood. A scraggly, graying black beard covered his face. His mottled hands shook with an unsteady draw of a withered bow.

"You're on the wrong side of the Raumelfr, Alfar." Fear shifted the old man's eye. Fear shook his hands as he pointed the bow at Rune and then Kallan.

"There's nothing but death on this side. What are you doing here?"

"We need to get to the Raumelfr," Rune said, making no movement. Blackened from grief, the old man studied the tapered ears and grand height of the Alfar with hardened eyes.

"Raumelfr, eh." His jargon slurred with exhaustion as he lowered his weapon. "You're a few days out of your way if you're looking for the Raumelfr."

Casting an eye over their camp, the old man seemed to assess their accommodations, lingering until his gaze fell to the pendant fastened at Kallan's neck.

It was a long while before he spoke again, unable to tear his eye from the tri-corner knot.

"You need food? Shelter?" He grumbled the words more than asked, and slumped away. His back, too long laden with burden, arched under the weight. "Come with me," he growled and was on his way through the thick of the wood from whence he came.

The Alfar collected their things and extinguished the fire.

"I heard a scream. It's why I came running," the old man said thickly as they joined him. "I'm Bern." He didn't bother to ask for their names.

Away from the path of the river, through the dark of the forest, they marched, led by the ramblings of the old man. Dead branches on the ground cracked beneath his feet as he stomped, clearing a somewhat crude path.

"I was sitting with my wife," he tried to say. "Well, maybe it's luck that I found you...maybe in time," he muttered.

"Is someone sick?" Kallan asked, eager to forget her own grievances.

With each hollow step, his torchlight flickered.

"Not sick." Bern pulled back a branch. "Dying."

The old man said no more until they reached the end of the wood where the land stretched out ahead beneath the moonlight. Black shadows spanned a vast clearing, throwing silhouettes into the dark. Mounds were strewn about mingled with barren land that seemed to end at the base of a mountain.

In the distance, through the mounds, the only sign of life spilled through the slip-shod planks, blanketed in peat moss and lichen in what was the dilapidated remains of a long-house. Orange streaked the black of night where the faintest cries carried through the air.

"My wife, Halda," Bern said. Grief shook his tone.

"What's wrong with her?" Rune asked as they made their way into the distance.

"It's Svenn, our son," he said, his voice cracking.

Kallan looked at Bern as he forced himself to explain.

"Nearly a fortnight ago, Olaf came through, demanding we denounce Freyja. When we refused..." His words were lost to his grief.

Bern rushed through his tale while he still had the nerve to speak. "But our boy...he didn't die right away...and now he has the fever. We can't...It would be kinder to kill him, but Halda won't…She has hope, you see."

The sobbing was nearer as they came to stand before the dilapidated remnants of a charred longhouse starting to fall in on itself. Releasing Astrid's reins, Kallan pushed on what she could only guess had been a door.

The familiar stench was overpowering. Metallic and rancid, mingled with the strong scent of feces. The smell hit her stomach and she gagged back a mouthful of bile, knowing what it was.

Black blood soaked the charred, wooden planks. A two-week-old trail led to the wall where rows of wide benches flanked the sides of the longhouse. The central fire pit burned with glowing embers that cast shadows of orange and red over the black and ash, and on the wall, kneeling beside a small, pale boy about thirteen winters old, Bern's Halda hovered.

Waxen flesh was pulled taut over the boy's skeletal face as his brown eyes, glazed with death, stared beyond his mother to a point unseen by the living. Trembling, Kallan fumbled over the flap of her pouch, her eyes frozen on the boy.

Too long, Kallan searched among the pouch's contents. It was with a deathly grip that she withdrew the luscious treasure.

Dropping alongside Halda, Kallan unsheathed her dagger. The boy was breathing, but barely. With quaking hands, Kallan withdrew Idunn's apple.

Kallan sat unmoving, as she clutched the apple, barely hearing Rune's step behind her.

She could save him. With one drop, the boy would never again know pain, never again suffer, he would never die, with just one drop.

The lad was slipping. She had to do something.

Still holding the apple, Kallan grasped the boy and administered her Seidr, threading the golden strands through him. The Seidr flowed into the boy's mouth and down the side of his face. With shaking hands, Kallan pulled at his shirt and the pool of black that had fused to the cloth. There, the stench of decay was the strongest. The wound was old, and more than blood seeped from his gut.

Blood coated her hands, smearing the perfect gold of the apple with vivid streaks. Tremors jolted her fingers as she shuddered uncontrollably. She had no choice. The boy would die.

Unable to hold her hands steady, Kallan moved to cut a slice from the apple and nicked her thumb instead. Rune took a step, and held himself back just as Kallan abandoned the apple and placed her hand onto his wound where she poured her golden Seidr threads.

"Please," Kallan breathed then muttered the incantation below her breath.

Her body shook as she drained her Seidr, pouring everything she had into the boy. The red of her blood mingled with the gold of her Seidr and the black of his blood and waste. The bleeding slowed, but his staggered breath punched the air. Once. Twice. Then never again.

Still glazed, the boy's eyes stared at the invisible point above his bed.

Torrid cries filled the house, but Kallan heard nothing. With the last of her strength, she rose to her feet, deadened to the weight of her arms. White fingers caked in putrid gore relinquished the apple. With a thud, it struck the floor and rolled, stopping in a pool of dried blood at Rune's feet.

Consumed by the grief she could no longer fight, her feet carried her past Rune. Silently, he watched from the shadows and, knowing the look in her eye, he followed her out the door.

The night's darkness enveloped Kallan, suffocating her in the abyss. Stumbling in a vacant stupor, she dragged her feet into a barren clearing beneath the moon. There, she dropped to her knees.

The night's cold air invaded her lungs. Tightening her grip on the dagger, Kallan plunged the dagger into the earth, pulled the blade through, and counted.

One for Father.

Withdrawing the dagger from the soil, Kallan lunged and remembered the boy.

Two.

This time, her sorrow dug deeper as she stabbed the earth, rending the walls of her anguish.

"Three," she murmured, remembering Olga's son and Dofrar.

Four where Mother lay dead. How many more?

Kallan counted and stabbed again. Maybe if she dug deep enough, the boy would heal.

Kallan gouged the earth. Something in the soil could heal them. It had to. Memories of her father flowed from behind her wall. Tears mingled with the dirt and fell on her hands.

Three hundred for the lives of Austramonath.

Desperate to ease the pain, Kallan tilled the earth with every stab of her blade, convinced the next one would be enough, but each cut, each thrust could not fill the insatiable ache, and she dug deeper.

Tossing the blade aside, Kallan dove, burrowing her hands into the earth. With the tips of her fingers, she clawed, tearing at the ground as if looking for relief.

The ground was cold. It needed to be.

"Kallan."

Deeper. Almost there.

"Kallan."

Blood and earth covered her hands.

"There are no ships," she whispered. Tears blinded her.

"Kallan."

"It's just there," she said. "I can almost see it." Down to her knuckles, Kallan burrowed, desperate to find the end. "The boy must be burned. Father must be burned."

"Princess." Rune took her by the shoulders.

"Or the ravens will eat them...the ravens will eat them...and Odinn won't find them. Odinn won't—"

Kallan lunged again. A rock sliced open her finger and Rune pulled her into him.

"Please," she gasped, falling, and Rune caught her.

Sobbing, Kallan shook, digging her nails into Rune's arms.

"I want my father back. Please give him back. I'll let you go...I'll let you live..."

The crescent moon lit her eyes wide with tears as Rune cupped her face. His thumb brushed a tear and more flowed in its place.

"I can't," he said.

"Please," she begged, brimming with despair, certain he could fix this, certain he could mend it. "I have silver...please...I'll pay...give him back."

"Kallan—"

"I'll do anything. Anything. I want my father back."

And Kallan fell.

Giving her refuge where there was none, Rune rocked as Kallan cried until the latest hour, when the shadow ebbed and took with it the last of her wall. There, free of the anguish that bound her, Kallan slept.

Chapter 55

Kallan woke to the pop and crackle of a fire. With a deep sigh, she pulled in the warm scent of roasted venison. Walls of tanned hide formed a domed room where no fewer than sixteen poles were propped through a singular smoke hole blackened with soot. From the light that seeped through the opening, she assessed it was not yet midday.

Furs, blankets, and hides were placed in between the pole supports, providing makeshift beds and seating that was spaced around a small fire positioned in the tent's center below the smoke hole. Pots and baskets were scattered about with satchels, all bagged as if ready for travel. Beside a silent, single drum with etched figures, Rune sat, staring through the doorway. His arms rested comfortably on his knees with his back to Kallan, as if waiting.

Peace eased her worries and Kallan relaxed as she studied the curve of his back. Memories, too bold to forget for too long, surfaced and waves of tears pricked her nose. Kallan bit her bottom lip.

If ever she was to say anything...to tell him...

Kallan pondered, but couldn't bring herself to speak. A sigh she stifled emerged as a sniffle, and Rune turned with the inescapable look of relief holding in the silver of his blue eyes.

"You're awake," he said, but didn't smile and remained seated in the door.

Kallan rolled her head back and peered up at the smoke hole then dropped a wrist on her brow as if shielding her eyes from light.

"Where are we?" she said weakly, desperate to steer the conversation clear from certain topics. Rune seemed just as content to oblige.

"You're in a *finntent*," he said. "There isn't much left of the longhouse. We burned it."

The statement seemed definitive and Kallan nodded.

"If you're asking about the land," Rune said. "we're still in Throendalog, two days' march from Plassje where the Raumelfr begins."

"Plassje," Kallan repeated.

"It's what Halda calls it," Rune said, and looked out to the open once more, leaving Kallan to her bed and silence.

For a short time, Kallan wallowed in thought, allowing her mind to wander and drift. She remembered snippets of blood and earth from the night before and her spine stiffened as she braced for the usual barrage of sharp pain to stab at her chest and rob her of breath. When only a dulled ache came instead, Kallan's thoughts altered to Rune and a part of her softened with regret.

"Rune?"

Kallan heard him turn, but she didn't dare look away from the smoke hole. She stretched her thoughts to the iron wall where she stored her woes in the darkness, and, catching her breath suddenly, gasped.

She heard Rune shuffle away from the door, and fought to keep her eyes ahead. He sat alongside her, waiting, like he knew she would break.

"I don't..." A tear fell. By the time she opened her mouth to speak, the words she had amassed had fumbled apart. She gulped down a wave of cowardice to begin again. Another tear streaked her face.

"I don't..."

"You don't know what to say." Kallan met Rune's gaze as he spoke for her. "So you'll decide to say nothing. Then we'll both pretend you didn't want to tell me 'thank you' or that you were wrong or that you now believe I never killed your father."

Kallan bit her lip. Tears swelled and she looked to the smoke hole, avoiding Rune's eyes just as he looked her way. Knowing the time to be silent, she waited and listened, letting him do the talking.

"Instead, you'll lay there and nod."

Kallan nodded.

"And we will both pretend," he said, "for one small moment, that you did not want to thank me or kiss me."

Kallan whipped her face to his, her eyes wide with objection.

"I didn't," she said, but Rune was already smiling.

"You found your words," he said and caught her smiling before Kallan wiped it away.

"This doesn't change anything," she said and allowed Rune to see a smile lift the corner of her mouth.

As she exhaled, she released the temper, the anger, the hate she harbored just for him.

Rune grinned. "Of course it doesn't."

Half-gasping, half-smiling, Kallan shook her head and bit the corner of her bottom lip. Without a word, Rune stood and left Kallan alone in the *finntent*.

Sunlight pierced Kallan's eyes, forcing her to take a moment to adjust to the daylight. The stench of rancid, burning flesh and hair seared her nose and Kallan gasped.

A field of carnage spanned the whole of Bern's land from the hide flap of the *finntent* to the dilapidated remains of the charred longhouse that formed a pyre. At the base of the pyre, Rune stood watching giant flames devour the house and bodies of reindeer and cattle as streams of sweat trickled down his bare shoulders.

"The boy?" she asked, failing to force her eyes away.

It was a long while before Rune responded.

Exhaling, he passed his gaze over Kallan, and extended an arm to the distance. Stones now outlined the shape of a boat over the ground where Kallan had dug up the earth the night before. She didn't have to ask to know he had finished the job for her and put the boy to rest in the ground.

The sight twisted her insides and she averted her eyes from the grave.

"The animals..." Her voice cracked as she spoke. "The blood."

Rune nodded. "Olaf passed through."

The name stabbed at Kallan's chest. She was quickly growing to hate that man.

"Bern and Halda hadn't heard of his arrival," Rune said, not bothering to wait for the color to return to her skin. "They didn't know of the massacre of Odinnssalr or his tyranny in Nidaros. They didn't know that Hakon Jarl was dead." The longhouse creaked as it buckled under its own weight and Rune stared into the flames. "When Bern refused to denounce their faith to Freyja," he continued, "Olaf killed their livestock, burned their fields and home, and stabbed their child, leaving him to bleed out."

Another stab tightened Kallan's chest.

"But Olaf was heading south to Viken along the western roads through Upplond." Kallan rushed through the words. "It's the reason we came this way."

Darkness blanketed Rune's face as Kallan paused to think for a moment.

"What are his troops doing this far east from Dofrar?" Kallan asked.

"He came with a fraction of his men," Rune said. "Bern believes the majority of his troops still march along the road to Aeslo while he followed a different path with a selected few. Bern isn't sure."

"Rune."

Bern's voice diverted Kallan's attention to the human's burly form. In the darkness he looked menacing, almost wild, but in day's light, he looked old and worn, exhausted from grief. He waited until he crossed the carnage, seeming indifferent to what he passed.

With a weak smile and a brief nod to Kallan, he looked to Rune. "I'm almost through here, then Halda and I will start packing up the tent. Shouldn't take us more than an hour before we're ready."

"I'll be along to help," Rune said, dismissing Bern with a nod.

"Ready?" Kallan asked, studying the woman scurrying in and out of the finntent. The forty-year-old woman had tied back her long, black hair into a braid and had fastened her apron dress with hand-carved soapstone brooches.

"Halda is Finn," Rune said at Kallan's side. "Her people live off the reindeer and move when the reindeer move. She settled down with Bern ten winters ago."

Rune stepped over a pool of blood, and, when he walked, Kallan followed.

"With the boy gone, they've made plans to return to Finnmork," he said.

"Where is that?" she asked, peering up with an unusual gentleness in her eyes that caused Rune to stop and meet her gaze.

"Wherever the Finn call home," he said. "With Svenn's wounds too great, they couldn't travel."

Inhaling, Rune forced his attention out to the barren, blood-soaked plain.

"Now that he and the house are gone, nothing keeps them tied to this land."

With nothing left to answer for, Rune gazed at Kallan, who was, once again, fixed on Svenn's grave.

The blue in her eyes was vivid. The thin line of her neck drew his eye down to her collarbone.

"What?"

Rune jumped, unaware that Kallan had turned.

"Nothing," he said and pretended to not see the bit of a smile as he stared at the *finntent* behind her.

A solid *thunk* ended the peace between them as Halda and Bern dropped a shaft into a growing pile of poles. The tent was already half down and all their possessions placed onto a large stretch of bound leather.

"They'll accompany us to the lake where the Raumelfr begins," Rune said. "With luck, they'll find the Finn along the way. If not, we'll part ways at

the Raumelfr where they'll head north of Throendalog toward Naumudalr."

"And we along the Raumelfr," Kallan said.

Rune nodded.

"Hm." Kallan shrugged and bounced her way over
to help Halda with the sheets of hide.

Within minutes, the *finntent* was down. With several more minutes, they had the poles splayed upon
the hide, secured and wrapped into place.

"We usually fasten the harness to a reindeer bull,
but the horse should do," Bern said, untangling a
mass of leather straps as he and Rune approached
Astrid.

After many derogatory snorts from Astrid, the
straps were fastened into place while Kallan managed
to distract his disgruntled objections with an apple.

"He took to the harness well," Halda said as she finished tying down the last of their possessions onto
the hide bound to the harness. "For not being a
plough horse, I mean," she said nervously.

Too long, her eyes lingered on Kallan's pendant,
but before Kallan could ask, Halda was off, bounding
toward Bern.

With a hearty pat to Astrid's shoulder, Kallan took
up the reins at Bern's word and they started their
way back to the river that would lead them south to
Aursund. Passing gray clouds rarely permitted the
sunlight as they journeyed. Songs of birds carried

through the wood. At a distance, grouse drummed off as they took flight. The river was as wide as it was constant, leading them on without fail. Its banks housed a fair number of white-throated dippers that skittered and flicked across the surface, disappearing into the water to re-emerge again. They had walked for an hour in silence before Rune slipped to the back of the line, leaving Bern with Halda at the lead.

Kallan eyed him suspiciously as Rune fell into step beside her.

He extended his hand to Kallan. "Here."

With a furrowed brow, Kallan opened her palm, where Rune dropped four orange-white berries.

"Cloudberries." She looked at him.

"We aren't going to be able to stop and I figured..." Rune didn't finish.

Mouthwatering memories surfaced of sweet cloudberry cake interspersed with the bitter bite of the berry. A smile turned the corner of her mouth, but, by the time she looked up again, Rune was gone.

The first half of the river snaked its way through a plain that resembled a wetland despite being dry. On either side of the river, the land rose with the trees until the peaks of the hills were out of sight. The further they walked, however, the narrower the valley between the hills became. The land stretched to the sky until mountains boxed them in like a pair of hands cradling them between its palms, like a child cradles a glowworm.

The mountains pushed them on, forcing them to the river's edge where the water had almost no room to flow.

Within hours, the mountains rolled down off their peaks and opened the valley, granting them room to breathe. As Rune promised, they didn't stop. Not at midday, when the sun passed high overhead, nor five hours later at sunset. They walked in darkness along the river with less moonlight than they had the previous night, as if counting down the time Rune had left.

Within a quarter hour, Bern and Halda had pitched the *finntent* and rabbit roasted over the fire inside. They chattered idly amongst themselves about the farm, the war, and Halda's heritage. After they ate, Halda withdrew her drum and struck the softened hide pulled taught across the wooden frame while Bern pulled out his long smoke pipe, encouraging Rune to follow suit.

Around the fire they sat, saying very little as they listened to Halda's voice ebb and flow like the wind. She sang for more than an hour as Kallan, lulled into serenity, tucked her knees to her chest beneath the heavy overcoat.

At times, Halda's voice dipped so low, so soft, Kallan strained with her Alfar ears to hear the faintest hum. Smoothly, her voice would rise again like the wind passing in and out of the trees at a whim. At the end of the hour, when Halda set the drum to the side, Kallan dismissed herself and emerged from the tent, lost in endless memory that had awakened.

Purple lights moved overhead much like Halda's music. Free of the pain that had haunted her, Kallan remembered the streets of Lorlenalin all dressed for the Midwinter Jol, when the giddiness of the Raven's feast stirred the mischievous nature of the children, and she would run through the streets with Eilif, elated for the break in her studies.

She raised a palm and summoned a ball of gold, which spun on her command. Kallan remembered Gudrun and her Seidr lessons. She remembered her father's voice as he guided her through each sword lesson. The reprimand and scolding she and Eilif received when they overturned the table Cook had laden for feast one Disablot on the eve of Disting. The look in Kri's eyes when she and Eilif showed up one Jol with bowls of pudding.

Kallan smiled and flipped her palm about, encouraging the Seidr to obey as she recalled the day her father first tossed her onto Astrid.

"They're beautiful tonight," Rune said.

Kallan jumped, extinguishing her Seidr.

"Beautiful?" she asked, not daring to look at Rune.

Inhaling, he drew a breath through his long pipe as he settled himself down beside Kallan.

"The Valkyrjur."

Rune pointed to the cool blues and purple lights dancing in the sky. He released a long line of smoke. "The days are getting shorter," he said thoughtfully.

Kallan raised her hand and summoned her Seidr. The line of gold light filled her palm, captivating Rune's attention.

"What is that?" he asked.

"Seidr," she said, holding her gaze on the Seidr as she flicked her hand over once more.

Rune pulled another draw through the pipe.

"I thought the Seidr is what you light my back side with."

Kallan cracked a wide smile and shook her head.

"No." She afforded a glance to Rune. "That's fire. Seidr flame."

In silence, he watched, as if enthralled with her hand enclosed in threads like streams of gold.

"This," she said at last, "is Seidr...just Seidr in its basic form."

She flipped her hand over once more, commanding the light to pull up and around her fingers like flame.

"This is the energy I manipulate to create the fire I *try* to burn your back-side with."

Rune released the smoke. The moon was little more than a sliver.

"Two nights will be the new moon," he said, releasing another draw as Kallan played and pulled on her Seidr. She felt the shadow clearing her eyes, leaving behind a hint of kindness and she relaxed her shoulders, adding a pleasantry to the air.

She flicked her wrist and the Seidr obeyed as she proceeded to play with the ball of light, pulling back on the Seidr and letting it go.

Taking another long draw, Rune looked to the moon and released a long breath.

"Kallan."

Silence.

"I realize this is probably going to end with us locked in combat...but let's assume for a moment that a Ljosalfr didn't kill your father."

The wind passed by, ruffling the tension between them.

"Alright." Kallan's voice was gentle enough to encourage him to continue.

"The day he died...was there anyone else you may have seen?"

Kallan extinguished her Seidr and she felt Rune relax. Her chest rose and fell with the deep sigh she took and remembered: Daggon riding off after the warrior, the empty keep, her father and the black blood.

Kallan shivered.

"No," she said. "Just you and your kin."

"And what about your father?"

"You aren't suggesting—"

"No," he said. "I'm asking. Try to remember. Was there anyone?"

Kallan shook her head.

"Just Daggon."

"And Daggon wouldn't—"

"No. Daggon wouldn't." Kallan's voice was firm. "He was my father's captain before he was mine. Daggon held his allegiance without question. My father died—"

A flood of tears burned the back of her throat and filled her eyes before she could stop them from falling. Looking away, Kallan forced her worries in check and shoved the tears away.

"My men had orders to apprehend Eyolf and bring him back to Gunir alive."

Kallan looked at Rune. Disbelief twisted her face.

"I had hoped, with him there, we might commence negotiations," Rune said.

Kallan hugged her knees tighter and stared at the ground. She caught the sympathy in his voice when he added, "If one of my men did kill him, then it was against my orders."

Kallan dug at the exhaustion in her eyes.

"Did you see anyone?" he asked.

Kallan shook her head. "No one."

Rune sighed and pulled in another draw from his pipe.

"Am I meant to believe you?" Kallan asked, "That your orders weren't what killed my father?"

Rune met her eyes.

"I didn't do it," he said.

"Why should I believe the son of the king who laid waste to the Dokkalfar during the feasts of Austramonath?" she breathed.

Her voice had grown cold.

Images of the Austramonath Massacre flooded back: Dokkalfar women hewn in two at the foot of the pikes that impaled their husbands. Children that lay, left to die in pools of blood, and a single boy clutching the remains of his brother.

"Not one of the three hundred lives was spared," Kallan said. "Not even the children."

"Long have I suffered to shed my father's shame," Rune said. "Long have I yearned to share their anguish. It is the shame I and my brother bear."

Thick, dry tears burned the tip of Kallan's nose.

"Our cries carried over the massacre of Austramonath when we found what our father had done," Rune said.

Kallan stared, lost in what to say.

"It was in a fit of berserker rage that my father spilled that Dokkalfar blood," he continued. "When he came to, he realized what he had done and killed himself in hopes of rescinding his crime. He killed himself when his dead wife failed to utter words of forgiveness."

Stupid understanding, the kind that leaves you feeling small and insignificant, left Kallan wordless as Rune held her gaze.

"I am not my father's son," he whispered.

Kallan forced down the unease in her stomach.

"What will you have me do?" she said, fighting back the tears that swelled with regret from the blood lost.

"Believe that I did not kill your father."

Chapter 56

Kallan stared across the cold coals at Rune, who gazed back from the other side of the *finntent*. The strange, sporadic honk from outside was faint. The second honk was louder and accompanied the strange staccato of a series of quacks along with a kind of clicking that grew by the minute.

"Boar?" Kallan asked, perplexed, keeping her voice low.

"Too late in the season," Rune said.

"Not boar," Bern said, pulling on his boots and taking up the rope next to him where Halda still slept. "That's reindeer."

Quietly, he crept across the tent.

"If we get to the lake before we find Halda's kin, we'll be without horse or cattle," Bern said.

The quacking and clicking grew louder until the noise was too loud to continue whispering from across the room. From beneath the furs, Rune scrambled to his feet, keeping low before crouching down at the door beside Bern, who peered outside. More than nine hundred reindeer surrounded the camp, pulling at the lichen on the ground, honking and grazing, while others lingered at the river for a drink. The incessant calls of reindeer grunts were as deafening as a hundred wild boar rooting about in the ground, and, with every step of every leg, there was a distinct click.

"There must be a thousand." Bern studied the herd packed into the valley enclosed by the mountain.

"The gorge doesn't give them much place to run," Rune said, looking at the high walls of forest on either side.

Bern nodded.

"The only escape is back the way they came."

"Could be confusing should something leap out at them."

Eager to make his exit and launch his battle upon the prey, Bern readied himself to lunge like a king into battle.

"Let's go get one," Bern said, rallying his lone legion.

Enlightened with an epiphany, Rune clasped Bern's shoulder.

"Let's get two."

"What are you doing?" Kallan asked, putting a temporary end to their discussion. As she propped herself up, she peered at the men bouncing with eagerness on the balls of their feet.

"Hunting," Rune whispered and took up his quiver, which he fastened to his belt.

"Alright," Bern whispered, "but I'm roping mine. Halda and I can use it for hauling."

"Fine," Rune said, loading an arrow into his bow. "So long as I get to eat mine."

Bern unraveled the rope he was rearing to throw.

"Ready?" the Ljosalfr asked, preparing his bow.

"Ready."

Throwing back the hide flap, the men charged the herd, releasing their battle cries and sending four black wood grouse into flight followed by their calls. The reindeer bolted, making slow progress as the herd of ten hundred all picked a direction to run and promptly went nowhere. The few who succeeded in rearing up, landed their front hooves onto another's back, while those along the outside edge managed to make it around the herd.

By the time Rune had dropped his pick of the bulls and administered Freyr's blessing, Bern had roped a large, six-pointed female reindeer, a cow of abundant stature. Panic had taken her and she ran circles around her captor, limited by the confines of the rope tangled in her antlers.

"Easy now...Easy," Bern soothed.

Rune grinned at Bern's lassoed reindeer.

"Come on now," he said. "Mine's behaving rather nicely. Get yours in order."

Bern pulled in the rope for less give, as the cow changed directions.

"Mine is a bit more nervous than yours," Bern said while affording a glance to the dead bull.

Bern's reindeer tried to leap, desperate to rejoin the herd that had sorted themselves out and bolted.

"Sh. Sh. Sh," Bern hushed. "Easy, girl. Easy." But she persisted and Bern allowed her the room to change her direction and circle again until she had run herself to exhaustion.

Only then did Bern shorten his leash, hushing and reeling until he was close enough to touch her.

"Easy, girl," Bern whispered, stroking the fur already thickened for the winter ahead. His fingers sank into the coat up to the first knuckle. Save for the prominent patch of brown that covered her shoulders and the curve of her back, her body was white and contrasted her black and brown face. Her antlers, still covered in a thick coat of velvet, had not yet begun to shed. Holding her head down, the reindeer heaved. With mouth agape, her tongue hung to the ground as she panted to regain her breath.

"Easy." Bern gently patted her shoulder.

From the *finntent*, Kallan and Halda watched as Rune cut the bull open and began the process of preserving the blood for storage while Bern administered another run of hushes.

The delay cost them well over two hours in which they collected the blood from Rune's bull, fashioned a second harness for Freyja, and strapped the carcass to the crude sled to be harvested later at the lake. Once Bern secured the final strap around the *finntent*, they were off with the cow in tow.

Too soon, the sun passed overhead with too little road behind them. By late midday, they pushed through the last of the river, walking as they ate fruit, berries, and salted meats. Before the sun vanished behind the last mountain, the light of day touched down on the waters of Lake Aursund.

"The Raumelfr." Bern pointed to the west where the lake stretched on. "It flows from the lake there." He shifted his hand to the southwest. "You are exactly where you'll need to be for tomorrow."

Nothing but lake could be seen, spanning the distance.

Eager to find a clearing to secure camp for the night, they moved toward the edge of Aursund, but before they had advanced five paces, Bern's arm flew up.

"There," he said, pointing to a single pillar of smoke rising from the ground.

Rolling earth buried in lichen extended over the land, save for a distinct line of smoke that billowed from a hill of moss. Rune and Kallan narrowed their eyes and gazed upon the fireless smoke emitted from the ground. Hoping for an explanation, Kallan looked to Bern as Rune studied the smoking knoll.

"Halda," Bern called, but she had already seen and was off. Flying the rest of the way to the mount, Halda ran on ahead.

"The Finn didn't migrate and plunder to settle on this land," Bern said, tugging the reindeer alongside him after Halda. "They were born here long before my elder father's elder father explored these parts."

"*Aed 'ne!*" Halda cried. Her voice was barely audible in the distance.

"Long before the high king ruled your Alfheim," Bern said, "the Finn had mastered this land. Their culture flourishes here, untouched by kings who usurp the rule of jarls. They are indifferent to the laws set by outsiders and hold no regard for our *Thing.*"

Halda was almost at the smoking mound when she called again.

"Aed 'ne?"

"They have their own laws to abide by," he said, "their own gods to answer to, but you'll find, in most cases, they have no need for such things as laws. They live for the Nature, and abide by Her ways."

"The smoke," Kallan asked, still eyeing the top of the hill where the pillar billowed at the base.

"That," Bern said, nodding to the knoll, "is a *gamme*, much like the *finntent* here, though not exactly portable."

As Bern and the Alfar drew nearer, it was easier to make out the earthwork that could only be a makeshift hut formed out of earth. Years of overgrowth had camouflaged the abode completely. If it had not been for Bern's explanation and the smoke, they would have passed it by without notice.

Out of the earth, a wooden door lined with moss flew open. Swaddled in thick fur clothes matched with fur hats and moccasins, two tiny girls with ebony hair hanging free to their waists emerged from the ground. In a blur of white and brown reindeer fur, they bombarded Halda's legs in a swarm of hugs, all the while giggling.

Halda scooped up one of the girls and squeezed her back. Bern and the Alfar made their way across the various reds and greens of the ground that rolled up and over the gamme.

"Their homes are built from the earth," Bern said as one of the girls holding Halda's legs released a high-pitched squeal of delight. "The inside is braced with planks of birch. The earthen roof and mud walls are lined with moss, holding the fire's warmth."

A sudden, sharp bark laden with softened syllables silenced the giddy girls as a woman emerged from the smoking moss. With hair flowing freely, her round face and high cheekbones matched the girl's with a deep nose bridge set between their eyes. Their eyes, like Halda's, were as blue and as clear as the Lake Aursund.

Keeping their distance, Rune halted the horses as happy tears flowed down Halda's face. In a soft dialect sharpened by the occasional consonant, Bern called out to the women and children, his cow in tow behind him.

Curious to see what the ruckus was about, a man emerged from behind the *gamme* with four reindeer, the sixteen knees all clicking with each step. The man had tied back his long, ebony hair, adding definition to his round face. A deep nose bridge matched his wide brow. At nearly six feet, he stood beside a young boy, no more than four winters, with hair that shone in the sun's light like black water. Save for a hat, the boy wore the same browns and whites as the giggling girls, and held a bucket as wide as his shoulders.

With a grin, Bern ruffled the boy's head and released a rush of fluid words. Calling to the *gamme*, the man smiled, giving a firm slap to Bern's shoulder, all the while exchanging the same fluid dialogue Rune and Kallan could only guess to be salutations. More words accompanied smiles and happy tears when Bern swept his arm in Kallan and Rune's direction.

Silence fell over the dwelling, leaving behind the quiet wind and a single click of a reindeer's knee. It was a long while before the Finn man spoke, emitting a single decipherable word.

"Alfar."

With eyes still fixed on the Finn, the creek and closing of the wood door broke the silence, drawing their attention to an elder woman standing in front of the domicile. With black hair streaked with white and aged lines etched into her face, the elder woman stepped to embrace Halda, and Kallan gasped.

With hunger, the Beast rose to attention while Rune stared dumbfounded at the elder woman. Seeing what only Kallan could see, he snatched Kallan's arm as she made the substantial effort to stand. Like he, she battled her breath steady as they gazed at the golden light that weaved its way through and around the elder woman. Mesmerized, Rune stared, knowing the Seidr lines he felt, the lines he knew Kallan saw.

With a second glance, the elder woman stared back at Kallan then Rune, just as enthralled, just as dumbfounded, as if she was unsure which of the two Alfar fascinated her the most. And, all at once, she burst into a smile and exploded into a round of unfamiliar syllables. She exclaimed, clasping her hands, and made her way over to Rune and Kallan.

With a warm greeting matched with a smile, she extended her arms and embraced the Dokkalfr, the top of her head barely reaching Kallan's shoulders. Halda smiled as fluid sounds flowed from the elder woman's mouth. With a laugh, the elder woman reached with her frail fingers and took up the elding tri-corner knot hanging from Kallan's neck.

"She's happy to know you," Halda said, refusing to budge from the place beside the younger woman. With a great affection, the elder woman turned the charm over before releasing it to rest against Kallan's skin.

"This is my elder mother, Sarahkka." Halda grinned, her eyes still ripe with tears. "She is our *Naejttie*."

Kallan ran her hand through the lines Rune felt through the Beast, who growled impatiently but didn't move. The lines flowed around the woman and gave way, twisting around Kallan's wrist as Rune fought to ensure the Beast—ever ready, ever hungry—obeyed. Enraptured, Sarahkka laughed.

"*Naejttie*," Kallan whispered as if remembering something.

Sarahkka nodded with a delighted grin that became a long, warm laugh.

"*Naejttie*," Kallan repeated. "She's a Seidkona."

"I thought humans had forgotten the Seidr," he asked.

"They did," Kallan said. "I mean, I've never seen—"

Sarahkka clasped her hands in jubilation and buried her old fingers into a hide pouch tied to her side. It wasn't until her bony fingers vanished into the pocket of fur that Rune even noticed the pouch.

While speaking excitedly, Sarahkka withdrew a small, white seed, and, cupping Kallan's hand, dropped the seed into her palm. In a tune much like Halda's song, the *Naejttie* mumbled a rhythm with words. The Beast within Rune stood and roared. Unleashing its hunger, it reached and slammed into Rune's will. He held it back while he felt Sarahkka's Seidr strengthen and move into Kallan.

In wonder, Rune watched Kallan stare as the Seidr encompassed the seed as if cradling it. The seed coat swelled then split, and a root emerged, extending out into the world until its leaves formed, pushing back the husk as they opened. Like spring follows the winter thaw, the sprout reached toward the light of the setting sun, oblivious to the cold that would soon blanket the world.

As her incantation ended, Sarahkka grinned and the Beast calmed, allowing Rune to relax his will.

The sprout's leaves rustled in the breeze, and as Kallan studied the veins of green flowing with gold, she gasped and curved her mouth into a smile.

"This is the Seidr," Kallan said, still eyeing what Rune determined was the Seidr he felt encompassing Sarahkka.

"What is?" Rune asked, squinting and trying to see what Kallan saw.

"You don't see?" she asked, tearing her eyes from the *Naejttie.*

At once, he realized how close she was. Her eyes glanced at his mouth. When she raised her face to his, he studied the wonder that brimmed in Kallan's gaze.

"She wasn't always like this," Halda said from beside the woman. "Only after we came to this land many harvests ago and found the Seidi—"

"Seidi!" Sarahkka exclaimed.

"Seidi?" Kallan said and, with a fresh wave of enthusiasm, the *Naejttie* launched into an onslaught of syllables neither Alfar could understand.

After a slew of phrases, Sarahkka lifted the sprout from Kallan's hands and placed it onto the ground. Her withered palm folded into Kallan's and she pulled, urging the Dokkalfr to follow. But a worry visibly took hold and, digging her feet into the ground, Kallan snatched Rune's hand with the same conviction.

Sarahkka turned back and glanced at Kallan's hand interlocked with Rune's. With a series of fervent nods, she burst into a new fit of laughter. Waving her hand, Rune and Kallan could only interpret her actions as an invitation to follow together.

Rune walked alongside Kallan as she pushed her way over the moss and molehills, one hand yanking free her skirts that caught on the shrubs and branches as they walked and the other clutching Rune's hand as if afraid to let him go.

Sarahkka continued her excited monologue five steps ahead as she led them into the trees. She stopped once or twice and burst into laughter she quelled with a shake of her head. After a moment, she restarted speaking in a language neither Kallan nor Rune could understand.

The trees thickened until a forest had formed, forcing them to slow their pace and the Beast within Rune paced. Kallan stopped pulling her skirts free, and began holding back the low hanging branches as they pushed their way through the wood.

After several minutes, Sarahkka stopped, giving Rune and Kallan time to catch up. They stood, taking in the surrounding area. The *gamme*, the horses, the reindeer, and Finn were far from sight. With a smile, Sarahkka uttered a few words and placed a twisted finger to Kallan's mouth then pulled back the last of the thick branches. Pushing aside massive fronds, as tall as two Alfar, Sarahkka stepped into a vast clearing, waving Kallan and Rune to follow.

Kallan and Rune eyed the foliage, taking care to run their hands up the firm, slender leaves as wide as their hands. The Beast hastened his step. Rune reasserted his will. With difficulty, Rune and Kallan took their turn bending the fronds away and joined Sarahkka in a moss-covered clearing encased in tall pines and peppered in slender birch, where a brook flowed from a wall of bedrock. With their hands still clasped together, Rune and Kallan took one look at the ground before them and gasped.

Plum marsh orchids that could fill Rune's palm climbed giant stalks. Blossoms of martagom lilies hung from their stems like large luminescent floral saucers. Toadflax and hop clover, made gold by the Seidr light emerged in bunches throughout the clearing. Bouquets of oblong blossoms, vibrant pink, protruded on a single stem. Each bloom elongated a span and was cocooned in a white, silk webbing that covered the plant from the ground to the tips of each rounded blossom. And ferns—grand, green ferns, more than two men in height—filled every corner, every crevice of the clearing.

Interspersed with the flora, oversized butterflies with wings of smoky cobalt blue, wings painted iridescent greens, and white wings dabbed with abalone, fluttered about the massive blooms. At the base of the trees, red spotted mushrooms clustered around fungi with pristine caps and stems. Both varieties, as long as a man's arm, glowed gold in the Seidr light. Along the brook, a pair of dippers dipped and dove into the water and emerged after a minute with their beaks clamped on over-sized water insects and larvae. Among the foliage and flowers, red squirrels as large as ship cats scurried about the trunks of the conifers. Tufts of fur extended off each ear, and their tails, twice the length of their bodies, trailed behind them as they scurried up and down the tree like Ratatoskr.

"Do you see this?" Kallan breathed as Rune held back the Beast that clawed at his will.

Both gaped, unable to tear their eyes from the ground where golden light twisted its way through the tiny fibers of moss, making its way toward the *Naejttie*. There it mingled with the glow surrounding them.

"What is it?" Rune asked, unable to pull his attention away from the earth and the lines of Seidr that moved on the wind.

"It's a Seidi," Kallan said. "Sacred ground where springs of Seidr emerge from the earth."

A smile lifted her face. With a nod, the *Naejttie* moved to the center of the clearing and dropped to her knees, splaying her palms out on the moss where the light flowed. Releasing Rune's hand, Kallan knelt opposite Sarahkka and mirrored her.

With the fountain between them, the old woman mumbled a series of indecipherable words. The Seidr grew brighter, stretching like hundreds of vines across the ground, contorting itself up the trees with every word Sarahkka muttered. The Beast screamed and threw itself toward the lines. As if starved, it clawed and bit, held back only by Rune's determination to keep it from feeding its insatiable hunger.

The Seidr twisted its way up the women's arms and over their backs, until they were enveloped in a blanket of gold and the Beast released another scream. Sweat formed on Rune's brow and Kallan gasped as the energy flowed through her. The Beast pushed and Rune bore down. He felt himself losing to the hunger. Its cloak of Shadow seeped out, breaking through Rune's will and streaming into the lines of Seidr. It snaked its way to the first of the lines and Rune fought with the creature inside him.

It linked itself with Kallan's Seidr. More Shadow drained as Rune's strength waned. Hungrily, it lapped up Kallan's Seidr, connecting her lines to his. Startled, he jumped, almost losing the fight, when he could hear an old woman's words clearly from within Kallan's mind.

"You're fighting it, Kallan. Allow it. It's there...ready to be a part of you."

Sarahkka spoke. The fluid breath of her dialect interrupted Kallan's thoughts, breaking Rune's concentration, and more of the Beast broke through Rune's weakening barrier. A mischievous light glistened in Kallan's blue eye. At once, Rune understood. The Beast was up on its hind legs now, snarling and snapping at the Seidr, drinking more in as it flowed. He would not be able to hold it back much longer.

Gasping, Kallan re-positioned her palms on the ground and, re-establishing her center, reached into the bottom-most depths of her core, beyond the ends of her own Seidr where the earth's power began and hers ended. From there she pulled the energy inward, trembling beneath the magnitude. A flood of strength swarmed her and the light from the ground doubled, pouring faster into the clearing. In a rush, the Seidr flowed and held her to the ground. The Beast shattered the last of Rune's will as it threw itself at the Seidr.

Corporeal Shadow, blacker than umbra, flowed from Rune like the Seidr that poured from the spring. Unleashed, the Beast drank its fill while the sudden surge of Shadow and Seidr pinned Rune to the ground. Unable to move, he stood as the Beast pulled the trail of light from the wind to his feet, through the ground and into him, and Kallan knelt at the fountain with her eyes closed, oblivious to Rune's Beast of Shadow.

Kallan pulled the Seidr as it mingled with that of the Earth's, providing far more Seidr than Rune's Beast could ever devour: so much Seidr that Kallan and Sarahkka remained oblivious to the Beast's presence or how much it drank.

From the spring, the Seidr flowed until the whole of the clearing filled with light, far more than the Beast could drink, until the air itself glistened and gold streams rose up the trees like ivy and blanketed the wall of bedrock, taking the form of a wall of fire and flame that rose from the ground. And the Beast ever drank.

Over the wall of bedrock, into the sky it stretched and thinned, growing until the very ends of the Seidr became an endless stream of blue flames that ended where the edge of the flame glowed white. The tips flickered and licked the air, compiling until it formed a bridge that reached to the heavens.

Sitting back on her legs, Sarahkka released the ground and smiled, delighted at the depth of Kallan's focus as the Seidkona absorbed the earth's Seidr. Pulling it through her, Kallan fueled her own energy, oblivious to the bridge that had formed from the tiny spring that yielded the Seidr.

"Kallan," Rune said, gaping at the bridge before them. He tried again to move and failed.

"Kallan," he said, louder this time, hoping to break her concentration. When she didn't respond, Rune slipped his own consciousness along the threads of Seidr and entered her mind.

Sudden comprehension awakened within, sudden realization that had not been, making Kallan aware of how unfocused and dim her thoughts had always been. The fog cleared within her mind and in the moment that she saw, she understood.

As vivid as the Seidr surrounding the *Naejttie*, Kallan saw the blood consumed by flame settling into the sea. A contorted face screamed as a man, a giant, rode into the horizon, crying out for war to Asgard as the edge of his silver sword ran with blood.

The image faded and changed, reappearing with flames that stretched to the sky, licking the air like dragons' tongues. The screams rose with great plumes of black smoke and Kallan and Rune saw a pair of ageless, gold eyes smiling through the burning towers that was Lorlenalin.

With a start, Kallan gasped and released the ground at once, severing the ties that bound Kallan to Rune and the Beast. Seidr settled on the wind, leaving the bridge in view. Rune restored his will and manacled the Beast, which recoiled. The energy that held Rune to the ground released and he dove, catching Kallan before she fell face-first into the dirt. Beaded sweat fell from his brow and Kallan's widened eyes met Rune's.

"Lorlenalin," she gasped, looking about with madness. A single tear streaked her cheek.

"She's fine," Rune said, knowing the images she had seen.

Kallan's eyes shifted from side to side as if watching the memories play over, keeping her steeped in panic.

"Heimdallr!" she shrieked and sat up, reaching for the burning bridge. "Heimdallr!"

"Kallan, no!" Rune lunged, barely grabbing her in time to stop her from diving head first into the fire.

Her strength had doubled. Struggling more than ever to contain her, Rune wrapped both arms around her, holding her back.

"The Bilrost burns!" Rune shouted over her madness.

"Release me," she said. "I have to warn him!"

"It wasn't real!"

Kallan shoved his arms aside and lunged for the fire. With all his strength, Rune threw himself into Kallan, taking her to the ground with him as Kallan shrieked for Heimdallr. With two sharp syllables, the command of Sarahkka's voice cut through their tussle, forcing their voices silent and their attention to the Finn. Entranced, Sarahkka rose to her feet.

With mouths agape, they stared in awe at the floor of fire and wall of flame. Atop a horse of golden flames that whipped and licked the leather reins, untouched by the fire that twisted and burned, sat Heimdallr, guardian of the Bilrost.

Chapter 57

Clad in black elding boots that protected his feet from Bilrost's flame, Heimdallr lowered himself from his stallion, Gulltoppr. With a muscular build that matched his proportions, the god stood a head taller than Rune. Already dwarfed in comparison next to the Alfar, the *Naejttie* appeared like a small child before the god.

Encrusted with gems and gold, Heimdallr's sword, Hofud, hung at his side across from Gjallarhorn, the grand golden horn ornately decorated with runes and images. He had tied back his long, blond hair and his iridescent skin shimmered as it reflected the fire's glow of Bilrost. Heimdallr's hardened eyes, like golden baubles, stared as if warning the careless challenger to think twice before raising arms to the guardian of Bilrost.

"What brings the Alfar to this side of the Vingul-mork?"

His smooth voice boomed with a hallowed grace that exceeded the tales told, but his eyes were cold and menacing. His stance was anything but forgiving. Kallan was the first to break from her trance, forcing the awe aside. Ignoring Rune, she pulled her arm free and approached the Bilrost.

"Heimdallr, please," Kallan begged. "Where is Loptr?"

Heimdallr tipped his head in question.

"The Deceiver." His words, not quite a question, brushed the air and carried over the burning bridge. He tightened his grasp on the hilt of his golden blade.

"Where?" Kallan asked, not bothering to adhere to formalities.

Lost in the depths of his thoughts, Heimdallr stared through Kallan's eyes as if trying to reach into the back of her mind.

"Chained," he said at last. "Where the All-Father left him, bound to the roots of Yggdrasill where Nid-hoggr feasts."

His answer did little to ease her worry.

"Kallan?" Rune gently clutched her arm, coaxing her out of her daze. "It wasn't real."

With her eyes centered on a fixed point in the distance, Kallan recalled the images as the Seidr had flowed through her. In a series of pictures that flashed through her mind, she searched for a comprehensible explanation of what she saw.

"He's free. He rides on the sea to Asgard." Kallan's voice trembled, but broke through Heimdallr's hardened stance. Worry widened Heimdallr's eyes and his shoulders dropped beneath his gold armor.

Her trance broke and she looked to Heimdallr. "He brings an army of dead and rallies the giants from the west. They ride to destroy Odinn," she said. "They will succeed."

Heimdallr shook his head as if perplexed by the Dokkalfr's warning.

"None can cross Bilrost," he said, but doubt weighed heavily in his words.

"Bilrost will be destroyed," Kallan said. "It will sink into the sea."

Her words honed Heimdallr's attention and, as the words left her lips, she saw Heimdallr, fallen and impaled by a silver sword. With a start, she shook the vision from her head and opened her mouth to warn him, but stopped, taken aback by the living Heimdallr, unwounded and standing before her.

A tear slipped from her eye, and, in silence, seeing her failure in his eyes, she turned from Bilrost, the horse, and the god.

"Alfr," Heimdallr said.

Kallan looked back. A cold, distant worry held in his eyes behind a kind curiosity. "How is it you have come to be here in Midgard?"

"The Dvergar," Kallan said. "They carried me from Alfheim to the gates of Svartálfaheim."

Heimdallr's sallow skin drained of blood. His bottom jaw dropped slightly.

"The Dvergar entered the land of the evening sun?" he asked.

"Led by the Dvergar king himself," she said.

"Motsognir." The name left Heimdallr's lips as a breath.

Without another word, he mounted Gulltoppr and steered the horse around.

"What will you do?" Kallan asked.

"Odinn must know," he said. "I will ride to his hall and tell him what you've told me here."

Grimly, Kallan nodded. With a cry, Heimdallr sent Gulltoppr back up the flames of Bilrost.

Her nerves ached with the need to speak to Gudrun and throbbed with the knowledge that she could not. More than ever, she was alone, and trembled at the shiver that ran up her spine.

"And they shall disappear into flame and rise from the sea," Kallan spoke and another tear streaked her face.

Raising her voice over the thunderous hooves that pounded the Bilrost, Kallan called to Heimdallr. "Beware the Deceiver!" And her shoulders slouched, knowing he failed to hear her.

Chapter 58

Sigyn forced her hands steady as she balanced her weight beneath the snake. The venom dripped, forcing the collected poison in her bowl to ripple. The wood sizzled at the renewed contact made with the fresh wave of poison as it ate through its sides.

"Is it full?" Loptr asked, panting heavily and pulled taut on his back.

"Almost," Sigyn said, forcing back a wave of sobs and biting her bottom lip hard.

Just one more, she thought. *Just one more and then...*

Tears burned her eyes and she bit her lip again.

There would always be one more.

"Sigyn."

Loptr's voice rolled over her, penetrating the deepest core of her grief, and the tears flowed. Forcing her arms steady, she permitted a glance to the gentle eyes beneath her.

"Sigyn." He smiled, unnerved by the burns that covered his face where the venom had eaten his flesh. "I'll be alright."

Another drop followed by another tiny wave rippled the poison and the wood sizzled.

"Go ahead," he urged.

The smile was gone, but the softness in his eyes was still there.

She tasted sweat that burned her lips. Every time, her response was the same. She listened. She obeyed. She never argued and hated herself every time the venom fell.

Carefully, so as not to spill a single drop, Sigyn lowered the bowl as near to his wrists as she could. As stable as the awkward position would allow, she poured the venom onto his shackles.

The elding hissed, protesting the abuse as the venom flowed over the metal chains and onto his wrists, raw from his metal bonds. Gritting his teeth, Loptr quelled a howl with a grunt, and Sigyn eased up on the flow.

Loptr howled over the pain.

"Don't stop!"

Blinded by tears, Sigyn poured, and Loptr screamed. Dumping the last of the venom onto the chains, the poison flowed onto and over Loptr's bound wrists. The metal hissed and the giant arched his back, muffling another scream between his teeth.

With a hollow thud, the bowl struck the stone as Sigyn stood and gathered her skirts, ready to race to fetch the next bowl before another drop could fall.

"Sigyn," Loptr said.

Sweat flowed down his brow as he gasped.

"Yes?" Her voice was frail from relentless tears. The word scratched her throat.

The exhaustion and grief weighed heavy on her, never allowing her peace, and still she waited on him at all hours between batches of venom and meals with ointments to aid his healing. She would argue. She would refuse, but he had thought of this long and hard. There were no other options.

"I need you to ride to Muspellsheim. Meet with Surtr. Send for him."

Sigyn gasped.

"Muspellsheim," she said, her weariness more visible than usual.

"Speak to Surtr," Loptr said.

"But every second I'm gone, the venom burns." Sigyn clasped her hands to resist their shaking.

Loptr tried to shrug and smiled. "I can handle it," he said. "Besides. It keeps things interesting."

"Interesting," Sigyn gasped, her eyes widened with the insanity that was setting in. "Loptr...Surtr...The Muspell dwellers—"

"I am their kin," Loptr said, knowing the protests had begun. "They'll come. Now go..." He flashed a smile that somehow eased her worry, and filled her with the confidence only he could exude in the darkest hour. "And come back before I realize you've gone."

Within a heartbeat, she was on him, moving her lips over his and leaving a tear on his cheek when she stood again. His eye caught the hem of her skirt as she pulled herself onto Svadilfari. Before he could change his mind and call to her, the black stallion was gone.

The venom dripped. His flesh sizzled and, arching his back, Loptr howled, shaking the earth as he pulled against his chains wrought with pain.

Gasping, he collapsed back to the stones that sliced his back. The ointment Sigyn had applied had already worn off. Loptr glanced at the snake overhead, studying the next drip that would fall. He rattled the chains that held him. They would never budge. He knew that. Motsognir had supplied the metal forged by Volundr himself, but the snake...

Loptr studied the specimen once more. If there was a way to use the snake, then maybe he had a chance, and for that, he would need Surtr.

Chapter 59

The fire crackled in time to the snoring of Olaf's elkhound. On the rug, Vige slept, sprawled out by the fire. Pouring over the map splayed out on the table in front of him, Olaf stared at the minute speck that was Nidaros. His gaze followed the Raumelfr that trailed down from Throendalog through Heidmork to Viken where his eyes rested on one word. Vestfold. There his men waited. There he would make his next move.

A blast of cold forced Vige to emit a groan from the rug, confirming Thorer's return. Digging the tips of his fingers into the table, Olaf forced his eyes steady on the map.

"We found them," the captain said, pride dripping in his voice.

Olaf straightened his back while his eyes lingered on Vestfold. After a time, Olaf snatched the mead that had been resting at the corner of the map and poured himself a drink.

"Where?" Olaf asked once he returned the tankard to the table.

"The border of Heidmork," Thorer said. "They will enter Raumariki in two days."

A crooked grin stretched over Olaf's face, easing the captain's tension enough to continue.

"Do you want us to bring them in?"

Olaf shook his head.

"No," he said into his drink and sipped. "Why bind and blind them to carry them along the road they walk willingly to Viken? We'll wait until they're almost through Raumariki. Then we'll move in to redirect their path to Vestfold."

Releasing the table, Olaf stood, straightening his back as he helped himself to the ale.

"Keep an eye on them for now. Notify me of any changes."

With a nod, the captain pulled back the pelt flap to leave.

"And, Thorer," Olaf said.

Thorer stopped at the door.

"Send word to Vestfold," Olaf ordered. "Advise the men to be ready to take up arms. I expect no less than a blood bath from the Seidkona."

"What of her companion?" Thorer asked, clutching the pelt over the door.

"He is useless," Olaf said, taking another thoughtful sip. "Kill him."

Another nod confirmed his understanding and Thorer closed the flap behind him.

Silence settled over the glistening stones of Lorlenalin, leaving a deadening stillness in its wake. The thunder of Livsvann's waters filled the cavernous stable with a dulled echo. Feet scuffed the stone and colossal shadows of black and orange etched the walls of the grotto.

Gudrun pulled her cloak tighter.

Within moments, Gudrun had saddled, bridled, and tacked the saddlebags on Daggon's stallion. She took up Thor's reins and doused her lantern light, submerging the stables in a bluish glow that seeped in from outside.

Before she had taken two steps, she stopped and slipped her hand into her robes.

"That's my horse, woman." Daggon's voice matched the thunderous rumble of the waterfall, blending with the water's roar. Gudrun jumped then relaxed, leaving her Seidr staff safely tucked in place.

"And it's too early for an evening stroll," he said.

"Go back to bed, Daggon," she grumbled, continuing toward the exit.

"I'm involved now," the captain said, leaning against the corral's support beam and crossing his ankles as he crossed his arms. "You know I can't turn my back on this."

Whipping around, Gudrun released a flash that grazed his shoulder.

Daggon impassively glanced at the blackened beam. Inches from his face, the wood sizzled. He studied the slender Seidr staff extended from Gudrun's palm. A line of smoke rose from the tip.

"Huh," he said. "You must be really pissed to bring that out."

"I'm going after Kallan," Gudrun said. "Now mind your own."

Her words wiped all the gaiety from Daggon's face as he stared down the Seidr staff pointed at his heart.

"You are my own," he said, pushing himself off the beam, undeterred by the threat she posed, "and so is she."

Heavy with grief, Gudrun dropped her arm as she battled back the sudden rush of worry.

"Does Aaric know?" Daggon asked.

With a derisive snort, Gudrun shook her head.

"I can't say that I blame you." His voice rolled like rich amber as he studied the weariness in her golden eyes.

With a tug of the reins, she pulled Thor toward Livsvann Falls, but Daggon took hold of Thor's bridle. There had been no mistake, the insurmountable wall of unspoken thoughts poised behind her stilled tongue.

Daggon leaned closer, forcing her eyes on him.

"You know something, woman," he said.

"Where does your loyalty lay, Captain?"

The night's blue light seeped from behind the falls and spanned his face, etching black shadows across the lines of scars.

"I've sworn to protect Lorlenalin," he said.

Dismissing her challenger, Gudrun wrapped Daggon's knuckles with her Seidr staff and gave a tug to the reins.

"Humph." Gudrun pushed Daggon aside. "Then your place is here with your keeper."

The clop of the stallion's hooves filled the stables.

"You, of all others, know I would die for that girl," Daggon said.

Thor stopped alongside Gudrun.

"You have the gift of Sight, Volva," Daggon whispered, clasping Gudrun's shoulders. "What do you know of Kira's daughter?"

Gudrun released the reins and sighed.

"Aaric has abandoned all efforts to find Kallan," Gudrun said. "He has proclaimed her dead."

Daggon dropped his brow and gave a slight shake of his head.

"We know this."

"But I can not See," Gudrun said. "I do not know..." Her voice trailed off with her thoughts. "She's somewhere. Alive. I feel it in these bones of mine. I just don't know where."

"If she were dead..." Daggon said, coming to stand closer to better preserve their whispers. His own voice hushed as if afraid someone would hear.

Gudrun nodded.

"I could see where and how, but..." Her voice was faint. "This is different. She isn't dead. She's just...out of reach."

"In Gunir?" Daggon asked.

Gudrun was already shaking her head.

"They never made it to Gunir," she said.

Daggon's brow furrowed as he took a moment to think.

"Where was the last place you Saw her?"

"In the forest, off the road," Gudrun said, "between here and Gunir. But something has since interfered...blocked my sight somehow."

The thunder from the falls roared, filling the silence.

"I think Aaric tampered with it somehow. Blocked my Sight."

"Aaric," Daggon said. "How? Are you sure?"

"Ever since that night...there are things that don't make sense," Gudrun said, dropping her voice lower and forcing Daggon to lean in to hear. "I remember being in my chambers. I fell asleep, but remember almost nothing before then. I don't remember falling asleep, or even being tired. But there's more. When I woke, my Sight was...blocked somehow. And I see it in your eyes. When you speak about the Ljosalfar king taking Kallan, you have the same look in your eyes that I know is in mine." Gudrun shook her head. "We're not remembering right."

"Why would you think Aaric—?"

"I know the spell that would be used. Aaric is the only one—" Gudrun swallowed the lump in her throat. She couldn't tell Daggon that she suspected the spell had come from Under Earth. Only Aaric and she knew of such places. "I gave Aaric an elixir for such an occasion if a situation ever arose that needed it."

Daggon thought for a moment, assuring her that he believed her lie.

"Where were you going to look?" Daggon asked.

Her grief vanished as her convictions hardened. A finger twitched on her Seidr staff.

"You will not stop me," Gudrun said.

"I'm not here to stop you," Daggon said, undaunted by her ferocity and matching her absolution. "I'm here to join you."

He flashed a smile, but before his next footfall touched the ground, Gudrun snatched Daggon's arm and held him at her side. Aaric's cold glare emerged from the shadows that had been empty moments ago.

"I made my orders clear," Aaric spoke through a tightened jaw. "My answer was precise."

Gudrun tightened her grip on Daggon's hand, the Seidr staff weighed heavily in her other.

"You will not stop me, Aaric," Gudrun said. "My kin is out there."

Daggon squeezed her hand and Gudrun eased her grip on the staff.

"No one wishes Kallan were alive more than I," Aaric said, taking a step closer. Daggon glanced at the sheathed sword at Aaric's side, but the High Marshal made no move to draw it.

"Then let us look." Desperation lined her words. "You'll have lost nothing if we look."

Daggon shifted his eyes from shadow to shadow and concluded that Aaric was alone.

"I'll have lost a healer," Aaric said.

"There are others," Gudrun argued.

"Kallan is dead!" Aaric shouted, forcing Daggon's attention sharp. "Lorlenalin is weak and I can not waste what man power we have searching for the dead."

"We are only two people," Daggon said.

"You are this city's captain." Aaric took a step closer.

"Then I'll go," Gudrun said. Her hand tightened on Daggon's arm.

"You will stay." Aaric took another step.

"I am Volva!" Gudrun's voice rang through the cavern, adding to the thunder of Livsvann. "I have pledged allegiance to no one but my kin."

"Lorlenalin's people require your services." Aaric moved his hand to the pommel of his sword.

Gudrun twitched, and Daggon tightened his hold on her hand, keeping her beside him. Rage flashed red in her golden eyes.

"You have forgotten your place," she said.

Aaric's eyes darkened. "Mind your own."

"You have no home here, High Marshal." Her voice lilted in mockery at the title. "Go back to your keepers and your whore."

Aaric tightened his hand on the hilt of his sword as Gudrun's Seidr staff moved. A flash of red light and golden Seidr collided and the stable horses reared as the cavern filled with a deafening bang.

All was white.

Daggon's heart thundered in his chest. The room was silent save for the sound of air passing through his chest. Grappling on the ground, Daggon brushed the stone.

A magnified, sharp staccato drummed Daggon's head then rippled like a single drop of water. Its echo cleared, leaving the silence behind, then another...louder this time. His pulse banged his chest in between each drum. A boot struck the ground, and a third drum echoed. A blur appeared through the white. A black shape that became Gudrun's body formed in Daggon's sight and the white faded. The stables returned.

A long scrape of metal against metal rang in Daggon's ears. Blue moonlight glistened off the sheen of Aaric's blade as the high marshal raised his sword, rearing to strike Gudrun's unconscious form, and Daggon lunged, unsheathing his blade.

The sharp twang of his sword striking Aaric's confirmed he had moved in time. Beneath their blades, Aaric peered down at Kallan's Sentinel.

"You." Aaric creased his nose in disgust. "You dare cross arms with me?"

"She's an old woman," Daggon said.

Hate rolled from Aaric's eyes.

"There is no room in my court for deserters!"

With every bit of strength he had, Daggon shoved up and against Aaric's blade, knocking the high marshal back and off balance. Sheathing his sword, Daggon stood and lifted Gudrun from the ground while Aaric stared, stunned, unmoving, his sword hanging idle at his side.

Without a word, Daggon carried the old woman to the stallion, lowered her limp body into the saddle, and collected the reins.

"Nidingr!"

Aaric's voice filled the stables and Daggon stopped, his foot fall frozen to the stone.

Fingers curled into white fists as the word ripped through the captain. He knew what the challenge meant.

"Nidingr," Aaric said, holding his blade at his side, forgotten.

"You would have me choose between my queen and my citizenship?" Daggon's face contorted with rage. Then, without another word, he led Thor to the passage beneath the falls.

"If you set foot from these walls, who will remain to defend your honor?" Aaric cried.

Daggon was almost gone now.

"You will wander the earth! You'll be nothing but a rogue who has forsaken his honor!" Aaric's voice cracked a shy breath from madness. "Nameless!"

The waters of Livsvann swallowed Aaric's words.

"Fool!" Aaric cried. "Where will you go? Who will have you now that you've abandoned Lorlenalin?"

Peering over his shoulder, Daggon met Aaric's madness with the cold emptiness of his own resolve.

"My queen is lost to the world," he said. "I will walk the world over to bring her back so long as she requires my aid."

"She is dead!"

The waters of Livsvann roared, filling the void between them.

"Until I see a body," Daggon said, carrying Gudrun's own vehemence in every word, "I will be found in Kallan's services."

Daggon vanished into the darkness beyond the echo of Livsvann Falls.

Chapter 60

Bergen studied the black sky, engrossed with the single thought that had plagued him since the waning moon. His whitened knuckles gripped the stone of the window's sill, paying no mind to the silent shuffle of Geirolf's footfall.

Geirolf stopped beside the berserker and looked to the sky for the answer to his question.

"The sky is black," Bergen said. With a smile, he looked at the old man. A glint of mischief gleamed in his eye. "We ride."

With a subtle jump in his step, Bergen strode from his sitting room to his chambers. Bottled energy from weeks of waiting burst from his chest. Geirolf doubled his pace to keep up.

"Bergen."

"Wake the men," Bergen called, not wasting the time to look back. "We leave now."

With a nod, Geirolf closed the door of Bergen's bower and descended the steps to the Great Hall.

After lacing his boots, Bergen fastened his trousers and buckled a piece of leather armor over the tunic he slipped over his head. With a final glance back, he took up his great sword emblazoned with "Uthbert" and closed the door behind him after Geirolf.

The castle was already awake and buzzing by the time Bergen plodded down the stairs, eagerly bouncing off every step. He crossed the wide Great Hall while he finished strapping his sword to his back. With a boom, he opened the doors wide and entered the courtyard.

"Bergen!"

The shrill voice came from a petite woman with sharp cheekbones and a narrow nose. Her skirts swept the stone as she marched at him head on. Her hair, usually twisted and fastened to the top of her head, flowed freely in streaks of silver and brown down her back. Diverting his path, Bergen hastened his pace and met the woman in a wide embrace.

"Lady Torunn," he cried, picking her up by the waist.

Barking a laugh, he spun her around and lowered her back to the ground, kissing her hard on the mouth before letting her go again.

"Keep those off of me," Torunn scolded. "Odinn knows where they've been."

With a second laugh, Bergen added a skip to his step and was on his way again with Torunn quick on his heel.

"Geirolf tells me you leave tonight," she said.

"Right now," Bergen said, flashing his smile.

"Where will you go?"

"Wherever I need," Bergen beamed.

The warmth of the stables and sweet scent of hay enveloped him as he passed through the open doors. Several war-men saddled their horses, while others led theirs from the stables.

"I figured we'd take the horses across the Klarelfr into the valley," Bergen said as he saddled his slate-gray destrier, as black a gray as the fire worms of Muspellsheim. "Then, if we need to, we'll take our search to the ships and go beyond the Raumelfr."

"And what of the throne?" Torunn asked as she scuttled behind Bergen.

"Well, I wasn't going to bring it, but if you think we shoul—"

"Bergen."

He tugged at the saddle's strap and matched Torunn's stern brow.

"I've left it to Geirolf," he said somberly.

Lowering her eyes to the stable floor, Torunn nodded and squeezed her fingers nervously. With a smile, Bergen clasped Torunn's knotted hands.

"Don't fret."

She glanced up at the scar glistening on his brow.

"Be well," she said then shuffled from the stables. He was busy again with the saddle, when Torunn called back from the door.

"Bergen."

He met her round, gray eyes.

"Come back with Rune," she said.

Bergen grinned. "Always."

With a smile she quelled too often, Torunn left Bergen to his horse. The saddle was buckled, the reins secured, and Bergen's back, slapped by Geirolf.

"The kitchens are ready with stock," he said, dropping a pack of dried pipe leaf into Bergen's hand. "All who ride with you are waiting or getting ready."

Geirolf leaned closer, his previous jubilant energy, replaced with a solemn tone.

"Where will you start?" he asked, keeping his voice low.

Bergen flipped the flap of a saddlebag closed and pulled the rope taut.

"The forest of Alfheim where I saw him last," Bergen said with a darkness that enhanced the black of his eyes, "then on to Swann Dalr."

"Rune left a moon ago," Geirolf said. "Any trail left will be gone."

Bergen finished the final buckle on the bridle, tugging at the strap to ensure it was secure.

"I'm not looking for a trail."

"Bergen."

Bergen swung the reins over the mare's head, and began stuffing some final rudiments into his pack.

"Torunn worries," Geirolf said.

"Of course she does," Bergen retorted. "She's a woman."

"Bergen." The old man dropped a hand onto Bergen's shoulder, forcing his full attention. "There are reasons why Rune hasn't returned. She insists something went wrong."

"Don't think I haven't reached the same conclusion," Bergen said.

The light-heartedness was gone from his voice.

"You're as worried as the rest of us," Geirolf said below his breath. "Be cautious. Be ready." He gave Bergen's shoulder a shake.

With a nod, Bergen strapped his pack to the saddle, and took up the reins.

"Alright, Zabbai..." Bergen said and patted the mare's neck. "Let's go."

Leading Zabbai from the stables, he pushed through the crowded stalls of rider and horse. The cold night air punched his senses, rejuvenating his jovial energy. With a final once over and adjustment, Bergen pulled himself onto his horse as the last of his riders filed out of the stables.

"Bergen," Geirolf called, coming to stop at Bergen's side. "He may have crossed into Midgard."

Bergen looked across Gunir's yard to the tall, stone gates. Beyond the fortress and the bailey, longships lined the docks in the lake where the Klarelfr cut through and around Gunir. Further still were rolling fields riddled with rivers that met the pines of the Alfheim Wood, and at their end, the Raumelfr divided the Alfar from Midgard. "The world of Man is not like ours," Geirolf said. "Things change quickly there."

Bergen grinned down at Geirolf. "You're beginning to sound like Torunn."

"Bergen." Geirolf's tone forced the berserker to be still. "You brothers...You're all we have left..." Geirolf pursed his aged, thinned lips. "Come back to us."

Nodding, Bergen raised a hand, signaling his men, and sent his horse into a light canter toward the gate.

"Before the moon is full," Bergen called over the thunder of horses' hooves as they vanished into the black night.

Cradled between the mountains, through the woodlands of Heidmork, Rune and Kallan trekked along the banks of the Raumelfr that twisted through clusters of birch and patches of reindeer moss. As Rune slogged along, clutching Freyja's reins, Kallan passed the days atop Astrid trying to germinate the seeds from her golden apples. Each attempt barely swelled the seed coat, leaving Kallan more frustrated as the hours slipped by. At the end of each day, after filling their stomachs and resting their feet, Kallan returned to her lessons.

The green of the Northern Lights streaked the clear sky, casting an emerald hue overhead. Kallan huffed and tucked her knees to her chest. Three days of incessant practice, hours of endless concentration, had yielded almost no change in the latest apple seed.

Atop his bed of furs, stretched out with ankles crossed and arms folded under his head, Rune peered across the fire. Kallan stared into the flames, the seed clutched in her hand.

"How goes it?" he asked.

Kallan sighed.

"It was easier when it was just pouring out of the earth." She looked the seed over for any sign of growth. "It feels locked, somehow, like it's there, but I can't get to it."

"You need to rest," he said, positioning his arm over his eyes.

Kallan rested her chin in the crook of her knees.

"What I need is Gudrun," she mumbled.

Exhaling, Kallan released her legs and settled herself back onto the pile of furs. With the seed still closed in her hand, she pulled the leather overcoat to her neck.

"The elements are the same," she said, staring up at the lights, "passing through the air, the water...moving through the earth."

The silent, red lights spilled across the sky like ribbons.

"I can feel it," she whispered. "It's there, just...out of my reach."

"You're tired," Rune said, his arm hung over his eyes. "You've been putting in hours every day since we left. You hardly stop to eat before jumping back into more hours working on this."

"I'm so close."

"You need sleep, Kallan." Rune said.

Still plagued by dampened spirits, Kallan stared at the Valkyrjur's Lights.

"Goodnight," she bid though her eyes were still wide and alert, her mind still laden with thought.

"If you say so," Rune said.

The frogs chirped. An ember popped. The sound of a picked blade of grass broke the evening's chorus. Rune shifted his arm and gazed at Kallan.

Idly, she twisted the blade between her thumb and a finger.

"How long before we see Alfheim?" she asked.

Rune covered his eyes with his arm again.

"Tomorrow we leave Heidmork," he said. "Then we pass through Raumariki. Within half a fortnight, we'll be in Viken."

"And Alfheim?"

"Alfheim is across from Viken," Rune said. "We'll have to pass through Vingulmork before we see Alfheim."

Kallan pulled the overcoat closer as red light flowed like a river across the black sky.

"There's no moon," she said.

"No. There is not."

"The Lights of the Valkyrjur are much clearer here," Kallan said.

"They are."

Kallan lay, gazing upon the lights. She wasn't ready for sleep.

"Rune?"

"Hm?" Rune grunted, keeping his arm splayed over his eyes.

"Have you ever heard of the Seidr Sionnach?"

Rune sighed.

"Kallan...until you and Gudrun came to Alfheim, no Ljosalfr had ever heard of the Seidr, let alone a 'Sayth Shonach'." He ended the word on a botched guttural sound.

Kallan grinned.

"The Seidr Sionnach," Kallan repeated. "The Sionnach were a pair of foxes twice as tall as a man and strong enough to pull a sleigh across the snows of Jotunheim." She stared at the lights of Odinn's Valkyrjur. "They loved each other beyond this world until one's release was the other's breath. They roamed wild and free, wreaking havoc, nonsense, and all sorts of mischief among Men. All who looked upon the Sionnach feared them and so...despised them."

Lowering his arm, Rune lay and listened quietly.

"One day," Kallan continued, "Freyja looked down from Asgard and saw the Sionnach frolicking without worry of what Men thought. Their adulation became her conviction. And she loved them. She loved them so much that she gave them her Seidr. Freyja taught them how to wield it and the Sionnach grew in power and strength alongside her. Over time, they too grew to love her. Some stories tell of how they pull her chariot across the skies." Kallan grinned. "It was said that from the earth, the Sionnach, with their red Seidr flames trailing behind them, looked like two red cats bearing Freyja across the night."

Kallan grew silent as she stared into the ribbons of red dancing upon the black.

665

"Sionnach," Rune said.   "That word isn't of Alfheim."

"It's from Eire's Land," Kallan said, twisting her head around to better look upon Rune around the fire. "Gudrun brought the story back with her."

"Eire's Land," Rune whispered and returned his arm to his eyes. "I haven't heard a story from Eire's Land since..."

Rune's voice faded with his thoughts and he was quiet again.

Biting her bottom lip, Kallan stared across the fire.

"Rune?"

"Yes, Kallan." His voice was light with infinite patience.

"Do you think the children are alright?"

Rune inhaled.

"Yes, Kallan," he said, ensuring his eyes remained on the sky. "I'm sure the children are alright."

An owl hooted in the distance.

"Rune."

"Yes, Kallan?"

"I miss the children."

Rune pursed his lips.

"I know," he said.

The ribbons danced.

"Rune?"

Rune exhaled, renewing another round of patience.

"Yes, Kallan?"

"Good night."

A smile pulled at his mouth.

"Good night, Kallan."

Rune and Kallan awoke to a downpour on their last day in Heidmork. The storms added substantial volume to the river, tripling the water's roar as the droplets hammered the ground in a continual, sharp staccato.

By midday, they crossed into Raumariki where streams flowed through vast lakes that peppered the lands with blue. Despite the elements, Kallan busied herself with the Seidr, while Rune trudged over the soaked ground. The rains continued into nightfall as the gray day ended. Hunched beneath a low hanging pine branch, they spent the night huddled against the cold, wrapped in wet blankets and Kallan's overcoat.

The next morning yielded no mercy from the deluge and, unable to ride with a wet saddle, Kallan walked alongside Rune. They journeyed on much like they had been, staying close together and silent. When dusk blanketed them in blue and gray, they stopped for the night, too withered in spirit to walk.

Beneath a cluster of pines where wide branches blocked most of the elements, Kallan ignited a pile of dried pine needles and dead branches she had managed to dry out with her Seidr flame while Rune unsaddled the horses. Together, they did their best to wipe the horses dry with wet blankets then laid out their blankets, cloaks, and boots around the fire.

The fish sizzled in the firelight. Rune's stomach tightened with hunger as the aroma rolled off his dinner.

"Kallan."

He flipped the skewers.

The constant hush of rain swallowed his voice. He waited a moment longer, turning them over one last time, before placing the fish on a flat stone.

"Kallan," he called again, but no answer came.

After giving Astrid a quick pat, he made his way to the Raumelfr where he felt her Seidr with the Beast's hunger. There, on the banks of the Raumelfr, he stopped short at the sight of Kallan standing thigh-deep in the river. With her hair sleeked back, and her drenched gown clinging to her body, Kallan stood with extended arms.

In an enclosure of golden Seidr, she pulled and guided several strips of water from the river's course. Like glass ribbons, the minute streams twisted and flowed up and around and over until they encircled her.

Engrossed with her skill, Rune watched her every movement, mesmerized, as she raised her hands and flicked her wrists, commanding a handful of droplets to stop midair. Keeping her glass ribbons flowing, Kallan tapped a single drop with a slender finger, then another, commanding each, in turn, to fall. With a backhanded sweep, Kallan willed the next series of droplets to follow the direction of her hand. Like golden threads, the Seidr bound to each one and followed Kallan's instructions. With a final sweep, she raised her delicate hands and severed her Seidr. And, just as smoothly, the frozen droplets fell and the minute streams returned to the river and Rune's Beast quieted with the settling Seidr.

Standing soaked between the rain and the river, Kallan suddenly took notice of Rune.

"It's here," she beamed. "I didn't sense it before, but it's here."

With each breath, the water shimmered on her neck.

"The fish," Rune said, unable to remember what about fish he had to say.

"Fish?"

The water glistened on her lips.

"Yes," he said stupidly. "Fish."

"Is it ready then?"

She smiled. He watched her chest heave with excited breath.

"Yes."

Brimming with optimism, Kallan pulled herself to shore. There, Rune helped her back to land. She wrung the water from her clothes and twisted the rain out of her hair then did her best to warm herself by the fire as she ate.

By the time they had finished picking apart the skewered fish, the two-day deluge ended, leaving them eager for a dry night's sleep.

669

Rune stared into the darkness. The waxing sliver of the crescent moon provided almost no light. The orange glow of the fire's cinders had faded with the night chill. Rune whipped his head to the side and frowned.

Kallan's bedroll was empty again.

Already the Beast was alert and pacing, wanting the Seidr he felt from afar. With a sigh, Rune threw back the furs and, taking up *Gramm*, rose to his feet. Feeling the threads the Beast desired, Rune followed its appetite through the cluster of pines. Over foliage and forest debris, he followed the path of Seidr threads until a distant light glowed then flashed, directing him to an illuminated clearing ahead. Only then did he ease his shoulders with relief and Rune fought down the Thing inside of him with its ever-growing hunger.

Taking care to stay in the shadows, Rune slipped through the branches and trees. Content to watch Kallan from a distance, he peered through the forest. Enveloped in a golden light that twisted and warped its way around her, she stood as she had at Bilrost. She had kicked off her boots, leaving her bare feet, delicate ankles, and half shins clearly visible beneath the high hem of her skirts.

Pulling the Seidr through her, Kallan exchanged it for her own and positioned her hands, palm-side up, then released her energy from within, bathing herself in sheets and streams of golden Seidr.

A shadow blackened the forest behind Rune, and a whisper rose. Unsheathing *Gramm*, Rune shifted toward the darkness and raised the blade at the ready. The red pommel glistened in Kallan's light.

"You would raise my own sword to me?"

The guttural chill of a familiar voice forced a second look from Rune. Stepping into the Seidr light, donned in heavy black boots, worn trousers, and tunic, Ori emerged from the forest, taking the shadows with him. A threadbare travelling coat replaced the one given to Kallan, and a sword—simpler, plainer—replaced *Gramm*.

Rune relaxed his shoulders and lowered the sword. The Dvergr gazed at Kallan in the clearing, who was now busy tying eternal, complex knots with her Seidr.

"She's become her mother," Ori said, engrossed in the spells she weaved.

"Why did you come here?" Rune asked.

Somberness blanketed Ori's black eyes as he tore his attention from Kallan.

"I've been following you since Throendalog."

Rune clenched his jaw. Not once did he detect the Dvergr's presence and Rune pondered how that was possible. Where Bergen boasted his skills with the blade, he boasted his skills in tracking.

"If you're here to take her back—"

The Dvergr was already shaking his head.

"Motsognir insisted someone keep on your trail," Ori said.

"Motsognir?" Rune said.

"The leader lived, but barely," Ori explained. "If anyone else had volunteered to hunt you, Kallan would be in Svartálfaheim right now and you would be dead."

Rune stared through the little light provided by Kallan's Seidr.

"Your point is clear," Rune said. "At any time you could have taken her and didn't. Now what do you want?"

"I must be brief." Ori's words flew from his mouth in a hush. "There is more to say than I have time for. Olaf is here."

The words rent Rune's nerves.

"He's less than an hour behind you," Ori said. "Right after you passed through his camp, Olaf followed. He and his men hunt you."

Light from Kallan's Seidr brightened Ori's pale face, making his black eyes appear larger than they were in the dark.

"How did they—"

"The apple," Ori said, studying Kallan in the dark. "They saw her use the apple. They know."

Rune swayed with lightheadedness.

"Immortal apples," Rune said. Kallan's Seidr had grown, twisting in and around itself until he lost the beginning and the end of her complex knots. The Beast paced, eagerly waiting for Rune to drop his guard. "Every mortal who comes to learn of their existence will race to get their hands on one."

Ori nodded. "The secret's out and Olaf's racing."

"To the borders of Alfheim, he'll follow," Rune said, gazing at Ori. "He won't stop."

"Not with the campaign he's started," Ori said. "Not for this."

Rune eyed the Dvergr suspiciously.

"This is the second time you've helped me."

"Her," Ori corrected. "Never you."

"Who are you?"

Ori drew in a slow, steady breath. "Motsognir is my father."

The slits of Rune's eyes darkened.

"A Dvergar prince," Rune mused, "son of the king who murdered her mother. How can I be sure you aren't looking to finish what your father started?"

Anger blanketed Ori's eyes. "My father's decisions do not reflect my own."

Flooded by thoughts of his own father, Rune's judgment softened as Kallan swept her hands, extinguishing her Seidr and dispelling the knots of Seidr she had woven. Eagerly, the Beast waited. With a sudden flick of her wrist, a ball of blue flame burst to life in her palm. Mesmerized, she stared at the blue flame and turned it over as curious as a child inspecting a new bug.

"Why would a Dvergr risk death for a Dokkalfar queen?" Rune asked.

"Not a queen," Ori said, "a friend. One I owe my life to."

Ori shuffled his feet as he moved to leave.

"Ori."

The Dvergr paused.

"What does your immortal king want with Idunn's apple?"

The question held Ori just long enough to answer.

"Motsognir doesn't want the apples," he said. "It's the pouch my father is after."

Rune shrugged. "Without the apples, it's just an ordinary pouch."

"To you," Ori said. "To Kallan maybe. To Motsognir..." Ori's voice trailed off. Shaking his head, he turned back to the shadows. "There is no time."

The Dvergr vanished as he stepped back into the shadows.

"Get her out of here and stay on the move," Ori called unseen through the black. "They're coming."

Chapter 61

Rune stared into the darkness, replaying Ori's words. The earliest of morning birds had begun to trill when he stepped into the clearing. Cradling the ball of blue flame, Kallan rotated the sphere as she stared into its white center unaware that Rune watched from behind. The Beast remained at bay, obedient to Rune's wishes as Kallan extinguished her flame and withdrew her Seidr.

"Olaf is here," Rune said. "We have an hour, maybe less."

"How—"

"A raised guard goes a long way." His throat was dry.

Kallan nodded.

"We need to get a move on," Rune said, moving back to the trees.

"Rune."

Her smooth voice grated on him like a smithy's sandstone. Inhaling, he restored his patience and, cursing himself for knowing better, gazed back at Kallan.

"Your Majesty."

Kallan bit her bottom lip.

"When we get to Alfheim—"

"You'll be difficult, I'm sure," he said and, in hopes of discouraging further conversation, turned back to the wood.

"If I were to go with you to Gunir ..." Kallan's question trailed off.

A light smile pulled at the corner of Rune's mouth. Forcing his face stern, Rune gazed back.

"Wou—"

A sudden shuffle broke the night and Rune threw his hand up, silencing Kallan. Seconds too late, his steady hand flew to the hilt of his sword as a pommel slammed into the back of his head.

Rune caught himself on one knee, and unsheathing his sword, he swung *Gramm* through his fragmented vision blurred with darkness. Somewhere behind him, Kallan's Seidr light blazed.

"Ori," Rune called to the darkness, but a heavy boot caught his face and, just before the world went black, he spotted Kallan unconscious on the ground, her Seidr lines riddled with poison.

The fire's light splashed streaks of orange across Olaf's face as he threw back another large gulp of spiced mead. The thick, sweet beverage was quickly gaining his favor. From the chair positioned beside the map table, Olaf scratched the underside of Vige's ear. The dog leaned into him then dropped his chin onto Olaf's thigh, evoking a warm smile from his master.

With the creak of leather and the clink of a sword, a chill swept the room, with it the scent of pine.

"Your Highness," Warrior Egil said.

"News."

"We anticipate our arrival in Vestfold within the fortnight. Arrangements have been made for Thorer to meet us there."

Olaf shook his head and released Vige.

"Tell him not to bother," Olaf said, downing another gulp. "At this pace, we'll have joined Thorer's army before he finds us."

With a satisfied sigh, Olaf stared at the tarnished flask. He threw back his head and polished off the last of the mead.

"Is the witch talking yet?" Olaf asked.

"No," Egil said. "Havelock is with them now."

Olaf gazed at the warrior. Tall, burly, and almost thirty, the scar on his forehead exemplified his valor.

"Cut every last finger from her hand if you have to," Olaf said. "She'll show me how those apples work before the night is out."

Placing the empty tankard on the table, Olaf picked up a pile of letters, attempted to be interested, failed, and tossed them aside again.

"Did you collect their possessions?" Olaf asked, as the dog pulled his head from Olaf's lap.

"Havelock is," Egil answered as the dog circled the rug several times then settled itself down beside the fire. "There's something you—"

A second blast of cold threw their attention to a guard at the door.

"What is it, Havelock?" Olaf asked, irate at the interruption.

"My lord," Havelock panted. "We have a problem with one of them."

"So gut him," Olaf said. "We don't need him anyway."

"It's not him, sire."

Olaf looked to the soldier and waited in earnest for an explanation.

"It's the woman. We can't get near her, sir."

Before Havelock could say more, Olaf was up and out the door.

With blue flames alight in both palms, Kallan stood, poised for battle. A wall of Seidr glowed, securing a perimeter around her, shielding her. From warrior to warrior to Havelock, who clutched Rune's sword and her pouch, Kallan assessed her escape, clear and inviting, behind her.

With her back to the forest, a barricade of swords blocked her passage to the only thing that seemed to keep her there. Rune, forced to the ground, kneeled subdued by a pair of guards, who twisted his arms back and locked his elbows at the joints, ensuring the slightest pressure would break them.

Curious, Olaf studied the Seidkona whose escape was available should she abandon her companion. Olaf threw a careless hand toward Rune.

"What's the problem here, Havelock?" he asked. "Clearly we have leverage."

"Let him go," Kallan said, uninterested with the man who had joined them.

"Hold your positions," Olaf shouted over Kallan's command.

Kallan gazed at Olaf donned in fine fur robes, and recognized him as the one who had the power to free Rune, or to break him.

"Release him!"

"I am this land's high king," Olaf said. "And you stand in my realm. I alone order my men, witch."

Kallan's face tightened as she forced herself calm. Prepared to lunge, Kallan dug her feet into the soil.

"Havelock. Pouch," Olaf said.

Without hesitation, Havelock tossed Kallan's pouch to Olaf, who snatched it midair, then threw back the flap and pulled an apple from its contents.

Torchlight glistened off the golden skin reflected in Olaf's eyes as he turned Idunn's apple over.

"Show me," Olaf said, glaring at Kallan.

She clenched her jaw to seal her lips.

Coldly, Olaf threw the apple to the ground. It came to land at Rune's side.

"Show us," he said.

Undaunted by his empty promises, Kallan stayed steadfast.

"Apparently, you need to be motivated." Olaf came to stand beside Rune. "Show us how these work, or..." Olaf buried his fist into Rune's ribs and his guards released the Ljosalfr.

A flash of silver caught Kallan's eye as Olaf pulled his fist away, and Rune fell to the ground clutching his chest. Blood pooled in the dirt and Rune's face fell white.

A sudden burst of Seidr radiated from Kallan's hands as panic and rage pulsed through her. Streams of flame engulfed the barricade of men and they scattered, fled, or attacked. With a second stream, Kallan broke through the barricade, throwing a ball of flame toward Olaf while maintaining the Seidr-shield around her.

For a moment, her Seidr glowed white from her hands and formed a corporeal sword she grasped at the hilt. Kallan poured her blue flame from the white, and slashed the air with her Seidr-sword as she battled her way to Rune.

Dispelling the sword, Kallan fell to her knees and expanded her shield over Rune. Blood and dirt caked her hands and she pushed him onto his back. She snatched the fruit from the ground before panic could block her senses, and dug her nails into the apple's flesh. She was muttering the incantation before the apple surrendered its juices.

"Please," she whispered, angling the apple's nectar to flow into his mouth, Rune battled to keep his breath. Sweat poured from her pallid brow and, with trembling palms, Kallan called on the only thing she knew could save him. Her mind cleared, the Seidr swelled, and, placing a palm onto his wound, she pulled from her core, guiding her Seidr into him and through him, all the while muttering under her breath.

In silence, Olaf and his men stared at the golden light that seeped from the Dokkalfr, out and through the prisoner. With each word, the spell drained Kallan's Seidr, weakening her shield until it faded then vanished.

Rune eased his breath and the color returned to his face as his flesh sewed itself together, erasing all evidence of the wound. Only then did Kallan cease her muttering.

"You should have let me die, princess," Rune whispered darkly.

Olaf purred with a grin, his own pensive gaze fixed on Kallan.

"Egil. Their possessions."

Obediently, Egil picked up a small bag and Kallan's dagger from the pile of satchels and blankets that had been stripped from the horses. "There is also this," Egil said, extending the elding handle of *Blod Tonn* to Olaf.

Olaf eyed the black detail before shifting his attention to the pouch. With fluid movement, he dumped its contents into his hand. Kallan's pendant fell into his hand alongside a pair of rings. With acute interest, Olaf's eyes widened as he pushed the rings over with his thumb.

The fire light revealed the detailing of a silver signet ring engraved with the figure of a boar's head encircled with runes.

"A silver ring with the head of a boar," Olaf said. "How did you come by the mark of Gunir?" He narrowed his eyes. "Unless..." Olaf turned the ring over in thought, eyeing the runes encircling the boar.

"You are Rune Tryggveson," he said, restoring his gaze to Rune. "The blood of Lodewuk flows in you."

Olaf turned his eyes to Kallan.

"Which makes you..." He looked the Dokkalfr over, clearly assessing the tattered gown, iridescent eyes, and the Seidr that flowed from her hands.

"A hired bodyguard, perhaps?" he asked. "One of the Varingjar?"

Kallan's hands twitched with desire to kill.

"But the Ljosalfar don't dabble in the Seidr arts and would never hire a woman to fight for them." Olaf turned over the second ring.

"Elding," he thought aloud, eyeing the three eternal triangles crossed with a hammer.

Olaf raised his eyes to Kallan's as understanding clicked into place faster than words could form.

"What is your name?" His dark stare dared her to lie.

"Emma of West Seaxna," she said.

Olaf closed his hand over the jewelry.

"Your lying tongue betrays you," Olaf said, "for I have lived on the shores of West Seaxna, witch." Olaf shook his head. "You are not born of Alfheim."

He looked at her as if pondering the accent, the lucid shade of her pale skin, and the tapered points of her ears.

"You are of Svartálfaheim...though you lack the rancid stench of Dvergar filth. No..." Olaf shook his head and met Kallan's gaze. "You were born to the White Opal. You are Dokkalfar."

With a wave of Olaf's hands, the guards were on them, swords poised at the Alfar's throats.

"An elding signet ring," Olaf said, pouring the treasures back into the bag and exchanging the bag for *Blod Tonn*. "An elding blade..." He unsheathed Kallan's dagger. "And a pendant marked with the knot of Eire's Land."

Kallan watched the Northern king with elusive eyes.

"You are Seidkona." Olaf eyed her knowingly. "You are Eyolf's daughter."

Kallan's shoulders stiffened at the mention of her father's name. Her shock didn't escape Olaf and he lifted his face with smug victory that glowed with regal arrogance.

"Kallan, daughter of Eyolf...Lady of the White Opal...which makes you..." He looked to Kallan as the final pieces slipped into place. "Queen of Lorlenalin."

Kallan held her head high with contempt, refusing to confirm, refusing to deny his conclusions.

Olaf swiped her blade, slashing Kallan's face with her dagger.

A guard dropped his hand to Rune's shoulder as he shifted to leap, keeping Rune in place on the ground. As hot blood flowed down Kallan's face, a smile stretched across Olaf's.

"Both monarchs of the divided Alfheim," Olaf mused. "The only stretch of land that has managed to escape Danelaw this side of the Kattegat."

Olaf couldn't hold down the grin that stretched his square chin.

"What would the King of Gunir and Lorlenalin's queen be doing in the middle of Midgard?" He directed the question to Kallan, who allowed her hate to flow, refusing to satisfy his game with an answer of any kind.

"Bring them both!" Olaf spun on his heel and marched back to his tent. "Alive!"

Chapter 62

Olaf's troops were on the move before the morning sun had a chance to awaken the wildlife. Rune panted through the thick, stagnant air left for him within the bag shoved over his head. He had no doubt that they had marched until the sun was high and hot.

The rustling clinks of mail and sword accompanied the dulled clop of the caravan's footfall as they forced their way through the forests of Raumariki, every step taking them farther from the river's edge. Conversations peppered with foreign tongue surrounded him like one continuous, garbled hum. The day wore on as Rune caught occasional mention of Vestfold.

The early evening sunset confirmed the fast approaching winter. Rune's shackles weighed him down until the darkest hours of the day when Olaf's army stopped for the night.

A hurried bustle engulfed the camp and Rune listened as soldiers built their fires and prepared their beds beneath the stars.

Within minutes, a pair of hands dragged him to a tent and secured him to the center pole. Before the last guard finished securing Rune's bonds, a rush of cold and light struck his face as the bag that blinded him was ripped away.

Rune scanned his surroundings, taking in every crack and crevice of the tent. There were no pleasantries, save for that of a single lantern and the stale company of a lone guard, his sentinel. Clad in armor with a large scar across his temple, he stood, glaring down at Rune with his beefy arms folded over his chest.

Just outside the tent, a familiar ruckus disrupted the silence and the tent flaps were thrown back as a pair of warriors hauled Kallan into the tent squirming, kicking, and cursing.

"Kallan," Rune said.

"Rune?" Kallan asked amid her squabble from within the bag tied around her head.

"I'm here," he said, already fixed on wriggling out of his bonds.

With her hands and feet still bound and harder than necessary, the two warriors dumped her to the ground then took their leave, paying no mind to Rune, who had begun fidgeting with his bonds.

"Can you see where we are?" Kallan asked.

Rune peered at the silent sentinel standing beside the exit.

"I don't know," Rune said. Bowing his head, he focused on his fingers, blindly working the intricate knots. "There is talk of Vestfold."

"Vestfold will delay us a full fortnight," she said.

"I know." He seemed indifferent to her objection, choosing instead to focus on the ropes that bound his wrists.

The tent fell silent, the lone guard sulked, and Kallan squirmed until she exhausted herself.

"Rune?" her gentle voice did little to ease his tension.

"Hm."

"How did you know?"

Silence filled the tent again as she waited for his answer. An occasional grunt and the strain of the rope's fibers were his only response.

"Know?" he said finally.

"You said Olaf was tracking us." She attempted to refresh his memory.

Rune gave an extra yank against his bonds before giving up for the moment and relaxing his shoulders with a sigh. He stared again at their silent sentinel. He seemed uninterested in their conversation for the moment.

"I must not have known much seeing as how we're here, in a tent that reeks of island rats and ale."

"You said he was an hour behind us," Kallan said. She had gone limp on the floor.

The tension in the tent thickened as Rune listened to the settling commotion outside that ensured Olaf's men were bedding down for the night. Kallan continued, paying no mind to the sudden silence.

"Which means the information you had was not your own, or you would have seen he was right behind us and we never would have stopped."

With a huff, Rune dropped his head against the pole.

"How did I not see them?" Rune muttered.

"You assumed he was a day off because someone told you he was," Kallan said as if uninterested with Rune's question.

Silence.

"Who misinformed you?" she asked when it was apparent Rune wasn't going to speak.

"Kallan," Rune said. "Can you reach the ropes with your hands?"

Kallan stiffened against the question, seemingly waiting for the sudden bark of a guard, but nothing came.

"He doesn't understand us," Rune said. A proud lilt stuck to his voice and Kallan relaxed enough to hunt for the ropes at the end of her hands.

After a few more attempts at loosening their bonds, Rune decided to answer.

"Ori has been trailing us since Jotunheim."

"Ori," she whispered.

The name stabbed her memory like a smith's poker that brought back every vivid stench of Dvergar filth and she remembered her dreams in the mist of corridors and dragons. Her fingers fell limp with a sickness that weakened her nerves and loosened her grip as the darkness enveloped her once more.

Beyond the world of dreams, Ori had found her there in the deepest chasms of a prison she once believed had no end, but that which death would bring. She struggled to see anything beyond the bag blindfold that left her alone in the dark.

"He approached me last night and warned me of Olaf's progress," Rune said.

There was silence.

"How do you know of Ori?" Kallan asked. Rune could hear the rage stifled behind her teeth.

"He lent us aid after I freed you in Jotunheim," Rune said.

"And you accepted?"

"You were wounded, dying, and bare to your skin in the middle of Jotunheim," Rune said. "You would not have lived without it."

"You accepted help from a Dvergr?"

"He came to me," Rune said.

"After knowing what they did to me, you accepted his aid," she shrieked.

"I had no choice," Rune said as a second guard entered the tent. Rune watched as the two guards exchanged words in their native tongue.

"Guard!" Kallan shouted. "Untie me! Untie me!"

The silent sentinel moved toward Kallan.

"Leave her! Leave her!" Rune cried.

"You, filth," Kallan said, tugging at her bound wrists, visibly desperate to stand and fire. "You—" She stopped with a gasp when a blade pressed to her neck and the sentinel cut the ropes from her ankles.

"*Swige, witch,*" the sentinel said, his speech punctuated with a foreign blend of syllables unfamiliar to the Alfar.

Pulling Kallan to her feet, the guard gave a violent shove that sent Kallan stumbling across the tent and into the second guard, who pushed her through the door.

Kallan squinted against the sudden white light that burned her eyes. The scent of venison and stuffy tent air engulfed her like a warm blanket as the light faded to a softened yellow-orange emitted by firelight and lantern. Tossing aside her blindfold, the guard released her, leaving her arm bruised from his grip.

The large build and wide shoulders of Olaf seemed to fill the entire tent riddled with spears, furs, and maps. A large elkhound, lost in the wonders of dreaming, slept on the floor at the foot of a bed and kicked the air with a hind leg.

"Leave us," Olaf ordered of the guard, who bowed before taking his leave. Cautiously, Kallan eyed Olaf, who poured himself a glass of mead, disinterested with her company. His lowered guard flaunted his confidence and her urge to slap him intensified.

"Two guards stand outside," Olaf said, scanning the platter of food and drink before him. "If anything happens in here, they have orders to kill your comrade out there."

"What do you want?" Kallan said coldly.

Olaf took a trial sip from his drink.

"To wipe out every last Seidkona from this earth," he said.

"Are you to kill me?"

Olaf leisurely trailed his eyes from her face down to her shoulders, following the slender gown to the hem at her shins.

"That has yet to be decided."

"And its factor?" Kallan asked.

"On whether or not I need you," he said, lifting his gaze to her hardened eyes. "For the moment, my curiosity is what stays my hand."

Olaf polished off the mead and dropped the empty cup to the table.

"I was born to this land and raised on the stories merchants and pirates told of the Alfheim War and the Conflict..." An endless cold descended into his eyes as Olaf spoke. "How your father launched such few numbers against the thousands in Gunir and won." Olaf picked at a small berry and popped it into his mouth. "That the armor and craft of your people has yet to be matched by any who wasn't born to the mines of Svartálfaheim."

Steering away from the food, Olaf sauntered to the map table where Kallan's possessions lay with Rune's. He picked up *Blod Tonn* and unsheathed the blade. "How King Tryggve massacred hundreds with such a cool, insatiable rage that the stories reached as far west as the Hag's Head in Eire's Land," Olaf said.

Kallan clenched her jaw and the gash on her face pulsed.

"Yet here you stand the daughter of Eyolf, joined at the side of Tryggve's son. And, what's more...you seem to reserve a form of fondness for him." Olaf grinned. "Oh, how children are fickle. But I must ask. Does he share in your affections?"

"What madness is this of yours that you would keep me imprisoned only to inquire of my girlish fantasies?" Kallan asked.

Olaf's grin widened.

"It is not the reason for your imprisonment, but I can not deny that I am amused."

"Amused?" A cold smile began to lift the corner of Kallan's mouth. "Or interested?"

Olaf shrugged and something in his gaze softened.

"I will not deny the advantage of having a Seid-kona's foresight on my side," Olaf said, "nor would I reject the hand of a queen of Alfheim to wife."

Kallan's face split into a gentle grin.

"And together we would vanquish our enemies," she mused, catching the firelight in her eye, "starting with the bloodless whelps of Gunir, I suppose."

"And on to the Dani," Olaf said, and Kallan cocked her head. A lock of long hair spilled over her shoulder.

"While riding on the life granted by my golden apples," Kallan lulled in wonder, smiling.

Olaf eyed the curve of her bosom and the slender lines of her neck.

"Together, we could do such extraordinary things," he said.

Kallan turned her smile down and coldly stared across the fire.

"If you were to extend a dying hand to me in the deserts of the Nordic plains," she said, "I would turn my back, leaving you to die at the mercy of the Fire Giants." With every word, Kallan pulled the grin from Olaf's face. "If you were cracked and bleeding, parched with want for drink, I would not so much as spit on you lest it quench your thirst. Nor will I sate your curiosity, that you may live in misery...perplexed and plagued by unanswered questions."

In an instant, Olaf's hand was on her neck, throwing her back against the table behind her. He bore his weight down, crushing her beneath his body.

There was a blast of cold and Olaf growled. "Get out!"

The guard blinked then scurried outside.

Olaf pushed his mouth to her ear.

"Don't think I haven't pondered the amount of silver a she-Alfr would fetch at market," he said, his venom burning her with his hot breath. "There are corners of the world where even you have a marketed value, and there are those who would pay a fine price to add an Alfr to their collection. In the right market, it's too easy to mistake an Alfr for a Slider." Horror, masked only by her anger, filled her eyes. "I have half a mind to keep you with me and trade you at port if I didn't fear your stubbornness wouldn't cost me half of what you're worth."

With a kick of his leg, Olaf pushed harder against her, digging his hipbone into her leg. Kallan winced despite glaring with an adamant hate he could not break.

"Even now, will you not gleam a sliver of fear?" Olaf whispered.

"I would not give you such pleasure," Kallan said.

"Other pleasures can be taken," Olaf said, grinding harder.

"I would die by my own hand before allowing my enemy to decide such fate, and you're wasting my time," Kallan said.

"Your time?" Olaf grinned between short, sporadic bursts of laughter. "A prisoner dare speaks of wasted time?"

"What do you want?" Kallan said, her patience spent.

Olaf relaxed his weight and released her. Appeased, he watched as Kallan gasped for air and fought to stand.

"I want to know where the apples came from," Olaf said as he walked the floor, granting her an arm's length of space to lick her wounds.

"The apples," Kallan whispered.

"They are one of the coveted treasures of Asgard," Olaf said, getting down to business. "Grown and tended to by Idunn herself."

Olaf folded his hands behind his back.

"The Bilrost is lost," he said. "No one knows the way into Asgard these days. So how is it you came by one of her apples?"

"One of..." Kallan gasped. "It was a gift," she said.

"A gift," Olaf repeated. "And who gave it?"

"An old hag who earned Odinn's favor," Kallan said.

Olaf snorted and slammed his fist into her face. Grabbing her neck, he pulled her from the floor to his face.

"Don't taunt me, witch. I've done worse things to women far more valuable than you. Where did you get the apple?"

Kallan stared, not budging as the black of her swollen eye filled in to match her cheek, split and bloodied.

"Go and serve your dues to Hel," she spat.

Olaf's grip tightened and he pulled her body against his.

"The moon is new tonight," he said, "and I have only need for one of you. Do you think your comrade will be so willing to risk his life for yours? Do you wish to test him?"

Kallan remained unbending and cold.

With the back of his hand, Olaf struck her again and Kallan fell to the floor.

"Guard," Olaf said to the door.

A cold blast of air grazed Kallan's wounds.

"Take her to the lake," Olaf said. "Let the depths have her."

Chapter 63

Campfires lined Rune's path in the dark as he fought the guard with every step through the camp. With a growl he couldn't understand, the guard pulled back the hide flap and pushed Rune into Olaf's quarters.

As the guard removed his shackles and took his leave, Rune examined the furs and armaments. Ignoring the dog, the man, and the buffet of fruits and meats splayed out on a table, a wave of discouragement settled itself as Rune realized Kallan wasn't there.

Donned in a set of simple red frocks of the finest cloth, Olaf stood beside the large fire that burned in the center of the tent, casting shadows of orange and black about the room in a myriad of patterns. Rune eyed his host suspiciously, as they stood inspecting each other. With his hands folded behind his back,

Olaf moved with a regal condescension that illuminated his composure.

The Dubh Linn prince untwisted his hands from behind his back never once lowering his bearded face from Rune. He studied his rival with a pensive curiosity that masked his innermost thoughts before addressing his guest.

"Far too long I've moved my army into position toward my one goal," Olaf said. "Far too long I've spent my days fervently fixed on one man: to bring Forkbeard falling from his throne, scathed and defeated." Olaf pulled himself from his ponderings and gazed upon a bored Rune. "Your lands could serve as a fine solution to the rule and fall of Dan's Reach. For so long, I've desired to speak with you. I've started a number of letters requesting your council...letters I've thrown aside with less than satisfactory diction and suddenly here you are before me.

"Rune, son of Tryggve..." Veneration flowed from his words. "King and Lord of Gunir and Alfheim...descendant and last of Lodewuk's line." In awe Olaf beamed, admiring Rune's station as he settled his weight down onto a table strewn with maps. "Too few hold claim to the title bestowed upon you by your fath—"

"What do you want?" Rune asked.

Olaf tightened his jaw and visibly forced a smile.

"You are not a prisoner here," Olaf said. "Please, eat."

He waved an open hand toward the feast that filled the tent with aromas of sweet meats and honey mead.

697

Rune glanced at the food with apathy. It was with a heavy, dispirited sigh that Rune spoke at all. "I've played host to many a monarch who danced graciously around the true matter at hand, wasting my time with court etiquette and hollow gestures. I have no interest in feigned hospitality that masks blatant betrayal." Olaf's false grin fell. "End your illusions of friendship and state your business plainly," Rune commanded with the sternness of one looking down at a usurper bearing gifts.

The fire popped.

"My father lost rule to this land when it was taken from him fifty years ago," Olaf said, visibly forcing aside his illusions of joviality and feigned friendship. "He was killed before he had a chance to reclaim his birthright."

"I remember," Rune said, stifling a yawn.

"My elder father led his campaign into these lands and left behind my father to reign in his stead."

"My father had him fed to Solve Klove." Rune maintained his regal rigidity as he spoke.

"You remember." The words rolled from Olaf's mouth with a gleam of admiration as he looked upon Rune with a fresh wave of envy. "How I pine for a fraction of the life only granted to you Alfar."

Rune said nothing, but kept his patience while he entertained his own agenda. Olaf turned and poured himself a drink.

"Solve Klove and his kin were bent on ridding my father's land of our bloodline," Olaf said. "That Sea

King would have given up the lives of his sons to avenge the death of his father and uncle."

"Where's Kallan?" Rune asked.

Olaf's mouth curled into a smile.

"She is Dokkalfr," he said. "Or have you forgotten that?"

"What do you want?" Rune asked, weary with being the subject of his host's sport.

Olaf returned his untouched drink to the table.

"The throne of Danelaw proffers a constant threat waiting to make its move," Olaf said. "Forkbeard grows stronger. You, of all others, must know of the constant threat to our lands." His words were quick and smooth, and his voice dripped with certainty.

"You seek to make me your puppet king."

"I seek to offer an alliance," Olaf corrected.

Rune's irritation slipped away as the surmounting opportunity spilled into his lap.

"With our combined forces, you can bring down the Dokkalfar," Olaf said, "rend every stone of Lorlenalin that defaces the mountainside. With our strength, we can squash the festering rot that sulks in the mines of Svartálfaheim and as one, we can take back Northumbria...return her to the glory that answers to the realm of Dubh Linn."

Rune's attention filled with Olaf's vision.

"Dubh Linn," Rune said.

"We can wipe out the Dani."

Rune stared beyond the flames, entranced by the world proposed by Olaf. The food and drink lay forgotten on the table.

"The use of that army would more than make up for the numbers lost to the Dokkalfar," Rune muttered aloud in thought. He pulled his eyes from the fire. "You seek to hand Northumbria back to the Uí Ímair."

Olaf smiled with a tip of his head.

Rune relaxed his shoulders and set the room at ease.

"And from there, I suppose, you would have us march north to Alba...Then on to take Dubh Linn for yourself?"

"The house of Amlaib Cuaran already answers to me," Olaf said. "They have long since recognized me as the King of the North and have already sworn their allegiance. Upon my word, they will fight...and with their strength, we can defeat the insipid filth of Dan's Reach."

Rune lowered his eyes to the flames. Within the red of those flames, he saw the brave new world laid out to him. Three clans, three nations joined against the might of the Dokkalfar, led by the sons of Ivann the Boneless himself. A union that strong would prevail against the magnificence of the Empire. Regardless, his gut churned with unease.

"And when the last of Danelaw has been rid of this land..." Rune said, returning his gaze to Olaf. "When your people are victorious and look to reap the spoils of this war, will you still look to share this land with my people?"

Olaf smiled and returned his attention to the table laden with food and drink.

"We both desire a world that would deliver peace to our people." He found his cup and took a sip. "I would give you all of the North if it meant the fall of Forkbeard."

Olaf ended his soliloquy and waited with tension in the air for the answer that would unite their people in arms.

Rune stared back into the flames.

"Think of it," Olaf said. "A world without the Dokkalfar...Without the Empire!"

"A world without war or fallen comrades."

"I have seen the hand of Forkbeard and how far it reaches beyond that of Dan's Reach," Rune said. "I was there at the Battle of Hjorungavagr. Why, by the fires of Muspellsheim, would I ever subject my kin to a massacre like that again? Why would I risk the lives of my people to anger the greatest power since Otto's Empire in the south, who serve the imperial god and senselessly slaughter my people?"

"We have so much to gain as their victor," Olaf said.

"Forkbeard turns a blind eye, discouraged by the wars of my people," Rune said. "A challenge would awaken his green-eyed interest in my land...one that my fathers and I have managed to avoid. We sit beyond the desires of Forkbeard's throne, and I intend to keep it that way."

Rune turned for the door. In a single step, Olaf desperately grabbed Rune's arm.

"Why do you believe leaving that sleeping giant alone will keep his interests away from Alfheim?" Olaf asked, his patience clearly waning.

"I have the wars of my own people to put ahead of the greed of a dethroned king. Now..." Rune yanked his arm free from Olaf's grasp. "If you won't tell me where Kallan is, then we are done here."

Olaf pursed his lips, seemingly readying himself to start again, but stopped at the sudden clamor raised outside. Both kings paused and listened. The silence that had fallen over the camp was gone, replaced with the muffled chaos of distant cries. Exchanging glances, they abandoned their argument and, as one, started for door.

A sudden series of tumultuous cries ended when the tent flap flew back and Egil fell to the floor of Olaf's tent. Black blood seeped from his right side. His white hand trembled as he struggled to hold a gaping wound closed.

Dropping to one knee, Olaf pulled Egil's hand away. Streams of blood pulsed from the wound, leaving Egil pale and waxen.

"An ambush, my lord," Egil said. "We didn't see them coming...thousands...from the shadows."

"Forkbeard." Olaf said.

"No..." Egil shook his head. "There is no mistaking the black of that hair...the death in those eyes staring back from white faces."

Rune's spine became rigid as he suddenly found himself starved for a weapon.

"Dvergar," Olaf said. His face had turned white as the last of life left Egil staring into the distance beyond what the living could see.

Taking up his servant's sword, Olaf rose to his feet and joined Rune in the march to the door. The chill of the night air pierced their faces as they pulled back the hide and stepped into the night.

Swarms of Dvergar infiltrated every crevice of the camp, wielding axes against Olaf's men, who raised steel swords against them. Burning tents peppered the darkness and drowned out the sounds of the fallen.

"It isn't too late, Ljosalfr," Olaf said, clearly eager to avenge his comrade. Egil's sword rang out in declaration as he unsheathed the blade. "Take up arms alongside me this day. Fight with me."

"Where is Kallan?" Rune called over the screams of the fallen and the fires that spread.

An elated grin was Olaf's reply before he plunged into battle, impaling a Dvergr along the way, crying out to his men in encouragement. Rune turned his thoughts to his only goal and, dismissing the battle around him, skimmed the burning camp.

The fragile, steel blades crafted by the smiths of Dubh Linn were no match to the elding blades forged in the mines of Svartálfaheim. Men bearing the mark of naudr buckled beneath the Dvergar's might.

After selecting the clearest path, Rune lunged into battle, skirting along the forest's edge. The flames passed from tent to tent, lighting up the camp as Rune weaved in and out of the chaos. He stopped frequently to reassess his path before moving on to the next cover, twisting his way through tents and dashing behind barrels as he went.

"Kallan!" he cried over the chorus of clinks and screams of sword and shield. His sanity ebbed with every moment as the purr of the flames grew, drowning out the battle cries.

"Kallan!"

"Stand your ground," Olaf called from across the battlefield above the clash of swords and the fire's roar. Whipping around, Rune met the cold, hardened eyes of Olaf.

In that brief moment, the conversation they had started in Olaf's tent ended along with temporary truce. With a single nod, Olaf revoked his offer and accepted Rune's rejection as the battle raged on. Rune proceeded along the forest's edge, leaving Olaf behind to fight the shadows and darkness.

Behind a wagon filled with barrels, Rune stopped and assessed his next move. A flash of silver half-buried beneath the body of a slain soldier caught his attention. Rune glanced about to confirm there was no immediate threat and emerged from behind the wagon. With a grunt, he pushed the corpse off the blade and took up the dulled iron sword.

"Kallan!" he called with a flood of panic on the rise.

His desperation caught the attention of a Dvergr, who charged at him, his axe raised at the ready. With a pivot, Rune dodged the blow and countered with a thrust through the heart. With a kick, Rune shoved the body off his blade and peered through the smoke and the dying strewn about on the ground.

"Kallan!" he cried, not bothering to wipe the blood from his blade.

Something grabbed his ankles and pulled him down, slamming his shoulder into the ground. Before he could find his bearings, the something dragged him into the forest behind him.

With a wide swing of his blade, Rune rolled onto his back, freeing his ankles. The wild, black mane and flash of clear ebony was enough to mandate a second swing of his sword.

"Be silent," the Dvergr said. "She doesn't have much time."

The familiar voice forced Rune still and, all at once, he recognized the wide, black eyes of Ori.

The cold water engulfed Kallan's body, stabbing at her like a thousand knives. Gagged by the rags Olaf's men had stuffed into her mouth, she failed to gasp against the cold of the lake. The weighted shackles cut into her wrists as she wriggled and fought to break her bonds. Kallan's consciousness waned the deeper she sank to the lake's bottom. She forced her eyes open despite the cold, and looked into the black nothing around her.

Battling back the panic clouding her mind, Kallan gave a final jerk at her arms secured behind her back. Her body shuddered and the last of her breath left her to the black fathoms of Lake Mjerso.

Chapter 64

Golden light wafted beneath the waters in slender strips of ribbon. It twisted itself behind Kallan, encircling her with the glittering gold of soft light.

She reached to touch it, but it bowed and arched away from her, teasing her, egging her to follow. The bands widened into tiny rivers that flowed in a steady stream down, deeper into the black chasms of nothingness. There, in the depths, nothing mattered. Nothing else existed there where the world she left behind ended, and this one began.

Kallan pushed herself down, closer to the light and it mirrored her, pushing down deeper, twisting upon itself until it doubled back and wrapped itself behind her. She thought back to the *Naejttie*, Sarahkka, and Kallan wondered if this too was a Seidr-spring lost and forgotten beneath the lake.

"Kallan."

She ignored her name, eager to pursue her curiosity, and gave a hard kick, propelling herself closer to the light. It had branched itself out into thousands of strands, whipping and flowing, bending and forming as it moved with the water.

"Kallan!"

She forced her mind clear and tried to move closer, but the rivers of light were flowing too fast. She struggled to keep up.

"Kallan!"

With a deep gasp, Kallan opened her eyes and stared into the black night speckled with starlight and the lights of the Great Hunt. The lake wind rushed over her soaked body and she shook against the sudden cold. Her breath punched the air in a series of gasps. Her body convulsed against the chill.

"Stay with me!" Rune's voice barely penetrated the thick wall of her consciousness. "Kallan?"

She looked about, disoriented at first, until her eyes found Rune leaning over her. Droplets of water fell from his face and his black hair was matted to his neck and brow. A wide smile broke across his face as her breathing settled and confusion cleared.

Throwing her arms around Rune's neck, Kallan gasped with relief. Lake water glued her gown to her skin as each granule of sand beneath her dug into her legs. Ignoring the discomfort, she crushed Rune in a hug, taking solace in his warmth that permeated the chill and regulated her pulse.

He was as drenched as she was, but Kallan tightened her grip and buried her face in his neck as she waited for the disorientation to pass. Astrid snorted and pawed the ground beside Freyja and Kallan peered over Rune's shoulder. The lake stretched out like black glass, reflecting the blue and purple ribbons of the Valkyrjur's Lights overhead. The forest resumed where the beach ended and pine trees clawed the sky. A pair of clear, black eyes, framed in the mass of black hair stood vigilant alongside Astrid with reins in hand.

"Rune," Kallan said, moving so as to not prematurely provoke the Dvergr. Flicking her wrist, Kallan poised her arm, and aimed as she moved to fire.

"Kallan, wait." Rune threw himself into her, slamming them into the ground as she unleashed a stream. With a thud, they hit the beach, knocking the air from Kallan as Ori ducked. The tree behind him sizzled and the fire died.

"Get off," she said as she opened her claws to Rune and he rolled with her.

"Kallan, be still," he said.

"What are you doing? That's a Dvergr!" Kallan pointed a finger at Ori. "He's one of them!"

"He helped me find you!" Rune said.

"I know what he is," Kallan said.

"You're alive because of him."

Kallan studied Rune's face for lies.

"He's been following us since Jotunheim," Rune said. "He saw where they took you and led me from

Olaf's camp. It's because of him I was able swim out to you before you were even in the water."

"Rune, they're coming," Ori urged.

"We don't have the time," Rune said. "The Dvergar are here."

"If they're here, it's because he has led them here," Kallan said.

"Listen! Foolish! Woman!" Rune punched each word with a tone that forced her to hold her tongue. "They are here because Motsognir brings his army. He has not stopped. He is here."

"Three thousand ride from Svartálfaheim," Ori interjected, walking closer with Kallan's dagger suspended from his hand. The color drained from Kallan's face as she lay, not moving, waiting. "Rune, we have to go."

Rune shuffled to his feet and extended a hand to Kallan, who slapped it away then pushed herself from the ground. After brushing off the clumps of sand that had caked onto her clothes and hair, Kallan took up her skirts and wrung out the excess water.

With a huff, Kallan released her gown and sneered at the Dvergr whose unreadable ebony eyes met hers. Without a word, Ori made his way back to the horses. With a blank look, Rune joined the Dvergr, leaving Kallan to bring up the rear with a huff.

As Rune gathered Freyja's reins, *Gramm*'s silver filigree hilt and red pommel caught Kallan's eye. In an instant, she moved. Unsheathing the sword from Rune's side, Kallan swept the blade toward Ori, stopping the tip at his throat.

"Do not turn your back, Dvergr," Kallan said, daring him to move. "The scars inflicted upon me are too bold a reminder of what your kinsmen did to me. Some wounds run too deep," she warned.

With a nod, Ori held her gaze. "I understand," he replied.

Slowly, Kallan lowered the blade, grimacing as she moved to take Astrid's reins.

"Hold it."

Kallan turned her attention to Rune, who snatched Kallan's dagger from Ori. Without a word, he took two steps toward Kallan and yanked back his sword, sheathed *Gramm*, and handed *Blod Tonn* to the Dokkalfr. As Rune shuffled through the saddlebag, Kallan tightened her grip around the black hilt.

Almost immediately, Rune withdrew Kallan's pouch and handed it to her. As she busied herself with the strap, Rune pulled Ori's black leather overcoat lined with rabbit fur from the saddle and dropped hard onto her shoulders.

Kallan buckled beneath the weight. As he lifted himself into the saddle, Kallan tossed a final scowl at Ori, who seemed indifferent to her disapproval. After slipping her hand into Rune's, he hoisted her up in front of him. Taking up the reins, they started into a light canter that carried them along the lake's shores with Ori and Freyja following right behind them.

710

With every softened footfall, Kallan frowned at the Dvergr walking alongside their mount, until the frequent shift of her eyes became one constant grimace permanently fixed over Rune's arm.

Ori ignored her venom and took care to avoid her eye. Indifference glazed his expression, angering her more. Despite Rune's continuous efforts to block Ori from Kallan's view, she made several adjustments in the saddle to regain a clear path in which to peer down from her seat upon Astrid.

After an hour, Rune pulled back on the reins.

"Ori," Rune said, sliding from the saddle with a nod. Ori returned Rune's nod and walked back down the path alongside the lake.

Taking Kallan by the waist, Rune pulled Kallan to the ground, ensuring his grip stayed in place. Kallan shifted, but Rune's hands tightened, adding a jerk that maintained her position. He waited, keeping her in place, until the last of Ori's foot falls vanished.

"What the Hel are you doing?" Rune asked as soon as they were alone.

"What am I doing?" Kallan asked, attempting to shove his hands from her waist. They did not budge. "You're the one picking up friends among enemies wherever you can find them. What's wrong with you?"

"We need him," Rune said. A twinge of his regal demeanor burned in his eyes, and a flicker of respect pinched Kallan's nerves.

"There is nothing I will ever need from a Dvergr," Kallan said, digging at his fingers holding her waist.

711

"His king knows where we are," he said. "They know we are heading to Alfheim. They know the path we take. It is not a question of if they find us. They will find us. They will catch up."

Kallan glanced at the lake, knowing he was right.

"What then?" he asked when she didn't answer. "What plan do you have to hold off a army of three thousand?"

"Regardless of what I can do to evade them, travelling with one of them can be of no help," Kallan said, looking back to Rune.

Rune's grip tightened on her waist.

"He hopes to head off the scouts and redirect the troops. If he can convince them we took a different path, it may buy us the time we need to enter Alfheim."

"And why should they stop at Alfheim?" she asked.

"Motsognir is convinced you have kin looking for you at the borders of Alfheim. If they see him, if they suspect your abduction was linked to the Dvergar, Motsognir fears the Dokkalfar will launch an army against Svartálfaheim."

With a creased brow and anger ebbed, Kallan studied Rune's face. "Why would he think I have kin waiting at the border?"

Ignoring her question, Rune continued.

"I am certain, if we can get to the border before Motsognir catches up—"

"We'll be free of their huntsman," Kallan finished for him, suddenly aware of how close he had pulled her in.

"Yes," he said, releasing his grip from her waist.

Kallan stared out to the lake. Lost in the darkness and her thoughts, she rolled through her options. Her clothes were damp from the lake, leaving her chilled to the bone. With a shiver, she pulled Ori's overcoat tighter around her shoulders.

"Very well," she said, "but I will not drop my guard. I will not sleep in the presence of that...that..." She pointed to the general direction taken by Ori. "That!"

Kallan turned on her heel and marched back to Astrid, leaving Rune with his sighs of exasperation.

Chapter 65

Kallan lay awake, listening to the lake water lap the land as it flowed with the wind. Rune's breath had already settled into the slow, steady rhythms of sleep. As Kallan flopped and shuffled into numerous positions to induce sleep, the scent of fish still clung to the air. She glanced to Rune across the fire. The Dvergr had not returned and she found herself wishing he would.

From the shadows, she feared his betrayal and waited, prepared for the moment when he would suspect them asleep, but no attack came. Instead, Kallan watched and waited with guard raised as the night passed by.

Wide-awake and irate, Kallan kicked off the hide and sprung to her feet. Creeping around the fire, she snatched up *Gramm* from Rune's bags and fastened

714

the sword to her waist. As she plodded off on the balls of her feet, running into the thick of the forest, she failed to see the slit of Rune's eye watching from the fire's side.

The black forest battled the Seidr light from Kallan's hands. Repeatedly, Kallan directed the flow of her Seidr through the seed. Repeatedly, she tried once more.

She had managed to tame the Seidr that naturally flowed through the earth beneath her feet and pulled from the waters as she came to streams and lakes, but the Seidr in the air, always there without structure or elements to direct its flow, was still too far from her reach.

With another attempt, Kallan failed again and started over, pushing every bit of Seidr she could collect into the seedling in her hands. After several minutes, she opened her hands.

"What are you doing?"

Kallan jumped and dropped the seed to the forest floor. Flashing Ori a grimace, she gathered her skirts and kneeled, pulling apart each blade of grass and upturning each crumpled leaf in search of the apple's seed.

"What are you looking for?" Ori asked.

Refusing to entertain his inquisition, Kallan shuffled through the mulch and grass. His armor rustled as he walked and dropped to his knees in front of her.

After a moment, he was silent again and she risked a glance up from her work. Kneeling and hunched on the ground before her, Ori pushed his fingers through the pine needles, leaves, and earth as she separated the grasses.

"What are we looking for?" he asked, searching the ground.

"A seed," she said, feeling the cold in her voice scrape her throat.

Ori froze and set his impenetrable, cold stare on her. Pausing, Kallan glanced up. His eyes, cloaked with grief, forced a sudden wave of discomfort through her and she hated him more for it.

"What were you doing out here so far from camp?" he asked after she resumed her search.

She didn't answer.

Ori shook his head with an affectionate chuckle. "You still find every moment to run off alone, don't you?"

Kallan's hands paused on the grass. "What do you know of me?" she said through the hate that dripped from her words.

Sincere hurt shone from the black of Ori's eyes. "You really don't remember, do you?"

Kallan's cold eyes remained unaltered.

"I thought that the drugs had suppressed your memory," Ori said, "but you don't remember."

Her palms tingled with the temptation to set him ablaze right there.

"And what, Dvergr, am I supposed to remember?"

"The halls of my father that flowed with rivers of silver, and opals so abundant they could be cut right out of the rock face. Veins of elding so hard, only our smiths could shape those ingots..." Solemnly, Ori seemed to search for the glimmer of someone he once knew within Kallan's iced eyes. "And mines so deep, our labyrinths descended into the earth beyond the roots of Yggdrasil down to the gates of Helheim. Do you remember nothing?"

Kallan hesitated, forcing a civil composure.

"What I remember...are the cold weeks I spent bound by your elding chains that burrowed into my wrists. And that pungent tang that robbed me of my senses, my reason...my will to live as I dangled at the end of a leash! Days spent cowering in the shadows while I was forced to endure those insipid rhymes meant to torment me!"

Kallan sat back on her heels, forgetting all thought of the seedling lost to the forest floor. "The boot of your comrade smashing my face, crushing my hand, and breaking my nose, and the constant stench of bat buried in the bowels of the caves where you kept me chained like a Slider rolling in its own filth! That," she spat, "is what I remember."

Ori's face fell, weighed heavy with a loss Kallan dismissed without a care. It was with a disheartened voice that Ori spoke, each word carried by his hope.

"We were lost in the mazes of Nidavellir's mines, chased by the dragons we had found. Your father and mine had exhausted the realm's army in search of

717

us...and when they found us, you insisted the dragons were there."

With widened eyes, Kallan listened, enslaved by
the sudden colors of forgotten memories that merged
one into the next until the colors became unblem-
ished images she could identify.

"He scolded us...we argued and stood our ground."
Ori spoke with a stronger voice that commanded her
audience. "We insisted the dragons were real."

The pictures were clearing and Kallan remembered
her father standing before them, glaring as he so often did in those mines. She saw the browns and tans
and blacks of the fur cloak he always wore and the
leather of his boots, the silver sheen of the sword hilt
at his side.

"How..." she tried to ask, muddled with images that
struggled to refine themselves.

"Before the war," he said.

Kallan narrowed her eyes, staring beyond the
Dvergr where the images formed as she forced the
memory.

"There was a prince," she said, "and dragons, deep
within the chasms of the Svartálfaheim mines...in Nidavellir."

Ori sat patiently while Kallan pushed through
dozens of memories, countless memories that fought
to surface. She could see the mines again, streaked
with their rivers of silver. She could hear the echoes
of her laugh resonate through the caves, and the
warm, black eyes of a boy, with a pale face untouched
by the warmth of the sun. The black of his hair

gleamed in the torchlight. As they crawled through the labyrinths, he cried out from somewhere in her memory.

"Kali! He's here! I've found him. I've found him! Look, there's his tail!"

"He's there! I see him, Ori! Catch him! Catch him!"

Her forgotten words echoed from within her head and she could hear, so clearly, the dormant memories awakened.

"By all the fires of Muspellsheim," her father had roared. *"Kallan, that's a newt!"*

"It isn't a newt, Father! He's a dragon! I saw him myself climb out of the fire!"

Daggon's laughter had boomed from behind as the young princess had tried so desperately to hold onto the gray Northern newt.

Eyolf had done well to hide his grin beneath the mass of his black beard.

"Ori, stop telling her they're dragons! Daggon, stop laughing!"

"But he could be! He could be! Sometimes the dragons are real!" Little Kallan had shrieked and the memory faded.

"Ori," Kallan whispered, still kneeling on the ground in the grass, and the Dvergr smiled. Narrowing her eyes, Kallan studied his face through the dark for a hint of the boy she had forgotten.

She didn't see the shadows move behind Ori, nor did she see the wild black of the crazed eyes flash as Motsognir's scout launched from the blanket of night. By the time Kallan rose to one knee, coddling a

719

blue flame, Ori had unsheathed his sword and stood, impaling the scout, who slumped to the ground. The prince wiped the blood from his blade, panting with even breaths.

"Were you looking to save me?" Ori asked, taking a step toward Kallan.

Ori moved and a second Dvergr lunged with raised sword from the shadows. In a torrent of black hair and ebony eyes, he charged then stopped only inches away. A single arrow shot clean through his heart interrupted his advance, and he fell to the earth with the look of victory frozen on his face.

Kallan and Ori whipped around as Rune lowered his bow to his side.

"They're here," Ori said between breaths.

Rune nodded and the Dvergr grinned.

"I'll be blaming you for this," Ori said, pointing at the bodies with his blade.

"I figured you might," Rune replied with a tone that radiated his respect. "Kallan," he called, offering her his hand. "Come."

His gentle voice coaxed her and she took his hand. With a heavy numbness, she slid her hand into his as he pulled her to her feet. With a slight tug, Rune urged her to follow and led her into the darkness, back to the horses and camp.

"Rune," Ori called. "Take care of her."

With a contented smile, Rune nodded and tightened his grip on Kallan's hand, guiding her back to the banks of the river.

Lost beneath the forest floor, unbeknownst to them all, a single seedling lay among the forest mulch. Its tiny stem had swollen and broken free from its prison shell. Four tiny apple leaves stretched themselves out like little arms reaching toward the heavens for light.

Smoke and ash billowed into the air as Rune rolled up the beds. After saddling the horses, they were off, riding hard down along the lake's edge. They transitioned between full gallops and light canters, and stopped only long enough to rejuvenate and heal the horses with Idunn's apples. Through the night, they rode with little said between them until the sun rose over Midgard and spilled its light onto the lake.

Mid-day came and went as the tip of the lake narrowed into the wide river that drained Lake Mjerso.

Rune turned the skewered salmon steaks he had propped over a fire.

Kallan stared into the flames. "Salmon."

"Again," Rune said.

Kallan hugged her legs into her chest, resting her chin on her knees. She released a weary breath.

"I miss Gudrun's *flado*."

Rune's eyes grew wide. "Oooh, *flado*," he exclaimed at the thought of sweet, golden creams molded into beautiful bowls and topped with preserves.

"Yeah!" Kallan's face lit up with excitement. "Gudrun makes the best *flado* from the juice of Idunn's apples. She calls it Idunn's Nectar."

"You know what I miss?"

"What?" Kallan asked, giving an alternating tap with her feet.

"Cook's boiled blood pudding," Rune said and Kallan puckered her lips with relished delight.

"Gudrun makes that with cloudberries," she beamed. "Oh, and blood cakes with imported sugared pears drowning in mulberry sauce."

"Boiled pork," Rune said. "And—"

"—Black Soup," they both exclaimed.

Kallan sighed and looked to the stars. "Lingonberry jam," she said.

"With boiled pork." Rune bobbed his head and hungrily licked his lips then dropped his gaze to the skewers of unseasoned salmon propped over the fire.

Kallan dropped her chin back to her knees.

"I hate fish."

They watched the salmon and waited until Rune took up each skewer. Quietly, he passed a stick to Kallan and, in a daze, she peeled off the skin of her fish as her thoughts filled and emptied with memories of silver streams that riddled the mines of Nidavellir.

The wood fire crackled.

"We're not stopping for long," Rune said as Kallan picked off another piece of fish. "Ori may have managed to divert Motsognir, but Olaf can't be far behind."

Kallan rotated her fish as she lost her thoughts in the mazes of Svartálfaheim caves.

"So my thinking was this," Rune continued, "I can head out when I'm done here and hand myself over to Olaf."

"What?" Kallan said, jerked from her thoughts.

Rune shrugged.

"Astrid will ride faster if he's only carrying one of us," he said. "So I figured you could take him on ahead to Alfheim."

"Are you mad?"

A smile stretched Rune's face. "Now that I have your attention," he said, "what's really on your mind?"

Kallan chuckled lightly, shaking her head after tossing her meal's carcass onto the fire that devoured her fish bones.

"I can see them," she said.

The fire whipped its flames into the air.

"Them?" Rune asked.

Kallan leaned back against the pile of saddlebags. Astrid crunched on the grass behind her as his bridle jingled.

"Have you ever had the pleasure of seeing Nidav-ellir?" she asked, staring past the fire into her memories.

"The Dvergar city within Svartálfaheim?" he asked.

Kallan lifted her eyes from the flames.

"No." Rune shook his head. "But I know someone who was once imprisoned there." Kallan quelled her questions for later. "He spoke of their mazes, their labyrinths...their culture."

Kallan nestled her chin into her knees.

"The Svartálfaheim mines," she said, "were sculpted around the metals and stones flowing through the ground. Endless streaks of silver and black glisten in the fire's light...a majesty I've not seen duplicated since."

Kallan paused, allowing herself to get lost in the beauty known only to those halls.

"And those metals..." Kallan gasped at the memories Ori had awakened. "I would watch for hours as Volundr wielded the silvers and blacks of their elding."

Rune straightened at attention.

"Volundr," he exclaimed. "The Smith?"

Kallan smiled and nodded. "*Gramm*'s maker."

"By the fires of Muspellsheim," Rune said, leaning back on his bedroll.

Kallan watched him through the flames.

"My father could only tell us tales," he said, staring up at the stars.

Kallan shuffled herself around, stretching out on her stomach and staring off into the darkness with her chin resting on her arms. Sleep was beginning to find her and she closed her eyes in submission.

"What I wouldn't give to see him work," Rune said.

The fire crackled as she listened to Rune shuffle into his bedroll. Dreams came quickly as she drifted off in thought of raw opals twinkling from beneath the earthen walls.

"Kallan?"

"Hm." She could feel his eyes on her and she smiled, allowing the comfort of his vigilance to sooth her.

"When we cross into Alfheim tomorrow..." Rune paused. "Will you go with me to Gunir?"

"Hm hm," she agreed with a smile, allowing her own petty desires their moment as she drifted off to sleep.

Chapter 66

The next morning, sunlight spilled over the mountains. Seated atop Astrid, Rune and Kallan made their way along the river streaked with beams of light. Desperate for the first glimpse of Alfheim in nearly a full moon and a fortnight, Kallan beamed with an eagerness she couldn't contain. Her wide-eyed zeal had become anxious jitters as she looked from the horizon, to the waters, to the forested land. As if worried they had somehow strayed and lost their way, she looked about in search for a road or land bridge that would open up and carry them into Alfheim.

"Soon enough," he said and wrapped an arm around her, forcing her still.

Astrid's steady pace carried them through the forests along the river's edge, dragging the day behind them.

"Where is she?" Kallan asked as the mid-day sun began to rise.

"Eager to get underway?" Rune asked with a grin.

"Our deal stands, Ljosalfr."

Kallan sensed the continued battle that brewed as Rune tightened his hold on her waist.

"What will you have me do...to convince you to come to Gunir?" Rune's voice was near a whisper.

Kallan scoffed then glanced over her shoulder to better direct her insults toward him.

"Only a fool would willingly follow an enemy to their home," she said.

"Am I still your enemy?" Rune asked, pulling his eyes from the road.

With mouth agape, Kallan spun around to rebutt, but Rune suddenly fell forward, dropping his weight onto her. Clenching his teeth, Rune bit back a howl and pushed himself up again as Kallan caught a glimpse of an arrow's shaft protruding from his shoulder.

With a slap of the reins, Rune sent Astrid galloping in and out between the trees down the riverbank ahead of a volley of arrows. Reaching around, Rune grasped the arrow and broke the shaft in two, leaving half of the arrow still embedded in his shoulder and that was when he saw them: lines of archers in the distance standing behind lines of spearmen, who charged them. And in the distance, atop his horse, sat Olaf among his archers.

"Olaf," Rune said and, before the color finished draining from Kallan's face, Rune had untied Freyja's reins from the saddle horn and sent her galloping into the forest along with most of their possessions.

Rune whipped Astrid's reins, and the stallion fired into a torrent. The pines thickened and Rune veered Astrid away from the river where the banks rose into sharp cliffs. The woodland thickened, hiding them from Olaf's arrows and forcing Rune to ease up on the gallop. A sliver of light pierced the wood, beckoning them on ahead. With a final bound through the trees, Astrid emerged from the wood and Rune pulled back hard on the bridle, putting an immediate end to their chase.

"The river..." Kallan muttered.

The river they had followed east for two days, the river that should have led them to the open fields of Alfheim, abruptly ended as it joined with a second river that flowed from the north. The waters of the Raumelfr, wide enough to comfortably hold three longships, stretched out in front of them.

With his legs jellied, Rune slid down from Astrid, and briskly walked along the land that hugged the banks of the Raumelfr, forming a blunt point before trailing up the other side of the east river and shaping the land into a peninsula. Together they stared out across the conjunction, gaping at the other side.

"We're blocked in," Rune said. His heart pounded like a drum, burning his shoulder where the arrow rested. The charge of soldiers behind them grew louder.

"Rune?" Kallan said. She looked to him, awaiting an answer, but his attention had settled on the land across the Raumelfr.

"That's Alfheim," Rune said.

"What?"

"We're on the wrong side."

"What?"

"We're on the wrong side," Rune's voice rose the more the realization settled in.

"We're on the wrong side?"

"We're on the wrong side! Alfheim is there!" Rune pointed to the wooded plains ahead.

"We have to cross this?" Kallan shrieked. "That's the width of an arrow's shot!"

"We have to cross this," Rune said.

"We can't cross this!"

"I know we can't cross this!" Rune shouted back.

"We can't cross this," Kallan said. "How can we be on the wrong side?"

"We were at the wrong lake." Rune's voice sharpened as he realized his error.

"The lake?" Kallan said.

"I thought it was Lake Mjerso."

"Then what was it?" Kallan asked.

"We must have been further west."

"What do you mean further west? You didn't know?"

"No, I didn't know!" Rune shouted back.

"I thought you've been here!"

"I was, but that was a long time ago!"

"You mean you don't remember?" Kallan said.

"No! I don't remember!" Rune shouted.

"Rune..." Kallan gasped. "We can't cross this."

The march of the soldiers grew louder, forcing them to abandon their argument. Before she could disagree, Rune grabbed Kallan's hand and bolted up the west bank of the Raumelfr.

"Rune," Kallan managed between breaths, "we can't run all the way up the Raumelfr."

"I know that."

Rune came to a stop and looked about for a place to escape, a place to cross, a place to hide.

"What do we do?" Kallan asked.

"I don't know." Rune looked from left to right for a solution. Deciding on one, he pulled Kallan back to Astrid. "Come on."

Lifting her up, Rune hoisted Kallan into the saddle. After pulling himself up behind her, Rune looked about for Olaf's men then snapped the reins, forcing Astrid into a full gallop up the banks of the Raumelfr.

Undaunted by the advantage Kallan and Rune gained from atop their mount, Olaf's men charged with spear and axe. Rune pulled back on the reins and studied the far side where the spearmen left an opening. Directing Astrid toward the banks of the Raumelfr, Rune steered the horse to the only opening ahead. Within moments, more spearman moved in, closing ranks and forcing Rune to reconfigure his escape.

After re-examining the scenario for another opening, Rune sent Astrid across the peninsula. Flying ahead on his command, desperate to outrun the war-men, Astrid rounded the tip of the land and Rune veered the stallion up the banks of the east river, but the spearmen were waiting with Olaf.

Forced to a full stop, Rune looked for any opening that could lead to an escape, but the army had barricaded them in and the only open path was down a sheer drop into the Raumelfr.

Rune wrapped an arm around Kallan as she flicked her wrists. Rune snatched Kallan's hand.

"Don't," he said. "There are too many."

The first of the spearmen closed in, cutting off the last of the space between them when the blast of a war horn and a call to arms filled the wood around them.

Everyone looked to the trees.

Moving as one and clad in armor, a legion of Alfar warriors emerged from the forest sporting sword, shield, and spear. Olaf's spearmen tightened their grips on their arms. Confusion settled in as they looked about, studying the warriors surrounding them. Untouched by the fear of man's mortality, the faces of the Alfar were hardened with the coldness possessed only by those born to the halls of Alfheim.

Kallan looked from face to face. Rune felt her tremble as she leaned into him like she was desperate to sink through him and vanish. She slipped her hand into his and folded her fingers down with such strength as if terrified he would suddenly be ripped from her side.

Rune searched the innumerable faces and scanned the crowd of troops for a single pair of obscure eyes.

From the line of Alfar, a single warrior stepped into the opening and Rune ended his search, relaxing onto Astrid with a wide grin.

Clad in black and seated, almost bored, upon a charcoal mare with an elding great sword fastened to his back, the berserker emerged from the line of Alfar. His dark eyes fell on Kallan.

"Olaf!" Bergen bellowed above the confused mass of murmurs that had fallen over the troops. "Stand down!"

Olaf addressed the challenger, throwing all of his hate to this Ljosalfr, this berserker.

"You stand on the grounds of Viken," Olaf said and Bergen unsheathed his sword with a flourish. "With what warrant do you contest the king and lord of this land?"

"We are here for our king," Bergen said, "and are prepared to take him back..." With a flick of his wrist, Bergen readied his great sword and grinned. "Or to avenge him."

Olaf smiled widely from atop his horse.

"Have you so many lives to spare that you can send them to their deaths in vain?" Olaf asked.

The Dark One waited for the echo of Olaf's taunt to fade before answering.

"Ten thousand," Bergen said with the cold calculation of a strategist. "Ten thousand stand strong awaiting our return in Gunir. They have orders to march to your precious citadel and rend your fortress to the ground where she stands if we don't." The smile fell from Olaf's face. "Are you prepared to amass your troops in defense against our vengeance?"

"Your falsehood is plain," Olaf said. "Your numbers have significantly depleted."

"Will you gamble your stronghold on false assumptions?"

The weighted silence fell over the troops, each awaiting their commander's orders. Kallan and Rune shifted gazes from Man to Alfar. After a long moment in which Olaf and Bergen exchanged glances, Olaf called to his men.

"Fall back!"

In a wave that passed over Olaf's troops, they lowered their arms and withdrew to the woods as Olaf kept his eyes fixed on his challenger. Olaf steered his horse about and rode to the front of his order without a glance behind.

Exhaling, Rune barked a loud laugh.

"Bergen," he said, swinging a leg over Astrid and dropping his weight to the ground. With wide strides, he hustled toward the bear-like mass of Bergen, who beamed.

"Rune," Bergen said and matched Rune's lead.

Sliding from his horse, Bergen sauntered out to meet his king. They embraced, punched each other in the shoulder, and exploded into a set of laughs that left tears in their eyes.

Clutching Astrid's bridle, Kallan followed a great distance behind Rune, careful to keep her guard raised and her focus on Bergen.

"The full moon was a fortnight ago!" Bergen roared, adding a second jab to Rune's unwounded shoulder.

"We were detained," Rune said.

Several yards behind him, Kallan came to a stop as Bergen's eyes met hers and the grin on his face fell.

"By the fires of Muspellsheim," the berserker cursed.

The tips of Kallan's fingers drummed the air, aching to pull on her Seidr. The movement caught Bergen's eye and he risked a glance to her palm, knowing very well what she was. Cautiously, his hand slid from the pommel to the hilt of his sword, his eyes ever fixed on hers and they moved in the same instant.

A flame erupted in Kallan's hand as Bergen raised his sword and Rune jumped between them, his arms spread between them both.

"Stand down," Rune shouted. "Stand down. Bergen, sheath your weapon. Kallan—"

Kallan glanced at Rune then restored her attention to the berserker who stood arms raised with great sword poised. After a heavy pause, Bergen slowly lowered his blade, careful to match Kallan's pace. Rune exhaled and Kallan, ever vigilant, extinguished her Seidr.

"Now then," Rune said with a relieved huff. "Kallan, daughter of Eyolf, Queen and Lady of Lorlenalin, this is Bergen, Son of Tryggve, Lord and heir of Gunir. He is my brother."

Kallan looked to Rune, to Bergen, to Rune, and Bergen pulled his helmet from his head, freeing the long, black braids that fell to his waist. Kallan gazed at the berserker. Her attention lingered on the deep scar above his right eye: a souvenir of their earliest encounters. Aside from the length of his hair, his eyes, the scar, and Bergen having spent a considerable amount more time in the barracks, the berserker matched his king's appearance in almost every detail.

"Kallan will be accompanying us to Gunir," Rune spoke, cutting an air of regality through the tension that hovered between the lady and his brother.

"Like Hel I will," Kallan said.

"I don't see how you've a choice," Bergen said.

"I'll not be dragged about by this *uskit*!"

Bergen raised his sword and Kallan relit her Seidr.

"Lady Kallan," Rune said, "has been invited as my guest."

"I decline," Kallan said, balancing her blue orbs.

"She will accompany me to Gunir as my guest..." Rune furrowed his brow at Kallan, forcing a civil tone in his voice. "...or be taken there by force...with rope."

"Gladly," Bergen said. Rune shifted a warning look to Bergen.

"There..." Rune gave the same warning look to Kallan. "...she and I will assemble to discuss our terms for peace."

Kallan shifted her attention to Bergen and then to Rune before finally lowering her arms and extinguishing her flames.

"Now," Rune said with a great effort to bring about their reconciliation. "Shake hands."

Kallan and Bergen didn't move.

"Shake hands, Kallan," Rune said.

With a silent glance from one brother to the next, Kallan extended a hand to Bergen, who took it, shook once, then snapped their hands down with vehemence.

Rune grinned with a finality that put the topic to rest.

"Kallan has agreed to ride with us," Rune said visibly delighted.

"Sail," Bergen corrected with a tone that sounded as displeased with the arrangement as Kallan looked.

Rune furrowed his brow. "You brought the ships?"

In the distance, a warrior led Freyja by the reins to where Rune and Bergen stood.

"There is no direct water way from Gunir to the Raumelfr," Bergen said. "And there is no crossing the Raumelfr without ships."

With her defenses raised, Kallan toggled her attention between the brothers, and backed into Astrid.

"How far are we?" Rune asked, accepting Freyja's reins from the warrior.

"Three days without favoring winds." Bergen's answer forced Kallan's attention that neither noticed.

Rune nodded. "Then we shall embark."

The command sent the men back through the wood toward the shores ahead.

Clutching Astrid's reins, Kallan remained immobile, and moved only when Rune stopped and extended an open hand to her.

A cold in her eyes had settled in.

"Don't think this changes anything, Ljosalfr," Kallan said and Rune lowered his hand to his side. "The first chance I get, I'm going home."

Rune dropped his shoulders. "Does what we've been through mean nothing?"

"Should it?" There was a bite in her words.

"No." Rune nodded and clenched his fist. "I guess not."

After several moments, Kallan pulled on Astrid's reins and, with a cold shoulder, followed Bergen down to the ships that would carry her to Gunir.

Epilogue

Olaf sat hunched at his desk. He clutched the tankard in his hand and let his blond hair cover the map. His eyes lingered on Dan's Reach, where he stared, unable to pull his musings away from the southern lands and Forkbeard.

He would win back the land of the Northern Way and the people there. They would follow him, abandon their gods, or die. The Empire would hear of his deeds and they would support him. He was certain.

A sudden sharp chill made him scowl, but before he could bark 'get out,' a thick sleep invaded him and he felt his anger ebb. A drugged complacence took its place and he turned to the Seidkona with hair as black as a raven's wing and eyes as gold as the desert sun.

"Well?" Fand said with her slick grin poised so perfectly on her lips. They were the color of plums he had seen from the far east. "Where is it?" she asked and his arousal subsided.

"I lost it," he growled and turned back to the desk, his map, and brooding.

"You lost it," Fand whispered and slid across the carpet of the lavishly decorated tent.

"We were ambushed," Olaf said. He threw back his tankard and downed the rest of his mead. "We lost everything, including the witch."

"So..." Fand was no longer grinning. "Go get her."

"She's in Alfheim."

"She's in...No matter. It shouldn't be too hard to retrieve her."

Olaf stood, shoving his chair back as he came to his full height. As if boasting his power, he shoved his face into Fand's and studied the gold that encircled her irises.

"You never told me she was Lorlenalin's queen."

If Fand ever looked off guard, it was in that moment, just before she smiled and emitted a soft laugh. She stroked the yellow strands of his beard as if patting it down into the fur lapels of his coat.

"Does it matter?" she asked, not bothering to look in his eyes.

"It matters," he said. "My army isn't equipped to take on the Dokkalfar. She'll come after me and my men and not even your poisons can hold her back."

When she refused to look at him, Olaf caught her by the wrist, forcing her eyes to his.

"I am organizing a war against Forkbeard," he said. "We are in the middle of an invasion. I don't have the resources to defend myself against the Alfar armies. Their numbers are too great. You want the pouch?" Fand yanked her wrist free. "Go get it yourself."

"You would give up your chance for eternal life?" she asked.

"Once I have reclaimed my father's land, I can move on Alfheim and strip the queen of her pouch, her virtue, and her pride," Olaf said. "Once I have taken back what is mine, then I claim eternal life for myself. Until then, my goal is Forkbeard."

Fand turned her back and strode to the door, taking the thick air with her.

"You will never see your father's land," Fand said, stopping at the door, "so long as I have breath in me."

She pulled back the hide and a gust of cold engulfed the room as she peered at the king.

"Forkbeard will be the death of you," she whispered and, releasing the hide, she took the form of a raven and flew from Olaf's tent before the hide fell back. The cold caw of the raven lingered like death upon his throat.

Thank you for your support. May the kindest of words always find you.
– Angela B. Chrysler

Congratulations! You have unlocked "Beneath the Mountain." Go to:

http://www.angelabchrysler.com/beneath-the-mountain/
and enter the password "Elding Stone" to access the special features reserved just for you.

tap-to-fling-dance-delusion-beyond-the-reunion-the-pavement-telling-show-in-seek-light-a-new-day-bright

About the Author

Angela B. Chrysler is a writer, logician, and die-hard nerd who studies philosophy, theology, historical linguistics, music composition, and medieval European history in New York with a dry sense of humor and an unusual sense of sarcasm.

Website: http://www.angelabchrysler.com/
Twitter: https://twitter.com/abchryslerabc
Goodreads:
https://www.goodreads.com/user/show/36016085-angela-chrysler
Google+:
https://plus.google.com/u/0/+AngelaBChrysler/posts
Facebook:
https://www.facebook.com/pages/Angela-B-Chrysler/
755206654548539

Pronunciation Guide

A complete list with audio is available at
http://www.angelabchrysler.com/pronunciation-guide/

Alfr (Alf) Elf
Alfar (Al-far) Elves
Alfheim (Alf-hame) Elf Home
Bergen Tryggveson (Bear-gen Treeg-vay-son) Ljos-alfar and berserker
Caoilinn (Kway-linn) Ljosalfar
Daggon (Day-gon) Dokkalfar
Dokkalfr (Do-kalf) Dark elf
Dokkalfar (Do-kal-far) Dark Elves
Dubh Linn (Doov Linn) Dublin, Ireland
Dvergr (D-vare-g) Singular
Dvergar (D-vare-gar) Plural See

"http://www.angelabchrysler.com/regarding-the-dvergar/"

at www.angelabchrysler.com

Eilif (A-leef) Dokkalfar

Eire's Land (Air's Land) Ireland

Elding (El-ding) A mysterious metal infused with the Seidr only used by the Dokkalfar and the Dvergar.

Elding (El-ding) The age in which the Alfar reach full maturity and stop aging.

Finn (Fin) The Old Norse word for the Sami

Finntent (fin-tent) The Old Norse words for a portable teepee-styled tent still used by the Sami

Fjandinn (Fee-yan-din) The old Norse equivalent to the Christian word "Devil" used by Norsemen prior to the introduction of the Christian culture.

Freyja (Fray-ya) Norse goddess

Gamme (Ga-may) The Old Norse word for an earthen home still used by the Sami

Ginnungagap (Gi-noon-ga-gap) The Great Gap

Gudrun (goo-droon) Dokkalfar

Gunir (Goo-neer) The Ljosalfar city in Alfheim

Hel (Hel) Loptr's daughter, Hel, guardian and over-seer of Helheim

Helheim (Hel-hame) The Norse version of the Under-world where Loptr's daughter, Hel, resides.

Idunn (I-thoon or I-doon) Norse goddess

Jotun (Yo-toon) Giants

Jotunheim (Yo-toon-hame) The home of the giants

Kallan Eyolfdottir (Ka-lon A-olf-do-teer) Dokkalfar

Loptr (Lopt) The Old Norse name for Loki

Lorlenalin (Lor-len-a-lin) The Dokkalfar city in Alfheim

Ljosalfr (Lee-yos-alf) Light Elf

Ljosalfar (Lee-yos-al-far) Light Elves

Midgard (Mid-gard) Literal translattion "Middle-Earth." Midgard is the human realm.

Nidingr (Ni-thing) Literal translation: "Nothing." The status of "outlaw" given to a dishonorable coward who has been stripped of his station, property, and citizenship in Norse culture.

Odinn (O-thin or O-din) Norse god

Olaf Tryggvason (O-lof Treeg-va-son) Historically, the first king of Norway.

Note: Olaf Tryggvason has no relation to Bergen or Rune whose last name is Tryggveson. The name of Olaf's father was "Trygg" while the father of Rune and Bergen is "Tryggve."

Seidr (Say-th or Seed) The life source bound to the elements and all living things and referred to as "magic" in the Deserts.

Seidkona (Say-th-kona or Seed-ko-na) Old Norse for "Witch"

Surtr (sert) Lord of the Fire Giants

Sigyn (See-gin) Loptr's wife

Svartálfr (Svart-alf) Black Elf

Svartálfar (Svart-alf-ar) Black Elves

Svartálfaheim (Svart-alf-a-hame) Home of the Black Elves

Thing (Thing) The Norwegian Parliament still in existence today in Norway.

Tryggve (Treeg-vay) Ljosalfar

A look into Fire and Lies:
The Seidr Cycle Book #2

Chapter 1

Rune followed Bergen down to the water's edge. Before they reached the shore, Kallan could see the masts of six wide, longships stretched from the beach where Bergen had them pulled to land with roller logs. The water lapped their sterns causing the wood to whine against the current.

The keel of each ship rose up and out of the river, reaching to the skies at each end, where they curled into themselves at the top of each bow and stern. Several of the men had settled the yardarms into the trestles and were preparing the sails while others raised the final mast. With a series of ropes, raw strength, and the aid of the mast step, the Ljosalfar pushed the mast upright and secured it into the keel-son within the hull.

Ljosalfar collected fresh water from the river, pouring it into large barrels for drinking while others were busy dumping their weapons and mail into their sea chests onboard.

"Your majesty...here!" cried a man with an aged and unscarred face. He waved fiercely from the farthest boat in an attempt to attract Rune's attention. With a nod, Rune pulled a saddlebag from Freyja's pack and dumped it on the ground before moving to take Astrid's reins from Kallan who tightened her grip and scowled.

"Well, you don't mean to leave him here, do you?" Rune asked in reply. He tried again and, succeeding this time, snatched the reins from Kallan.

She watched as Rune led Astrid and Freyja down to the water's edge where a lone ship had docked parallel to the shore. Following the other, Freyja, then Astrid, stepped over the side of the longboat, tipping the entire boat high onto its side. As the horses stepped in, the boat rocked with vigor, forcing the old man to cling to the mast for balance. After accepting the reins from Rune, the old man gave an affectionate, but hearty pat to Astrid's deep russet neck and gave Rune a welcomed nod.

He paused for a moment to ogle the unusual breed that was Astrid before running his hand through Freyja's white, silken locks. Paying more mind to the horses than his footing, the old man caught his ankle on a large mass of orange and white as a cat scampered across the ship in pursuit of a rodent. With a slew of curses, the old man recovered his balance and led Astrid and Freyja to the center of the boat. There, he tied their reins to the mast alongside a handful of fjord horses and a charcoal gray, courser mare.

"That is Gunnar."

Kallan jumped, unaware Rune had returned to her side.

"He is our horse master," Rune said, throwing the load over his shoulder.

With interest, Kallan watched as Gunnar the horse master offered a bucket of grains to Astrid, who ate graciously, happy for the change from apples and grass.

"He couldn't be in better hands," Rune assured her. "Come."

When she refused to take his hand, he wrapped an arm around her back and cautiously, led her down to the boats, stopping at the nearest ship.

The edge of the water sloshed onto the sands as Rune led Kallan to the gangplank. She took in the ropes and the tie lines, and the grand oak strakes that overlapped each other. Men had taken their seat on top of their sea chests and others had already positioned their oars through the oar ports. A few were preoccupied with fastening their shields to the side of the boat.

The instant weight of seventy sets of eyes turned her way as her foot touched down on the deck of the boat, and she lowered herself from the gangplank into the first of her enemy's territory. Kallan raised

749

her face to the sudden silence that blanketed the ship and slowly took in every face staring back with as much hate as she harbored for each.

Without a word, she released the gunwale as Rune came up behind her. Stopping long enough to acknowledge his men, he extended a hand and directed her to the ship's stern. Her muffled footfalls sounded too clearly over the river's gentle waves as Kallan continued to shift her eyes from port to starboard taking in every face that condemned her presence on their ship.

With a jerk, Kallan stopped too suddenly as she neared the aft of the ship. Bergen's bare back greeted her. Thin, pale scars made visible in the sun's light, marred the length of his spine. He bustled with a rope at the side oar, unaware of her arrival. Behind her, Rune closed in, preventing her from bounding back the way she came and running, full speed, back to shore. Her face rose in a sneer as she clenched her fist with the urge to fire. The cold stares of the Ljosalfar soldiers bore down with reminder that, at one point or another, she had attempted to kill each one of them.

Kallan had nearly finished plotting the dash to Astrid and her escape route, when Rune jarred her thoughts and pulled her out of her daydream with his own petty bickering.

"Don't make me remind you who is king," Rune said.

"By a random chance granted to you by a few seconds and Freyr's sense of humor," Bergen retorted.

"I have to shove this damn arrow head through my shoulder and I'd prefer a heavy dose of mead to do it, now give me the booze!"

Bergen flashed Rune a grin.

"Father always did warn mother she was too soft on you," Bergen said, tossing a flask to Rune, intentionally forcing him to catch it with his impaled shoulder.

With a wince, Rune stifled a groan and pulled off the stopper with his teeth. A second later he downed half the flask. Exhaling through the incessant pulsing in his shoulder, Rune delivered a swift vexed kick to the collection of furs he had dumped into a pile against the stern-side trestle where the men had stored the roller logs.

"Kallan." He spoke gently, dropping himself into the pile of furs with a groan.

Grateful for the chance to ignore Bergen, Kallan kneeled on the furs behind Rune and quickly, gratefully, went to work. Rune was already talking to her over his shoulder when she rolled up her sleeves, withdrew her seax, and positioned the flat of the blade over the broken end of the arrow in his back.

"Alright, what you'll need to do—"

Rune howled as Kallan slammed her palm into the blade, driving the arrow through the Rune's shoulder. Happy to be busying herself with her hands, Kallan shuffled herself around to Rune's front and took hold of the arrow's tip, pulling the rest of the arrow out. The wound bled freely.

A second helping of curses rambled free from Rune's mouth as Kallan proceeded to tear up strips of cloth she used to dab at the wound, saying nothing as she focused on her work. Throwing his head back, Rune gulped down the rest of Bergen's mead. The sweat on his forehead beaded as he dropped the empty flask to his lap.

"You couldn't use an apple?"

Kallan raised a hateful eye to Rune and ripped another strip of fabric.

"Where did you find the cloth?" Rune asked dragging his tongue through his stupor.

Again, Kallan met Rune's glossed eyes as she ripped off another strip. Behind her, Ottar led a wave of grins that passed through the ship and ended with Bergen, each warrior understanding what Hel Rune was in for as Kallan made rags of Rune's tunic.

Throwing back the empty flask before remembering it was empty. Rune suddenly realized the severity of his drunken state.

"Hey, Bergen," Rune slurred, "What's in this stuff?"

Kallan sat herself down against her pile of furs as Bergen flashed a grin that matched the gleam in his eye.

"What happened to your shirt?" he asked dropping himself at the tiller as Rune examined the frayed ends of his tunic.

"Move out!" Bergen bellowed content not to answer.

One by one, with gangplanks raised, the ships pushed off from shore and several men waded waist high in the water, passing the logs from shore to the rowers. With fluid precision, the rowers passed the logs overhead and laid them into the trestles. After climbing on board, the last of the men settled themselves into their places along the hides and floorboards.

Thirty rowers lined each side of each ship. Those who climbed from the water slogged to their sea chests and settled in place as the rowers took up their oars and pushed off the land while the seaside oarsmen began rowing. They found their rhythm and, within minutes, the river's current carried them. The wind picked up and shortly thereafter, they found a favorable wind.

"Drop the sails!" Bergen shouted from his seat at the side oar.

In unison, a handful of those who had raised the roller logs proceeded to untie the sail fastened to the yardarm. They took up the halyards and, together, hoisted the yardarm to the tip of the mast, where the flag of Gunir, encrusted with the boar's head encircled with runes, snapped in the wind.

Before they could finish tying off the lines and securing the sheets, the sails billowed. The increased speed was instant and, for the moment, Kallan forgot Rune's drunkenness, his bloody shoulder, or the Dark One sitting behind her, coddling the tiller like a boy happy with a new stick.

With a newfound eagerness, she studied the ships behind them. Each followed suit and one by one, their sails unfurled, catching the wind that pushed them with ease through the water. In the far distance behind her ship, she found Astrid unconcerned with the sea voyage as he happily buried his head in his bucket of grains. She watched Gunnar with peeked interest as the old horse master inspected a fjord stallion. Giving Gunnar a playful swat, the horse whipped his black and white tail as the old codger averted his interests to the unusual strands of Freyja's coat.

After patting the stallion's hindquarters, Gunnar walked to the charcoal gray, courser mare. As tall as Astrid, she radiated with a black sheen that matched her sleek tail and long mane. Kallan lost herself in the serenity of that ship, where only the rowers and a man at the side oar were present with Gunnar and the horses.

She exhaled, slowly releasing her breath through her nose in an attempt to remain unnoticed by Bergen's men. The wind whipped her hair about as she looked to the vibrant greens of Alfheim, almost within an arm's reach along the banks of the river. Ahead, the Raumelfr captivated Kallan's attention. The lands rose and fell with the river, moving and twisting with it as the winds carried them through the water.

"You've never been to sea before," Rune said as drowsiness, pain, and liquor took the better part of him.

The interruption brought her dazed dreams back to the boat, reminding her of the company she kept aboard her enemy's vessel. Quickly, she slunk back down into the pile of furs.

With the sails billowed, the rowers pulled in their oars and deposited them onto the floorboards, filling the ship with a collection of thuds and clunks. Stretching out among the barrels, sea chests, and ropes strewn about on the deck, Kallan watched, horror-stricken, as the Ljosalfar men on board proceeded to scratch, amuse, and relieve themselves overboard.

Quickly, Kallan readjusted her seat, settling for a view of the stern, where Bergen sat, relaxed and bare-chested. Rune's head bobbed about sleepily as Kallan shifted her gaze from Bergen to the gunwale, to the hem of her skirts, and to Rune, who gave a sudden jerk of his head to force himself awake. The gnawing awareness of her enemy's presence nagged at her consciousness.

At last, with much hesitation, Kallan raised her eyes to Bergen, who had fixed his full attention on her like a mountain cat stalking a lone, limp deer. The massive black of his eyes glared, loathing her presence there on his ship, as much as she hated being there. Despite shifting her position to better face Rune, Bergen's dark eyes continued to dig into her.

Rune dozed again. His hand clutched tightly to the empty flask as Kallan clasped her hands to contain the urge to attack. Bergen's scowl burrowed deeper, until the side of her head burned from his glare. Abandoning all regard, and embracing her resolve, Kallan snapped her eyes to Bergen and mirrored his dead, cold stare.

They glowered in silence, their scowls saying so much more than any throng of insults could ever say. Both held their stance, neither willing to break, both daring the other to be the first to weaken, to break the silence, to—

"Enough!" Rune barked, "We have three days ahead of us and I'll be damned if I spend every bit of this voyage with the two of you snarling at each other!"

Bergen broke his grimace first and Kallan lowered her eyes. Catching a flash of fur and the tip of a tail of a white ship cat, for a moment, Kallan was relieved for the distraction.

Revived from whatever stupor Bergen's mead had induced, Rune pushed himself up onto the furs, wincing, before settling himself back down against the trestle.

From the corner of her eye, Kallan peered at Bergen, who was suddenly interested on a certain point at the head of the ship.

"Ottar!" he called.

While picking at his fingers with the point of his dagger, a wide-shoulder man glanced up from where he leaned against the fore trestle. Pushing himself upright, he ambled to the stern. A large scar carved into his right shoulder flashed as he moved, holding Kallan's attention longer than she had intended.

Stopping over Kallan, he turned his hateful eye down with a cold glare.

"What is it, Dokkalfr?" he growled. "They don't grow real men in that Mountain City of yours?"

Kallan dug her fingers into her skirts and, with all her will, forced her head low. While scowling, she attempted to calm the sick in her stomach as Ottar continued on toward Bergen. After a quick shuffle, Bergen passed the tiller to Ottar, who took Bergen's seat.

Glancing away from the side oar, Kallan raised her face just in time to see Bergen unfasten his belt. Heat climbed her neck as she lowered her head and closed her eyes. Anger grated against the resounding laugh that eructed from Ottar.

"Something wrong, Princess?" Ottar jeered with rich vulgarity. "Did they neglect to teach you an appreciation for men?" He released another bout of laughter and Kallan balled her fists.

"Ottar," Rune said against the trestle. "That's enough."

The big brute swallowed mid-guffaw and, with resumed silence, governed the side oar. Confounded, Rune gazed at Kallan's grimace as the heavy clomp of Bergen's boots returned.

In a torrent of billowed skirts, Kallan rose to her feet and, slamming her shoulder into Bergen's, plodded to the front of the ship, paying no mind to the catcalls and jeers as she went.

"What did you do?" Bergen asked, watching the wind whip Kallan's hair into the folds of her skirts as she came to stand near the ship's bow.

"I'm not sure." Rune stared, his brow still furrowed.

Stupidly, Bergen's face stretched into a wide grin.

"You know how to pick them, don't you," Bergen said, shuffling his seat to the furs beside Rune. Exhaling, he dropped to the floor and leaned into the trestle.

"Why not let her go, Brother?" Bergen said, leaning in and dropping the amusement from his tone. "She doesn't want to be here anymore than she's wanted here. You could send an arrow to her back or I could pluck her off tonight while she sleeps."

"She won't sleep," Rune said as he watched Kallan hug herself against the chill. "And she has to come with us."

"Well, of course, she has to come with us." Bergen scoffed dismissively. "But why take a bothersome prisoner to kill on ceremony when we can just kill her here? It'll boost the men's spirits."

Rune kept his eyes fixed on the fore, watching, guarding, to ensure none of his men stepped out of line.

"There are greater enemies out there with greater happenings than any of us are aware of," Rune said. "And unless we combine our efforts..." Rune tore his gaze from Kallan. "...we will never see the end of this conflict."

Bergen leaned closer, eager for the moment to speak privately.

"I know you," he said with a darkened look to his eye. "You don't go gallivanting after wenches."

Bergen added a subtle nod toward the front the ship where Kallan stood. "What goes on, Brother?"

Rune shook his head.

"I don't know. Not yet."

"The least you could have done is let her sail with Gunnar," Bergen said. "He hates everyone equally...unless they're a horse."

Without a second look to his brother, Rune made his way to the bow, stepping over men who slept and sulked, stretched out on the deck.

Grabbing the mainstay to keep his balance against the jostling ship, Rune came to stand beside Kallan who stared into the cold winds, grateful for the whistling that drowned out most of the comments behind her. She stared ahead, refusing to acknowledge his presence, the wind drying the bite of her tears from her eyes.

The boat's stern cut into the river's surface as it pushed on through the waters. The spray of the sea added to the chill, but she didn't budge against the ruthless winds of the Nordic air.

"I am responsible for their behavior," Rune said. "They mean no harm, really."

He shifted his gaze to Kallan and followed the pale curve of her cheek, to her ear and down the lines of her neck. The only movement was of her hair whipping wildly about by the wind. With a sigh, Rune looked back to the river.

"Men aren't as temperate as women," he said. "We like our comforts and get crass when we lose them."

He waited for her to answer. When she didn't, he looked back to Kallan who stared, still idle, still unmoving, distant and dead to the world around her. His jaw tightened as she withdrew, back into the black chasms of her mind where she harbored the remnants of her iron wall. Without a word, Rune trudged back to the stern and dropped himself back onto the pile of furs, ignoring the banter of laughs exchanged between Bergen and Ottar.

At the bow, Kallan stood, giving no sign that she lived or was aware of her surroundings as she sank back into the vacant depths of her mind.

Dear reader,

We hope you enjoyed reading *Dolor and Shadow*. Please take a moment to leave a review, even if it's a short one. Your opinion is important to us.

Discover more books by Angela Chrysler at

https://www.nextchapter.pub/authors/angela-b-chrysler

Want to know when one of our books is free or discounted? Join the newsletter at

http://eepurl.com/bqqB3H

Best regards,
Angela Chrysler and the Next Chapter Team

Dolor and Shadow
ISBN: 978-4-86745-460-2 (Mass Market)

Published by
Next Chapter
1-60-20 Minami-Otsuka
170-0005 Toshima-Ku, Tokyo
+818035793528
30th April 2021